THE CONTINENT OF
GALLINOR
I0817728
WARDWELL
VALLENVOREN
ALDERFELD
THE SPINE OF
SABLEMIRE
THE NORTHERN ISLES
THE FALKERON CLOISTERS
N
W
E
S
CAWDER
MARROWGATE
CAIATHOS
BIG DEEP
BLIGHDON
THE TORDELL CLOISTERS
BATHYN
THE SEA OF THE DAWN
EAST TO AIDURRA
Brightrun River
BEROGES

PRAISE FOR THE MIDDLEMIST TRILOGY

"A lush and bewitching gothic romance where the inner lives of the characters are just as intricately crafted as their sumptuously magical world. I was completely swept away."

—Ava Reid, #1 *New York Times* bestselling author of *A Study in Drowning*, for *A Song of Ash and Moonlight*

"Claire Legrand at her best! This page-turner of a book will leave you on the edge of your seat, with searing love, furious battles, and twists you'll never see coming."

—Beth Revis, *New York Times* bestselling coauthor of *Night of the Witch*, for *A Song of Ash and Moonlight*

"*A Song of Ash and Moonlight* sets achingly genuine characters against a stunning world and lush mythos, expertly counterbalanced by a heart-wrenchingly sweet romance. Claire Legrand is a master of sweeping, intricate fantasy."

—Sara Raasch, *New York Times* bestselling coauthor of *Night of the Witch*

"As usual, Legrand leaves her readers breathless and dazed. Her Middlemist world is exquisitely immersive, and the pages sparkle with a tender tale of intrigue, romance, and extraordinary mythmaking."

—Roshani Chokshi, *New York Times* bestselling author of *The Last Tale of the Flower Bride*, for *A Song of Ash and Moonlight*

"This is the type of book that stays with you—like an imprint on your heart. Claire Legrand crafts a heart-achingly beautiful story that's captivating, thrilling, gritty, at times spooky, and utterly magical."

—Kate Dramis, *Sunday Times* bestselling author of *A Curse of Saints*, for *A Song of Ash and Moonlight*

"Claire Legrand has created a vibrant, ruthless world in which the magically anointed aren't always blessed and the burden of responsibility carries with it sacrifice and grief. A lush story a reader can fall into and never want to emerge from, where entire worlds exist in the details and the characters are people we want to know and love. A masterful fantasy romance by the talented Legrand."

—Grace Draven, *USA Today* bestselling author of *Radiance*, for *A Song of Ash and Moonlight*

"Spellbinding... Legrand is a polished painter of word pictures. Luscious descriptions bring the story alive, making it immersive and fun even when it's uncomfortable or excruciating."

—*Associated Press* for *A Crown of Ivy and Glass*

"*A Crown of Ivy and Glass* is full of high stakes for her characters and detailed fantasy world-building with interesting mythology for readers."

—*Library Journal*

A ROSE OF BLOOD AND BINDING

THE MIDDLEMIST TRILOGY • BOOK THREE

Also by Claire Legrand

The Empirium Trilogy

Furyborn

Kingsbane

Lightbringer

The Middlemist Trilogy

A Crown of Ivy and Glass

A Song of Ash and Moonlight

A ROSE OF BLOOD AND BINDING

THE MIDDLEMIST TRILOGY • BOOK THREE

CLAIRE LEGRAND

Cover design by Stephanie Gafron/Sourcebooks
Cover illustration © Nekro
Map illustration by Travis Hasenour

Sourcebooks and the colophon are registered trademarks of Sourcebooks.

Published by Sourcebooks Casablanca, an imprint of Sourcebooks
1935 Brookdale RD, Naperville, IL 60563-2773
(630) 961-3900
sourcebooks.com

Cataloging-in-Publication Data is on file with the Library of Congress.

Printed and bound in the United States of America.
MA 10 9 8 7 6 5 4 3 2 1

for those who long to go home, and for those who never can:
may you find a new home, of your own resolute making,
wherever your journey takes you

Author's Note

Though this is a fantasy novel, its characters face very real challenges. Please note that this story contains discussions of self-harm and both passive and active suicidal ideation.

Prologue

Twelve Years Ago

When Petra shook Mara awake, and Mara opened her eyes to the dark world, her first thought was one of relief, for her dream-addled mind, soaked in its own wild hopes, suggested that someone had finally come to kill her.

"It's happening," Petra whispered, her eyes twin fireflies in the candlelit shadows. "Get up."

Petra's voice trembled with fear, and excitement, and something feral that made Mara sit up, wide awake. Since coming to the priory of Rosewarren weeks ago—no, since being *taken* to Rosewarren, since riding away from Ivyhill in the Warden's black carriage, since hearing the sobs of her baby sister, Gemma, and her mother, Philippa, fade away on the wind—since then, Mara had spoken only to Petra.

At first, no one had made her talk at all; no one had made her do anything. So she had said nothing and done nothing, nothing but lie on her little cot in the barracks with eleven other new recruits, and listen idly to their chatter, and think of home.

Sometimes she woke from a troubled sleep, and for one panicky moment, she couldn't remember what Ivyhill looked like, or the steady tone of Farrin's voice, or what Gemma's soft curls felt like against her cheek when she crawled into Mara's bed after a nightmare, whispering tearfully about knives lodged deep in her bones.

Then Mara would remember everything in a rush of feeling that pummeled her like fists, and remembering was a relief, and remembering was awful, because what good is it to remember things that hurt you?

So she slept, and lay there, and refused to eat, and only when she started to feel faint would she take small sips from the cup of water on her bedside table that someone kept refilling. Some instinct pushed her to sit up, to move her arm, to raise the little tin cup to her lips. She imagined the Warden finding her starved corpse and smiled in grim satisfaction.

But after a few days, Mara could no longer ignore the pangs of her starving stomach. She'd never felt such pain and thought she might be going mad. Her thoughts were fevered, her dreams desperate. She grabbed the sleeve of one of the girls rushing past her at the sound of the dinner bell—another girl who had been taken from her home, another daughter stolen in the name of the queen—and said, "Can you please bring me some food?"

The sleeve belonged to a girl named Petra, just one year younger than ten-year-old Mara, with ruddy skin and freckles and auburn hair that flew every which way. Petra had the kind heart of a loyal hound. She took one look at Mara, her mouth twisting, and nodded once, briskly, and a little while later she came back with a leg of roast chicken and a hot buttered roll wrapped in a napkin. She sat next to Mara while Mara ate, reminding her to slow down or she would get sick, reminding her to drink water.

And then, once Mara's hunger was diminished, her mind felt a little clearer, and her grief rose up in her like a wild animal finally let loose from its pen, and she cried. She cried so hard and for so long that some of the other girls started to complain, but Petra hushed them with a fierce look and a few harsh words, and because she was kind and good, and well-loved for her humor and her speed with a knife during training, everyone obeyed.

Petra spent that night in Mara's bed, holding her while she cried, and that became the way of things every night thereafter. The two of them exchanged stories of home, and Petra told Mara about everything she missed. Sometimes, when Mara couldn't sleep, Petra wouldn't either. They would clasp each other's hands and touch their foreheads together, and Mara would describe the vines of Ivyhill, how they coated the house in a glossy green carpet, and Petra would tell Mara about the rocky northeastern shores of her home, where the waves crashed against the cliffs and everything smelled of salt.

Petra even persuaded Mara to join the other girls for chores in the long hallways of Rosewarren, with their soft red carpets and soft dim lights, and outside in the stables and on the grounds, where everything shimmered silver from the nearby Middlemist. The first time Mara went outside, she squinted for a good five minutes. She had forgotten what daylight felt like, and even the Mist-shrouded sun seemed to warm her inside and out.

But now Petra was climbing out of bed, hopping around on her right foot to pull on her left boot. The other girls—northern and southern and from the heartlands and the Mistlands too, all eight, nine, ten, eleven years old—were scrambling from their beds and throwing on their cloaks, tugging on their stockings.

Mara watched for a moment, listening hard to the whispers darting through the room.

Initiation, they said. *The trials*. Some girls were ashen, wide-eyed; others were practically frothing at the mouth. *Finally*, they said. *It's been long enough. I thought it would never happen. I want to go home.*

Don't be a coward. Hurry. There's no time to dress. They're right outside! They're waiting!

Petra held out her hand to Mara, her eyes grave but her voice gentle. "If you stay here, I don't know what the Warden will do to you."

"It might be funny to find out," Mara said, but she took Petra's hand anyway and stood to find her cloak.

Petra laughed and grabbed Mara's boots. "You're so odd. I think that's why I like you."

Odd? Mara thought. She didn't feel odd. She felt very little, really. Sometimes when Petra laughed, Mara felt a twinge of something that could have been gladness. It came and went quickly, like a bird looking for a perch, but Mara's branches were no good—brittle and bare—so the bird wheeled around and flew off. That was what it felt like. A darting bright bird, gone too soon.

Mara let Petra lead her out of the barracks. A sea of whispers roiled against her skin as her fellow initiates pressed in on her from all sides. Her heart began to pound.

They were going to a lake, some of the girls were saying. They were going, at last, to the Old Country.

Two adult Roses, somber in hooded cloaks, their shadowed faces unreadable, led the girls through the priory, past alcoves and doorways where still more Roses gathered to watch them scurry by. Then they were out on the grounds: two columns of six recruits in nightgowns and stockings, boots and cloaks, with the two hooded Roses in front. The night was damp and cool, and the black trees stretched like a dark spider web across the silver sky. The sun had set long ago, but the Mist had its own light, like that of a bright full moon that never waned.

They passed through a gate in the wall that surrounded the priory, and then into the wild woods, where the ground was lumpy with moss that swallowed all sound. Here, the Mist slithered thickly. The milky air hissed and snapped like flames in a hearth, and one of the girls ahead of Mara choked out a scream.

Petra grabbed Mara's hand. Her palm was clammy, and her fingers trembled. Mara had never seen Petra look afraid before.

Am I *afraid?* Mara examined her body piece by piece, as her father had taught her to do. Her heartbeat was fast. Her jaw felt tense; she relaxed it and paid attention to her breathing until it was steady and deep. Her skin was a bit prickly. She felt a little like she wanted to run, but in a good way, a strong way. All her senses glinted bright as knives.

Even as the two hooded Roses led them into a greenway, and then another, and then *another*—twisting, violent passages through gnarled thickets and deep forests that reminded Mara, awfully, of home and all her mother's ivy—even then, in that mire of hungry magic, Mara felt ready. Ready for what, she didn't know.

But she did know that she wasn't afraid.

Mara glanced at Petra, whose skin had gone pale and shiny, and then at the other girls. Their faces told her everything: eyes glassy, lips tight and thin, every line of their bodies taut. Someone retched; someone else stumbled and let out a soft, startled sob. Greening magic, Mara knew, could disorient you if you weren't used to it. And not everyone came from Anointed families, as she did; not everyone could afford to hire wayfarers and travel through greenways as often and as simply as others used roads of stone and dirt.

And then there was the matter of her blood. Her father's voice echoed through her memory, strong and dear. *You are a sentinel, like me. We are warriors, Mara. We are hunters. We do not feel pain as others do. We do not become afraid as others do. But that doesn't mean we cannot be hurt, and it doesn't mean we should not sometimes fear.*

He had told Mara that long ago, when she was four years old and had begun to train with him out on the grounds at Ivyhill—racing deer in the game park, smashing boulders with quick kicks of her small, booted feet, plunging into the ice-cold lake to see who could hold their breath longer. At the time, Mara hadn't understood what he'd meant. She had only wanted to run faster, run farther, break more rocks, dive twenty, eighty, two hundred more times. And anyway, how could someone not be afraid but also feel fear?

But she had said, "Yes, Father," as patiently as she could manage, waiting breathlessly for him to suggest something else: let's climb a mountain, let's race to the top of that tree and then jump down, let's run all the way to the capital and back.

Now, though, Mara understood. She wasn't afraid of what was happening, not like the other girls were. Their breathing came in terrified little bursts; hers was steady. They stumbled; she didn't. They looked sick; she had never felt stronger. Her heart pounded as anyone's would in the face of such uncertainty, but she didn't panic. As she sucked down the silver air and allowed yet another greenway to tug her past the watchful older Roses, Mara felt, for the first time since arriving at Rosewarren, like her old self, a strong and clear-eyed girl, and not a pile of sadness trying feebly to hold on to its bones.

But then everything fell quiet. The Mist was gone; the ground was dark sand. Unfamiliar stars spangled the sky. The air was sharp and cold on Mara's skin, and on her tongue was the taste of silver coins. Then the tang of bright purple fruit. Then the gritty smoke of charred meat. With each breath came a new flavor, a new seduction of taste and aroma.

Old Country magic, Mara guessed, feeling a little wild. It tasted better than she would have thought.

Nearby, other girls were getting sick and crying. Petra's hand was cold, her breath thin. Mara shuddered, feeling chills of bliss all over, like she'd just sunk into a steaming-hot bath. Her muscles, neglected for so long, seemed to lengthen inside her like jungle cats stretching awake, ready to prowl. She fought not to smile; she didn't want Petra to think she was laughing at her for being afraid.

Overhead beamed a full moon, the path of its reflection glimmering across a black lake. A long wooden pier jutted out into the water; a raft bobbed alongside it. Scattered across the beach were stones and branches, driftwood, rusty hatchets, frayed ropes, broken staffs. Mara's skin tingled. *Weapons.* Not far from the tree line roared a bonfire, and around the bonfire, masked figures carrying spears paused in their revels to stare at them. Horrible noises rattled beyond the fire, beastly and furious. A rattle of metal, a jangle of chains. Mara squinted past the flames. Cages?

And at the shore, where the water lapped at the earth, stood a figure Mara had never seen before but would know anywhere. The whispered tales about her skittered across the continent of Gallinor like spiders. She was a pale woman with dark hair, wearing a black gown with a high collar and square shoulders, and she stood as still and tall as a pine.

The Warden. The woman who oversaw the priory, who had ruled Gallinor's Order of the Rose for decades upon decades. Ageless, ruthless, secretive. Feared. Adored.

Mara's breath grew quick. Her arms and face turned hot, then cold.

We do not become afraid as others do. But that doesn't mean we should not sometimes fear.

And she *did* feel fear in that moment. She felt it like she could feel the shape of her own body. But while the other girls gasped and startled or even turned to run away, Mara was quiet and watchful. Her fear kept her sharp. In this strange place, with Old Country magic washing over her like waves, she felt ready to run, to fight, to climb mountains, or even bring them crashing down. The Mara of earlier that night—despairing in her little cot, aching for home—felt like a bad dream.

Mara watched the Warden's eyes rake over all of them and land on her.

The Warden smiled. *At me*, Mara thought, readiness charging through her veins like lightning. *She's smiling at me.*

Then, with a voice like black stone worn smooth by a thousand rivers, the Warden said, "Welcome, little ones, to your night of trials. If you survive, you will be formally initiated into the Order of the Rose, and your placement will determine your rank, your duties, your room assignment. If you do not survive," she added gravely, "know that your sacrifice is not in vain. Everything we do, even these trials, is in the service of the Order and our queen."

Shock made the fine hairs on Mara's nape stand up. Death? That was not in the stories she'd been told. As far as she knew, the Warden was strict but not cruel. The trials were rigorous but not fatal. She crouched slightly; her muscles coiled, ready to spring. Petra began to cry quietly. Another girl wailed, "Survive? But we thought—"

The Warden raised her arms, cutting her off. "It's time to begin."

At her words a shudder of magic bolted through the air, swift and cold. The cage doors beyond the fire clanged open, and monsters tore free of their chains—five hulking chimaera, mottled with scales. Out of the lake burst a great watery fist. *A water titan?* Mara thought frantically.

The figures around the fire leapt across the beach, spears in hand, feet bare, hair streaming from under their masks. *Are they Roses?* Mara wondered. *Or fae from the deep Olden forests, or figments, with their powers of illusion?* The other girls were losing their minds—bolting away, screaming, throwing shaky magic at their attackers.

Mara took quick stock of her fellow recruits, remembering Petra's introductions from the barracks. There were three beguilers, who could work spells; one beholder, who could see through masking spells, like glamours, to the truth that lay beneath. A silvertongue, good with languages. A vissera, who could gather information and even glimpse shades of the future by reading animal remains. None of them were Anointed, and the remaining five were mere humans who could work no magic at all, including Petra, who was swift and clever but now looked as helpless as a lamb.

Mara spared a single angry thought for how unfair this seemed, how outmatched they were, and then bolted into action. She darted across the beach to the two nearest weapons—a hatchet and a stone the size of her head—and brought them back to the group in five seconds flat. Her muscles were mighty storms, her feet fast as falcons. The other girls gaped at her. Someone pointed over Mara's shoulder and shrieked, "*Chimaera!*"

Mara whirled around on her heel and flung the stone as hard as she could. It crashed into the chest of a rearing chimaera—a small thing, but ferocious. Feline, scaly, with a nasty mouth of fangs. With a horrible crack like lightning, the creature fell, its chest caved in, its ribs broken.

Smiling grimly, Mara shoved the hatchet into the hands of a brown-skinned girl with wide dark eyes and then turned to Petra.

"Take the other humans out onto that pier," she ordered. "Get on the raft and go out as far into the middle of the lake as you can."

"But the titan!" one of the girls protested, her face streaked with tears. A gurgling roar answered from the lake.

"It'll ignore you if you're boring enough," said one of the other girls—the vissera. She was maybe twelve years old, with a pale, square jaw, bright eyes, and a lean body built for running. "Titans don't like working for anyone, no matter how much they're paid for it."

Impressed, Mara nodded. "And we'll distract it, draw its attention. Now, go!"

Petra hurried the others away, throwing one quick glance at Mara over her shoulder.

Mara jerked her head at the vissera. "Are you fast?" she demanded.

The girl nodded once.

"Go collect as many weapons as you can. I'll cover you."

Then Mara ran straight for the nearest chimaera, who was bounding their way with mean yellow eyes. Enormous bat wings, face like a naked bear, paws carving huge divots in the sand. White neck, bare and exposed. There was a glint of silver on the ground: a knife. Not big, but something.

The chimera pounced with a snarl. Mara leapt to meet it, heart pounding hard, lungs screaming with joy—this exertion, this *force*; she was made for it. She squared her shoulders, lowered her head, then twisted her body in midair and jammed her elbow into the creature's soft neck. Together they crashed to the ground, the chimaera wheezing out a choked roar. Mara rolled, avoiding its flailing claws, grabbed the knife, and spun around to plunge it into the chimaera's left eye. Deep. Hard. Blade against bone.

Blood spurted, steaming and rancid. The creature shrieked its agony. Mara wrenched the knife from its skull, shook her head to clear her spotty vision, and ran back to the others. The vissera girl tossed a staff to the girl nearest her, then grabbed a thick branch and put her whole weight on it to snap it in two. She kept one for herself and shoved the other into the hands of the silvertongue girl—short, shaking, ashen. Then the vissera whirled back around to find Mara, and her eyes widened.

"Look out!" she shouted.

Mara felt the titan before she saw it. The ancient creature's might sucked at the beach under her feet like a violent tide. She shoved the others away, the force of her push flinging them thirty feet across the beach, where they skidded to a stop. An instant later, the titan's furious water came crashing down like a fist, knocking Mara flat. She went swirling underneath the waves, kicked hard, and surfaced, dodged another blow of a huge rippling fist, caught a glimpse of an angry, glaring white eye.

Mara swam for the beach and tore across it the moment her feet hit sand. The vissera girl ran up to her, fierce and soaked, her branch clutched in her hands. She jerked her head past Mara.

"Look at them," she said tightly. "They're running away. Why?"

Mara whirled around to see the masked figures racing into the woods, spears in hand. They crowed gleefully, as if there weren't a titan pummeling the beach or a chimaera chasing after them. One of them easily dispatched the small wolfish chimaera with a sharp kick to its side. The creature yelped and went flying.

And then Mara realized that these masked figures were women. She was close enough to see their bodies in the roaring firelight and caught a rose tattoo flashing on a shin here, a shoulder there. A chill climbed up Mara's arms. These women were *Roses*, and none of them were attacking Mara or the other recruits. They certainly *looked* menacing, with their masks and their jerky movements, like they were performing some strange dance. Mara's first instinct was to lunge for one, fell her, and steal her spear.

But it was all a show, she began to comprehend. None of them had used their spears on the recruits. And that woman had kicked away the chimaera as a normal person might a ball.

A sentinel. Mara's heart jumped in recognition.

She ran after the woman, ignoring the warning cries of the other recruits. The woman raised her spear and crouched as if to strike, but Mara kept running, then slammed to a stop right in front of her. *May all your thorns drip poison.* The phrase emerged from the hazy memories of those long days in the barracks when she had wished for death. She had heard some of the others talking about it, including Petra, before they'd become friends. It was a thing the Roses said to one another before battle—a wish for blood, for victory, for a safe return.

Mara reached out and grasped the woman's forearm. Her nerves fluttered, but she thought of her father and held on to her courage.

"May all your thorns drip poison," she said, her voice small but strong, and when the woman raised her mask and smiled, her face streaked with paint and her cropped blond hair soaked with sweat, Mara couldn't help but smile back.

The woman grasped Mara's other arm and squeezed, gentle but firm. She looked several years older than the recruits. "And may your bones always know the way home," she replied with a keen look. "I'm Brigid."

"I'm Mara."

"Oh, I know. We've heard about you."

Mara bit back her delighted questions and instead said breathlessly, "Will you help us?"

The woman grinned. "We thought you'd never ask. Just tell us where to go."

Then she turned and whooped over her shoulder—a battle cry, Mara realized, her skin prickling with excitement—and the other Roses shed their masks, tossed them joyfully into the trees, and followed Mara back onto the beach, spears raised to defend her.

Following me, following me, Mara repeated to herself as she ran. Letting herself grin felt like unlocking a secret door buried deep in her grieving heart. *They're following* me.

"Any elementals here?" Mara called over her shoulder.

"Here!" one of the women cried.

"And here!" shouted another.

"Go distract the titan. Keep it away from the humans, don't let it near their raft."

"And the rest of us?" asked Brigid.

Mara shot her a smile. "We'll take care of the chimaera."

She couldn't *stop* smiling. These women at her back, these women flying across the beach at her orders—they were all so strong and fearsome, and they were all Roses. Like she would be. Like she *was*.

May your bones always know the way home. As Mara whirled into battle, flanked by hollering Roses, the fleeting thought came that maybe, if she couldn't return to Ivyhill, the priory wouldn't be such a terrible prison after all. Maybe, someday, it could even feel like home.

It was the last thought she had before a great inky blackness swooped across her vision—jagged and dark, like feathers spread wide—and the world around her disappeared.

When Mara came to, she was in the trees. *High* in the trees. The stars were closer, the air quieter. Quickly she assessed her surroundings: she was on a sturdy wooden platform affixed to a pine's thick trunk. An Olden pine, fatter and taller than any she had ever seen. The cold air brushed across her skin with a sensation like someone was painting her with silver fire. On her tongue, the taste of smoke. Olden magic, ripe and swollen.

And she was not alone.

A dark figure perched on the platform's edge, looking out over the world.

"I need your help, Mara," it said.

The Warden. Mara recognized her at once, though her voice was deeper now, rounder, like bells so huge and old that their chimes could shake the earth.

The Warden raised her long feathered arm. *Feathered*, with curling talons and iridescent bird down that gleamed in the moonlight.

Mara's breath caught. The Warden had transformed into her avian form, as Roses did during battle. *Real* battle, against real Olden enemies. Mara wondered what it looked like when a Rose transformed from woman to bird. She had always wondered.

Mara approached the Warden slowly, her heart beating at the back of her throat, her mouth dry. She thought of her father's voice. She would fear, but she would not be afraid. Fear could be helpful; it warned, it advised. She forced her racing mind to slow down and observe. Yes, here was the Warden, crouched on the platform's edge like one of Ivyhill's grinning gargoyles. Her gown was gone; in its place was the naked skin of a pale woman and the feathers of a great dark bird. Her hair flowed loose and wild. Fierce black feathers framed her golden eyes.

Owl. The resemblance was obvious.

The Warden was pointing down at the beach below. Tiny bonfire, tiny darting shapes. A faint chimera yowl. The answering holler of a Rose.

"You did well," the Warden said. "Look at all of them fighting together. Seasoned Roses and raw recruits. Fresh little buds. They're frightened, yet they fight." The Warden's head swiveled unnaturally as she turned to stare at Mara. "You did that, Mara. You gave them orders, made them brave. Instead of desperately fighting everything that looked like an enemy, you had the nerve to ask for help. Many would have died without you. Now all of them live. How does that make you feel?"

Mara pried her gaze from the scene below and forced herself to meet the Warden's unblinking stare. "Proud," she replied. Her blood ran hot and fast under her skin. "And happy."

"Happy. Do you enjoy violence, Mara?"

"I am a warrior. A hunter." *Like my father before me, she thought, with a pang of homesickness*. "I'm good at fighting. I like doing it." She paused. She sensed that it was wise to be careful. "And I'm happy that everyone survived the trials. We'll all be Roses now. Isn't that right?"

The Warden cocked her head. "Fierce child. The trials have only just begun. Look, out there on the water. What do you see?"

Mara obeyed. Waves churned at the shore, where the elemental Roses battled the titan. Beyond that, a raft drifted steadily across the water. When Mara squinted, she saw a single figure atop it—a girl with auburn hair.

Petra.

Mara's stomach turned. "I don't understand. Where is Petra going? Why is she alone? I told her to take the other humans out onto the lake."

The Warden did not answer.

Mara looked to the pier, and what she saw froze her blood. The other four humans—the girls Petra had been tasked with protecting—remained huddled on the pier's edge, abandoned. Mara's sharp sentinel hearing brought her a desperate sound. One of the girls on the pier was calling after Petra with a sob in her voice, pleading with her to come back. Petra had *left* them there.

"Petra is very brave," Mara said calmly. She did not feel calm. "I don't know why she left the others, but there must be a good reason. Maybe she's going for help."

The Warden hummed quietly. "These are Olden forests. Help is rare and comes at a cost."

"She's trying to distract the titan, then."

"That titan doesn't care about one lone girl when he has a whole beach full of people to entertain him. Perhaps," she added delicately, "Petra thought too many girls would sink the raft, or that she was safer on her own. One girl on a raft is surely less appealing to a titan than four girls stuck on a pier."

"She's just afraid," Mara offered. She curled her fingers around the ends of her sleeves. "There's nothing wrong with fear, and of course she's afraid. You're making us fight monsters."

"True. But I don't see you paddling away, leaving the others to fend for themselves."

Suddenly Mara's anger returned. This wasn't fair. She turned to glare at the Warden. "I could be down there helping them, but you brought me here instead. Why?"

For a moment, the Warden was still. After a moment, she said quietly, "The binding magic that ties me to my duty as Warden, and ties all of my Roses to *their* duty and to me, is ancient and unkind. It is hungry. It needs blood to do its dark works. And no one has died yet today. Thanks to you, Mara, everyone is safe. Look, even now"—she nodded at the water—"the titan's attack is subsiding. The chimaera are dead. And away across the water floats Petra the coward. Listen to the others beg her to return. How frightened they are."

Mara shook her head. "I don't understand."

"You do. The trials are meant to cull the weak. Weak hearts poison the magic we must use to fulfill our duty, to serve our queen."

An oily slick of dread curled inside Mara's stomach.

"What should we do, Mara?"

The Warden's voice was gentle, patient, sad. It brought Mara no comfort.

"She was kind to me," Mara insisted. "I won't do anything to hurt her."

"Even if that means others might hurt instead? Even if binding her to us weakens our magic? Even if making her one of us means it will be harder for us to protect our country?"

Mara hesitated. Words stuck in her throat, words she refused to speak.

The Warden sighed. She stretched her sinuous neck, shifted her weight. Her slender feathered feet ended in black talons as thick as Mara's wrists.

"Very well," she said. "We'll bring her back to shore. But I hope, Mara, that as the trials continue—and they will continue, for as many nights as are required—you will make the wise choice, for all our sakes."

Mara looked up at her stern visage, feeling small and cold. "But why must *I* choose?"

"Because you are strong," the Warden replied, "and the binding magic will therefore relish your decision. In thanks, it will bolster you. You and your fellow recruits will enjoy a particularly steadfast connection. You'll grow into a mighty squadron. Someday you may even be the soldiers who save us all." The Warden looked out over the water, tracking Petra's raft with her golden eyes. "Is that blessed chance to save your country, your queen, something you would give up, all for the sake of one cowardly little girl? To save her, you would welcome rot into our bloodline?"

To that, Mara had no answer. Her mind turned and turned, looking for the right thing to say, the right thing to feel, to do. She worried it might go on spinning forever.

The Warden sighed once more and opened her wings. "Come, child. The next trial awaits. Remember what I have told you."

Mara could not protest. She couldn't even recall her father's voice. She stepped into the Warden's feathered embrace and hesitated, unsure where to put her hands.

The Warden's laugh was harsh. "I have lived lifetimes in this world. A few pulled feathers won't pain me. Hold on tight."

Mara obeyed. The feathers were black silk against her palms.

"Will I have to be the one to do it?" Mara whispered. "After I make the choice. Will I have to be the one who hurts her too?" Her cheek pressed against the warm skin right above the Warden's downy breasts. The scent there was familiar, maternal. Mara pushed hard against the rising thoughts of home.

"What do you think the magic that binds us would most enjoy?" the Warden asked. Bitterness soured her voice.

It was a question that needed no reply, for the answer was obvious. Mara closed her eyes tight. She would not cry, she would not cry. The Order's old magic, she suspected, would scorn her tears. She locked her shaking legs around the Warden's feathered hips and held on tight as the night air rushed around them. Their flight was silent, swift. Below, on the beach, the bonfire still burned. Roaring. Waiting.

Chapter 1

It was a rare quiet morning at Rosewarren, dawn only just beginning to brighten the windows and the air crisp with the coming winter. A beautiful morning, really, if one cared about such things.

I did not.

I stormed out of the priory and strode across the grounds, the frosty grass crunching beneath my boots and my blood burning bright with fury.

I had just come from the infirmary, where I'd left one of my fellow Roses, Cira, with Nanette, our head nurse. Cira was fifteen and strong, far more resilient than her reedy frame would suggest, and the wound in her shoulder was minor. Nanette wasn't concerned; neither was Cira. Injuries were to be expected. We were Roses, after all, and our country was at war.

But in the twelve hours since the arrow had pierced Cira's shoulder, I hadn't been able to stop thinking about the man who had fired it.

Just before I entered the stables, I threw an irritated glare at the nearby Middlemist. Its soft light that morning—a silver glow beneath the rising dawn—felt like a cruel taunt. I hadn't seen it so tranquil in months. Not since before my sisters and I freed Talan from Kilraith, before any of us knew that the late Queen Yvaine had been a godly being called Ankaret.

Before the war that now governed our every decision, every meal, every hour.

That morning, however, even with blood from the night's battle still spattering my arms, I hardly thought of the war. I could only think about Gareth. Gareth Fontaine and his foolish friends, one of whom was apparently a fantastic shot with a crossbow even when he was drunk.

I took to one of our new mares with a curry comb, hoping a few minutes of vigorous brushing would calm me. A list of tasks awaited me—writing reports, training our new recruits, running through my daily conditioning exercises—and I wouldn't be able to focus on any of them until my anger quieted.

Before even a minute had passed, however, Posey found me. One moment she wasn't there; the next she was, in that uncanny way of the Olden fae.

"You look terrible," she remarked, regarding me over the mare's shoulders with her bright silver eyes. "What happened to Cira? I heard something about an arrow wound."

"We were on patrol in the southeastern canyons yesterday evening," I replied, eyes focused on my work. "An intoxicated ass thought she was a game bird and shot her with his crossbow."

Posey snorted. "What kind of game bird is as large as a Rose in flight?"

"I think we can blame that miscalculation on the aforementioned drunkenness."

"I suppose he could have thought her a harpy or a chimaera. Neither is as unlikely as it once was."

"If he were smarter, he would have given me that excuse," I said grimly. "Alas."

"Did you kill him?"

"The thought crossed my mind. But then a piece of Mist fell. Even that far south, we could feel the aftershocks. We left, we fought the invaders, we secured the break, we came home." I pressed my lips together, remembering how bravely Cira had fought, even with her injury. "If her wing is permanently damaged..."

"Then you'll kill him?"

"Perhaps."

Posey began combing her fingers through the mare's mane. "Who was he, anyway?"

"Some librarian from the capital. A friend of my sister's friend. I don't know his name. But Gareth will tell me, or else I'll make him tell me."

"Gareth? He's your sister's friend?"

"Gareth Fontaine." I punctuated the words with a brisk stroke of my comb. "A professor and librarian at the university, and a breaker of many ladies' hearts, if I am to believe Farrin's stories, and I have no reason not to."

Posey looked at me with new interest. "What sorts of stories are those?"

"I came out here for peace and quiet," I said, "not vulgar storytelling."

"I don't think you're allowed peace and quiet if you're the Warden's favorite."

Something about the tone of her voice made me lower the comb and look at her.

"What is it?" I said. "You've come to tell me something."

Just then a small falcon glided into the stable and alighted on the mare's stall door. My angry heart lifted to see the familiar brown feathers of Freyda, my falcon and familiar. Posey turned away from me to stroke Freyda's speckled white breast.

"The Warden wants you," Posey said, holding up a curled piece of paper. "And if you don't go quickly enough, she'll take it out on me. So please go quickly. If she asks why you're late, blame it on Gareth and his friends."

I sighed, set down the curry comb, and came to Posey's side. Freyda watched my approach with a stern yellow glare. Never mind that she was my bonded familiar and I would never love another creature the way I loved her. I hadn't sought her out upon returning to Rosewarren, as was our custom, and it was clearly important to her that I understand how upsetting that was.

"When you say the Warden will take it out on you," I said to Posey, "what does that mean?"

Posey handed me the Warden's message and raised one elegant silver eyebrow. A row of elaborate pearlescent earrings glinted in each of her long, pointed ears, and her green-tinged skin gleamed in the torchlight.

"She doesn't beat me," Posey said coolly, "if that's what you mean. I can tolerate a lot, but not that."

"And if she did decide to beat you, how would you fight back, exactly?"

"A captive fae is still a fae. There's some strength in me yet."

"If we were talking about any other human, I'd agree with you. But the Warden is…"

"A horror?" Posey offered sweetly. "A brute?"

I wasn't in the mood to joke about the Warden. "She's also the reason you're here and not dead."

That surprised her. A wave of hurt crossed her face before she could hide it, and she began fiddling with the small silver locket she always wore at her throat—a familiar nervous habit of hers. As impossible as it would have once seemed to me to befriend a fae, I had done it anyway over the last few weeks, after convincing the Warden to offer Posey asylum in exchange for aiding our intelligence efforts. During that time, I had seldom been short with her.

"I'm sorry," I said after a moment. "That was unkind."

I rubbed my forehead, wincing a little. I could feel a headache coming on. We'd all been getting headaches more frequently. Headaches, fevers, tremors, random stabbing pains. Soon those symptoms would spread far beyond the Mistlands. The gods had made the Middlemist, and they'd also made all of us who lived in the human world of Edyn. Now the Mist was falling, and if we couldn't save it, so would we. It was inevitable.

All of this was inevitable. At least it felt that way to me. I hadn't been able to make my own decisions since I was ten years old and the Warden had taken me from Ivyhill, with a few notable exceptions. And even those—going into the Old Country with my sisters the first time we fought Kilraith; sneaking them into Rosewarren for more visits than they were allowed—had felt like stumbling into decisions that someone else had made for me.

The only thing I'd done completely of my own volition was collect my morbid cave treasures: corpses affected by Mistfires, artifacts belonging to people who had been infected by the failing Mist and gone mad. I could barely stand to think about that Mara of months ago, so earnestly determined to shoulder some of the Warden's burden and unravel the growing mystery behind the Mist's condition herself.

A whole lot of good that had done.

Posey put a hand on my arm, wresting me from my dark thoughts. "You should ask the Warden for some time to yourself. You need rest." Mischief curled her voice. "I wasn't joking earlier. You do look terrible."

I smiled a little. Teasing I could handle. "Rather unfair, coming from a fae. Is it even possible for you to look ugly?"

"Certainly not. I'm offended that you would even ask such a thing."

The knots in my shoulders eased the slightest bit. I pushed aside the pain of my headache and took the Warden's message from her.

Posey watched me with an uncharacteristically grave expression on her face. "I mean it, Mara. You're no good to any of them if you're exhausted."

Them. The other Roses. The tired elders, the frightened littles. More and more littles these days. With our dwindling numbers, we could no longer afford to be choosy when recruiting, and the new draft law issued by the Royal Conclave told us we didn't have to be.

"I'll think about it," I lied, giving Posey a reassuring smile.

"That is the worst fake smile I've ever seen."

"Go have some breakfast. You'll get the freshest rolls."

Posey made a face. "Rolls. Good gods. How I miss fae food."

As I strode across the stable yard back toward the main house, Freyda flew after me and landed lightly on my shoulder. The pinch of her talons reassured me. She gave a few strands of my hair one of her familiar sharp tugs. I'd been forgiven, it seemed.

I reached up to stroke her belly, wishing I could retreat to my room and draw her close, tuck her little head under mine, and breathe in the scent of her feathers. Most falcons would tolerate no such behavior. But like me, Freyda was far from ordinary.

"Thank you," I whispered. It was so much easier to face the Warden when Freyda was with me—and easier to ignore thoughts of home, which seemed to arise much more swiftly when I was tired. Ivyhill, Farrin, Gemma, Father. Mother, sequestered up at Wardwell. I still wasn't used to thinking of her as a god. For so long I'd tried not to think of her at all. I'd tried—and failed—not to think about any of them, though with every breath I missed them a little bit more. Over the years, they had come to visit me once a month, as all the Roses' families were allowed to do, and every time they left, it was like they carved out a piece of me to take with them and I was left a little less whole.

Freyda's talons squeezed my shoulder again, bringing me back to myself. She always knew when the shadows were coming for me.

I scratched her belly once more, then opened the Warden's note, expecting it to be a summons to her office upstairs. But reading it made me stop short.

Come to the Stillhouse at once, it said in her precise, cramped penmanship. Nothing more.

Freyda ruffled her feathers and gave a soft chirp, disquieted by my sudden unease. The Stillhouse was cruelly named; there was nothing still about the place. It was where we kept our most dangerous prisoners. No matter how diligently we scrubbed its walls, we could never wash away the stains.

Thinking of those mean, dark rooms turned me cold. I stood at the edge of the stable yard and focused on the rhythm of my breathing until I'd squashed my rising dread and paved over it with stone.

The Warden's message could mean only one thing. It was time, once again, to interrogate the harpy Nerys.

A horrible shriek burst through the air just as I stepped into Nerys's cell. I was glad I'd left Freyda up above, though I'd almost been cowardly enough to bring her with me. The scream of a harpy is a terrible thing—multitonal, discordant, loud enough to make one's ears bleed if the harpy is at full strength.

Luckily for me, Nerys was hardly more than a deflated bag of skin and bones on the floor. She had few feathers left, her wings small, fleshy, and pocked with sores in their absence.

Even at the grisly sight of her, I didn't break my stride once. What a model Rose I was. I closed the door behind me and headed down the stone stairs to join the Warden. She crouched over Nerys, staring into her cloudy yellow eye. In her hand she held a glass syringe of bright green liquid.

"The tip I received indicates that the creature Kilraith could be hiding in the Cold Barrens," the Warden said quietly, "building an army out of the scraps of Mhorghast. Planning his final offensive. That's where you were born, isn't it, Nerys? A hatchling harpy taking her first awkward flight among the frost-trees."

If I closed my eyes, I'd be able to imagine her speaking to a small child. I could convince myself that perhaps she was telling a bedtime story.

I did not allow myself to close my eyes.

"Nerys," the Warden said, wheedling, "I know you don't want me to give you more of this serum. I know it hurts. I don't like causing pain, if you can believe that. So don't make me do it. Let's have a conversation instead. Tell me where in the Barrens someone like Kilraith might hide."

The Warden waited, statue-still. The only things that moved were her black eyes, darting across the harpy's mangled skin. Cataloging every wound we'd inflicted on her, every infected scar.

What was she thinking? I wondered. What was she *feeling*? If she felt anything, that is. After twelve years with the Warden, I still couldn't be entirely sure what made her tick.

The only thing I knew for certain was that as frightened as I was of her, I loved her even more. And I wanted her to love me.

It was my greatest triumph—and the source of my deepest shame—to be the Warden's favorite Rose.

"Nerys, talk to me about the Barrens," she continued. "I've been there myself hundreds of times, but I know harpies love their secrets, and I know somewhere in that harpy mind of yours are hiding spots that even I've never seen. Describe to me exactly where they are."

For a long time, Nerys was still. The silence was awful, heavy. The vials of poison sitting on the little wooden table to my right glowed like gems in the torchlight.

I fixed my gaze on the harpy's unblinking eye. The flesh around it was ghastly, swollen and abused; she could barely open it. She was quiet for so long that I began to think she was dead, or close to it. *Die,* I thought, directing all my energy toward her. Maybe some scrap of my mother's godly power would rise up within me and sap the life from this poor creature. *Please die. Give up. There's nothing left for you here.*

Finally, Nerys shifted to look away from the Warden and right at me instead. Gemma would have been horrified to see the left half of the harpy's face, where flesh and muscle had been scraped away to expose her bones. Farrin would have excoriated me for allowing such treatment.

But at the sight of Nerys's wounds, I felt only a small ripple of disgust that I tamped down immediately. *May all your thorns drip poison,* came the thought.

And here we were—the Warden and me—dripping our poison just as we were supposed to.

Nerys cracked open her dry, lipless mouth. All her sharp teeth were gone. Her gums were black and green with infection.

"Kill me," she rasped, looking right at me with the one eye she had left.

"Never," the Warden snapped. "I will keep you alive for the rest of my life, and I have many decades left in this world." Then she plunged the syringe's needle into the sagging flesh of the harpy's neck.

The Warden's poisons worked quickly. Nerys's body seized before I could draw another breath. Once she had been massive and powerful, requiring dozens of steel chains bolted to the floor to contain her. Now all the chains were gone. We'd broken her so thoroughly that they weren't necessary. She twitched and screamed between us on the cold floor, each stone stained black with her blood. Weeks of it, layers upon layers.

The Warden leaned closer, put her mouth right above Nerys's

ragged, tufted ear. "Tell me about the Barrens, Nerys," she shouted, implacable. Harpy screams were nothing to her. "Tell me, and I'll make it stop. Are there underground caves? Strongholds in the mountains? Vaults cloaked in Olden magic? The Great Mother Harpy has always been fascinated with fae. Did she strike a bargain with one of the clans? Are they hiding Kilraith? Are they hiding He Who Is All?"

"Please," Nerys moaned. Her limbs bent unnaturally, jerked out of alignment by the poison. A wrist snapped; a wing inverted. "Kill me!"

I did not look away. I'd seen worse, and my dread was safe beneath all the stone inside me. I imagined a smooth winding road of it stretching from my tongue down to my throat and then to the panic bubbling in my gut. Quieting me. Coating me with cool stillness.

The Warden tossed away the syringe with a sharp curse. "Mara, get over here. And bring the Box."

I was ready to obey until she mentioned the Box—the nickname for a poison so vile that I'd seen it used only once in all my years of service. That stopped me in my tracks, startling me out of the cool, still place I'd been standing in.

At my hesitation, the Warden rounded on me. "The *Box*, Mara."

I don't know what made me do it. Maybe I harbored a scrap of my mother's power after all, indignant at the treatment of one of her sister Neave's creatures. Maybe it was my exhaustion, or the shadows on the Warden's haggard face that betrayed her own. She was not herself. None of us were. The breach bells rang every hour. The Mist was falling. The queen was dead. And we trained new Roses every morning while burning the corpses of dead ones every night.

"Madam, we can't," I said quietly. "The Box is meant for—"

"I know what the Box is for," she said, rising to her feet. Her voice was chillingly quiet. "I designed it. And I'm telling you to bring it to me right now."

She could have easily retrieved it herself. It sat there on the table with the Warden's other tools of torture: a single drop of dull purple liquid in a slender glass vial.

But now it had become an order. A challenge, a test. The Warden held out her hand, watching me, waiting.

Maybe there was a drop of pity or kindness left in me, no matter how hard I'd worked to rid myself of such things, especially over the last few blood-soaked weeks.

"There are other ways to find information about the Barrens," I suggested, trying for reason. "We can dispatch a scouting squadron, send Posey with them. They can act as her prisoners if they need to."

"We don't have soldiers to spare for yet another dangerous scouting mission," the Warden said. "And I'm tired of playing games with this creature. Bring me the Box."

"It will take you many weeks to brew another batch." I was getting desperate. "What if a dire situation arises tomorrow and we need what we have left?"

"Then we'll brew more."

"Madam, we don't have the resources—"

"We'll find the resources!"

"It will kill her," I said sharply. My skin was hot with anger, with fear. I should not have come here without Freyda.

"It won't, and you know it. Did you hear that, Nerys?" The Warden crouched, hands on her knees. "This vile substance I'm about to feed you will make you think you're dying, but it lies. You'll think you're finally passing into the Great Dominion, where the gods were born, where you can finally find peace—but then you'll find yourself right back here before me, with noxious fire burning you from the inside out and the memories of everyone you've ever killed screaming in your head. And you've killed a lot of people, haven't you? Do you wonder what they felt in their last moments, as your talons tore into them? As your venom choked their lungs? Soon you will no longer have to wonder."

With every sentence, the Warden pressed closer to Nerys. Her voice climbed in both volume and pitch and began to fracture. To my horror, I thought I heard a wave of tears amid all her fury. The sound shocked me into moving toward her—to comfort her, to lead her away from this death-drenched room. She needed a drink of water; she needed rest.

But as soon as I got close enough, she grabbed my forearm, yanked me toward her, and twisted me around to face Nerys. I tried to squirm away, but the Warden's grip was strong and cold as ice.

"Look at her," she commanded. "Look her in the eye and tell her to answer my questions."

My shock left me speechless. Long weeks ago, I'd been here in this very room with Farrin and Gemma, manipulating them into using our collective influence to pry more information out of Nerys. Because we had Kerezen's blood in our veins—the blood of the goddess who had created sirens, incubi, succubi; the goddess of seduction and beauty—our mere presence had made Nerys talk.

I didn't see how it was possible for the Warden to know about this. Had someone—my family, Gareth, my sisters' lovers—betrayed our secret? My thoughts immediately flew to Wardwell, where Mother had hidden herself away.

"*Tell* her, Mara," the Warden said, watching me carefully.

"I don't see how me asking her questions will make any difference," I managed to say.

"You're lying. You've been keeping something from me."

It took all my strength to meet her dark gaze with a look of what I hoped was genuine confusion. "I don't lie to you, Madam."

"You do when it serves your interests and that of your sisters," she replied, then pushed on before I could speak. "Do you think I'm oblivious to the rumors of what happened in Mhorghast? Most of the stories I've heard are useless gossip, but some give me pause. And I can read between the lines of the report you gave me. You shouldn't have gotten out of such a place alive, much less unscathed. You've fought Kilraith twice now, and though he still lives, he hasn't managed to kill you. Why?"

"We've been lucky," I said quietly.

"Yes, the wicked sort of luck that blesses fools and liars." Suddenly the Warden's expression softened. She didn't release me, but with her free hand she cupped my cheek. I leaned into her cool touch before I could stop myself, my heart fluttering madly. Not even I, favored Mara, was immune to the allure of the Warden's affection. Her touch was rare, a precious gift.

"It saddens me that you don't trust me with the secrets you carry," the Warden murmured. "You know that I think of you as my own daughter, don't you? All of you are my daughters, but you especially."

I didn't know what to say to that. The weight of her attention was unbearable, the kind of pain that bordered on bliss.

"I trust you," I whispered. "I am yours, Madam. I serve you with all my heart."

She watched me for a moment longer, holding my face gently in her hand. Then something dark crossed her face, a gutting flicker of sadness. She shoved me away and stood, glaring down at Nerys.

"Someday you'll stop lying to me, Mara," she said quietly. "Until then, know that every day you persist in deceiving me is like a knife to my heart."

Then she retrieved a sword from the shadows and with one swift stroke severed Nerys's head from her body.

"There," she said, her voice flat and dull. "A gift for you, Mara. Her long suffering has ended. Am I not merciful?"

Her disappointment in me was physical, a blow that stunned tears from my eyes. In a moment, I would tell her everything, if only to banish that look from her face. The words danced on my tongue.

"Leave me," the Warden said, saving me from myself. "I need to clean this up. And there is much to do." She brought a shaking hand to her temple, pressed her fingers to her hairline as if to stave off a headache. "Always so much to do," she repeated quietly.

I turned and fled up the stairs. Only when I burst out of the Stillhouse and my boots touched the grass did I feel like I could breathe again. Freyda swooped down from the trees, and when I opened my arms she came to me, fussing at me as if I were an errant child. I held her to my chest and pressed my brow to her silken head until my eyes were dry once more.

Chapter 2

After three afternoon training sessions with new recruits and an evening patrol to assess the state of the Mist in my assigned territory, I was in no mood for company.

I'd sustained a nasty knock on the head from a terrified young mountain nymph who'd fallen through a hole in the Mist and had been only too happy to be driven back into the Old Country where she belonged. My joints ached, and I'd been unable to stomach lunch or dinner after the incident with the Warden, so I was ravenous. The idea of a quiet few minutes in the privacy of my room with some stew—and more importantly, some bread—was the only thing keeping my legs moving forward.

But my room was occupied.

Cira and Brigid turned as I opened the door. Cira was sitting cross-legged on my bed, and Brigid was reading in the corner chair. Both of them were in their nightclothes, and both of them looked far too eager for such a late hour.

"I know, it's late, but don't kill us just yet," Cira said, holding up two sealed letters with a grin.

My breath caught. "Are they from…?"

Brigid closed her book and smiled. "They are. Both of them."

I set my dinner on the bedside table and took the letters from Cira with suddenly shaky fingers.

"You're trembling," Cira observed. "What happened? Is Nerys—"

Brigid hushed her with a sharp hiss.

The first letter I opened revealed Gemma's handwriting, the second Farrin's. I held each of them for a long moment before I could bring myself to start reading. The sight of their penmanship alone was enough to make me feel weepy again, and I'd already felt weepy more than enough for one day. I wasn't used to the feeling.

"Can you tell us what they say?" Cira asked.

Brigid made an irritated noise. *"Cira."*

"I was just *asking*."

Quickly, I read each note three times. I could hear their voices in my head—Gemma's clear as a bell, Farrin's steady and sharp. Then I fed the letters to the fire and watched the flames until my sisters' words were ashes.

"No news," I said flatly. Farrin and Ryder were still in the capital, working with the royal councils to oversee military operations and secure housing for the refugees fleeing south. *Come and find me,* Ankaret had said before her death—and Farrin had tried, as hard as she was able to with all the world on her shoulders. But there had been no sign of our late queen in either of her forms. And Gemma and Talan were still searching the country for signs of the awakening gods, but they still had no leads, not even a whisper of one. Soon it would be winter; traveling would be more difficult and dangerous, even for them. The cold made people desperate. So did war.

And their letters hadn't even touched on the *ytheliad,* the curse that had allowed Kilraith to gain such strong footholds in both Edyn and the Old Country. Our theory was that five objects anchored the curse. The first was the Three-Eyed Crown, which had bound Talan to Kilraith and was now hidden at the university, being studied. Then there was the egg that had been hidden inside the human host of Jaetris, god of the mind, which my sisters and I had taken from Mhorghast. It too was safe in Fairhaven, the capital city.

Gareth and his team at the university had been studying each of these anchors for weeks—their markings, the strange movements of their clockwork parts, the shadowy images that darkened their jewels—and if their interpretation was correct, three anchors remained: a key, a goblet, and a black lake under a full moon, the only anchor that was not an object.

But scouring the shores of every lake in Gallinor had revealed nothing. I'd even led teams of Roses to Olden lakes—including the vast black lake at which the Order conducted our recruiting trials—and we had found nothing there either. I was beginning to worry that Gareth and his team had made a mistake, that the image of the lake was meaningless and there was an unknown fifth anchor somewhere for which we hadn't even begun to search.

My worries these days were plentiful, and my concern for my sisters' safety ate at me more than any other.

"Every day I worry the letters will stop coming," I muttered to the fire. "Every day I wonder if I should tell my sisters to stop sending them. Contacting me puts them in danger. And if the Warden—"

I stopped, cursing my mistake. I hadn't yet told either of them about my true lineage and hoped I would never have to. A fool's hope, but I clung to it anyway.

"If the Warden what?" Cira demanded.

"Nothing." I rubbed my forehead hard. "It's nothing."

"We heard you went to the Stillhouse today," Brigid said. "What happened? Something did. I saw it on your face the moment you walked in."

That question seemed safe enough. I turned to face them. The firelight kissed Cira's brown skin, black braids, and bandaged shoulder with gold. Brigid, nearing thirty-five and the oldest Rose in service, was solid as a tower, tall, and pale with white-blond hair cropped short.

I could hardly stand to look at either of them, especially Brigid. A thirty-five-year-old Rose was unheard of. Her marvelous luck would run out one of these days, and I didn't think I would be able to survive the blow.

"Nerys is dead," I told them simply.

"Good," Brigid said at once. "That should have happened long ago. She hasn't given us relevant information in weeks. There was no reason to keep tormenting her."

"The Warden enjoyed it though," Cira said, watching my face. "What changed her mind?"

A vision of the Warden flashed through my mind—her hand tight around my arm, her fingers brushing my cheek. Her eyes hard and black, furious. *Know that every day you persist in deceiving me is like a knife to my heart.*

"I did, I suppose," I said, trying to push the memory out of my head. "She wanted to use the Box on Nerys. I told her she shouldn't, and things became strained."

After a moment, Brigid asked quietly, "Did she hurt you?"

I scoffed, retrieved my dinner, and sat on the floor to eat. "Why does that matter? She has hurt all of us many times."

"It matters because I've seldom seen you this upset."

"I'm not upset. I'm tired."

"Mara, come sit on the bed," said Cira. "It's softer."

"I don't want softness," I snapped, and then, as I chewed ferociously on my bread, something inside me broke open, and the tears I'd been fighting all day spilled out of me. I wasn't a loud crier; one moment I was eating, and the next my eyes were burning. A tight pain in my chest made it hard to breathe.

Brigid gently took my tray and helped me to my bed, then pulled her chair close while Cira curled up beside me and wrapped her arms around one of mine. The gesture reminded me so unexpectedly of Petra—my first friend at Rosewarren, and my first kill—that I nearly shoved her away. But her warmth was too comforting to spurn, and after a few minutes, my eyes had dried.

Then Cira said, "The Warden is quite unwell, isn't she?" When no one answered, she added irritably, "She really ought to hurry up and have that child she's supposed to bear."

Brigid blew out a sharp breath. "*Cira*, now is not the time."

"Tell me I'm wrong, then."

"I said it's not the time, not that you're wrong."

Cira released me and sat up. "The sooner she has a baby, the sooner the baby can grow up and train, and the sooner the Warden can pass on her magic to her daughter and make *her* Warden, and then she can die and leave us all in peace."

"Hold your tongue," Brigid said. "We're not going to talk about the Warden dying right now, or even talk about her at all."

"You'll agree, though, that she's not herself. Yelling at everyone, stalking around the grounds talking to herself, going to the outposts for days at a time without warning, leaving Mara to run everything on her own. And just look at her, she's exhausted!" Cira gestured indignantly at me. "None of this is the behavior of a stable Warden. Did you know that of all the Wardens in the history of the Order, her tenure has been the longest? By *decades*?"

"She's just tired," I said wearily. "And I'm not on my own. I have all of you to help me."

"But Mara, when *you're* tired, you don't terrorize your students."

"That's enough," Brigid said. There was a sharpness to her voice that hadn't been there before. "We all need rest, and dawn patrol is only four hours away."

I buried my face in my pillow. "That is not nearly enough hours."

"Fine," Cira said with a huff. "No more Warden talk." Gingerly she settled back down beside me, and after a long moment of quiet, she said, "Tell me the story of Ankaret and Kilraith again."

"I'm going to scream," Brigid said blandly.

"Listen, just yesterday I was shot by a very stupid man, and now my shoulder hurts. I like the story, and I deserve a treat. And anyway, the more we hear it, the likelier it is that we'll uncover some helpful piece of information hidden inside it." Cira looked at me. "Don't you agree?"

At the sound of those two names, uttered so casually by Cira's youthful voice, a little chill raced down my body. Ankaret and Kilraith: two accidental children born of their gods' destruction. One a beloved queen who remembered nothing of what she had once been, one buried for centuries in the dark sea, stewing in hatred.

I could still remember the hoarseness of Farrin's voice as she'd told us all the story that day in Ivyhill, after the destruction of Mhorghast. How gaunt she had looked, as if receiving the memories of the god Jaetris before he died had drained half her life away. If Ryder hadn't been beside her, helping her stay upright, I'm not sure she would have been able to find the strength to speak.

"Are you saying you want a bedtime story?" I asked Cira. "Aren't you a little old for that?"

"No one's ever too old for bedtime stories," Cira said promptly, a sentiment I couldn't bring myself to argue with.

But before I could say another word, the room exploded with the peal of the breach bells. The *full* breach bells, which meant that not just the squadron on duty would be deployed; *all* of us would be. The walls shook suddenly, as if a huge fist had slammed into the priory; my tray toppled off the bedside table, and the stew splashed across the floor.

"Shock wave," I muttered, bolting out of the bed. Since the collapse of Mhorghast and the death of Ankaret, the Middlemist had grown more unstable every day. By now we knew quite well what it felt like when part of the Mist fell. The impact resonated for hundreds of miles.

"Godsdamn the godsdamned Mist and everything it touches," Brigid grumbled mutinously.

From outside in the corridor came the sounds of running feet and barked orders as Roses ran to their stations. Ripples of magic spilled through the air; they were transforming, and so were we. Already I could feel my body elongating and the sharp pinpricks of pain that marked the bloom of feathers along my spine.

Brigid strode toward the door, downy gray feathers cascading across her skin. "What's happened?" she shouted.

"Mistfall," came the answer—Danesh, one of my fellow squadron captains. Her changing voice split in two. "Sector Three is down!"

"*All* of it?" Brigid asked, incredulous.

I bolted to the door, Cira just behind me. Sector Three housed two small settlements and an Order outpost.

Sleep would have to wait.

It was time for battle.

Chapter 3

When the greenway spit us out into Sector Three, a nasty storm greeted us—typical for an area affected by Mistfall. Pelting rain, constant lightning. The second we emerged from the greenway, gusting winds slammed into each of us, blowing us off course.

I turned into the wind, beating my wings furiously to stay upright, and spent a few seconds up above the chaos, assessing it all. Freyda raced past me, along with the other avian familiars who had accompanied their Roses. They would catalog the damage, give us a picture of the Mistfall's true scope. The terrestrial familiars followed them from the ground—foxes, ermines, lynxes—leaping across chasms and between huge crags of earth that had been thrust up through the ground like a new range of mountains. A range of *moving* mountains, shifting atop a burning underground sea.

And across this chaos poured the Mist—a roiling silver ocean, no longer contained by the gods' ancient magical boundaries. In its wake, the ground split open with great yawning groans.

Cira hovered to my left, her slender face crowned with speckled brown feathers, her eyes huge and golden. "Earthquakes and thunderstorms!" she shouted. "Lovely. My favorite combination!"

Brigid, to my right, flung out one of her massive gray wings to gesture toward the watchtower in the distance. "Graystone burns!"

Graystone: an Order outpost now submerged in Mist. Only the burning watchtower was visible. I glanced quickly in the direction of the nearby settlements—the tiny, stubborn towns of Two Bluffs and Oakvale that we planned to forcibly evacuate next week. Even through the rain and wind and Mist, I could see that they teemed with darkness and hear their villagers' distant screams.

Invaders. Each of my heightened senses prickled. What would it be this time? Shifters? A titan?

Kilraith?

There was no time to wonder. I whirled about in the air to face the waiting squadrons.

"Red Team, secure Oakvale; Blue Team, Two Bluffs," I roared as the rain lashed my face. "Green Team, follow the familiars and eliminate any hostiles in the open Mist. Gold Team, you're with me. We'll secure Graystone."

In an instant, they obeyed—four squadrons, sixty Roses. I watched them tear off like arrows through the storm. Black and gray and brown, beautiful and deadly efficient. Red and Blue Teams, led by Danesh and an older Rose named Wenna, sped toward the villages; Green Team dove into the Mist in unison, their wings matching each other beat for beat. Every formation was precise, every captain belting out clear commands.

I spun around and followed the rest of Gold Team toward Graystone. A quick, dark thought came flying at me: How many of us would die on this mission? How many of us would return home?

Such thoughts were not new to me. But the Warden's words tickled the back of my mind, stoking unfamiliar flames of fear: *It saddens me that you don't trust me with the secrets you carry*. The image of her tired black eyes, the silent strength of her sword arm. The head of Nerys rolling across bloodstained stone.

I pushed hard against the memories, refusing to let them take hold of me no matter how clever their grasping fingers. I was a soldier; I could not afford distractions.

As we approached Graystone, we dove beneath the Mist's canopy to get a better view. Cold raked across our feathers like a thousand icy fingers as we slipped through the silver. Confused whispers snaked into our ears, urging us to stay, to sleep, to run, to hide. The Mist had many things to say these days, much of it nonsense that contradicted itself. It was as if the knowledge of its own destruction was slowly driving it insane. But we knew these tricks and flew on.

"Hold!" I ordered, switching from the common tongue to one of the coded languages we used in the Order.

My team pulled up around me, our wings beating hard to remain stationary in the howling wind. I scanned Graystone for signs of hostiles and saw nothing; there were no Roses either. Were it not for the blood-curdling screams rising up to greet us, I would have thought the place abandoned.

Then I realized with horror that the screams were coming from inside the outpost's burning buildings.

"Fire nymphs?" Cira shouted from my left.

I hoped so. If it were fire titans—much more powerful than nymphs and far less human, much harder to reason with—we were in trouble. One squadron alone wouldn't be enough, even with three elementals in our ranks.

"A Unit, take the eastern buildings!" I shouted. "B Unit, the western buildings! C Unit, with me to the main house! Eliminate all hostiles, and rescue all the Roses you can find. Roses priority, staff disposable!"

No one hesitated. It was protocol, and the humans we'd allowed into our ranks over the last few weeks—to support the war effort and relieve us of our more menial duties—knew it as well as we did. If necessary, we would save ourselves and each other before we would save them.

Another flutter passed through me, a chill of bad feeling. Nerves? Memory? I kept expecting to see the Warden's face rise up out of the darkness to stare at me in disappointment. A wild image flashed before my eyes: the Warden standing over me, prying open my mouth with both hands and pleading, "Tell me your secrets, Mara!"

I shook myself, furious and spooked. What was wrong with me?

"Mara?" Brigid cried from my right, a rare note of uncertainty in her voice.

I nodded sharply at her, then roared, "Deploy!"

As one, we dove ten feet and then split into three groups, hurtling toward the burning buildings below. My unit slammed into the front doors of the main house three times before they finally flew open. Someone had barred them from the inside. The entrance hall was deserted, but we heard screams from the corridors on either side, calling to us from deeper within the outpost.

"Caralind?" I shouted over my shoulder—one of the low-magic elementals on my team, and a good one. Earth was her affinity, not fire, but I hoped she would be able to read the signs well enough.

"Searching!" she replied, already surveying the room on quick gray wings. After a few seconds of examining the flames, she reported back breathlessly. "This fire is definitely nymph-made, not titan. But there's something else here too. A magic I don't recognize."

The word *Kilraith* slithered through my mind with a vicious smile. I squashed it flat. I'd beaten him before; I could do it again.

"The nymphs who did this should be nearly burned out by now," I said. "They won't be much of a threat, but the fire will. Pair off in Ruby Formation. Each pair takes a hallway. You have your orders."

I flew up the stairs, my partner—Caralind—racing up behind me. The air was scorching, the splintering floor even worse. Our feet were feathered and bore gleaming black talons, but they weren't impervious to damage. Flames crawled up every wall; groaning rafters crashed to the floor. We turned a corner and recoiled, barely evading a small firestorm thundering down the hallway. I glimpsed a grinning face within its flames. Godsdamned *nymphs*. They couldn't just let their fire be fire; they had to show off and *animate* it.

Each room we came to was empty, and as we plunged deeper into the outpost, the flames grew and grew. The heat felt physical, a smothering force. A burning rafter crashed down right behind us, throwing us both to the floor and showering us with sparks.

"We have to turn back!" Caralind shouted, shaking embers from her wings. "The walls are buckling!"

She was right, but I couldn't leave yet. If the Roses in the outpost were all dead, where were the bodies? And if they had fled, who was screaming? The shrieks were turning desperate, bordering on animal.

I pushed down the hallway toward the sound, raising one of my wings to shield my face. Through the smoke I saw a door I hadn't noticed before, split in two by a section of fallen ceiling.

"Mara, get back!" Caralind cried.

"Someone's in here!" I shouted back at her, hoping I was right. I peered into the room, and my heart dropped when I saw them: ten young girls, all new recruits I recognized at once. We'd sent them to Graystone earlier that week to prepare for their trials. And now they were huddled in the middle of the room, encircled by a ring of fire clearly controlled by the nymph standing in front of me. Except for her hair of flames, her fiery fingertips, and her impossibly bright blue eyes, she looked human. And on her face was naked desperation.

"Don't come any closer," she hissed. She thrust out a hand at me, the flames dancing at her fingers coalescing into a ball of flame. "I don't want to kill you, but if you take another step, I'll do it."

My own fingers, hidden under my wings, itched to draw one of the arrows from the quiver strapped around my torso. Caralind spat out a low curse. I felt her elemental magic simmering behind me. She could use it to shift the ground under our area of the house, throwing the nymph off-balance. Then I could lunge and fling her against the wall so hard her fire would vanish and she'd never wake again.

"Please, help us!" screamed one of the recruits. They were drenched in sweat and tears, stained with smoke, overheated, coughing. I thought of Farrin as a child, how frightened she had been as Ivyhill had burned around her, and felt a spike of rage.

"Let them go," I said, "and I'll consider sparing your life."

The nymph shook her head slowly, and with a slight turn of her wrist, the ring of fire around the recruits shrunk, roaring closer to them. The girls screamed, sobbed, clung to each other.

"I didn't want to do this," the nymph said. "He gave us no choice."

The brightness of her hair and hands flickered, and her eyes dimmed. The effort of maintaining the ring of fire was draining her. Nymphs' affinities ran in their blood, and they had only that to draw upon to manifest their elemental power. If she didn't stop soon, she could burn herself out, even to the point of death.

I just had to keep her talking.

"Who gave you no choice?" I demanded, my mind shivering with his name. *Kilraith, Kilraith.*

"I cannot tell you," she said, her voice cracking. Her eyes flared white, then blue again. "I want to, but I *can't*. Do you understand?"

Some sort of spellwork had hold of her tongue. I nodded. "Release the girls. You don't need to die today."

"Oh, but I'm going to." Tears of fire coursed down her face. "Whatever happens here, I will die today. I know it. Take my daughter, and I will let them go."

A small burst of light flared, and a girl—even smaller than my recruits—peered around the nymph's legs. She was paler than her mother, and fresh jagged scars striped her body.

"Coming here was the only way I could get her out," the nymph continued. "Not all of us are loyal to him. You are a Rose. You know this."

She was right. Not every Olden creature wanted the human world destroyed. Posey was proof enough of that. And not even all of the Oldens who did want us dead were loyal to Kilraith, though many were. According to our intelligence efforts, his supporters numbered in the thousands.

"I knew you'd come for them." The nymph was fading, her voice warped and ragged. She moved her wrist again, and the ring of fire shrunk once more. The recruits were practically climbing on top of each other to dodge the flames.

"I'll do it," the nymph whispered. "I'll use whatever's left in me to kill them and you."

"And yourself and your daughter too?" Caralind snapped from behind me.

"Better death than what we faced there. Take her back with you, keep her safe, and I'll let them go."

I hesitated. The Warden wouldn't like yet another Olden refugee sheltering under our roof. But better to take in an orphaned nymph than lose ten recruits.

"Five seconds and they're dead," the nymph cried out.

"We have an agreement." I held out my hand to the nymph child. "She'll come to no harm with us, and we'll take care of her as best we can. Release the girls, now."

The nymph waited until her child was beside me. The poor silent thing looked numb, as if she were walking through a dream. I took her hand in mine—smooth and warm like a sunbaked stone—and her mother, looking blankly at us, grief etched in harsh lines all over her glowing face, blew out a wavering breath. The ring of fire vanished, and the recruits stumbled toward me, weeping and wild. I was about to draw the nymph child under the shield of my wing when suddenly a sharp twang pierced the air behind me.

The child's hand spasmed in mine; her body jerked. She slumped to the floor, her eyes frozen in shock and Caralind's arrow lodged deep in her chest.

"*No!*" the nymph howled. With her last breath, she flung a raging fire toward us, an inferno so large I knew it would kill her. It was too swift, too strong. I couldn't move quickly enough to shepherd the two remaining recruits past me to safety.

As I watched, helpless, the flames engulfed them.

Their deaths were quick, their screams of agony brief. And then they were ashes.

"Mara, *move*!" Caralind yelled, four recruits clinging to her in utter terror.

My shock, the heat, the ashes coating my lips—for a moment I couldn't breathe, couldn't think. Then I felt the other recruits tugging at me, heard their terrified cries.

I whirled around and helped the girls climb over the shattered door and out into the hallway. "Grab on to me!" I cried, and they obeyed, clinging to my torso, my legs, my slick feathered arms. I flew down the hallway as fast as my wings could carry me. Caralind's shape sped ahead of me, shimmering in the heat. Death was following us, licking at our tail feathers. A roar of fire and a wrenching explosion of sound chased us out into the courtyard just as the walls began to fall. A cascade of splintering wood and crumbling stone, a final cloudburst of fire and smoke, and we were free.

Across the courtyard, Roses from the other teams were fighting Olden hostiles, the shapes of which I couldn't make out amid the smoke and Mist. I heard roars, mad laughter, the clang of swords, the lethal zip of arrows.

"We've got to get them to Rosewarren," Caralind was saying, her voice coming to me as if from a great distance. "We can't afford to lose eight more recruits. We've already lost two."

I whirled on her. "We wouldn't have lost two if you hadn't shot the child!"

Caralind looked at me as if I'd grown a second head. "You didn't actually trust what that nymph was saying, did you? It was a trap."

"I'm the commander of this operation, not you. I was making the exchange, and you should have honored that."

But Caralind wasn't listening to me. Her gaze had fallen to my torso in confusion.

I looked down.

Petra, my first friend at Rosewarren—auburn-haired, freckled, nine years old—was in my arms, staring up at me, glassy-eyed and frozen with death. Blood stained her chest, and in the middle of that red circle stood a knife, buried deep in flesh and muscle and bone. I knew the knife well. I remembered the weight of it, how my hand had curved around the hilt.

The world tilted under my feet. I staggered back and let her drop to the ground. Her body hit the dirt with a grotesque thud. A couple of the recruits clinging to me screamed. I closed my eyes, opened them again.

Petra was gone. It was the nymph child staring up at me now, just as dead as Petra had been, and just as small. An arrow had killed her instead of a knife, but the result was the same: bloodstained chest, eyes frozen in their final expression of shock and betrayal. I must have scooped her tiny corpse up into my arms as I fled the room upstairs.

I couldn't look at Caralind. I could feel her eyes on my face and didn't like to imagine what she saw.

"You're right," I said tersely. "We'll take them home at once." I glanced down at my four recruits, not really seeing them. My heart was pounding so hard I thought I might be sick. My feet were throbbing from minor burns sustained while running through those fiery hallways. *I will need a poultice,* I thought automatically.

"Hold on to me," I muttered to the recruits. "The greenway will be a rough passage."

As soon as I felt their little fists tighten around my feathers, I launched into the air, Caralind just behind me. The other teams would secure what was left of Graystone, save whoever they could from Two Bluffs and Oakvale. The nymph child's corpse would burn or rot.

I didn't look back once.

Chapter 4

The Warden called me into her office a few hours after we returned to Rosewarren.

Nesset brought me the message this time. I was helping our healers tend to the human refugees the other squadrons had rescued from Two Bluffs and Oakvale. The earthquakes, the storms, and the onslaught of Olden hostiles—chimaera, specters, a trio of furiants that had used their power to hurl boulders as big as houses—had left the towns in ruins. Dozens were dead, many of the survivors were severely wounded, and we'd lost two Roses from our rescue squadrons—two littles Danesh had been training for the past eight months. The ten Roses who'd been stationed at Graystone were dead. The eight recruits Caralind and I had saved were the outpost's only survivors.

Nesset came to me in somber silence. The infirmary reeked of blood, and one of the dead littles had been a favorite of Nesset's—Gertrid, a wiry northern girl with a talent for spear-throwing.

"The Warden wants to see you," Nesset said quietly. Her dark eyes were clouded from crying. Her rough gray-brown skin, sewn together with flowers and moss, looked patchy and raw, as if something had scraped layers of bark off a gnarled tree. Maybe Nesset herself had done it.

I looked away. I couldn't see the Vilia without thinking of Gemma, who had saved her from her abusive revenant masters. How fiercely Nesset loved my baby sister. If Gemma died, would she peel off every scrap of her skin to show her grief? Would I do the same?

I took the Warden's summons from Nesset, crumpled the square of paper in my fist, and strode away from her, ignoring the curious gazes that followed me as I passed through the crowded rooms. By the time I knocked on the Warden's office door, my mind was clear, my throat paved with stone.

I stood before her desk with my hands behind my back, staring straight ahead—past her, past the wall, past the priory and the Mist. I imagined nothingness. I was a blade, polished and ready, waiting for the breach bells to ring.

The Warden watched me for a long moment. "Caralind told me what happened at Graystone," she said at last.

That was all it took to sweep away my calm and rake me open. Petra's dead face flashed before my eyes. Then it became the face of the dead nymph child, golden and stained with ashes. I gritted my teeth, clasped my hands together more tightly.

"Yes, Madam."

"Her report was startling, to say the least."

"Yes, Madam."

"She has been punished, of course, and will continue to be, for going against your orders. If she had followed them, our two recruits would still be with us."

Another image: two terrified little girls running toward me, reaching for me, their faces dissolving into ashes right before my eyes.

I nodded briskly. "Yes, Madam."

Silence fell, and then the Warden sighed. "Mara, look at me."

I obeyed, keeping my expression carefully blank.

"My brave, strong girl." Her face was full of pity. "Caralind said you carried the child's corpse out of Graystone. Why? She was dead."

My surprise rattled me. Foolishly, I hadn't expected the question, but of course Caralind had told her this detail too. I'd held a dead child's body in my arms without realizing it. I'd looked at her face and seen Petra's. I was sure I'd said Petra's name aloud. I must have looked like a madwoman, covered in ashes and staring down at the ghost of a girl I'd killed twelve years ago. Surely Caralind had heard the tale of my trials. Even Roses liked a good scary story.

"I'm not certain, Madam." I resisted the urge to scratch an itch on my left temple. "I can only assume I was in a state of shock. The two recruits, the way they died…" My voice caught. Suddenly, in my memory, each of the two recruits was Petra, and it was her face dissolving into ashes, her screams of agony snuffed out like candles.

I shook my head, looked down at my boots, cleared my throat. "They made me think of Petra. I was caught quite off guard."

I don't know why I confessed such a thing, but once I said it, I couldn't take it back. I stood there, tense and miserable, until the Warden sat back in her chair with a little hum of concern.

"For the next two days, you'll be off duty," she said after a moment.

I jerked my head up to stare at her. "No, Madam, please—"

"I've made my decision, Mara. For the next two days, you will rest, you will eat, and nothing more. No training, no patrols."

The thought of being relegated to my room for any time at all, much less two whole days, horrified me. I needed to keep moving—tending the wounded, counseling the frightened recruits, comforting any Roses who needed it in the wake of our newest losses. There were duty rosters to look over, patrols to complete. The ruins of Graystone—and of Two Bluffs and Oakvale—would require excavation and retrieval procedures to ensure that no survivors remained trapped in the rubble.

"Sector Three is vulnerable," I protested. "We stopped the first wave of hostiles, but more will come, and Topthicket is a mere twenty miles away. The Mist will reach them in days, maybe hours. They'll need—"

"What *I* need," the Warden said, talking over me, "is for my best soldier to rest. You're no good to me right now. What if, instead of picking up the body of a dead child, you'd picked up your sword, swung it through Caralind's neck, and not realized what you were doing until you heard her head hitting the ground?"

I bit the inside of my bottom lip. "I'm not *ill*, Madam."

"You're not well either. And I understand." Her expression softened, as if she'd let go of some internal lever, and all at once I could see her weariness, the lines of age in the taut, pale skin around her eyes. "Ours is a hard life even in peacetime. And now…"

She let the words hang for a moment, then stood and closed the packet of papers on her desk with a quiet snap.

"Rest, Mara," she said, and then she turned to look out the window behind her desk, her arms folded across her chest. "I can't lose you. And if you won't take care of yourself, I'll do it for you. Dismissed."

It was a kindness, I suppose, and I was glad that she'd seemed more like herself than she had in the Stillhouse, but nevertheless, I left feeling like a scolded dog. Somehow I reached my room without anyone trying to talk to me. I lay on my bed, staring at the ceiling, but that was no good. Everywhere I looked—the ceiling, the walls, the sketches stacked beside the easel in the corner—I saw the recreation of Ivyhill I'd begun years ago, when I turned fifteen and was given my own room. Whenever I had a spare moment, I added to the mural: a bird here, a sprig of ivy there.

My chest tightened with sadness so overwhelming that it became anger. I turned off the oil lamp on my bedside table, but darkness was no help. I knew it was there, somewhere past the black: the house I was born in, the home to which I could never return.

Suddenly I couldn't be in the room any longer. I sat up, still dressed, and grabbed my coin purse. My skin was roiling as if it weren't skin at all but a sheen of upset insects instead. Skittering, clicking their shiny sharp mandibles.

When I felt like this, only two things were sure to settle me. One was training, but that was no good. Someone would spot me and report me to the Warden.

The other lay in Fenwood.

Long ago, I'd resolved never to love another person—not in a romantic way, at least. That sort of love invited heartbreak I couldn't afford.

I'd done it once before, at seventeen. I'd fallen for an older Rose, Crellin, who'd taught me about my body with gentle patience. She had made it clear that our arrangement was purely physical, a way of releasing tension, and that I should have learned these things long ago. Doing so was a matter of practicality and safety in our line of work.

But I was seventeen and stupid, and of course I had fallen hopelessly in love with her.

Then, on a mission to the Old Country, I'd lost her. One of the four Olden Winds—elusive, nebulous beings that spent most of their time in the skies—had swooped down to attack us, furiously howling some insult about the foolishness of trespassers. Not that the changeable, territorial Winds ever needed a reason for their violence. This one flew down upon us like a hurricane, picked up our squadron in one mammoth iridescent fist, and threw us through the forest. Crellin slammed into a rocky hillside and cracked her head open. I was the one to find her broken body, and once I returned to Rosewarren and finally stopped crying, I resolved never to love again. I'd kept to that resolution ever since.

But a purely physical exchange with someone I'd never see again was safe enough, and a dependable remedy for an unsettled mind when I wasn't in the mood for violence.

◆◇◆

The town of Fenwood was the closest settlement to the priory, and long ago, the Order had come to an agreement with its citizens: our protection, our reinforcement of the nearby Mist, in exchange for their discretion.

This arrangement worked marvelously well. As a Rose, I could go to Fenwood and do anything, seek anything. No one would question or stop me, and they would keep their judgments to themselves. Locals impressed the importance of these rules upon visitors, and visitors delighted in being able to sell Roses their bodies, their drugs, their information, all without consequences. Over time, humble Fenwood had become a treasure trove of secrets and illicit delights, if you knew where to look.

That night, I entered my favorite tavern, the Black Stag, wearing a hooded cloak simply out of habit. I could have strutted through town wearing a bright red gown and crowing my intentions for all to hear, and no one would have batted an eye.

I made straight for the barkeep, a woman named Imelda whom I'd known for years. She could look at someone—even a visitor she'd just met—and know immediately whether they were looking to bed a Rose. They came from far and wide—thrill-seekers of a sort. Collectors. It was an honor to be chosen by one of us, one of the grandest boasts a person could possibly bring back to their friends. And if the Rose transformed into a monster halfway through? Even better. What would that feel like? Would they somehow become a monster too?

Imelda had exquisite taste and knew my own quite well. She took one look at me, then nodded toward one of the room's far corners.

"That one over there," she murmured, hardly pausing as she wiped down the countertop. "He's been waiting around for hours. Sweet man, despite his looks. Sailor, I think."

I followed her gaze to the hulking man crammed behind far too small a table. He had ruddy skin, rough from the wind and sea, dark hair, a strong jaw. When I got closer, I saw that his fingernails were clipped and clean.

Good enough.

I took him to my usual room upstairs and wasted no time, which I think surprised him. But I'd been wet since I left Rosewarren, and I felt almost feral with impatience. It wasn't the act itself that aroused me; it was the promise of the relief that would come after. The buzzing, liquid quiet.

His hands shook when he touched me, as if he couldn't believe his luck. His fingers brushed against the rose tattoo that spanned my right thigh, then traveled up my torso. In the small mirror on the wall, I caught a glimpse of my lean, pale muscles, my long dark hair, his erection, his big hands palming my breasts.

"Gods," he rasped, "you're beautiful. What's your name?"

"No names," I bit out, and then I tugged on his arm, bent over the bed, and looked back over my shoulder. "Hurry up. Please," I added.

He obeyed at once—put his meaty hands on my hips, thrust into me from behind. I fisted the bed's quilt and closed my eyes. A mistake. Behind my eyelids were roaring flames, screaming girls, the memory of Petra's flesh giving way to my blade. Nesset, howling with sadness, peeling off her gray skin in long strips. Gemma and Farrin—dead, flayed, dismembered, disemboweled. My whirling mind was a festival of violence.

"Harder," I commanded. "Faster."

The man hesitated, panting. "Are you sure?"

"You won't hurt me." I pressed back into him, taking him deeper, making him moan. Immediately he grabbed hold of my hair and drove into me so hard I cried out—in pain, in delighted surprise. My eagerness encouraged him, and he kept going, more confident now. Sharp, hard thrusts, his hands digging into my flesh, his groans buried in my hair. He was big; I'd be tender in the morning, probably bruised. But that was what I wanted. That kind of pain I could bear.

This time, when I closed my eyes, I saw nothing but welcome warm blackness.

Chapter 5

The next morning, I awoke before dawn and left the sailor snoring in bed. A few coins and a note of thanks on the bedside table—the men especially liked mementos to show their friends—and I was gone. His snores followed me down the hallway. I'd worn him out. I envied the complete abandon of his sleep.

I was nearing the border of Fenwood, watching the sky for signs of what the Mist's mood would be that day, when a dark figure caught my attention. It moved swiftly through the shadows wearing a hooded cloak like my own. I knew that gait and that silhouette, even draped in fabric.

The Warden.

I nearly pressed on back to Rosewarren. I needed a bath, a tonic from the infirmary to guard myself against infections, and some sleep. And I was in a wonderful mood that I didn't want to give up, all my bad thoughts rigorously scrubbed away by the sailor and his impressive stamina.

But remembering Cira's recent musings gave me pause.

The Warden is quite unwell, isn't she?

She really ought to hurry up and have that child she's supposed to bear.

It was entirely possible, of course, that the Warden was here in

Fenwood for any number of reasons that had nothing to do with taking a lover into her bed. My curiosity, though, was too eager to ignore.

I followed her down the main road at a safe distance. On either side of me was the sleepy morning bustle of the town waking up: a baby crying out, the bleat of a goat, the clang of kitchen tools, the smell of baking bread. A girl darted out of a tall, narrow house, followed by her little brother. I stopped with a flinch. For a moment, the girl's hair was auburn, not black. For a moment, it was Petra giggling, Petra whirling around to hug the little boy, Petra catching me staring and throwing me an uncertain smile.

I hurried around the next corner, the taste of ash on my tongue, and stopped just short of barreling into the Warden.

"Madam," I blurted out. I ducked my head in a sharp nod. "Good morning."

"Good morning, Mara," she said, a twist of amusement in her voice. "I trust you slept well? I know you always do when you spend the night in Fenwood."

Her comment should not have shamed me. I was far from the only Rose to seek comfort in the arms of Fenwood strangers. In fact, the Warden encouraged it. But a flush crept into my cheeks, and I was certain she could hear my pounding heart. I made myself look at her anyway.

"The best night of sleep I've had in weeks," I replied.

Her smile widened. "Excellent. I'm gratified to see that you're taking my orders to rest so seriously."

With that, she glided past me, and I should have let her move on unbothered, but I was in a strange state. The little girl had smashed into my calm like a great stone, and now there were cracks all through it. For a moment I lost my head.

I grabbed the Warden's arm and said quietly, "May I ask you a question before you go?"

The Warden's eyebrows rose. She glanced down at my hand around her wrist; I immediately released her.

"Very well," she said smoothly. "Ask me."

My mind raced. I had to be careful here.

"The last few weeks," I began, "I've noticed that you've seemed more tired than you usually do. And after the battle in Sector Three, a thought occurred to me." I gathered myself with a shallow breath, then met her narrowed black gaze. "With these increased attacks and the regular Mistfall, the likelihood of something getting past our defenses, even at Rosewarren, is greater than ever. And with exhaustion comes mistakes, as you were wise enough to point out to me. If something were to happen to you before your successor is in place..." Another steadying breath. I lifted my chin slightly. "What would happen to us?"

"Oh, Mara. I'm touched by your concern." She took my chin in her hand and looked steadily at me. "This is what happens when you stop moving, isn't it? All the mean thoughts wriggle in."

I swallowed the urge to apologize. "It's a reasonable question, Madam. If there are contingencies in place, I should know about them."

The Warden tilted her head, appraising me. Even in her human form, the manner of an owl hung about her. After a moment, she nodded slowly and released me. Only then, my jaw aching, did I realize how tightly she'd been holding me in place.

"Perhaps you're right," she said. "I'll consider what you've said. And in the meantime, try to put thoughts of my daughter out of your mind. I'll introduce her to all of you when the time is right. Oh, and since you're here, I have something for you."

From the pocket of her dress she retrieved an envelope bearing the royal seal, which had already been broken. "The councils are holding a ball this weekend in Fairhaven. To boost morale, they say. A foolish waste of resources, but as long as they keep sending new girls to us, I'm afraid we must tolerate their idiocy. You'll attend as a representative of the Order, make nice with your sister, charm anyone with heavy purses. I'll give you a list of formal requests for the war council. Consider this an extension of your leave."

I took the offered envelope, feeling a little unbalanced. The abrupt change of topic left a sour taste in my mouth, as did the thought of attending a royal ball. Even in peacetime, I wasn't one for dancing. And I was still fixated on what she'd said about her daughter: *I'll introduce her to all of you*. Had she already borne the child?

"And Mara," the Warden added, already turning away, "make sure you bathe well, and soon. That man's stink is all over you."

Then she was gone, and my surprise left me standing there for a solid minute. *I'll introduce her to all of you when the time is right*. I thought back over the past few years, searching my memory for clues of the Warden's pregnancy, and found nothing. And even though the road back to Rosewarren was empty except for me, and I'd walked it thousands of times, I found myself looking over my shoulder like stalked prey. Each time, I thought for certain that I'd find the Warden slowly trailing after me, a girl with matching black eyes beside her, holding her hand.

But it was only me and the Mist and the quiet air. Embarrassed to be so jumpy, I hurried on.

⟡

Three days later, I was standing in a corner of the Pearl of the Sea Ballroom, drinking my second glass of wine in ten minutes, pretending to admire the palace's architecture, and wishing everyone would stop staring at me.

They were coy about it, but a Rose was an object of desperate fascination, especially during wartime. The night had just begun, and already I'd turned away two Anointed lords, a wealthy tradeswoman who was worried about how the continuing conflict would affect her profit margins, and three writers for various town bulletins, all of whom wanted reassurance in the form of a snappy quote.

The only one I was willing to give them was far more boring than they would have liked, and no doubt not reassuring at all: *The Order is working around the clock to reinforce the Mist and fight off as many Olden invaders as possible. We appreciate the sacrifice the country is making by sending us their daughters and entrusting us with their safety as we all band together to stop this unprecedented threat.*

The Warden had told me to be charming, but that was Gemma's skill, not mine. And even though that tradeswoman and the two lords undoubtedly had funds to spare, they wandered away looking disgruntled, and I made no effort to stop them.

I just needed to speak with Farrin, I told myself, maybe sit with her awhile. Then perhaps I'd find the will to paste on a smile.

I set my empty glass down on a sideboard and wandered the room, searching the crowd for my elder sister while the wine loosened the knots in my shoulders. At first glance, the party seemed normal enough. The royal orchestra played a lilting waltz from the stage at the far side of the room. Guests wearing glittering gowns, brocaded waistcoats, and fur stoles spun past me. Others gossiped in corners while picking at their plates of food. Outside the windows, stars were beginning to twinkle in the early winter sky. The Mist hadn't reached this far south. Not yet.

But every now and then, I saw people glancing at the windows with sparks of nervousness in their eyes, as if they expected the Mist to come roiling through the city at any moment. The soft coral-and-periwinkle banners hanging around the room, bearing the royal crest, were each flanked by two panels of gauzy black. A gorgeous oil painting of the late queen Yvaine hung above the grand staircase.

It was a party, yes, but in a country at war and in mourning.

For a moment, I stood at the bottom of the stairs, nursing my third glass of wine and gazing up at Yvaine's portrait. Her eyes—one violet, one gold—were soft and sweet, her smile beatific. She wore a lavender gown, and her voluminous white hair was gathered up into a knot, around which sat a slender silver crown. The prim, dainty image was so at odds with what I now knew about Yvaine that I laughed a little into my glass.

Ankaret. Memories of Yvaine's true form—a creature of fiery feathers and starlit eyes—whispered in the back of my mind. In Mhorghast, she'd fought so bravely to defend us, the reds, oranges, and golds of her body incandescent beside Kilraith's angry storm-cloud colors. I remembered her rearing up to shield us from his blows, the brilliance of her enormous wings. Woman and avian and Olden, just like me.

"Do you really think she'll come back somehow?"

I'd sensed someone coming to stand beside me but didn't realize who it was until he spoke.

I sighed, took another sip of wine, and kept staring up at the queen. Another person I didn't particularly want to talk to: Gareth Fontaine, he of the drunken crossbow-bearing friends.

"Stranger things have happened, I suppose," I said.

"Farrin believes it with all her heart."

"I'm glad she does. Hope can be a great comfort. Ryder will pull her back if she grows obsessive about it."

He hummed a little in agreement, then cleared his throat. "Mara, I know you don't like me very much. And I don't blame you, really, especially after that incident with your friend Cira the other day. But I'd like to change that, or at least try." I heard a smile in his voice. "I'm not entirely hopeless, you know. Do you think Farrin would like me so much if I were a true scoundrel?"

Finally I turned to face him, and when I did, I almost couldn't believe my eyes. I'd heard all about Gareth's rakish ways; I'd even gotten a small taste of them myself during our travels to Wardwell earlier that fall, when he'd fawned over me like a smitten schoolboy at the tavern in Vallenvoren.

But I'd never seen him done up so nicely. Of course he was able to reel in woman after woman, looking like that. His blond curls were artfully tousled, his green eyes sparkled behind his gold-rimmed glasses, and though his gray suit was unassuming compared to some of the other guests' extravagant garments, it was tailored to perfection. I'd not realized until that moment how pleasing a form he had. Tall, lean but solid, with a boyishly lanky quality that I found rather charming. It must have been the wine, or his elegant long fingers, or that sharp turn of his jaw. His collar was slightly undone, his tie loose and rumpled. As I took him in, he grinned.

"Why, Mara," he said, "you flatter me with such attention."

I raised an eyebrow and shrugged, determined not to react to that smile of his. "Even Roses can appreciate a handsome man. We're not monks, you know, scurrying about in our Cloisters muttering prayers day and night."

"Certainly not." He was looking me up and down. Fair play.

"Well?" I prodded. "Do I pass muster?"

"Let me see." Gareth circled me, holding his chin as if deep in thought. "Quite a nice gown, I must say. That deep violet color suits you. And it bares your shoulders in a way some might find provocative."

"Bared shoulders are provocative?"

"Absolutely, when they're as lovely as yours."

My cheeks warmed at the compliment. The wine had truly gotten to me. "These *lovely* shoulders often carry weapons into battle, you know."

"Even better."

I swallowed a smile and closed my eyes. "And my hair?" I asked, turning up my chin to pose.

"Wise to wear it gathered at your nape," he answered at once. "It shows off your skin, the lines of your neck."

Gareth was passing behind me then, and with my eyes closed and the orchestra's waltz spinning through the air, I convinced myself that soon he would come closer, put his hand on my waist, and press a kiss between my shoulder blades.

The image was absurd enough to shake me out of whatever tipsy madness had taken hold of my senses. I opened my eyes to glare at him, hoping he wouldn't notice the goose bumps prickling my skin.

"What do you want, Gareth?" I said sharply. "Did you come over here just to flirt with me?"

"If so, I'd say I'm doing a pretty good job of it," he replied jovially.

"I've seen better."

He put a hand on his heart, flashing me another mischievous grin. "I'd be honored by the chance to try again. Practice makes perfect, they say."

For a moment, I felt tempted to give in to whatever was happening here. Gareth was attractive and certainly smarter than most men I'd taken to bed. It was rare for me to feel pretty, and I did that night, especially with him looking at me like that, with his eyes twinkling and his clever mouth promising clever kisses. Maybe bedding a professor would strengthen the Order's relationship with the university. The Warden *had* said to be charming.

But then Gareth's gaze moved past me, and his expression darkened. "Oh, for the love of all the gods," he muttered, raking a hand through his hair. "Can I have the rest of your wine?"

I raised my eyebrows and wordlessly handed him my glass. He downed the last bit in a rather violent gulp, then turned to smile at the young man approaching us. He looked to be about twenty, with tawny brown skin, loose black curls, wide brown eyes, and an air of the fawn about him, skittish and guileless. But he carried a notebook and pen, and on second glance, those sweet eyes held an avid light that put me on my guard at once.

"Reynard Farrington," Gareth said lightly. "Enjoying the party?"

"Oh, yes. My first royal ball. I've never seen anything like it."

"And you may never again, depending on how the next few weeks unfold." Gareth glanced at me. "Have you met Reynard Farrington of the *Fairhaven Courier*? Reynard, this is Mara Ashbourne of the Order of the Rose."

Reynard's eyes widened. He opened his notebook and began jotting something down. "Gods remade, a Rose," he murmured. "I've never met one before."

"A veritable feast of new experiences for you tonight," I replied. "It's a pleasure to meet you."

"Likewise, likewise. If you don't mind, Mara, I'd love to ask you a few questions after I finish with Professor Fontaine."

The casual way he said my name, as if we were old friends, amused me as a precocious child might, but Gareth looked outraged.

"I already told you everything you need to know," he said.

"On the contrary, you answered only two of my questions."

"Yes, and then I walked away from you. Most people would read that as a dismissal."

"Most people don't write for the *Fairhaven Courier*. And if you're going to attend a royal ball, eat all this fine food, and dance the night away while thousands of your fellow citizens huddle in camps throughout the city, chased away from their homes by Olden forces or evacuated against their will…" Reynard shrugged with a sheepish smile. "It seems to me that the least you could do is answer a few questions for a writer just starting his career."

"This ball was arranged to raise morale and funds for the war effort," Gareth said tightly. "It isn't a frivolous affair."

"And the people who could benefit most from heightened morale are not here." Reynard nodded at the windows overlooking the city. "Instead they're out there, watching the golden festivities from their huts and their borrowed rooms and wondering if they'll have homes to return to when all of this is over. Or if they'll even still be alive."

This sort of talk was getting dangerously close to unwarranted criticism of my sister. "The refugee villages are clean and comfortable," I said mildly. "I toured them myself. The councils and the Senate have worked hard to provide for those who have been displaced."

"The councils, the Senate, and your sister, Lady Farrin Ashbourne?" Reynard looked at me keenly, pen poised over his paper. "What do you think of the fact that the late queen Yvaine bequeathed so many of her assets and responsibilities to a woman who has no governing experience?"

An easy question. "I think she chose admirably," I replied. "Farrin is wise, fair, and knew the queen intimately. What Queen Yvaine would have done, Farrin will strive to do."

"Yes, they did have quite a close relationship from what I've heard," Reynard murmured. "Some have speculated that's why the queen chose Lady Farrin as her successor. An exchange of favors, if you will."

The idea was so absurd that I had to laugh. "You can't be serious."

"Farrington, if don't stop talking right now and walk away," Gareth said, his voice low and furious, "I will shut you up myself."

Reynard's smile was full of pity. "Under normal circumstances, I would consider it most unseemly for someone of your status to threaten a humble journalist. But given what you've been through, I suppose such erratic behavior is to be expected."

Gareth flinched. His brow was a little damp now, and I saw in his eyes a flash of animal fear that I recognized all too well. I'd seen it on the faces of countless Roses over the years: the assault of unwelcome memories.

And suddenly I understood that Reynard Farrington had been trying to ask Gareth questions about his time as a prisoner in

Mhorghast—something I wasn't sure Gareth had even told Farrin about.

"I dare say that Gareth is behaving much more graciously than you would in his position," I said mildly. "Have you ever been a prisoner of war, Reynard? Have you ever seen someone killed before your very eyes?"

That startled the man, though he recovered quickly. "No, I haven't. But—"

"Pray you never do. Sometimes the gods listen. And meanwhile, Professor Fontaine and Lady Farrin and I will continue the work that keeps you safe at your writing desk."

I put my hand on Gareth's arm and started to gently lead him away, but Reynard Farrington was insatiable. He followed us eagerly, and I barely resisted the urge to kick him aside.

"My contact at the university," he went on, "says that the Committee of New and Emerging Magics is hard at work on a number of dangerous experiments that could aid the military's efforts tremendously. Professor, do you think it wise for a man such as yourself, who has been compromised by the enemy, to be a part of such important and sensitive work?"

Gareth whirled around, spitting a curse and clenching his fists, but I darted between the two men before he could strike. I put a hand behind me, urging Gareth to stay back, and fixed Reynard Harrington with a cool stare. He looked quite taken aback at my speed and swallowed hard.

"I suggest you return to the party and enjoy your evening, Reynard," I said quietly. "It would be a shame for you to spend the whole night working."

The man snapped his notebook shut, his lips thin with frustration, but he gave us both a curt little bow and left without another word.

A few small groups of people nearby were whispering and watching us, tittering nervously or throwing Gareth and me silent looks of trepidation. I wondered which they found more unsettling: a survivor of Mhorghast or a Rose in a gown.

"Thank you," Gareth said. "I could have killed him. Especially because he's not wrong about any of it. Well, except for Farrin and Yvaine. What scum, to insinuate that." He dragged a shaking hand through his hair. "But there *are* thousands of refugees outside these walls, and we're all in here, dancing the night away and pretending everything will be all right when of course it won't be. And I shouldn't be at the university, I should..."

He trailed off. He'd gone pale, and now it was easier to see the shadows of exhaustion under his eyes.

"I should go home," he said dully. "Far away from all of this. My mother would crow about it until the end of her days. Can you imagine?"

"I haven't met her," I replied.

"Lucky you."

He tried to take another swig from my wine glass, but it was empty, and the realization seemed to break him. He stared at it in dismay, his eyes distant and empty, flat as dull stone. It was a look that did not suit him, and it felt eerily familiar.

Gently I took the glass from him and gave it to a passing servant with a murmur of thanks. Then the orchestra launched into a new waltz, and since apparently the wine hadn't released its hold on me quite yet, I grabbed Gareth's hand and briskly led him out onto the dance floor. When I turned to face him, he looked as if he'd been given the shock of his life.

"What?" I said, putting one hand on his shoulder and holding the other up for him to grasp. "Don't you want to dance with me?"

"Well, of course, but—"

"Then put your hand on my waist, and let's dance."

Other couples whirled around us, their skirts and tailcoats a flurry of color, but Gareth hesitated, clearly still shaken.

"You said you wanted to practice your flirting," I prodded. "What happened to all of that? Have my provocative shoulders rendered you mute?"

That made him laugh, suddenly and with joyful surprise. Smiling brought some color back to his face, and when he put his hand on my waist, pulled me a bit closer, and wrapped his other hand around mine, I felt him relax. The very air around him seemed to let out its breath.

"Thank you," he said quietly. He finally looked down at me, his green eyes softer than I'd ever seen them. "For that, and for this."

"You can repay me by helping me find Farrin after this dance is over."

"One dance?" he asked as we spun into the waltz. With each gliding step, he seemed to become more like himself. "You wound me, Lady Mara. That's all you'll give me?"

"Until you prove yourself worthy of more."

"Will proving myself worthy to you involve me finding new friends?"

I laughed at that, which startled me. I couldn't remember the last time I'd laughed. I wasn't used to the sound. It was like hearing myself suddenly speak in a different language.

"It certainly won't hurt your chances," I replied. "Or at the very least, allow me to put the current ones through a rigorous training course that will make them never want to pick up a crossbow again."

"Now, *that* is a wonderful idea, as long as I can also receive the benefit of your instruction." He leaned in a little, his breath hot against my ear. "I may be a professor, but I'm also an excellent student."

"If you think you're getting me into your bed tonight, you're sorely mistaken."

"Ah, but the night is young, and my flirtations have only just begun. Allow me to demonstrate: Mara, has anyone ever told you how beautiful you are?"

"Quite often, actually. You'll have to do better than that."

He laughed once more, with genuine delight, and my heart fluttered a little at the sound. I tried to ignore it. No matter how nice it felt to have his warm fingers splayed across the small of my back, firmly holding me to him, the very last thing I needed was to enter into any sort of dalliance with Gareth Fontaine.

CHAPTER 6

Gareth didn't push his luck; once we finished our dance, instead of trying to charm me into another one, he gallantly fetched me a glass of water. I had just taken my first sip when a young freckle-faced page found us with a summons from Farrin and murmured, "If you'll please follow me."

He brought us to a chamber close enough to the ballroom that even with the door closed, I could still hear the orchestra's cheery waltz. There were several people in the room—council members, I supposed, few of whom I recognized—but I had eyes only for Farrin. My Order training prompted me to scan her for signs of injury, illness, or undue stress. Was she haggard? Had she been eating and sleeping enough?

She sat behind a table piled high with papers, her golden-brown hair in its usual braid. Her dress was simple but elegant, and its sumptuous dark blue shade warmed my heart, for I took it as a sign of her new devotion to the House of Bask—or at least to its son.

Ryder stood behind her, wearing a fine gray tunic with rolled-up sleeves and charcoal-black trousers. He was reading over her shoulder with a frown on his bearded face, his dark hair pulled back in a tidy knot.

I liked the sight of them together—Farrin sitting straight and tall in her chair, Ryder looming beside her like a great bird of prey, watchful and alert. When we entered the room, they both looked to me at once, and Farrin's brown eyes lit up in a way that made my stomach hurt. She said my name and stood, and I went straight to her and pulled her into my arms.

For a moment we were children again, the carefree ones who'd spent our days romping about the grounds of Ivyhill. I didn't allow myself to think of home as often as I once had, but in Farrin's arms I couldn't help it. She even smelled the same as the girl I remembered: the same soft hint of lavender, the same warm Farrin smell in her hair. And I was gratified to realize how strong she felt in my arms, nothing like the harried wisp I feared I might see. Ryder must have continued her training. When she started to pull away, my instinct was to draw her even closer, but somehow I managed to let her go.

"Oh, Mara, it's so good to see you," she said, holding me by the arms. "You look wonderful. I'm so relieved. The reports we've received..." Then she glanced behind me and smiled. "Oh, and you'll never guess who's here—"

Something slammed into me from behind, the air suddenly flush with a familiar floral scent. Arms wound tightly around me and squeezed.

"You might find returning to Rosewarren rather difficult," said Talan, coming forward, his smooth voice rich with amusement, "what with that wild Gemma attached to your back."

Grinning, I gently dislodged my baby sister's vise grip and turned around to return her fierce embrace. I couldn't believe it: both my sisters, here in the same room. It had been only a few weeks since we'd last seen each other—at Ivyhill, after the destruction of Mhorghast and the death of Ankaret—but it felt like years. I wanted to grab them both and hold on forever. I wanted to hide them away with me, somewhere no one could find us unless we desired it. Fiercely I wished for this. I prayed for it.

"You're lucky I didn't spin around and deck you for that," I said with a smile. "Haven't I told you to never sneak up on a Rose?"

"You're not a Rose," Gemma said, her voice muffled against my shoulder. "You're Mara."

It wasn't the first time she had said those words to me, but it was the first time they'd hurt me. I bristled in her arms, but before I could decipher the feeling, she stepped back to inspect me, a beaming smile on her face. I took her in greedily. There were the golden curls I'd known since I was two years old; there were her sparkling blue eyes. Our mother's eyes, but softer, sweeter. She wore a plain gray dress that I assumed she'd borrowed from someone. Even in a drab, ill-fitting gown, she was resplendent.

"That color," she declared, "is marvelous on you. You should wear purple more often." She glanced at Gareth, then back at me. Questions danced in her eyes. Part of me was curious about what she saw on Gareth's face, but the better part of me won.

"You're too thin," I observed, eager to stop talking about what colors suited me as soon as possible. I looked over at Talan. "You are too."

Gemma reached out to Talan, who took her hand gently. Even travel-weary and in borrowed plainclothes, he cut an extraordinary figure in the firelight: pale as ever, his dark eyes soft and tired, his hair falling in dark brown waves to his chin. But I didn't like the exhaustion I saw on his face or the new gauntness of his cheeks.

"Well," Talan said somberly, "we have much to tell you." He looked around at all of us and at the council members seated at several round tables scattered throughout the room. "I suppose now that we're all here, we should begin."

"The sooner we begin, the sooner we can adjourn and all of you can have some time alone," said the man seated nearest Farrin's table. I watched him as we took our seats. He had deep brown skin and cropped white hair, and he looked tired. I recognized the great sadness in his dark eyes. He kept it tightly under control, but I was too well versed in loss to miss it. He wore the black-and-gold robes and tasseled cap that marked him as a member of the Royal Conclave—the late queen's most intimate council of advisors. Thirsk, it must have been. Farrin wrote of him often. He'd been one of her closest allies in the capital since Yvaine's death. The queen had been dear to him.

"I'll keep this brief," he began. "Those of you who are interested in looking at the details of these reports may do so after we've finished here. But the long and short of it is that we are running out of time, both to find and apprehend the being known as Kilraith and to protect our people against an invasion from the Old Country. Lady Goff?"

One of the other black-robed advisers looked down at her notes. "As of yesterday, we have accepted ten thousand refugees into the capital and its immediate surroundings, and hundreds more arrive every day. Our food stores are adequate for now, but we'll need to recruit new elementals—or those with earth-leaning affinities of any kind—if we are to increase the underground hothouse yield and survive the winter months."

A man seated to my left, decked out in the crisp blue dress uniform of the Upper Army—comprising both Anointed and low magicians—grunted softly. "I cannot spare any more soldiers, Thirsk, no matter what sort of magic they possess. You'll have to find help somewhere else."

"With all due respect, General Haldrin," said Ryder, "if the people you and your soldiers are fighting to protect end up starving, then what is the point of protecting them?"

"Your tone doesn't sound very respectful to me, Lord Ryder."

The woman nearest him, wearing a dress uniform of her own,

put her hand on the general's arm. Her jacket was the rich chocolate brown that marked her as an officer of the Lower Army, which had only humans in its ranks.

"His point is valid, Haldrin," she said. "But Lord Ryder, as I'm sure you've heard, the state of the Mist is deteriorating rapidly. Every week another village falls. Every day new storms, earthquakes, and floods ravage the land. The Mist has flooded the Mistlands and will come for the heartlands next. The coastlines are shattered, and most of the main roads are ruined or clogged with refugees fleeing south."

General Haldrin grunted in agreement. "And General Pallien hasn't even mentioned the invaders. The cascading effects of the falling Mist means that the very fabric between the worlds is thinning. More and more Oldens are worming their way through. Every day the old magic keeping them where they belong grows weaker. We are fighting a war on *many* fronts, the likes of which we've never fought before."

I stiffened. Of course I knew all of this already, but to hear it said so bluntly put me instantly on the defensive. The general's words landed like an accusation: *The Order isn't working hard enough. If it was, things wouldn't be as dreadful as they are. The world would be safer, the monsters fewer.*

The woman—General Pallien—glanced at me, as if she sensed what I was thinking, and then looked at Farrin. "When we tell you we cannot spare anyone, we do not exaggerate. Perhaps if we send word to Vauzanne—"

Farrin shook her head. "They can't spare resources any more than we can, nor can Aidurra. The Knotwood and the Crescent of Storms are also in disarray, though not as drastically as the Middlemist."

"All the more reason for them to send us additional supplies," said General Haldrin.

"They couldn't even if they wanted to," Ryder pointed out. "Both the Gloaming Sea and the Sea of the Dawn are death traps now, riddled with storms and Olden hostiles, both of which surface unpredictably."

Talan nodded in agreement. "The falling Mist, the growing Knotwood, the spreading storms in the Crescent—all of it combined is wreaking havoc on the entire world, not just Gallinor."

General Pallien sighed. "Nobody can take advantage of supplies if they're rotting at the bottom of the sea."

Immediately an image of Kilraith stewing in that very place came to mind. Farrin had told us the story. Right before my sisters and I had killed his tormented host's body, the god Jaetris had given her all the information he'd gleaned about Kilraith during his imprisonment. The story was terrible: a newborn creature of the gods, abandoned by his creators and separated from the only other being in the world who was like him. All of this happened in what would have felt like an instant to us, but to Kilraith—and Ankaret too—it had unfolded over the course of years and years.

The impact of his fall from the skies during the gods' Unmaking left him buried deep under the water in the cold, ancient stone that made up the foundation of the world. Unthinkable and confused, this creature of shadows and light remained trapped at the bottom of the ocean for centuries as loneliness and rage consumed him. Now he was free to take his revenge upon the gods who had made him and the humans they had loved.

And so far, he was succeeding.

Gemma's clear, crisp voice pulled me out of my dark musings. "I can take a look at the hothouses, Lady Goff. My mother's botanical magic has blossomed in me over the past few months. I am now quite adept at using my elemental affinity. Perhaps I can work with your teams to enhance the crop yield."

"Lady Gemma," said one of the other black-robed advisers, an impatient-looking man with a reedy voice, "while that is a kind offer, we cannot afford for you and Talan to linger. Our priority must be to find the awakening gods before Kilraith does. And your godly blood is key to tracking them down."

A third advisor spoke thoughtfully. "Perhaps we should redirect all of our efforts toward helping Lady Farrin and Lord Ryder find Yvaine. Or Ankaret, I mean." She glanced at Farrin with a small, hopeful smile. "If we can find her, she can help us with everything else."

An uncomfortable silence fell until Thirsk broke it gently. "Lady Bethan, I believe we decided prior to this meeting not to discuss that topic any further."

"Excellent decision," said General Haldrin. "I would prefer not to devote any of our time tonight to fanciful stories and wishful thinking."

I looked to my sister, dreading what I would see, but Farrin's expression was calm, her posture as poised as a dancer's. "It is no fanciful story, General," she said quietly. "Ankaret told me to come find her. Those were her last words to me."

"The last words of a dying creature, heard by only one distressed woman desperate for comfort."

The room rustled uncomfortably.

"You doubt Lady Farrin's account?" said Ryder, his voice dangerously quiet and his blue eyes blazing.

Haldrin was unperturbed. "What I doubt is that these efforts to find our late queen are anything but futile. You are chasing an outlandish children's tale, Lady Farrin."

"The gods are awakening," Talan pointed out, "and Ankaret is a child of the gods, more so than any of us. Why, then, couldn't she be awakening too?"

His gentle voice seemed to soothe everyone listening. I wondered if he'd dared to use his demonic power to calm the room's rising tempers.

"I know what she told me," Farrin said. Her voice was quiet, but her brown eyes—our father's eyes—were flinty. "I know the contents of her will, and for years I knew *her*. My search for her will continue until I have no breath left in me."

"And doing so will be a waste of your breath," General Haldrin replied at once.

"That is *enough*, General," Thirsk snapped, all the sadness suddenly gone from his face. "And you will never again refer to Ankaret as anything other than the queen. Even in death, she deserves more than the label of *creature*."

That silenced us all. I found myself smiling as I regarded the tired, white-haired Thirsk, who suddenly looked as fierce as any soldier. I could see why Farrin liked him.

After a moment, General Pallien cleared her throat. "*I* would say our priority is to find the other anchors of the *ytheliad* curse. We have the crown and the egg, but three more are yet to be found. If we can destroy these anchors of Kilraith's power, render him toothless both here in Edyn and in the Old Country, we can stop whatever he's doing to destroy the Mist." She looked at me. "Lady Mara, I imagine the Warden and the rest of the Order would agree, yes?"

"To be frank with you, General," I replied, "I'm not certain that the Warden thinks of much beyond surviving each day with as many Roses alive as possible."

"Nor should she," said General Haldrin. "The duty of the Order is to protect our country from Olden invaders, not to go treasure-hunting."

Talan smiled tightly. "You make seeking the anchors sound like a mere child's game, General. While I agree that the Order's attentions should remain fixed on the Mist, finding the curse's anchors is no easy task."

Now Gareth was the one to clear his throat. The sound startled me. He'd been so quiet since we'd arrived that I'd almost forgotten he was there. He was standing in the corner, leaning against a sideboard and drumming his fingers on his thigh, as if we were simply having an academic debate at one of his professorial salons. And yet to me his presence felt suddenly and inexplicably larger than it should have been, as if he were standing right next to me instead of several strides away.

"If I may," he began, "I have a suggestion regarding that topic. My team and I at the university have been working on several projects, as you know. One of them involves a rather complicated set of innovative spells designed by our top beguilers—spells designed to seek out traces of the *ytheliad*. But we've reached the limit of what we can accomplish in the laboratory."

He cleared his throat again, glancing quickly at me. I thought I saw a flash of embarrassment in his eyes. "I propose that my team establish a new base of work farther north, where Kilraith's magic—and the workings of the *ytheliad*—are more concentrated and destructive and therefore more overt."

General Pallien nodded. "And easier to track."

"In theory, yes."

Gemma glanced at Gareth, then at me, then back at Gareth again, her eyes dancing. "You want to bring your team to the Middlemist, don't you?"

Gareth shoved his hands into his pockets. Unlike my sister, he was pointedly *not* looking at me. "I know it sounds extreme, but it's the natural next step in our work, and I believe it's where we can do the most good."

"Funnily enough," said Farrin, an odd look on her face, "the Warden has already sent for you, Gareth."

I turned to her in surprise. "I've brought no such summons with me."

"It arrived before you did," said Ryder. "She didn't tell you about it?"

I shook my head, accepted the note Farrin was holding out to me, and read it quickly.

Professor Gareth Fontaine: By the authority of the Order of the Rose, as bequeathed to me by the Crown upon the wishes of the gods, I request your presence, and that of whatever associates you deem necessary, at the priory of Rosewarren. I ask that you aid us in our search for the objects we currently understand to be "anchors" of the being Kilraith and facilitate further consultation on the transference procedure proposed in your most recent submission to the Academic Committee Councils. With cordial appreciation and expectation of all due haste.

The handwriting was certainly the Warden's, as was her scribbled signature and the message's somewhat sneering formality.

I looked up at Gareth with a glare. It seemed I wouldn't be able to ignore him any longer, and I felt unreasonably angry about it.

"Transference procedure?" I asked him sharply. "What is she talking about?"

"Another project my team has been working on is rather radical, much more so than our curse-tracking designs. The Warden has been particularly intrigued by the idea." Gareth took a breath. "To put it simply, we believe that it might be possible to transfer the essence of a god from one host into a stronger host."

Little gasps rippled around the room. I couldn't help but think of Mother up at Wardwell: the face and body of Philippa Wren, the spirit of the goddess Kerezen.

The impatient advisor scoffed. "Preposterous. Manipulation of a *god?*"

"Look what Kilraith did to Jaetris," Gareth pointed out. "Consider how long it took Kerezen, while living in the body of Philippa Ashbourne, to understand what she truly was." He shot an apologetic glance at Farrin, at Gemma, but not at me. My unreasonable anger returned, more at myself than at him. I didn't care one whit whether or not he looked at me.

"Clearly, as they reawaken," Gareth continued, "the nascent gods are in a weakened state and susceptible to being controlled by outside forces. And they have no bodies of their own, as they once did. Instead, they must inhabit someone else's physical form. At the moment, we can't predict how they will surface or in whom. But with a bit more time, I believe my team and I will be able to. At the crown's command, of course."

He began to pace, his eyes lighting up as he spoke. "So, for example, if we followed a lead to a child in, say, Beroges who has recently started acting strangely or performing uncharacteristic magic, and we determined that the goddess Neave was awakening in the child's body, we would be able to transfer the essence of Neave into a less vulnerable body. A burly soldier, or a trusted council member."

"And if this works," said Talan, "we could conceivably keep transferring Neave from body to body as she grows in strength?"

Gareth snapped his fingers. "Exactly. Making it harder for Kilraith or any of his allies to track her."

"Professor, what you're saying is extraordinary," said General Pallien. "How is such a procedure *possible*?"

Gareth opened his mouth, then shut it and ran a hand sheepishly through his hair. "Well, through an extremely complex series of spells conducted by a highly controlled team of Anointed magicians drawing upon an incredible power source, something even stronger than their combined magic. We haven't yet settled upon what that power source should *be*, exactly," he added reluctantly. "But the theory is sound." Then he glanced at Gemma with an apology in his eyes. "We would need an artificer to do the actual surgical work—"

Gemma went pale at the mention of an artificer—the same kind of being who had altered her body at our parents' command.

General Haldrin let out an incredulous laugh.

Even General Pallien looked shocked. "An *artificer*, Professor? You wish to bring an Olden being into a process as sensitive as this?"

"They'd sabotage the entire operation!" the impatient advisor blurted out.

"Not every Olden being is a bloodthirsty murderer," Gareth said, "as all of you know quite well. Their societies are as varied as ours."

He looked to me for confirmation. Reluctantly I nodded. "While that's true," I said, "we would have to rigorously investigate any artificer who offered their services, which would take time."

"And which my teams are fully prepared to do."

"*And* which I hope the entire council would fully support," added Gemma, "since keeping the gods safe from Kilraith is instrumental to winning this war."

Gareth shot her a grateful smile, which she returned. Talan took her hand, and she grasped it tightly while staring coolly at the generals, as if daring them to say another word.

"Once we have all the necessary personnel," Gareth continued, "the procedure itself is quite like a dance, although of course the entire operation is rooted in magical mechanics. If your goal, for example, is to transfer Caiathos from one body into another, those who possess magic of the earth would take the lead and be placed physically near each of the hosts. So, elementals, wayfarers—"

He stopped, catching sight of Farrin, who was giving him a wry look.

"But perhaps now is not the time to delve into the specifics," he said. "Though I'm happy to do so for anyone who might want to keep me company for a few hours after we adjourn."

He said this with the slightest plaintive hint in his voice, as if he dearly hoped someone would share his fascination and take him up on his offer. His enthusiasm was contagious, and there was no trace of sly roguishness on his face when he spoke of his work.

I couldn't help it.

I very nearly smiled.

Nearly.

"Wait a moment," said General Haldrin, rising to his feet with authority. "Before we send anybody anywhere, I must mention the thing that apparently no one else has the courage to speak of." His gaze landed squarely on Gareth. "Can Professor Fontaine be trusted with this work?"

Gareth's face fell. It was as stark a change as a cloud passing over the sun.

"Your complaints about Professor Fontaine have already been lodged, General," said Thirsk quietly, "and duly noted."

"Yes, but now you're talking about sending the man and his team of mad librarians to the Middlemist. To *Rosewarren*, for gods' sake—to the heart of the Order. How are we to be certain that *he* isn't an anchor of the *ytheliad*?" He looked around at everyone in disbelief. "Have any of you actually read the report of what happened in that wretched city? What Kilraith did to the people he held captive there? What *Professor Fontaine* did as well?"

Farrin watched the general through narrowed eyes. "Gareth has been thoroughly examined by multiple healers and by every member of the royal councils, General, including yourself. He has been deemed healthy, of sound mind, and free of all Olden influence."

"Nevertheless, the fact remains that Professor Fontaine was a tool of Kilraith and Jaetris while in Mhorghast. He has firsthand knowledge of the *ytheliad* anchors that none of us possess, with the exception of the demon."

"His name is Talan, General," said Gemma, her eyes flashing.

"And if you refuse to properly address him," Ryder added, "you will no longer be welcome in these meetings."

General Haldrin gestured incredulously at the advisors. "Thirsk, are you hearing this? This man has no authority here."

"No, but I do," Farrin replied. "And I agree with Lord Ryder. Talan will be addressed properly, or you will be dismissed. I will not tolerate any prejudice against him."

"Fine. *Talan,* then. He and Professor Fontaine are the only ones in this room who have been directly under Kilraith's thrall by way of the *ytheliad* anchors. And now you want one of these tainted men to set up camp among the Roses? This man with traces of gods-know-*what* lingering in his veins?"

"General Haldrin does have a point, Lady Farrin," General Pallien said quietly. "Kilraith is a being beyond our current understanding. We don't know what he's capable of or what latent weaponry he and Jaetris might have implanted in Professor Fontaine's mind."

Gareth shot her a sardonic smile. The happy light was gone from his eyes; in its place was a startling flatness, just as I'd seen in the ballroom, as if everything good in him had vanished.

"I assure you, Generals," he said, "if there were a dormant piece of foul magic living in me, waiting with bated breath to be awakened by some secret act of malice, it would have come to life during this conversation and flattened you both."

Ryder let out a choked laugh before he could stifle it.

I looked at Gareth with new eyes. Saying such a thing in front of the royal councils and the generals of both armies required nerve I hadn't realized he possessed.

"Gareth," Farrin said, a warning in her voice.

"Some might consider what you just said a threat, Professor," said General Pallien.

"Some might, yes, and I do," added General Haldrin. "And that right there should be enough evidence to convince you all of his inherent instability. May I remind you that he is a Fontaine? He would not be the first in his family to crack under pressure and become a danger to everyone around him."

Gareth blanched. I didn't know what the story was there—Farrin had never mentioned his mother—but his face told me enough. That was a deep, old wound. I hated the sight of his hurt. It was unfair. And this was an injustice I actually had the ability to correct.

"Are you a reader of the *Fairhaven Courier,* General Haldrin?" I asked. "It sounds as if you may have read one too many columns authored by an acquaintance of mine."

The general frowned, but before he could talk over me, I pressed on. "The Warden knows better than any of you the strength of the women under her command. She has read the Mhorghast reports, same as you have, and yet she has still requested the professor's presence. That should be enough to satisfy everyone here today. And," I added, "I must ask you, General: What of the soldiers under *your* command? What of the Roses under mine? The violence they have committed, the horrors they have witnessed—do these things make them dangerous? Should they, by your logic, be under lock and key along with Professor Fontaine?"

I hadn't meant to say quite as much as all that, but it seemed to do the trick. General Haldrin glared at me for a moment and then returned to his seat without another word. I was glad to receive that glare of his. It was fearsome, but so was I.

"Lord Thirsk," I said, turning to the man, "I will of course facilitate the relocation of the professor and his team to Rosewarren. Shall we consider the matter settled? I wonder what the next item on our agenda might be."

A soft wave of relieved laughter passed through the room as Thirsk began reading from his notes. I caught Talan's and Ryder's stifled smiles and the merriment flashing in Gemma's eyes. Even Farrin, dutifully stoic, looked ever so slightly amused.

And Gareth—I sensed him looking at me and couldn't resist checking his face. That was a mistake. When our gazes locked, the emotion in his was so raw and grateful that it embarrassed me. He gathered himself quickly and tucked whatever he was feeling behind a mask of bland attention. I did the same, determined to listen carefully to what Thirsk was saying. But my cheeks were warmer than they should have been, and for the rest of our meeting, I couldn't seem to cool them.

Chapter 7

I spent the next day at the university, helping Gareth and his team prepare for their journey north.

Their equipment—strange gadgets and sensors with clockwork pieces that whirred and buzzed—required protection from the barrage of wayfaring magic that would transport us to Rosewarren by greenway. I told them everything I could about the route, as well as what to expect upon arriving at Rosewarren. The priory was closer to the Mist than any of them had ever been, and they would need to be on the lookout for curious Roses and erratic Mist-touched magic alike. They needed to know everything: the layout of Rosewarren, our schedules, the procedure when the breach bells rang, and what would happen if a breach opened on the priory grounds.

I grew increasingly agitated the longer I spoke with them. It wasn't their fault; they were bursting with eager questions, every one of them thoughtful. But all day I'd been glancing out the windows at the dark northern horizon, where storms endlessly churned now that the Mist was in constant turmoil. What were my sisters in the Order doing? What new disasters had they faced in my absence?

The questions tore at me with quiet persistence. I hadn't been away from Rosewarren for so many consecutive hours in ages. The distance made me itch. Memories of flying sparks, ashen girls, and the nymph child's corpse in my arms kept tugging at the corners of my mind. It was worse when I had the rare moment to myself. What had the Warden said?

This is what happens when you stop moving, isn't it? All the mean thoughts wriggle in.

And I had so many mean thoughts. They clawed at the doors of my mind incessantly.

At least Gareth was so occupied with his own tasks throughout the day that I saw mere flashes of his messy blond hair and the occasional glint of his glasses, only heard his laughter and his hearty, teasing voice rise above the chaos a paltry few times.

Whenever I thought about the way he'd looked at me during the council meeting or recalled the sensation of his hands on me as we danced, my stomach clenched uncomfortably. A dangerous feeling, and one I hadn't experienced in years. What a silly thing I must have seemed to him, no better than any of the other giggling women he'd managed to seduce over the years. Me and my provocative shoulders. I scowled at the thought and longed for Rosewarren, where the Warden quite wisely allowed no beverages that made one lose their senses.

It wasn't until eleven o'clock that I finally retreated to the rooms set aside for me in the palace. We would leave at dawn. This time tomorrow, I would be going to sleep in my room at Rosewarren, and Gareth and his team would be doing the same in theirs.

I pinched the bridge of my nose and rolled out my aching shoulders. I couldn't decide who was likely to cause me more trouble: the intruding librarians or my curious fellow Roses. All I knew was that I wouldn't be able to sleep that night without first training or finding someone who wanted a quick tumble. But thinking about sex made me think of Gareth, and his pretty face was not welcome in my thoughts, nor were my mind's distracted musings about what he might look like underneath his clothes. So training it was. I would punch him right out of my head.

But when I reached my room, Farrin and Gemma were there in their nightclothes, talking quietly on a settee by the hearth. Farrin had her knees pulled to her chest and was staring at the fire. Gemma was braiding her hair.

"There you are!" Gemma sat up and scooted over. "Come sit. You look tired. Have some of these cookies I found in the kitchens."

"I'm really not hungry," I said.

"Just eat them," Farrin mumbled sleepily. "She'll keep pestering you about it until you relent. And they *are* quite good—laced with liquor of some kind. I actually feel a little drunk."

"Oh, I haven't been drunk with you in far too long. We'll have to set aside an evening for it the next time we're together. Mara, please come." Gemma patted the seat beside her. "You look alarmingly tense."

The chance to sit with them alone, privately, was a rare treasure, but I couldn't trust my mood. "I was going to train," I protested half-heartedly, joining them. "It helps me sleep."

"This will be even better, I promise you. Here." She held out the plate of cookies. "Try one."

I gave up and took one, and as soon as the crispy sweetness hit my tongue, I felt myself relax.

"Good, aren't they?" Gemma grinned, watching me. "Don't they remind you of the ones Mrs. Rathmont used to make?"

In fact, they did. Mrs. Rathmont, the head cook at Ivyhill, was famous in our household for her cinnamon-and-chocolate cookies. On stormy nights when I was a child—before the Warden, before the Order—Mrs. Rathmont would leave out a fresh tin just for my sisters and me, and we'd pile into Farrin's bed and eat so many we'd fall asleep feeling happy and delirious and a little bit sick. I closed my eyes, sinking into the memory. Lightning flashing outside the curtains. Farrin making shadow animals come to life on the walls. The smell of Gemma's cookie breath as she giggled beside me. Remembering was like pressing on a bruise; I relished the soft bloom of pain.

"I received the Warden's report about what happened at Graystone," Farrin said after a moment. "I'm so sorry, Mara."

All at once, the memory of home vanished. My eyes snapped open. "She sent you a report? What did it say?"

"It was a simple account of what happened, starting with the breach bells and ending with your retreat. It's standard procedure when there's a breach. You know that." Farrin paused, looking keenly at me. "Are you all right?"

"Did her report describe the fire nymphs?"

"Only that they set fire to the main buildings and held some young recruits hostage. You rescued so many of them."

"Of course she did," said Gemma promptly, squeezing my hand. "Brave Mara."

So the Warden had said nothing about my hallucination. I wasn't sure whether to be thankful or disappointed. Not until that moment did I realize how desperate I was to talk to someone about what had happened.

I swallowed hard. "Not all of them. I didn't save all of them."

"No one can save everyone," said Gemma.

"If anyone could, though," Farrin added, giving me a soft smile, "I think it would be you."

"I did nothing extraordinary," I said. Their kindness rankled me. I closed my eyes and reached for calm. But this time my memories did not cooperate. I was back in Graystone, the dead girls' ashes coating my fingers. I was at my trials, the blade in my hand and Petra's blood on my face. Sweat dampened my brow.

"It was just another battle in a long string of battles," I muttered. "I did my duty."

"That doesn't make it any less remarkable," Farrin said.

Suddenly the cozy stillness of our little spot by the fire no longer fit around me. Or perhaps it was me who no longer fit. My sisters were a sweet green meadow, and I was the monster who couldn't help trampling their flowers, no matter how hard I tried not to.

"Can we talk about something else?" I snapped. "Not Graystone, or Gareth's work, or Mother, or Mhorghast, or how Gemma and Talan are hunting for anchors, or Farrin's search for Ankaret. And I don't want to talk about Ivyhill either. I can't bear that. Not right now."

Gemma went very still. Even with my eyes closed I could feel Farrin watching me steadily.

"I know you've been working so hard," I added. "I've been frightened for you both." I opened my eyes and nearly lost my breath at the sight of Farrin's warm brown gaze. My sister. Both my sisters, here beside me. "But I'd like to just be with you. I'd like to pretend we're ordinary sisters. Please."

Farrin placed her hand softly on mine. "Of course."

"I know," said Gemma, lifting a cookie to her lips with a sly grin. "Tell her about your latest training session with Ryder."

Farrin dropped her head into her hands. "Oh, gods."

Gemma leaned a bit closer to me. "She's learning how to fight with a *sword*."

The change in topic was so abrupt and absurd that I let out a breathless laugh. "You're telling me that instead of sitting here by the fire, we could be watching Farrin wave a sword around?"

"I'm not terrible at it, you know," Farrin said. "Ryder is an excellent teacher."

"In more ways than one," added Gemma.

Farrin tossed one of the settee's pillows at her. A smile lit up her face. "You're a scoundrel. And I much prefer daggers to sword work.

I also prefer punching. And running away. And everything else that doesn't make me feel like my arms are going to fall off."

"But you told me singing helps lessen the weight."

"It creates the *illusion* that they're lighter," Farrin said, "which gets me through training well enough. The sword, however, remains a sword, and my muscles pay for it afterward."

I closed my eyes and smiled. The easy rhythm of their conversation was like a song. I was ravenous for it. "Tell me about Ryder. How is he? And Alastrina?"

"Alastrina has recovered nicely from her time in Mhorghast," Farrin replied. "She had trouble wilding for a few days, but that didn't last long. Half the time she's at Ravenswood, providing shelter to northern refugees, and when she's not there, she's at the Farrow estate."

"With her head between Illaria's legs, I hope," Gemma said.

I laughed. "And the other way around too."

"Of course! Illaria is endlessly generous. Much like a certain burly, bearded man we know."

Farrin threw another pillow.

I opened my eyes to relish the embarrassed color in Farrin's cheeks. The flush of love suited her.

"You wouldn't be talking about Ryder, would you?" I asked innocently. "Ryder...Bask, I think he's called?"

"The very same," Gemma said cheerfully. "And listen to this: the night before you arrived, Talan fetched me some of these very same cookies from the kitchens. That's how I found out about them in the first place. He's such a dear. Being here in the city with so many people around and so much magic in the air gave me terrible body aches, and the cookies helped, as they tend to do. Later I went to Farrin's room to share some with her, and I stopped right outside the door and *heard* them."

Farrin groaned and flung an arm over her eyes in mortification.

"They were deep in conversation, I assume," I said. "Discussing matters of state and the like."

"Oh, yes," Gemma replied. "And *quite* passionately too."

I took Farrin's hand in silent apology. "I'm glad for you," I said softly, and I meant it with all my heart. "It's clear when he looks at you how much he loves you."

Farrin's shy smile was like the sun rising. "Both of your crass insinuations notwithstanding, he *is* very…generous."

As Gemma burst into delighted laughter and Farrin scooted closer to press her leg against mine, I let myself fall into the comfort of their nearness, their voices, their familiar scents. My skin still itched, dark memories roiling in my mind and storms of worry rumbling just out of reach. But I concentrated on the warmth of my sisters and thought, *Let me be. Let me be with them tonight.*

And for a while, they obeyed.

Chapter 8

The next morning, at the mouth of the university greenway that would bear us all north, I found Gareth amid the chaos of his team—twenty librarians and professors, all their personal effects, and dozens upon dozens of books, trunks, and pieces of equipment.

They weren't being especially chaotic, actually, or annoying, and yet I found myself annoyed. If I couldn't hide away with my sisters as my heart of hearts desired, then I wanted to zip right back to Rosewarren and return to work as usual. Instead I was shepherding a passel of librarians and would have to get them settled in their rooms before I did anything else.

The very thought of that—and the cold reality of leaving my sisters yet again—made me want to run until I collapsed, or strike one of the punching bags in our training yards until my knuckles stung and my mind was clear.

Gareth must have sensed my agitation. He watched me approach with something like apprehension on his face and shooed away one of his colleagues without even looking at him.

"I'd like to make something clear before we leave, Professor," I told him sharply. "Just because I defended you against General Haldrin doesn't mean I like you."

A devastating opening statement, I thought, but Gareth just smiled and crossed his arms over his chest. "Your dancing, Lady Mara, suggested otherwise."

I pushed on, refusing to give him the pleasure of a reaction.

Refusing, too, to think about either dancing or the warm press of his hand on my waist. If I wanted a warm press of anything, I knew where to find it. And if my rebellious body was any indication, I needed to do so as soon as possible.

"The Roses are unaccustomed to strangers," I said. "Your arrival will cause quite a stir. But know this: If you set your sights on any of my Roses, I'll banish you from the premises, and your team too."

"Ah. Farrin has told you the tales of my many conquests."

"Some of them, anyway. Enough for me to be on my guard around you."

Gareth looked away, rubbing the back of his head. His smile faded, and when he looked back at me, his gaze was earnest.

"This assignment is important to me," he said quietly, "as is my work and what it could mean for all of us. I won't ruin it. You have my word."

He wouldn't soften me with those pretty green eyes of his. "Good. Life at Rosewarren is hard enough without piling heartbreak on top of all our other battles."

"I meant what I said at the ball, Lady Mara. I know you don't think very much of me, but I'd like to do whatever I can to change that."

"So you can study me? Or to ensure that your team gets the best cuts of meat at dinner?"

Gareth shrugged and gave me a small smile. "So we can be friends. It's nice to talk to someone who understands what it feels like to be… not entirely understood."

That shook me, though I wasn't certain why. Maybe because it was the most sincere I'd ever seen him. Maybe because I was tired and missing my sisters so much it hurt.

I turned away before he could read my face. He deserved a better response than that, but at the moment I couldn't give him one.

"When we get to Rosewarren," I said over my shoulder, "please stop calling me Lady. There are no ladies at the priory. There are only Roses."

⟡

I was flying beside the Warden.

I was flying beside *the Warden.*

Not ten minutes after I'd arrived at Rosewarren with Gareth and his team, the breach bells had rung. I'd reached the training yards at the same time as the other summoned Roses, all of our bodies halfway through their transformations—limbs lengthening, nails becoming talons, feathers sprouting along our unfolding wings. Cira's golden eyes had been eager as always. Brigid, though, had shot me a bewildered look.

I'd soon understood why.

The Warden had been waiting for us in the yard, already in her avian form—an owl, black and gleaming. At the sight of her, I'd stopped short. Freyda, just behind me, had landed on my shoulder and plucked restlessly at my hair.

But there had been no time for questions. The Warden had barked orders at us and launched herself into the air. We'd followed at once, the instincts of our training stronger than our confusion, and now I was flying beside her, en route to the human village of Sablemire in the northern Mistlands. Hostiles had been sighted. The village had called for aid.

It was an unremarkable mission. Such things happened every day in these times of war. And yet this time the Warden was with us, leading our squadron.

The Warden *never* flew with us on missions, nor did we expect her to. She was the Warden, not a general. It was up to the squadron captains, like me, to lead the Roses into battle.

I couldn't make sense of it, but I didn't try to for long. The Warden was remarkable, beautiful, her flight smooth and sharp. My nape prickled at her nearness. The entire squadron seemed reverent in her presence—no idle chatter, our formation flawless. Even our familiars were quiet, and Freyda flew closer to me than usual, as if sensing the moment's import.

Suddenly the Warden pointed with one taloned hand at the village on the horizon, from which smoke rose like storm clouds. She was so close to me that her black feathers brushed against my brown and gray ones, silk against silk. I shivered. I was *giddy*. I thought nothing of my sisters or of Gareth or of the little burning girls from Graystone.

I was a Rose about to dive into battle alongside the Warden, and that was all I knew.

"There," she said quietly. In the cocoon of her magic—the magic that bound us to her and her to us—I could hear her easily.

I saw it too—the village of Sablemire, one of the smallest and most remote ones in the northern Mistlands. It was a town for people who didn't much like other people. Sleepy, forgettable, isolated. Not even Oldens had touched it yet.

Until today.

"Separate and dispatch," the Warden said, reminding us of our orders. Not that any of us needed reminding. My skin itched with battle hunger, and I knew my squadron would feel the same.

"Two furiants," Cira said quietly, her voice carrying to all of us. She had the sharpest eyes of everyone except for me. "A figment, I think. It looks like a human man with a shimmer around him. Two shifters, a family of griffins. Wood nymphs? Possibly a siren. Gods, she's gorgeous."

"Maybe we'll spare her, at least," said Caralind.

A couple of the others laughed. I did not. The word *family* stuck in me like a splinter.

"A motley crew," Brigid observed. "That's odd."

"Enough chatter," the Warden said. "We'll dive on my command. Ruby Formation."

I couldn't let it go: a *family* of griffins.

Freyda, flying off to my left, suddenly let out a chirp and dove down into the Mist. A few seconds later, she returned with an urgent cry and pushed her head against my sternum, as if warning me away.

My blood turned cold. Something was wrong.

"Wait," Cira said, squinting. "I count twelve hostiles, no more than that. Far fewer than we thought. And they're not doing anything. They're just gathered in what must be the village square. I see humans, I see—"

"Children," said Brigid, her voice clipped. "Madam, your orders?"

The Warden didn't answer. We were close enough now that we could plainly see what awaited us: not a village in ruins, but one still standing. The columns of smoke were coming from chimneys. This far north, winter was in full force. Snow already blanketed the ground, and icy wind bit my cheeks as we emerged from the cover of the Mist, but I hardly noticed the cold.

My full attention was on the village below. The square was crowded with humans and hostiles alike, but as Cira had said, the hostiles were hardly that. No one was running or screaming. There was no violence here. And in the crowd I saw many small figures among the taller ones. There was a griffin bull with two pups clinging to his back. The siren Cira had seen held an infant in her arms. A quartet of wood nymphs stood nearby with pine needles in their hair and moss coating their feet. One was on the older side, her skin wrinkled and her posture hunched. The other three were much smaller. They couldn't have been more than five years old.

I scanned the rest of the scene frantically. The furiants, with their luminescent palms and glowing white eyes, weren't using their powers of the mind to hurl objects at the villagers. They were sitting at a table instead, sharing a meal with them. And the figment? When I found him, my heart sank. As Cira had described, a shimmer of illusion outlined the human male form he'd assumed, but he wasn't trying to deceive the villagers. He was sitting beside a small, pale child, beautiful and copper-eyed—a vampyr, though I could see no others of her kind. He held her hand while one of the villagers bandaged her leg.

Another man—a human man—had spotted us and was standing on a crate, waving his arms. He was hollering something, and though I couldn't make out the words, his meaning was plain enough. *Stop. Wait.* Others noticed him and began to do the same. The griffin plucked the pups from his back and stepped in front of them, his body a shield. The siren held her infant to her chest and ran. And even though my wings propelled me ever forward, I felt frozen with dread.

Somehow I managed to speak. "Madam, we must abort, they're not—"

"Now!" the Warden cried.

In an instant she was gone, diving fast toward the panicking crowd, and we all did the same, falling into Ruby Formation with the automatic movements honed by countless hours of drills.

But I broke ranks, going after the Warden instead. I would ram her if I had to. This was a mistake; her intelligence was wrong. These Oldens were not hostiles. They were refugees, and clearly the villagers of Sablemire had formed some kind of alliance with them. But the Warden was deadly fast, speeding out of my grasp like a shining black arrow before I could get close enough to stop her.

She went for the vampyr first. One moment the child was sitting between the healer and the figment, watching our descent with alarm. The next, the Warden grabbed her by the arm with her shining black talons and flung her into the nearest building. Her body hit the wall with a sickening crack before dropping to the ground. She did not get up.

I whirled around and spread my wings wide. "Abort!" I cried. "Abort, *now*!"

And for a moment the squadron obeyed. Cira drew up short; Brigid turned to block the others, echoing my command.

But then I heard a furious howl behind me. I whipped my head around to see the Warden darting through the crowd in a blur of black. The griffin reared up to meet her, but she was faster than he was, and he was a distracted father. She swooped around him, plucked one of his pups from the ground by the scruff of his neck, and seemed ready to toss him as she had done the vampyr child. But then she looked up and saw me, and she paused for a heartbeat. Her eyes locked with mine—hers round and gold, crowned with furrowed feathers—and I thought I saw the hint of a smile flit across her face.

Her hesitation gave the griffin bull enough time to whirl around and knock her from the air with one massive lion's paw.

The pup dropped into the cradle of his waiting wings, and the Warden went flying. She skidded across the ground and crashed through the door of a nearby cottage.

That was all it took: the sight of the Warden reduced to a limp pile of black feathers.

Behind me, my squadron let out a chorus of furious war cries. The blood fever that drove us through battle after battle, year after year, had seized them. Our Warden was hurt. And an Olden invader had been the one to do it.

The griffin lunged at us, claws outstretched. The furiants leapt to their feet, eyes and hands blazing, and flung their table at us with the force of a slingshot. Their chairs followed, then the doors they ripped from every building on the square using only the power of their minds. I threw myself to the ground just in time. A spinning windowpane zipped past my head before crashing into the building behind me. My fellow Roses tore past me, their familiars scurrying and flying alongside them. I could hear only the sounds of battle—the roars of my sisters, the roar of the griffin, and the roar of my own blood.

I had a choice to make and only a split second in which to make it.

I could stop this now, somehow, even though I feared the moment for that had died along with the vampyr child, or I could fight.

Behind me, Caralind screamed in pain. Brigid roared my name. She needed my help. The Warden still wasn't moving. And my bones were singing for blood, just as my training had taught them to.

If I tried to call off my sisters, I might lose them. I might lose the Warden.

I had lost enough. The furious thought ripped through me like lightning. I had lost *enough*.

It was like the world inside me switched from brightest day to darkest night in one breathless instant. And it was a relief to let the fever take hold of me. Fighting was familiar; fighting was instinct. I was good at it. And when I was fighting, I couldn't think of anything else. I couldn't hurt. I couldn't yearn.

The Warden managed to lift her head and push herself up on shaking arms. Our eyes locked once more. Hers were full of pain; her jaw glistened with blood. On her face was a silent plea: *Help me, Mara. Please.*

I whirled around with fire in my heart. I would help her. I *would*, and I would bring her safely home. I would bring *all* of the Roses safely home. If I couldn't manage that, what good was I to anyone?

If I couldn't manage that, what had all of this been for?

As I leapt into the fray, I saw no adults, no children. I saw only enemies. And I tore through them all like a knife through thin paper.

Chapter 9

We flew home in blood-soaked silence. As they always did after a battle, my ears buzzed with the echoes of screams and the slowly receding tide of my battle fury. It was a feeling I normally relished. It was the feeling of victory. Another battle fought. Another day survived.

But this time, each beat of my wings brought a cold sickness crashing down upon me. I felt so heavy that I could barely keep myself airborne. The others were quiet too. Our familiars, accompanying us, were silent shadows. Freyda stayed close, right above me and to my left, but I almost wished she wouldn't. She was too dear to me, and I didn't deserve her company.

"You did well, Mara," the Warden said quietly. She was in my arms in her wounded human form, unable to fly. We'd nearly lost her. Three times during the fight, I'd had to put myself between her and a hostile. Each time I'd barely been fast enough to save her.

Remember that, I told myself. Remember that, not the keening cries of the maimed griffin pups before Brigid had put them out of their misery. Not the slain wood nymphs, the granny nymph cut in half right across her gnarled middle.

I shut my eyes against the memories. I couldn't shake the feeling that something terrible had been done to me, even though the truth was that *I* was the terrible thing. *I* had slain children. *I* had lacked the courage to stop that madness from unfolding.

"Mara?" The Warden was looking up at me, studying my face. "What's wrong, child?"

I could hardly stand the sight of her. That she could bring herself to say the word *child* after what had just happened felt obscene. And yet I loved the weight of her in my feathered arms. So small, so fragile, so unlike her usual fearsome self. And she had asked *me* to bear her home. She was letting *me* see her so injured and vulnerable. Such intimacy was a gift.

I swallowed past the painful lump in my throat.

"Did you know?" I asked, fearing I already knew the answer.

"Did I know what?"

Her voice was deceptively mild. She would make me say it.

"Did you know that there were children among the hostiles?" I said. "Did you know that they…"

She waited, her eyes unblinking.

"They weren't hostile, Madam," I finally managed to whisper. "They were seeking refuge. No one would have bothered them in Sablemire."

"Can you be certain of that?"

"I know what I saw."

"It doesn't matter what you saw. What matters is your orders."

"But Madam—"

"Isolate and dispatch. You should need no further explanation than that."

"But did you *know*—"

"Did I know there were children among these hostiles? Did I receive a message from the Sablemire council alerting me to the presence of Olden invaders in their town and requesting asylum on their behalf? Yes, of course I did."

I couldn't believe what I was hearing. I felt like I was flying through a bog, each wing stroke a monumental effort.

"Then why order us to exterminate them?" I knew I sounded desperate, that I was treading on dangerous ground, but I couldn't get hold of my voice.

"Olden children can be as vicious as their parents," the Warden replied sharply. "You have seen it yourself many times. Olden beings can easily persuade and deceive. The council could have been coerced into sending me that request."

"They could have been, yes, but it wasn't a certainty."

"There is no room for uncertainty in times of war."

"But they didn't attack us until we attacked them!"

"And if we hadn't done so, we would have entered the situation at a tactical disadvantage."

"There was no *situation* for us to enter."

"You are out of line, Mara." The Warden's voice was quiet, but it still cut like a whip. "Clearly you weren't concerned enough about those creatures to defy my orders and try to save them. How many hostiles did you slay? Five, correct? All on your own? Why is it only now that you've decided to speak on their behalf?"

The question struck me so hard that only years of training kept me from wavering mid-flight. She was right. I could have tried harder to stop her. I could have done more to save the Oldens. But I hadn't. In the end, I'd done exactly as I was told. Because that was what I had been taught to do? Because it was easier?

I imagined what it would have been like to defy the Warden: attacking her instead of attacking the hostiles, turning on my fellow Roses if they didn't follow suit; turning on Cira, on Brigid. My stomach turned, and the truth came to me with such a hard quickness that it felt like I'd been punched.

I would not have been able to bear the disappointment in the Warden's eyes or the wounded shock in Cira's.

I was a coward. And I didn't even have the nerve to look my cowardice in the eyes and accept its judgment quietly.

The Warden shifted gingerly in my arms, wincing as she jostled one of her wounds. My silence seemed to placate her. She even turned into my body, nestling close to me as if for warmth.

"You did well, Mara," she said again. "I knew you would. I never doubted you. Take comfort in that."

The gentle heat of her palm resting on my breastbone quieted my storming thoughts. She touched no other Rose like this, I told myself, as if that were any kind of excuse. Greedy, craven, I reveled in the press of her hand.

I didn't sleep that night. Every time I closed my eyes I saw not the beings I had slaughtered but the Warden instead. The Warden smiling at me, the pride on her face, her crumpled body that *I* had rescued, that *I* had borne all the way home.

The next morning, I strode through the priory with a raging headache and my eyes burning from exhaustion. Gareth and his team were *everywhere*. I wasn't sure how twenty people could seem like two hundred, but somehow they managed it.

I went to the kitchens to grab leftovers from the breakfast I'd missed, and there was Gareth's friend Loudon Barnes, the pale and square-jawed sage who had shot Cira with his crossbow. Beside him sat his lover, Tarek Farber, a beautiful beguiler with brown skin and soft dark curls. They sat at a table poring over sheaves of notes while their eggs grew cold.

For a moment I considered joining them. My presence would certainly terrify Loudon, which might be amusing enough to distract me from my thoughts. But even Cira had admitted to me that Loudon had been more than adequately contrite since his arrival. She found it much easier to forgive than I did, and she would be unhappy to hear about me tormenting him. Bitterly, I left them in peace.

I passed through one of the reading rooms on the second floor and nearly knocked over a waif of a librarian—Fiacra Browning was her name—who for some reason thought it wise to stand not two inches from the entrance. She had been engaged in a heated debate with yet *another* librarian, Marvyn Blaine. I hated that I knew all of their names, which I recognized was an unreasonable thing to hate. That only fed my irritation.

"What is that doing here?" I said, gesturing at the table beside them. One of their little gadgets was perched there, spinning noisily. "None of your equipment is to leave your wing without express written permission from a senior officer."

Marvyn glanced nervously at Fiacra, who cleared her throat and then said, "Begging your pardon, Lady Mara, but the Warden did say it was all right just for this morning. This piece is rather sensitive, and we thought it best to—"

"Fine. Just don't let it out of your sight. And no one is to touch it except for the two of you."

"Of course, Lady Mara," said Fiacra. Then she and Marvyn exchanged a bewildered look, as if I were the strange one in this conversation.

I pushed past them and left before I could say something terrible. Words boiled at the back of my throat. I didn't trust them. I didn't trust myself.

Even in the barracks, where of course visitors weren't allowed, in every hollow of the central Heart Tree and through every door left ajar, I heard Roses whispering. *Do you know what they're working on? Why are they here? Is it something about Kilraith? Have you seen that man Gareth? He's the one in charge. What I wouldn't give to bring him back to my room some night and let him take charge of* me.

Whenever I heard Gareth's name, I flinched like I was a naughty child being disciplined. *Every time you say* Gareth *you'll get a rap on the knuckles.* But he was nowhere to be found, most likely ensconced in their converted laboratory and not thinking about me at all, which was exactly as it should be. How would he react if he could open me up and see the true beast beneath my beauty? How would Gemma and Farrin? The way they'd looked at me weeks ago during my interrogation of Nerys the harpy had been awful enough. *This is our gentle sister? This is what life at the Order has done to her?* And that had been merely a glimpse of the true horror I was capable of.

By the time I burst into the stables, my skin was crawling and images of death crowded the edges of my vision.

Brigid turned at my entrance, as did the three gaping littles beside her. She had an easy shift this morning, teaching some of our newest recruits how to groom the horses.

The sight of them dredged up a cruel memory. Twelve years ago, in those sad, quiet days before my trials, Petra and I had groomed the horses just like this. She had finally coaxed me out of bed and into the stables, where the first thing she did was teach me the horses' names. It was important, she had said, for me not to fall farther behind. And clearly, knowing the names of all the Order's horses was the highest priority. Petra hadn't minded when I'd walked away mid-lesson to cry in the corner. Neither had the horses.

I remembered every detail so clearly. Petra's curly auburn hair. The sweet smell of clean hay. The old gray mare mouthing gently at my arm as I wept and longed for Ivyhill. Garnet was her name.

I remembered too many things, and I wished I could forget them all.

"Good morning," said Brigid. "You look terrible."

The littles stared at me with unabashed fascination. One of them whispered to the others behind her hand. This happened with all the new recruits. My reputation was the stuff of legend.

I tried my best to ignore them. The sight of their fresh little faces—so young, so unprepared for what awaited them—was like a kick to the gut. And how do you respond to a kick to the gut? You either kick back or you collapse.

"I need to fight someone," I declared.

Brigid glanced down at her tiny charges. "Well, we're a little busy at the moment. But I'll be free at the hour."

Panic lanced through me. "I can't wait twenty minutes."

Just then, Posey entered the stables, balancing two pails of water on her shoulders. When she saw me, she stopped short. Her luminous, green-tinged copper skin and the silver cascade of her hair was such an outrageous contrast to the drudgery of fetching water for horses that I almost laughed. It occurred to me that perhaps I was going mad.

"Is it true?" she asked, staring right at me.

Brigid peered past Posey at the stone yard beyond, where Nesset was striding toward the main house. "Ah, Nesset! Do you have a spare few minutes?"

The Vilia turned, instantly on her guard. I didn't blame her. The forced cheer in Brigid's voice spelled trouble.

I returned Posey's stare. I was in no mood to pretend. "Is what true?"

"I heard about the mission to Sablemire."

"Well done, you."

Posey shrugged off her water pails. They hit the ground with a heavy thud, sloshing water everywhere. "They were just people. Just families. And you murdered them."

"That's enough, Posey," said Brigid. Her voice sounded suddenly very far away.

"They were hostiles in a volatile territory," I said, not taking my eyes off Posey's. "Isolate and dispatch."

I was a soldier. She didn't frighten me. Nothing frightened me. *You did well, Mara. I never doubted you.*

"*Volatile?*" Posey scoffed, her silver fae eyes bright with tears. Her hand flew to her throat. She clutched her locket in one angry fist. "No one cares about Sablemire. Not even the greediest fae clans bother with it. There's nothing there but rocks and goats. Those Oldens could have hidden there in peace, and clearly the villagers were letting them."

"There is no room for uncertainty in times of war," I said, realizing only after I'd said the words that they were the Warden's, not mine.

Posey shook her head slowly. "Will I be next, then? What if the Warden wakes up one day and decides I am too *uncertain*, too volatile? That my usefulness no longer outweighs the fact of my Olden heritage? If she orders you to isolate and dispatch *me*, will you do it? Or what about Nesset? She's a revenant, created by necromancers. That sounds quite Olden to me."

Nesset, whom Brigid had wrangled into the stables with no small effort, suddenly squared her shoulders. "I'd like to see anyone try and dispatch me."

"Thank you *so* much, Nesset," said Brigid, pressing a curry comb into her chest with one hand and ushering the three littles toward her with the other. "My helpers here are almost finished. Only Gray Gus remains. Don't forget that he can't hear very well out of his right ear, so mind that you don't sneak up on him."

Posey hadn't moved from where she stood. The puddles of spilled water spread slowly toward her toes. "You're not who I thought you were," she said quietly. "And neither is the Order. I thought your goal was peace, not extermination. I'm leaving."

"You can't," I said at once. "You know too much about Order operations. If you leave, we'll find you."

"And kill me."

"Yes." *None of us can leave*, I thought. *Not you, not me. We'll die in this place. Maybe tomorrow. Maybe today.*

Posey watched me for a moment, perhaps ready to say more, but then she glanced at the littles and stormed out instead.

Brigid took my arm and led me outside in the opposite direction. "Mara? Shall we?"

"As long as you stop using that voice, yes."

"Those littles don't deserve your bad mood."

"But they deserve to face death in their trials, do they?"

Once we were out of earshot, Brigid hissed, "Who told Posey about Sablemire, for gods' sake? When I find out who blabbed, I'll wring their neck."

"I don't see why everyone shouldn't know. The Warden didn't issue a black order."

We passed through the stone colonnade that led from the stable yards to the training yards. In the shadows, Brigid stopped me and made me face her.

"Talk to me," she said, looking right at me with those patient pale blue eyes of hers. "What's happened?"

"Yesterday was a mistake," I replied. I stared past her at the empty training yard and the practice swords leaning against the far wall. "Posey was right. Those Oldens wanted a safe place to hide from the war. And we slaughtered them without cause."

"We don't know that."

"The Warden told me as we flew home. The village council had submitted a request for asylum on the Oldens' behalf."

Silence. Then Brigid said, "Maybe that isn't the full story. She could have learned something else that superseded their request."

"I suppose."

"And anyway, once the Warden attacked, we had no choice. We had to be on the defensive after that. If we'd just stood there, they'd have killed *us*."

Even these few seconds of conversation were too much time spent standing still. I itched to grab one of the weapons awaiting us in the training yard. It was too immense, this dark space yawning open inside me, this deafening silence flooding my limbs. If I didn't move soon, it would kill me.

"Then she shouldn't have attacked," I said.

"Maybe not," Brigid conceded. "But the harsh truth is that we don't know what the Oldens intended. They could have been planning to turn on the village that very night, for all we know. Or other hostiles might have tracked them there and attacked, leaving the village in ruins and *everyone* dead."

I couldn't look at her. I was so desperate for solace that I would have seen her familiar face and believed her, and I didn't want the comfort that would bring. I didn't deserve to feel comfortable.

"You're right," I said flatly. "Staff or sword?"

Brigid put her hands on my shoulders. "Now, wait a moment. This is me you're talking to, all right? You can't put on that serene Mara mask and pretend I can't see past it. Let's go on a walk and talk this through."

I roughly shrugged her off. "Staff or sword?"

Brigid stepped back, frowning. "Fine. Staff. But we're talking about this later, once I've beaten this foul mood out of you."

She strode across the yard, grabbed one of the sparring staffs, and tossed the other one to me. It was like dangling a piece of fresh meat in front of a starving wolf. All the scattered, brittle pieces of my mind snapped back together. I caught the staff and lunged at her. She was ready, of course. Our staffs crashed together with a sharp crack, and then I pushed off of her to spin around and strike again.

And again.

And again.

It was bliss to fight someone who actually challenged me, and soon enough I couldn't remember who I was, *where* I was, or who I was fighting. All I knew was the weight of the staff in my hands and the strength of my muscles. I was fast, faster than my father, faster than anyone. And when I used my staff to strike, it was like bringing down an ax large enough to split mountains.

Dimly, I heard someone shouting my name, but I pushed on, ignoring the sound, because with the sound of my name came thoughts I didn't want to think, memories I didn't want to recall. And every lunge, every spin, every quick jab of my staff beat them back harder, faster, until all I could hear was my roaring blood and my panting breaths and the *crack, crack, crack* of my weapon finding its mark.

"*Mara!*" someone screamed right beside my ear.

I whirled around, my staff raised, but Cira ducked before I could hit her, and this—the sight of her cowering beneath me, shielding Brigid with her much smaller body—was what snapped me out of the gorgeous dark place into which I had fallen.

I stood there, in the training yard, in the pale, Mist-silvered light, sweating and panting and staring down at my friends in horror. Brigid was alive, but her nose was broken, and there was a gash across her cheek. Blood stained her collar, and her staff lay on the ground beside her, useless, broken in half.

I dropped my own staff and slowly stepped back from her, realizing only then that we weren't alone. At least a dozen figures stared at me from the perimeter of the yard—littles, servants, Roses my own age. I didn't look harder than that. I couldn't bear to see who else might have been watching.

"I'm all right," Brigid said, reassuring Cira. She pushed herself up. "Mara, wait—"

But I couldn't be there for a single second longer. I turned away from the sight of Brigid's bloody face and fled.

Chapter 10

Fenwood wasn't an option for me that day. What if I lost control of myself in bed, as I had just done with Brigid, and killed my unlucky lover?

I laughed to myself at the thought, though it wasn't funny. None of this was funny.

Getting to the Old Country from Rosewarren was easier now than it had ever been. The Mist was pocked with holes, many of them patrolled by Roses, and many others stitched haphazardly back together by the beguilers among our ranks. But those reinforcements would hold for only so long before the breach bells would ring again and we would have to start all over.

Until, of course, there was no Mist left to reinforce.

The entry point I chose that day was a thin patch of Mist two miles from the priory. It wasn't particularly dangerous since Rosewarren was so close; few Olden beings would take the risk. The Mist here swirled with darkness, as if a great storm was brewing just beyond its shimmering veil. Every few seconds, a violent flash of blue light illuminated the crisscross pattern of spells spanning the spot—a net of magical buttresses that kept this rift from getting worse.

Four Roses were on duty at the site. Gods only knew what they saw on my face, but it was enough to send them scurrying out of my way. They would probably report me to the Warden, but at the moment I didn't care.

I cared only about finding something to fight. Something big, something I could hurt with abandon. Something that wouldn't hesitate to hurt *me*.

But before I could enter the greenway's twisting spellwork, a familiar cry pierced the air, and Freyda swooped down to block my path. She landed on my arm, making no attempt to be gentle with her talons, and glared up at me, shrieking.

I felt the curious gazes of the four nearby Roses upon me.

"Freyda," I said sternly, ignoring them. "Leave me. Go to the aviary. Now."

Freyda, of course, knew what I intended to do, and she didn't budge, even though as my familiar she was meant to obey me, not the other way around.

I felt so desperate that I barely resisted the urge to shake her off me.

"Lady Mara!" a voice called out, followed by hurried footsteps through the grass.

Swallowing down a burst of irrational anger, I turned to see one of the pages who worked for Gareth's team—a serious teenage boy who always seemed to be in a hurry.

"Professor Fontaine requests that you join him in the laboratory," he said with a quick bow.

"Why?"

The boy quailed when he saw my face. "I don't know, my lady." Then he gave another quick bow, as if in apology, and hurried back toward the priory.

For a moment I stood in burning silence, reminding myself that neither Freyda nor this page nor the four Roses watching us deserved my ire.

Without a word I returned to Rosewarren. Each step was an effort; the greenway sizzling behind me, and the tendrils of broken Mist roiling at its edges, seemed to be calling my name.

⟡

By the time I reached the laboratory, I'd achieved a fragile calm. Freyda moved to my shoulder, her customary perch, and began cleaning her feathers. It was as if the little scene by the greenway had never happened.

But my throat was as tight as a fist, and my thoughts kept straying to the greenway and what lay beyond. Maybe I'd have found a chimaera to fight. Maybe the beast would have killed me.

I stopped in the open doorway of the laboratory, keeping my face impassive. Naturally, the first thing that met my eyes was Gareth, who stood at the front of the room. He was leaning back against his desk, one leg crossed over the other, his sleeves rolled up to his elbows and his gold, black, and blue professor's tie hanging loose at his collar. He insisted that his team dress in their university robes and ties here, just as they would in Fairhaven. Something about morale and institutional dignity.

Incredibly, the sight of him wiped my mind clean. His forearms were slender, his gesturing hands eloquent. Later, I decided, I would examine how concerning it was that I found the sight of an unremarkable rumpled tie so attractive.

"All right," Gareth was saying, "to remind everyone of tomorrow's agenda: Katra, Blaise, and Geddings will accompany the Order's eastern dawn patrol and set up a tracking station in Section Thirty-One, which will bring us to how many operational stations, Tarek?"

Tarek, who sat at a nearby desk taking notes, answered smoothly without looking up. "Three, out of a projected twenty-five."

The room deflated a bit at that number, but Gareth remained undeterred. "Right, so quite a lot of work left to do," he said cheerfully, "but I know you'll all rise to the occasion beautifully, as you've always done. And Loudon, what's your team's status?"

Loudon Barnes sat filing papers in a series of leather packets. "We've gotten through about one quarter of the notes we brought with us from Fairhaven," he replied distractedly.

Gareth raised his eyebrows. "Already? Well done."

Fiacra Browning, the librarian I'd nearly knocked over earlier that day, muttered, "It would go much faster if the priory's archives weren't so thick with spellwork."

"Ah, but we already discussed this with the Warden," Gareth said, "and you know what her answer was."

"Well, perhaps we should try asking her again."

"She won't change her mind," I said quietly from my spot by the door. Surprise rippled through the room at the sound of my voice. "The archives are warded for a reason. We're too close to the Mist to leave them unprotected for even a moment. Olden spies would steal them the second they were vulnerable."

"Spies?" Loudon stopped filing papers to stare at me.

"Certainly with all your professorial intellect, you could deduce that we are constantly under surveillance by any number of potential enemies," I said. "The Mist is right outside our doors, after all."

The uneasiness on their faces delighted me. I felt like I was regaining lost ground, somehow exacting payment for my thwarted plans. I watched Gareth steadily. *Go ahead and scold me,* I thought. *See what happens.*

But Gareth didn't take the bait. "Maybe we could replace the current wards with some that are a little smarter," he suggested. "More specific." His voice was pleasant, but his eyes were guarded. "Friendly to allies, unfriendly to enemies."

Tarek finally paused in his note-taking. "Absolutely not. We don't have the personnel to spare for yet another project."

Blaise Gardiner, the cheeriest of Gareth's friends, a stocky, ruddy-faced literature professor with a keen eye for finding useful information in allegory, looked to me hopefully. "You could persuade Her High and Mighty Ladyship, couldn't you, Mara? You're her favorite, or so everyone tells me."

Truth be told, I liked Blaise. His boisterous, forthright nature felt so out of place at Rosewarren that I found the novelty charming. But I couldn't help myself. It was as though I'd sprouted thorns, and they were hungry for a fight.

"What else does *everyone* tell you, Blaise?" I asked quietly.

Gareth pushed off the desk and clapped his hands. "All right, let's move on. You all have your assignments. Loudon's research team, let's meet back here after supper."

As the others gathered their things, Gareth came toward me with his hands in his pockets and a soft smile.

"It's good to see you," he said. "We've all been so busy since we arrived that I've only caught glimpses of you."

I refused to let him disarm me. "You sent for me," I said briskly. "I have a lot to do. What do you want?"

"I'd like to eat dinner with you."

I stared at him. "What?"

"You do eat dinner, don't you?"

"Of course I do," I replied, flushing.

"Then will you eat it with me tonight? We had so little time together in Fairhaven. And the days here are so full." He shrugged a little, sheepish. "I've missed you. I think about dancing with you every day."

I couldn't wrap my mind around what was happening. Not ten minutes ago, I'd been ready to abandon all of this and let whatever enemy I could find in the Old Country destroy me. And now here was

Gareth, flirting with me and being very sweet about it. The contradiction left me feeling unbalanced.

"I'm not hungry," I said, turning to leave. "I need to find Brigid."

Gareth, undeterred, followed me out of the librarians' wing and downstairs. Freyda sent a single grumpy chirp our way before flying off down the hallway. In her absence, my shoulder felt cold.

"Bad day?" Gareth asked.

"No worse than any other."

"How are you feeling?"

"Fine."

He nodded agreeably, taking off his tie and shoving it carelessly into his pocket. This had the unfortunate effect of leaving his collarbones on full display. I didn't know if I wanted to bite them or snap at him to button his shirt.

"Good," he said. "You certainly look fine."

His words sent a frisson of heat rushing down my arms. "Stop talking about what I look like."

"All right," he said. "If you're not hungry, maybe you'd prefer to spar with me first? We could work up an appetite together."

I stopped to stare at him. We had reached the empty central training yard, which was dusted with snow. Small flakes danced through the air, and the sky was a dark gray canvas, suffused with the light of the Mist.

"Spar," I repeated. "With you."

"I'm not a complete novice, you know," he said. "My parents were both soldiers."

"And *you* are a librarian."

He put a hand to his chest. "As if we librarians are limited only to might of the mind!"

"Fine." I stormed across the yard toward the weapons racks, feeling suddenly galvanized. If I couldn't fight a chimaera, I could fight him.

It wouldn't be enough—Gareth was no Olden beast—but if I didn't do *something* I'd burst, and if I got to knock that smile off his face, so much the better.

I retrieved my favorite sparring staff, realizing belatedly that it was the one I'd used to beat Brigid to the ground. Someone had cleaned it. Maybe Cira. The thought twisted my stomach, but I couldn't back down now.

A rustle of fabric made me turn to see Gareth stripping off first his professor's robe, then the collared shirt underneath. He tossed both garments aside, ran his hands through his tousled blond hair, then seemed to remember he was still wearing his glasses and set them carefully on top of his discarded clothes.

I tried, unsuccessfully, not to stare at his leanly muscled arms, the broad plane of his chest, his slim waist. My fingers itched to glide over the muscles of his back, which were certainly not the most impressive ones I'd ever seen but nevertheless hinted at a strength I would never have supposed he possessed. *This* was the man I'd danced with in Fairhaven?

My cheeks burning, I tore my gaze from his body and blurted out, "Why did you take off your shirt?"

I shouldn't have said a word. I shouldn't have rewarded him with a reaction. But it was too late now.

He shrugged, grinning at me. "I'm warm."

And so am I, now. I wanted to slap myself. "It's cold out."

Gareth grabbed a staff that someone had left leaning against the stone colonnade. Distracted, feeling a little wild, I made a mental note to remind my squadron of the importance of proper weapons care.

"What can I say?" Gareth said, still with that godsdamned grin on his face. "My blood runs hot."

Then he raised his staff and lunged at me.

My training kicked in, my earlier desperate anger roaring back to life. I met his staff with mine and shoved him hard, trying to knock him off his feet. But he was faster than I thought he would be and a smarter fighter. He stepped back right as I shoved at him, and the lack of resistance surprised me, making me stumble.

I recovered quickly, spun around, and struck just as he did. Our staffs crashed together, and our eyes locked, and for a moment I hesitated—shaken by his nearness, spooked by the memory of the last time I'd fought in this yard, not even an hour ago. Brigid's bloody, broken face and Cira's horrified one flashed through my mind.

And suddenly all I could think was, *Don't hurt him, don't hurt him.* Just a moment of hesitation, but it was enough. With a quick step back and a sharp thrust of his staff, he knocked mine from my hands. It went clattering across the yard and rolled into the shadows.

I raised my eyebrows, pretending cold approval. But my heart was pounding, and I felt short of breath, even though two minutes of sparring should not have come close to winding me.

"A son of soldiers indeed," I managed to say.

Gareth was panting, his skin flushed and already glistening with sweat, but his expression was eager, fierce. "A captain and a lieutenant general."

"Your mother is a sage, like you?"

"A stone elemental," he replied, following me with his eyes as I retrieved my staff. "Father was a sage. A strategist with a brilliant mind. Much like my own."

A meanness reared up in me. I regarded him coolly. "Do they know about what happened in Mhorghast?"

Gareth looked surprised. Then his expression hardened. "Mother does. My father died when I was a boy."

"Farrin never told me that."

"Well, now you know," he said, the biting tone of his voice bringing me a strange comfort. At least I'd finally managed to get to him.

"And what does she think of it?" I asked, unable to stop myself. I raised my staff to a horizontal position and circled him.

He mimicked my movements, matching my pace. "Who? And of what?"

"Your mother. What does she think of what happened to you in Mhorghast?"

A look of hurt passed quickly over his face. "She told me," he replied, his voice hard, "that I'd embarrassed her."

Straightening, I stopped where I was. "Why would she say that?" I asked.

"You don't believe me."

"She's your mother."

"And she has long wished that my father were alive and that I'd died instead. Father," he added darkly, "would have fought back. Father wouldn't have let himself be used in such a way."

His words evoked images I didn't want to see, questions I didn't want answered. On his face was that same awful flat emptiness that I'd seen come over him in Fairhaven, when General Haldrin had pointed to his time in Mhorghast as a reason not to trust him. His expression had looked familiar to me then, and now I realized why. I'd seen it on myself in the mirror, and on the faces of Cira, Brigid, Caralind, even defiant Danesh. It was the look of someone who lived under the weight of horrors—horrors inflicted upon them, and horrors they had inflicted upon others.

But I didn't want to feel sorry for him or for myself. I didn't want to feel anything unless it was pain being dealt either by me or to me.

"Was she right?" I said quietly, hating myself as I said it. "Did you let yourself be used?"

He came at me without a word, and I let him. The air around him snapped with anger, and I reveled in it. I didn't even raise my staff to defend myself, and when his clipped my shoulder, white-hot pain burst down my arm. I fell hard to my knees and waited for the next blow.

But it didn't come. Instead Gareth tossed his staff aside. It clattered across the stone. In quiet desperation, I watched it roll away.

"What is this?" he said, breathing hard. "What are you doing?"

"Keep going." The words shot out of me like arrows. "Why did you stop?"

"You're goading me. You let me strike you. You didn't even try to block me. Why?"

I shook my head, feeling a bit like I was going mad. "Why did you stop?" I whispered.

There was an awful silence, and then he knelt before me. He cupped my face in his hands and tilted it up to his. His palms were so lovely and warm against my skin that I couldn't help but lean into his touch.

His breath hitched. He stroked my cheek with his thumb, and then, without lowering his soft gaze from mine, found one of my hands and brought my fingers to his lips. The sensation was like a bolt of lightning—sudden, bright, breathtaking. Perhaps I should have scolded him for his presumptuousness, but I couldn't find the words. I could only burn.

"You are being unkind to me," he said quietly, "and you are not an unkind person. What are you trying to do?"

I'd never wanted anything in my life more than I wanted him to kiss me again—my fingers, my mouth, anywhere, *everywhere*. But I didn't deserve the gift of his touch. I didn't deserve the worry I saw in his eyes.

When I didn't answer him, he made a frustrated sound in his throat. "Mara. If you don't answer me, I'll start shouting for the whole priory to hear about how you've just confessed an all-consuming love for me."

My choked laughter surprised me. "I hurt Brigid," I whispered. "I didn't mean to. After what happened in Sablemire, I felt crazed. We fought, and I lost myself, and I can't allow that to happen. I'm so much stronger than her. I'm stronger than all of them."

"What happened in Sablemire?"

I shook my head miserably. "I can't tell you, or I'm going to be sick."

"Well, if ever there was someone who I wouldn't mind getting sick on me, it would be you."

"Don't." I shoved at him, pushing myself away and to my feet. It was agony to separate from him. Blinking back tears, I found my discarded staff. "Let's go again."

"Absolutely not," he said, still kneeling.

"But I need you to hit me."

He looked at me in astonishment. "What?"

"Gods, Gareth, get your staff and let's *fight*."

"I'm not moving until you explain to me what's happening."

Then he froze. Without even looking at him, I felt his understanding arrive.

"Farley said he found you by a greenway," Gareth said quietly. "An angry-looking one, he said."

Farley. The young page. I waited, hardly breathing.

"You wanted me to hurt you just now," he went on. "You're a hundred times more skilled as a fighter than I am, and yet you let me strike you. Where was that greenway going to take you, Mara? Where were you going? To the Old Country?

"I was on a mission," I said flatly. "The Warden sent me. I was to go alone so as not to endanger anyone else. It was a plan. An acceptable risk."

"An *extreme* risk, I'd say."

I laughed. "Welcome to life at Rosewarren."

"You're lying to me."

"And what if I am?"

"The Warden sent you to the Old Country alone, and then you decided to disobey her and come to my laboratory instead?"

I was rapidly losing control of this situation. Fumbling for words, I could manage only a shrug.

Gareth rose to his feet and came to me. Resisting the urge to meet his eyes left me feeling like I was going to split in two.

"Whatever you had planned," he said, "whatever you were going to do, please don't ever do it again. Too many people love you."

"People like you?" I finally managed to look at him, bristling. "You don't even know me."

"And you don't know me," he replied, just as sharply. "But I'd very much like to know you, and I won't get the chance to if you're dead."

I couldn't bear the rough sound of his voice. "You're just like all the others," I muttered, turning away.

"Oh? I've always thought myself terribly unique."

"You're far from the first moony-eyed southerner to obsess over a Rose. Most of them leave as fast as they can once they've gotten one of us into bed." I turned back to glare at him, making my voice as cold as I could. "Is that what I'll have to do to get rid of you?"

For a moment he watched me in silence. Then he retrieved his clothes and glasses and said evenly, "If you want to talk to me about what's troubling you, I'm happy to listen. If not, we're finished here."

My skin crawled with shame. A hundred muddled thoughts roiled in my mind. But I couldn't give voice to any of them. It would be like tearing open my chest and showing him my bare beating heart. I wouldn't survive that.

My silence spoke volumes. Gareth nodded, his expression unreadable. "Good evening, then, Lady Mara," he said quietly.

Then he turned and left, and I was alone. I let out a long, slow breath and tidied the weapons rack as the snow continued to fall.

It was better this way, I told myself. For both our sakes. Whatever this was between us, there could be no end to it but sadness.

Let him hate me. Let him think what he will.

But my fingers shook as I worked, and though I tried with all my might to forget the warmth of his touch, I couldn't do it. With those gentle hands, he had branded me. My cheeks felt as if they'd been kissed by the sun.

CHAPTER 11

Later that night, once dinner was long finished and the priory had grown quiet, I gathered my courage to go to Brigid, who was recovering in the infirmary. But Danesh found me first.

As I crossed the entrance hall, she emerged quietly from the shadows, as if she'd been waiting for me there, and matched my pace.

"Where have you been?" she demanded.

Danesh was two years older than me—pale, square-jawed, with bright hazel eyes that always seemed to be flashing with anger—and a squadron captain in her own right. Unusual for a vissera, even an Anointed one like Danesh. Reading animal entrails to glean information and prophesy was certainly useful, but those abilities usually didn't warrant a command position.

A fact Danesh boasted about at every opportunity.

I continued toward the infirmary without looking at her. I liked Danesh well enough, even admired her. We'd been in the same recruiting class. I'd spent more than half my life with her. But her arrogance rankled me. Confidence was a must in the Order; arrogance could get people killed.

Danesh's long ash-blond braid whipped through the air behind us. "I heard about what happened earlier today."

My stomach turned over with fresh shame. It seemed I possessed an endless supply of it. "Many things happened today," I said.

"Don't be coy with me, Mara. We've been in this together since the beginning. What's going on with you? Brigid's been in the infirmary for hours. It's not like you to lose control."

Danesh's words brought forth flashes of memory:

The two of us as children on the shores of the black lake.

Are you fast? The first words I'd spoken to her.

And hours after that, her words to me: *You did the right thing. Petra was a coward.*

I rolled my shoulders, shaking off the ghost of Petra's hands pressing against my arms. Trying in vain to stop me. Begging me for mercy.

"Just a bad day," I replied, lengthening my stride.

But Danesh was relentless, jogging after me. "The Warden told me about Sablemire. She's concerned about you."

"What about Sablemire?"

"That you're torn up about it for some reason. That it might affect your work going forward."

"It won't."

"Oh no?" Her voice was deceptively innocent. "Hasn't it already? Last I checked, you weren't supposed to completely incapacitate your sparring partners."

I squared my shoulders as we passed the wing housing the librarians, determined to react to neither Danesh's needling nor the nearness of Gareth. He was somewhere in those rooms. Working, probably, or maybe sleeping. I wondered what his face looked like when it was soft with sleep.

"Is there a point to this conversation?" I said.

"Whatever's wrong with you, resolve it," Danesh replied. "I don't want to go on missions with someone I can't trust to have my back."

That made me stop short. Not once in my years of service had anyone expressed doubt about trusting me.

"Did the Warden tell you to say all of this?" I said quietly, no longer bothering to hide my anger. "Or are you just scrambling to get on her good side yet again, since fucking her hasn't worked?"

Danesh grinned slowly, her eyes flashing with victory. "You should try it sometime. Might take the edge off."

I walked past her without another word, afraid of what I might do if I lingered. After all, Danesh was right, wasn't she? It wasn't like me to lose control, and yet I had.

It wasn't like me to be unkind, either, and yet look what I'd done to Gareth.

Once I was alone in the infirmary hallway, I paused for a moment, trying to clear my mind of all things—Danesh's words, Gareth's face. Then I pushed through the door and found Brigid sitting on a cot reading, propped up by several fluffy pillows. A cup of tea steamed on the table beside her. She took one look at me and set down her book.

Nanette, our head nurse, bustled in behind me. She was a stout, no-nonsense woman with cropped gray hair, gentle gray eyes, and a convenient talent for keeping secrets.

"No visitors right now, Mara," she said curtly, "not even you."

"Please let her stay," Brigid said. "I'd like the company."

Nanette pursed her lips. She cast a quick look at me, scanning me from head to toe. I met her gaze steadily. I knew what she was thinking. Gareth had interrupted that afternoon's trip to the Old Country, but there had been many others, and Nanette had discreetly patched me up after several of them.

I dreaded the day when she decided that she didn't like me quite enough to continue lying for me.

"Very well," Nanette said at last. "But I don't approve of this, and I'll only allow you to stay for an hour. Once I'm back from tending to the librarians," she added, pointing sternly at me, "you'll leave without a word of protest. Not a single word."

"The librarians?" I felt a thrill of nerves at the innocuous word, which had never once in my life thrilled me. "What's wrong with them?"

"Professor Fontaine has requested that they all be examined daily," Nanette replied. "The materials they're working with are volatile, he says. He wants me to look out for signs of strange illnesses." She scoffed, briskly gathering supplies from her shelves. "Strange illnesses. As if they won't get enough of those just being here in the Mistlands. And as if I don't already have enough to do these days. But he insisted. What a menace that man is. It's a good thing he's so handsome, otherwise someone would have beaten the lights out of him a long time ago, I'm sure."

Nanette hurried toward the door and stopped at the threshold to look back at me. "One hour," she said, and then she was gone.

Brigid broke the silence. She had always been braver than me and better in every way I could think of.

"What happened to you?" she asked. "You look awful."

I quickly took stock of her. The gash on her cheek had been stitched closed and was already fading. Her face was bruised brown and blue, but her nose looked straight, no longer broken. My heart sank at the sight of her wounds, but I made myself look at them anyway. "I'm fine."

"You ran off earlier. No one could catch up with you. Cira couldn't find you. Where did you go?"

I tried to smile. "I'm glad to know my speed records are safe for now."

But Brigid wasn't amused. She knew my deflection strategies far too well. "Mara."

"Don't press me on this," I said. "Please. I can't talk about it. Not right now."

Brigid watched me for a long moment. "Fine. I won't. But I'm not happy about it. And I could change my mind at any moment, at which point I'll pester you mercilessly until you break."

My mind provided an image of my body shattering, cleaved in two by some merciful villain. It would take something like that, I thought numbly, for me to actually die. Every wound I'd ever sustained, even mortal ones, had healed. Every broken bone repaired, every lost drop of blood restored.

"I'll never break," I said quietly. "Not really."

"You're still human, Mara. Even with that sentinel blood of yours."

A confession danced on my tongue. In the wake of everything that had happened that day, I longed with a sudden ferocity to tell her, to tell someone: *My mother is the goddess Kerezen.* Brigid would think it was some kind of strange joke and take a jab at my odd sense of humor.

"I'm so sorry about earlier," I said instead. "That's what I came here to say."

Brigid nodded in thanks. "No lasting harm done. Nanette patched me up quite nicely."

"I'm glad." I took a deep breath, exhaled slowly. "Brigid, I don't know if I could have gotten through all these years without you. It terrifies me that even with all of my training, I could lose control against you of all people."

"I just look at it as a sign that we've crossed over from the realm of friendship to that of real sisterhood," Brigid said. "Only around family can you truly be yourself."

That stung. I lifted my gaze to hers. "That isn't my true self. What I did to you today. That isn't me."

But it was, wasn't it? Even the shape of the words felt wrong on my tongue. *You're right, Brigid,* is what I should have said. *I am indeed a monster.* A monster with a god's blood in her veins. A monster who torments perfectly kind librarians and seeks out pain the way others seek out love.

Something of my thoughts must have shown on my face. Brigid softened. "I was only teasing," she said. "I'm sorry, I shouldn't have. Do you want to talk about anything? About Sablemire?"

"I can't think of anything I want to talk about less. Can I just sit here with you until Nanette returns? I'm so tired."

"Of course," she said, making room on the narrow cot. "But if you fall asleep with your mouth open, I'll kick you out."

I sat down beside her and nudged her gingerly with my elbow, feeling so grateful for her that I found it difficult to speak. "What about all that talk of family and real sisterhood?"

Brigid picked up her book with a smile. "That only applies until you start snoring."

Chapter 12

Three days passed, and I saw very little of Gareth.

Whenever I felt the sting of guilt about my behavior in the training yard, I reminded myself that I had done us both a great favor. I kept thinking of Crellin—her lifeless eyes, the pool of blood beneath her head, the long nights I'd spent crying over a broken heart.

No, life in the Order was not suitable for romance. I had learned that the hard way, as had so many Roses before me.

Gareth Fontaine was my partner in war, nothing more. Someday he would realize what I'd done and thank me.

I was pulling on my boots, preparing for an evening patrol, when Danesh burst into my room wearing a dark gray tunic and brown trousers, her ash-blond hair pulled back into a sweaty bun. Clearly she had just returned from an afternoon patrol.

"The Warden wants us in her office immediately," she said, her gray eyes alight with excitement. "Your fae friend brought us something useful for once."

I let the dig at Posey slide and followed Danesh upstairs to the Warden's office, where Gareth and two of his colleagues—Fiacra and Geddings—were already waiting.

Gareth glanced up at me as we entered. The weight of his gaze made me hot all over, but I resisted the urge to meet it and instead focused on Posey, who stood before the Warden's desk in dusty travel clothes. I hadn't seen her since our confrontation in the stables, and I was glad she didn't look at me now. If she did, I might see in her eyes the same judgment I'd seen that day. *I heard about the mission to Sablemire.*

You're not who I thought you were.

I pushed past the memory and looked beyond Posey to where one of my fellow squadron captains stood—Lorna, thirty years old, her brown skin riddled with scars, one eye missing. A sentinel like me. She gave me a brief nod, which I returned.

The Warden sat at her desk, hands folded atop it. "Speak, Lorna."

"Per your orders, Posey accompanied us on our intelligence mission to the northeast territories." Lorna paused, then glanced at Gareth and his colleagues. "An Olden region with ore and precious gems, constantly fought over by fae clans, who want the treasure, and titans, who often disagree about land rights."

Gareth nodded. "I'm familiar. The Emerald Fields, the Iron Mountains. Very near the westernmost border of fae country."

Lorna raised an eyebrow, impressed. "We stayed for a few days in the village of Oriak, near Brightfell, and used that as a base for scouting and surveillance." She glanced once more at Gareth. "The geography of these lands is constantly changing, especially over the past few weeks. We have to keep our maps as current as possible."

"Especially since the area is so rich in resources," Gareth added. "Which we trade for when we can."

Geddings, one of the younger librarians on Gareth's team, cleared his throat. "And steal when you can't?"

Lorna blinked at him. "If necessary. Some of these substances are too dangerous to allow Oldens to claim."

"Starstone, for example," Gareth added. "If harvested and processed properly, it can be forged into weapons that absorb whatever magic is nearby. And the northeast territories are flush with it."

Before I could think better of it, I chimed in to add, "And better for us to have control over such a resource than, say, fae sympathetic to Kilraith's cause."

Again I felt Gareth's eyes on me. Again I stared stonily ahead, cursing myself for jumping in on the tail of his words like that, as if we were partners used to finishing each other's sentences.

Danesh blew out a scornful breath. "Kilraith's cause. The cause of human extermination, you mean."

Posey didn't take the bait, ignoring Danesh's pointed glare.

"On a surveillance mission," Lorna continued, "Posey met one of her contacts and obtained intelligence I believe is worth pursuing."

Lorna looked to Posey, and she stepped forward. Her long silver braids fell to her hips, and even though I had grown used to her presence, her beauty still sometimes struck me anew, as it did now. She was so obviously not human—too beautiful for it, and too strange, with her green skin and pointed ears, her lissome grace.

"My contact is a young knight from the Cirrinoc clan," she began. "They are distant cousins of my own clan, the Frinthians. He said there have been whispers about a powerful object held in Cirrinoc. A great prize belonging to Lady Ifanna, Queen of the Veil, from a city where the only light is that of the moon."

At once my eyes flew to Gareth, who had gone very still.

"Cirrinoc," murmured Geddings. "Isn't that the Court of Shadows?"

Posey nodded solemnly.

"A city with only moonlight," Fiacra said. She glanced at Gareth. "Mhorghast, presumably."

His face was closed, but I knew what to look for: the shadows of Mhorghast turning in his eyes. I felt the dark touch of those memories myself. Though I hadn't been a prisoner in Kilraith's moonlit city, I had played one of his sinister games. I had stood with Nesset on the shores of the black lake—an illusion of Kilraith's design conjured from my memories. But it had been real enough. I'd heard his jeering voice as I'd endured trial after trial. Just as they had in reality, each one had ended with Petra's death. No matter how hard I had tried to change her fate, Kilraith hadn't allowed it. Every choice I'd made had led me down the same road with the same bloody end.

Gareth, when he spoke, sounded admirably calm. "If Lady Ifanna has a relic of Mhorghast, it could very well be one of Kilraith's anchors. Did your contact tell you anything else, Posey?"

She answered at once in a language that was obviously fae and too obscure for most of us to understand, which was certainly the point.

Danesh scowled, but before she could protest, Gareth spoke quietly.

"A bridge between nowhere and everywhere," he translated. "An unlocked door that no one can open. A tree that never sleeps."

Posey gave him a grudging nod. "So he told me. But I do not see the significance, and neither did he."

"It sounds like nonsense to me," Danesh remarked.

I looked to Gareth just as he looked at me. A thrill passed between us, lighting up his eyes.

"An unlocked door," I said. "That could refer to the key anchor."

"And a bridge between nowhere and everywhere," he said. "Perhaps that's Kilraith's ability to travel between the worlds and work his magic in either realm?"

"And a tree that never sleeps?" Fiacra asked, wide-eyed.

"Perhaps that's where the key is held," I suggested.

"Or it's something that guards the key," Gareth said. "This is a start, at least."

Geddings was scribbling furiously in his notebook. "I'll instruct our research teams to cross-reference these phrases against our project archives."

The Warden steepled her fingers at her lips. "So," she murmured, as if to herself, "one of the anchors of Kilraith's *ytheliad* curse is in the hands of the fae."

"Perhaps," Gareth cautioned. "This is simply a possible lead."

"The most solid lead we've had in ages," I added.

Danesh pushed off the wall she had been leaning on and straightened her tunic with a sharp tug. "Wonderful. Let's go get it."

Posey laughed. "Did you not hear the librarian? This is the Court of Shadows. You cannot simply *go get* anything that belongs to them, especially something this valuable."

"And if Lady Ifanna does have the key," I said, "or any valuable object from Mhorghast, she either stole it from Kilraith..."

"...or she is his ally," Gareth finished.

Posey's eyes flashed. The room rippled with a sudden heat, as if a gust of desert wind had swept over us. With the Old Country so fresh on her skin and in her mind, she was forgetting to tamp down on her fae instincts, which was one of the conditions of her stay at Rosewarren. I glanced at the Warden, ready to defend Posey's lapse, but she seemed strangely calm, her gaze distant.

"My cousins would not ally with that creature," Posey declared. "Other clans, yes. Weak ones, frightened ones. But the Cirrinoc-Frinthian bloodline would never agree to subservience."

"You did," the Warden pointed out quietly. "You serve us here at Rosewarren."

Posey's hands were in fists. "Because I do not wish to see Kilraith reign supreme over both our worlds. And I am not confident that such a thing won't happen without considerable help, given your apparent inability to truly defeat him yourselves."

"Say that again, Pointy Ears," Danesh snapped, "and I'll turn that green skin of yours black and blue."

I raised a hand to ward off Danesh. "She has a point. We haven't been able to defeat him, not permanently. But every anchor we dismantle further weakens his influence both here and in the Old Country."

Gareth rubbed his chin, his brow furrowed. "We have to retrieve it," he murmured. "This key, if it is the key. Or at least try to, no matter how difficult it may be. The Court of Shadows is aptly named."

"We've tried to track the Cirrinoc clan dozens of times," Danesh admitted. "It would be advantageous to have them as allies. But every path we've tried leads to a dead end."

Gareth's gaze flicked to Posey. "Could you get us there?"

"I am uncertain," Posey said carefully. "It has been a long time since I set foot in the veiled court."

"But you *could*," I prodded.

Posey hesitated and then finally looked at me, a flash of defiance in her eyes. She raised her chin. It was as if she was saying with only her expression, *You're not who I thought you were, and yet here I am, deigning to help you even so.*

"I could," she said slowly. "I think I could."

"But *will* you?" Danesh demanded.

Posey glanced at Danesh, a small smile playing at her lips. "If you promise me greater liberties upon our return."

"You are in no position to bargain, fae."

"Actually, I very much am."

"Quiet, Danesh," said the Warden. The room fell silent as she rose from her desk and withdrew a knife. "We will agree to one of your ancient oaths, Posey—the oath of exchange. I will give you my mother's knife, the only belonging of hers that I possess. You will give me something of equal value. On this exchange we will swear our bargain.

If either of us breaks our agreement, the item we have relinquished into the other's hands is forfeit and will be destroyed."

Her voice brought a solemn chill to the room. The oath of exchange was one of many fae oaths drilled into our heads as young Roses, but I had never seen it performed. At least one fae was required, as were certain key phrases. As the Warden recited the words, looking directly at Posey, the oath's magic began. All sound except for the Warden's voice disappeared. The air in the room grew warm and close, as if we were all trapped in a held breath.

Posey considered the Warden for an uncomfortably long moment. The walls seemed to tighten around us, and through the thick silence I began to hear the faintest rumblings, like those of a beast turning in its sleep. At last, Posey reached beneath her tunic and withdrew her locket on its thin silver chain. She opened it, revealing a lock of shining copper hair as brilliant as a polished coin.

"My sister's hair," Posey said quietly. "She died when I was a child. This is the only piece of her body that survives. The rest has long been burned."

The Warden nodded. "A fair exchange it is."

"And a fair exchange it shall be," Posey agreed.

"You will lead my teams to the Court of Shadows," the Warden continued. "You will protect them to the best of your abilities. You will ensure that they obtain and return with Lady Ifanna's prize."

"Upon our return," Posey agreed, "I will continue to aid the Order. You will limit my menial chores to two days a week. You will allow me to come and go from the grounds of Rosewarren as I see fit."

Danesh, looking indignant, opened her mouth to speak, then closed it. My skin prickled with relief. Any additional words could corrupt the entire ritual.

The Warden and Posey clasped hands. Two quick bursts of soft golden light snaked around their joined arms, and then it was done, the oath complete. The walls were themselves again, the air no longer oppressive.

But even so, I couldn't relax. Posey had hidden it quickly, but I'd seen the expression of naked fear on her face as the Warden had released her hand. And now she stood with her arms crossed over her chest, looking small and tired, staring at her boots. The silver gleam of her hair seemed dulled, her skin suddenly sallow. What had she felt or seen? Or had performing the oath simply tired her?

The Warden glided back to her desk. "Mara, Danesh, you will lead your teams on this mission. Professor Fontaine, you will accompany them with whatever personnel you deem necessary."

That got my attention. "Madam, I don't think—"

"We cannot make concessions for your comfort, Mara," the Warden interrupted sharply. "Retrieving and neutralizing this key may require their expertise."

I fell silent, my face hot. My comfort? What did she know? Was I so obvious? The presence of Gareth across the room suddenly felt twice as unbearable as before. I didn't even have to look at him. Simply knowing he was there pulled at me like the urge to breathe.

Danesh stepped forward. "And who is to be the senior commander?" She glanced at me. "Given recent events—"

"Of course Mara will be the senior, Danesh," the Warden snapped, "and if you ask me about it again, you will sorely regret it. Dismissed."

Everyone hurried out after that—Danesh storming away, Gareth already murmuring excitedly with Fiacra and Geddings, Posey after a moment of hesitation. Before I could follow them out, the Warden straightened, rubbing her temples, and a flicker of pain darted across her face. An instant later, the sky darkened, throwing the room into shadow. A sharp rumble shook the whole building; the Warden's teacup rattled in its saucer. From out on the grounds came the distant shouts of my fellow Roses.

"Section Eighteen," the Warden muttered. "Another breach." Then she rose from her desk and strode to the antechamber outside her office, where thick tasseled cords hung in an alcove set in the wood-paneled wall. She tugged on the nearest one sharply, and suddenly the air of Rosewarren rang with the sound of the breach bells.

I tensed out of habit, waiting for the signs of transformation—feathers pricking their way down my arms, the searing heat at each joint as my body grew longer, my muscles harder—but they didn't come. Other Roses had been summoned this time. For now, I would remain in my human form. Usually, this realization left me both disappointed and relieved.

But now, as I watched the Warden return to her desk, all I felt was a strange creeping dread. As she passed me, the black sleeve of her gown brushed against my fingers, and when she sat down, she leaned back in her chair and sighed, her eyes closed.

"I should send for my sisters," I offered, not knowing what else to say. I didn't know why I stayed; I only felt that I should, that something significant was happening here, right under my nose, though I couldn't quite name it. "All three of us were present when we collected the crown and the egg. I suspect our combined power will be necessary to obtain the key as well."

Because we are demigods. The words teetered on the tip of my tongue. The decision Gemma, Farrin, and I had made to keep that information from the Warden had seemed prudent at the time. The fewer people knew about us, and about Mother, the safer everyone would be. Power could be abused. Knowledge of power would make us targets.

But now I wondered if we were merely being selfish—or even worse, cowardly—by keeping our lineage a secret. Instead of tromping around the world searching for anchors and the ghost of Ankaret, we could have been holed up at Rosewarren all this time, or at Wardwell, putting every ounce of our energy into developing our power. How many dead Roses would still be alive if we had the full force of the Warden behind us, supporting us, helping us learn, perhaps even working side by side with Mother? Would the fire nymph child have lived? Would the littles who had burned to ashes? The griffin family we had slaughtered at Sablemire?

Petra had probably thought me a coward too in the last few minutes of her life. I set my jaw and pushed hard at the memory of her face. I needed to get out of this office. I didn't trust myself to stay silent for much longer. A nervy feeling I couldn't explain wriggled inside me like worms.

"Your sisters," the Warden replied quietly, neither moving nor opening her eyes. "Yes, of course you must summon them. An excellent idea."

First Posey had looked strange, utterly sapped, and now the Warden did too. The idea that something awful had happened during the oath was yet another worry I couldn't shake. And if the Warden was indeed secretly with child, should she even have attempted such a rite?

I cleared my throat. "Madam, I don't want to overstep, but is something wrong? You look unwell."

She laughed quietly. "I *am* unwell. And I won't be well again until this war is over." Then she opened her eyes, considered me for a moment, and came to me with a small smile. "My Mara," she said, taking my face in her hands. Her fingers were as smooth and cold as Gareth's had been warm. "You are sweet to worry. Do not fear for me. I am stronger than I look."

Then she leaned close and kissed my cheek, and before I quite knew what I was doing, I was hurrying out of her office, out of the priory, and across the grounds to the aviary. Once inside the squat redbrick tower, I leaned back against the wall and pressed my palm to my cheek, as if I could trap the feeling of the Warden's kiss like I would a fluttering moth.

It wasn't the first time she had kissed me like that. She was a mother to us all. She hugged us, she kissed our cheeks, she stroked our hair. But this kiss felt rare and precious, like a promise or a goodbye, and it frightened me. Suddenly I was a girl again, frightened and awestruck, clinging to the Warden's feathers on the night of my trials.

Freyda, who had been roosting on one of the many branches crisscrossing the tower, dipped down to alight on my shoulder and fuss with my hair. I breathed slowly, savoring the earthy scents of feed and warm feathers, and didn't acknowledge my familiar until my pounding heart slowed.

"The Warden is fine," I said. "The oath simply made her tired. We're all going to be fine."

Freyda gave an inquisitive chirp, but I said nothing more and instead strode beneath the branches to the far wall, where five Bask ravens roosted, preening. Ryder had wilded a dozen of them as a gift to the Order. Seven must have been out scavenging or on missions. At my approach, these five looked up and watched me with their eerie black eyes.

"I need you to retrieve my sisters," I told them, "and bring them here as quickly as possible, along with Talan and your master. Speak of this to no other Rose and no other creature." I glanced up at my familiar. In the absence of Ryder, her translation would have to suffice. "Freyda?"

Freyda ruffled her feathers irritably but obeyed, chirping at the ravens in harsh, rasping tones that mimicked their own cries. As one, their eyes shifted from me to her, and they listened intently for a few moments before launching into the air in a flurry of gleaming black feathers. I ducked outside and watched them go—one south, straight toward Farrin in Fairhaven, and the other four in different directions to search for Gemma and Talan.

Fresh snow had begun to fall, and the air held a sharp chill. I closed my eyes and prayed for the ravens' safety—not to my aunt Neave, goddess of the beasts, or to my uncle Caiathos, god of the earth. Given how strange and shaken I felt, even thinking about the gods seemed dangerous, as if doing so would reveal Mother's existence to an enemy I couldn't see. Instead I prayed to the ravens themselves, imagining that I could imbue their wings with some of my own sentinel strength. *Fly swift. Stay secret. Stay safe.*

A sudden cold feeling on my nape made me whirl around, hand on the dagger at my belt. All my senses tingled with battle readiness. Someone was near. Someone was watching me.

But when I searched the nearby evergreens, I found nothing but a pair of round yellow eyes watching me from the Mist-draped shadows.

A little shiver raced through me. It was Chella, the Warden's reclusive owl familiar.

I hadn't seen Chella in weeks, which wasn't unusual. She constantly patrolled the Mist, acting as the Warden's eyes and ears. And when she was home at the priory, she rarely showed herself to us Roses.

But here she was, showing herself to *me*. In the wake of the Warden's kiss, this felt remarkable, like a blessing.

Or a warning.

I took three slow steps toward her and bowed low in greeting, my heartbeat thunderous. When I straightened and looked back up at her, she was much closer, now staring at me from a branch of a nearby pine. I hadn't heard her move—no flap of wings, no rustle of feathers. But there she was, her feathered eyebrows stern and fearsome, her great brown-and-gray body at least three times bigger than Freyda's.

Her gaze held me rooted to the earth. Freyda, still perched on my shoulder, shrank back against me and buried her head in my hair. I wanted to reach up and comfort her, but my clammy hands felt heavy, weighted with a will that wasn't mine, and I couldn't lift them no matter how hard I tried.

A whine of fear, of warning, sounded deep inside my mind, bringing with it an instinct to run, but I didn't dare tear my gaze from Chella's. I opened my mouth to speak, considered bowing again—but before I could, the owl pushed off the branch and flew past me, scattering snow and pine needles. The tips of her wing feathers brushed against my cheek, right where the Warden had kissed me, and I couldn't help feeling that I had been tested in some way. Tested, and found wanting.

Chapter 13

One week later, I was sitting in the corner of one of the Order's many safe houses, very seriously considering the possibility of killing my baby sister.

The Order had many safe houses scattered throughout both Edyn and the Old Country, maintained and stocked by a rotation of Roses. I had never been to this one. It sat about seven miles west of Brightfell, a volatile mountainous region with nearly a thousand glacial lakes and waterfalls. In Edyn, winter was only just arriving; here, though, it reigned supreme. The vast forest surrounding the safe house was dense, quiet, and blanketed with snow. The Olden aurora was at its brightest this time of year, turning the sky into a shifting canvas of vivid color—aquamarine, violet, rose pink, sunrise gold.

Tomorrow our squadron would begin the search for Gothyn, the great fae city ruled by Lady Ifanna and the Cirrinoc clan. There were twelve of us: five Roses, including Danesh; Posey; my sisters and me; Ryder; Talan; and Gareth, to whom I hadn't said a word.

And at the end of this long day of hard, cold travel, when we all should have been bedding down for the night, Gemma marched into the center of the safe house's main room and thrust a bottle of wine into the air.

"Look what I found in the pantry!" she crowed. "The perfect way to relax before bed."

Danesh dropped the fur-trimmed bedroll she'd been untying and clapped her hands together. "Excellent. I was hoping someone had left us a bottle or two."

"Absolutely not," I said. "May I remind you that tomorrow we're trying to find Gothyn? Home of the most powerful fae clan in the Old Country?"

"Actually," said Posey, already heading up the stairs to the house's small attic with her own bedroll, "if you come before Lady Ifanna drunk or hungover, it might endear you to her. She loves nothing more than humans making fools of themselves."

"I'm going to ignore that little dig, Pointy Ears," Danesh called out, "but only because I really, very much want a drink."

I resisted the urge to rub the bridge of my nose and instead fixed Danesh with a glare, summoning enough sentinel strength to sharpen my voice and stature—a neat little trick I seldom used, lest it lose its power.

"Danesh, go to bed," I ordered. "Everyone, go to bed."

Danesh fell silent and backed away from me. I glanced at the other four Roses, all of them older than me but junior in rank, all of them Anointed. A beguiler, an elemental, a beholder, and an alchemist—magic I hoped would come in handy if we ran into trouble in Gothyn.

"Edra, Bette, Tressa, Glynis," I said, nodding toward the door, "that's an order."

Danesh managed a scowl but didn't protest. She retrieved her discarded bedroll, and the five of them retreated to the sleeping quarters at the back of the house. When they were gone, I closed the door behind them, sealing the rest of us into at least moderate privacy, and turned my glare on Gemma. As the others arranged their bedrolls and furs, she was serenely setting out six tin cups on the wooden table. After a moment, she looked up at me with a grin.

"Whatever are you frowning for?" she said sweetly. "We're not your soldiers. I thought orders didn't apply to us."

"On this mission," I said, "you essentially are my soldiers."

"With privileges?"

I rolled my eyes and started making up my sleeping pallet. A few seconds later, Gemma came up behind me, pulled me into a fierce hug, and kissed my cheeks over and over. "Dearest Mara, just a sip or two? Please? It'll warm us up. It's freezing in here."

I tried glaring down at her again, but Gemma was all innocence—her golden curls loose and her blue eyes bright and cheerful—and, unlike Danesh, seemed completely impervious to my irritation.

Talan rescued me, coming to retrieve her with a small smile in my direction. "Gemma, my wildcat," he said quietly, reaching for her, "we really should get some sleep." Then he leaned down to whisper something into her hair that made her blush and bite her lip, and she took his hand and followed him to their little corner, where Talan had already made up their bed.

"It *is* cold," Ryder pointed out. He was lying on his own pallet, one hand behind his head and the other rubbing tiny circles on Farrin's lower back.

My elder sister, undoing her braid beside him, looked apologetic. "Honestly, Mara, I could use something to settle my nerves a bit."

Ryder glanced at me, one eyebrow cocked. "Surely during your time at Rosewarren you've occasionally imbibed the night before a mission."

I was suddenly very aware of how outnumbered I was, and of the two couples in the room and how obviously in love they were, and of Gareth's quiet presence as he laid out his bedroll near the far wall. I felt irrationally furious that we'd decided not to bring any of his colleagues, who would have been useful distractions. But our party was big enough already, and the other librarians would have been liabilities. *None of them,* Gareth had said, *know how to handle a weapon as well as I do.*

To distract myself from that particular memory, I ruthlessly gathered my hair into a low, severe knot.

"*Very* seldom do we allow ourselves a drink when on duty," I told Ryder. "Personally, I'm not in the habit of clouding my senses before waltzing into certain danger."

"Oh no, you prefer waltzing into certain danger with both eyes wide open," Gareth said lightly.

I turned to glare at him, but Gareth merely pulled a red apple from his bag and took a crisp bite while looking right at me, a sharp glint in his eyes.

Gemma pounced on my silence. "And after all, we've come such a long way. And we're all together so rarely."

I sighed, finally giving in to the urge to rub my forehead, as if that would stop the raging headache blooming behind my eyes. She was right: we *were* hardly ever together, and gods knew what tomorrow would bring. Even if we succeeded in finding the city of Gothyn, something could happen to Gemma after that while she traveled with Talan in search of the gods, or to Farrin if some hostile Olden force managed to breach Fairhaven's defenses.

That we were all alive—that tonight we would sleep only feet from each other—was both extraordinary and terrifying. Their nearness was too precious and too easily lost.

"Fine," I muttered. "*A* drink, quickly and quietly, and then sleep."

Gemma jumped up from her pallet, pressed a quick kiss to my cheek, and began filling the cups before passing them around our little circle.

Gareth offered me mine with a tight little smile. "To your health, Mara."

I snatched the cup from him, ignoring the warmth of his fingers as they brushed against mine, and downed the wine in one violent swig.

Gareth raised his eyebrows and lifted his own cup to me with a grin. The look on his face—wry and triumphant, as if he'd won whatever battle we were fighting—pushed me toward the wine bottle on the table. I emptied the rest of it into my cup and returned to my bed without offering Gareth even a passing glance.

"Now that we've a chance to talk," Gemma said cheerfully, curled up against Talan's side, "tell us about your team's progress, Gareth. How has life at the priory been treating you?" She took a sip of wine and looked at me over the rim of her cup. "Has my sister been a gracious host?"

Talan nudged her with his elbow, but it was no use. Gemma was insatiably curious. She kept looking back and forth between Gareth and me as if trying to solve a most delightful puzzle.

Before I could think of how best to shut her up, Gareth spoke.

"We've set up several tracking stations with our new equipment," he said, a brightness to his voice that sounded false to my ears and ever so slightly angry. I took a deeply satisfied sip of wine.

"The magical mechanisms behind it all are very similar to ward magic, actually," he went on. "The clockwork is infused with seeking and warning spells, much like wardstones are when you set them to guard against intruders, and they constantly probe their territories for any trace of the *ytheliad*—abnormal vibrations, disturbed environments, and the like."

Ryder grunted and set down his empty cup. "Like hounds tracking a scent."

"Exactly," Gareth replied. "Our beguilers are truly brilliant. They've developed a method for infusing spells not just with instructions, but also *information*—in this case, every bit of knowledge we have about the *ytheliad* and its anchors. So our hounds are not just sniffing for a scent. They are going beyond basic magical instinct. They understand the context of what they're doing and why they're doing it."

The longer he spoke, the more eager he became, his eyes lighting up as they always did when he discussed his work. When he dragged a hand through his hair, sending a few wavy blond locks falling over his brow, the simple gesture made me flinch as if I'd stumbled off a step. I glared down at my cup and took another huge gulp. I couldn't bear to look at him anymore. Looking at him left my stomach in knots I feared I'd never be able to untangle.

"These spells, then, can actually find connections between seemingly disparate pieces of evidence," Gareth was saying, "and reach their own conclusions based on the information we've given them."

Ryder raised an eyebrow, impressed. "So, extremely *intelligent* hounds with the ability to reason."

"Not as well as we can, of course, but certainly better than your general workaday spell."

"Fascinating," said Talan quietly, his dark eyes thoughtful. "How much of this equipment do you plan to install?"

"Our goal is twenty-five stations," Gareth replied, "but we have enough resources with us to create at least five more."

Farrin shook her head. "You'll need a lot more than that if searching the Mistlands turns up nothing and we have to expand the search to, well, everywhere else."

"Oh, of course," Gareth said. "If these first stations are successful, we're hoping the royal councils and the Senate will approve funding for many, *many* more, a far greater number than we could create alone." He paused and raised his cup to Farrin with a cheeky grin. "And on that note, Farrin, may I tell you how positively radiant you look in the firelight this evening?"

Farrin, who was combing through her golden-brown hair with her fingers, stifled a smile. "Are you prepared to lavish that kind of flattery upon every councilperson in Fairhaven? I won't be the problem. They will."

"Not if we bring them results. They can't argue with success."

Ryder laughed. "You've been at Rosewarren too long. Some of the people in that godsdamned city seem set on doing nothing *but* arguing with success."

"Surely *war* is a convincing enough reason for them to agree," Talan said. "Once the anchors are destroyed, Kilraith's reach will collapse."

Suddenly I couldn't keep quiet any longer. If I did, I would combust, and the lack of control I had over the emotions raging inside me was infuriating. Even though he was several feet away from me, every move Gareth made, every breath he took pressed against me like a lover's touch.

"We *think* his reach will collapse," I said. "So much of this is conjecture. We don't know where Kilraith is, or who his allies are, or what other spellwork besides the *ytheliad* he may be using. We could destroy all the anchors and then learn that, oh, actually, Kilraith has five *more* ancient curses at his disposal."

Gareth clucked his tongue. "Come now, Mara, that sort of fatalistic thinking isn't very productive."

His condescension made me bristle. I made myself face him and kept my expression stony. "While professors and librarians may be keen to ignore reality in favor of the theoretical," I said, "soldiers have to consider every scenario so they can prepare contingency plans."

"Certainly, and of course we all know what a fantastic soldier you are." His words had a bite to them. He set his empty cup on the floor and leaned forward a little, chin in hand, as if we were engaged in the most stimulating of intellectual discussions. "But why worry about curses that *may* exist before you actually *know* they exist?"

"It isn't worrying," I replied. "It's forethought. A concept with which you may not be familiar."

Gemma cleared her throat and began to speak before Gareth could reply. "Farrin, could you convince a few of the more recalcitrant people on the councils to stay at Rosewarren for a while? Maybe observing the librarians' work firsthand would help loosen their purse strings."

I scoffed. "The last thing we need is more southern city folk crowding Rosewarren and draining our resources."

Gareth, his gaze still fixed on me, hummed thoughtfully. "Yes, and I wouldn't want to subject more of those poor southern city folk to the priory's harsh environment. So close to the dangers of the Mist and populated by so many short tempers."

"I do not have a short temper," I snapped.

Gareth sat up, his expression guileless. "I was speaking in the most general of terms."

"Enough bickering," Ryder said gruffly. "I'm tired, and the wine, very sadly, is gone."

"What's going on with the two of you?" Talan asked, his expression one of deep concern, as if we were squabbling children and he a patient, slightly annoyed parent. And the worst part was, I couldn't blame him.

I rose and went to the table to discard my empty cup. "Nothing's going on. I'm afraid the transition from academia to actual service has been quite a shock for Gareth. He doesn't have the constitution for it."

"In fact, I do," Gareth said, "and realizing that frightens you."

With a laugh, I turned to face him. "*Frightens* me?"

Gareth was serious now, his false smile gone. "Yes, because it means your insults have no basis in reality, so you'll eventually have to confront the real reason for this misdirected anger of yours."

"Whose reality are you talking about, Gareth?" I was past pride now, past our thorny gamesmanship. I squatted in front of him, his face mere inches from my own. "Your reality? Or mine? Because my reality is leading soldiers into mortal danger every time I leave the priory. Watching people burn and bleed out because of commands I've given. Wondering what each new day will bring—a breach in the Mistline and all the rampant destruction that comes with that? An invasion of Olden hostiles finally making it past our defenses and tearing Rosewarren to pieces? My friends not returning from their nightly patrols? The Mist breaching all its borders and flooding the entire continent because I wasn't strong enough to hold it back nor clever enough to repair it?"

I paused, my whole body tingling from anger, from the instinct to fight, from Gareth's awful, exhilarating nearness. "What is your reality, Gareth? Please do tell me."

For a long moment, Gareth said nothing. He simply watched me, his green eyes flitting all over my face as if searching for something elusive. "To answer your question, Gemma," he said at last, slowly, quietly, "as you can see, your sister and I have grown quite close during my time at Rosewarren. You might even say we're the best of friends now."

I couldn't let him have the last word. I stood, looking down at him. "You might, if you were delusional."

"True. One *would* have to be delusional to assume genuine affection when all signs point to that very thing." He paused, then snapped his fingers. "Wait, no. One would have to be delusional *not* to."

"Affection should not be confused with courtesy."

"Ah, so you were simply being *polite* all this time? Even when we danced together in Fairhaven? And what about the way you look at me when you think I won't notice, the way you leaned into my touch that day in the training yard—was that politeness as well?"

Gemma, watching us wide-eyed, said quietly into her cup, "I would very much like to hear more about that day in the training yard."

I barely heard her. Gareth was all I could see, all I could hear, all I knew. I wanted to tackle him, strike him, pin him to those furs and kiss him silent.

"You think too highly of yourself," I said, flicking out each word as if it were a blade, "and your imagination has betrayed you."

Gareth smiled sadly. "And your anger is betraying you."

"All right, *enough*," Farrin snapped, silencing us both. "We have a mission in the morning, so I suggest you act like the adults you are and quash whatever ill will exists between you. When we return to Rosewarren, by all means keep sniping at each other. But until then, I don't want to hear another word of it."

The room went quiet after that. The only sounds were the crackling fire, which had begun to die, and the rustle of fabric as we all settled into our beds. For a long time, I lay awake in the growing dark. I stared at the stone wall, my back to the room. An hour passed, then two, and finally my body relaxed enough that sleep seemed possible. But my sentinel senses were still restless, and as the fire quieted, the only other sound in the room rose up to take its place: the sound of everyone breathing as they slept.

I resisted the urge for as long as I could before turning my attention toward Gareth's bed. His breathing was steady, the slightest snore rattling on every inhale. I heard an echo of his voice in the shape and tone of his breath, and when he shifted, turning in his sleep, he let out a soft sigh, and my chest ached so much I could hardly breathe. I relived everything we had said to each other, torturing myself with the memory, until I could no longer ignore my exhaustion and fell hard into a troubled sleep.

Chapter 14

The next day, as we slogged westward through the snow-choked forest in our furs, following Posey's lead, I began to lose all sense of time, but I didn't realize it until Gemma, to my left, stumbled and nearly fell.

Before leaving the safe house, she had cast glamours around herself, Farrin, and me to disguise our godhood, which, as we'd learned, the Old Country's magic made far too obvious. The glamour's magic rippled against me with a quick lash of cold, faltering just as Gemma did.

Talan caught her arm and held her to him. "Gemma? What is it, love?"

She shook her head, leaning hard against him. Her face gleamed with sweat, and her skin was shockingly pale.

"I'm fine, I just need a moment. Something..." She looked around, squinting as if into a bright light. "Something has changed. My joints are on fire."

Talan glanced at me. "We have to stop," he said, his voice uncharacteristically annoyed. "We've been going for hours, she's exhausted, and I'm starving."

That surprised me and sent a chill down my spine. "But we just stopped to eat lunch."

"Did we?" Farrin touched her temple, frowning. "I don't remember eating."

Ryder bit out a curse. "I do, and it was only five minutes ago." He hefted his crossbow from his shoulder with a fearsome glare at the trees around us. "What in the name of the gods is going on here?"

Posey, who had kept walking, turned back to look at us from the top of a nearby ridge. "What's wrong? Why have you stopped?" Then she saw Gemma, and looked past us all at something in the trees. Her eyes widened with horror, and though I wanted to whirl around and prepare to fight whatever was coming for us, I couldn't. I was stuck in a mire, my limbs heavy and my senses dulled. I watched in a daze as Posey dropped her pack and sprinted toward us, yelling something I couldn't understand.

With the only scrap of strength I could find, I reached for Farrin and Gemma, and as my skin touched theirs, my mind cleared, and a current of rejuvenating power passed between us. Gemma's breathing steadied; Farrin stood a bit straighter. Their hands still in mine, I turned and saw Posey racing through the snowdrifts to put herself between my dazed Roses, who were wandering about as if in a dream—and a gaping chasm in the earth that I was certain hadn't been there moments before. The only Rose who still seemed to have hold of her senses was Tressa, our beholder, pale and freckled and small, her honey-colored hair in a braided crown.

"Stop! Don't you see? It's a trap!" She was shouting at the top of her lungs, desperately trying to guide the others to safety, but it was as if some inexorable force was pulling them forward.

Even with the strength of my sisters flowing through me, I was moving too slowly to help, my sentinel power dulled by whatever magic had ensnared us. "Help me," I said to my sisters through gritted teeth. "Concentrate."

Fresh power surged into me from each of their hands just as

Gareth pushed past us, staggering and unbalanced, and caught himself on Ryder's arm. When he spoke, it was in a fae tongue, the same short phrase over and over, and though his voice was hoarse and thin, it did the trick: Danesh and the other Roses stopped short only a couple of paces from the chasm's edge. Posey, breathing hard, guided them to safety as they returned to themselves.

"What just happened?" Danesh demanded. She glared around at everyone, her hands in fists. "What was that?"

"You nearly stepped off a cliff into a chasm," said Tressa, her arm around our alchemist, Glynis, who looked as if she'd just woken from a nightmare.

"Not just a chasm," Posey said darkly. "That was a trap. We must be close to Gothyn."

"We *must* be?" Danesh said. "I thought you knew where we were going."

"I'm trying my best to find it based on what I remember, but the borders of Gothyn—and its protections—are always changing." She glanced at Gareth. "The chant of unveiling—how do you know that?"

Gareth, still holding on to Ryder, pushed his glasses up his nose and took a shaky breath. "I read it a few years ago in a book of fae lore excavated from ruins in Aidurra."

Posey raised her eyebrows. "You can read the Unremembered Languages?"

"All seventeen of them, yes. Though I'm less comfortable with Hartha and Immendor."

"*I* can barely read Hartha." She looked him up and down, smiling. "No wonder you didn't see the need to bring any of your colleagues."

Ryder gave Gareth a bracing pat on his back. "The most useful know-it-all to have ever lived."

Gareth smiled ruefully, then glanced at me and caught me looking at him. In the wake of what had just happened, his face was unguarded, a flicker of hope in his eyes. He opened his mouth, then closed it and turned away from me, drawing up the hood of his coat once more.

A thank-you hovered on the tip of my tongue, an apology for everything I'd said last night just behind it. But before I could say a word, an eerie hush fell, cloaking the forest in silence. Darting shadows, tinged silver and gold, rushed out of the trees and snaked all around us. In the wake of Gareth's chant, my mind was clear, and my sentinel instincts caught fire. In the space of two seconds, I clocked the shadows, pulled my sword from its sheath at my hip, and whirled around, ready to strike.

My sword's blade met another, this one slender and slightly curved, engraved with strange markings.

"Careful, daughter of Kerezen," said the fae beyond our crossed blades. His skin was a beautiful inky black, his hair a wreath of elaborate silver braids, and his limbs long and knobby, like they belonged to the trees. "Drawing a sword in these woods is a challenge I doubt even you want to face."

My peripheral vision showed me that we were surrounded by at least a dozen fae, all of them clad, as my opponent was, in what looked like boiled leather armor dyed the colors of the forest. But I kept my gaze fixed on this one's violet eyes, my expression hard. *Daughter of Kerezen.* Did he know about Mother? Or could he simply tell from my speed that I was a sentinel?

I desperately hoped for the latter.

"I would not have drawn my sword if you had met us with courtesy," I said, "and not with tricks of light."

"Ah, but tricks of light are our specialty," the fae said smoothly. He glanced past me. "Frinthian cousin, you are green of skin and far from home. And why are you in the company of humans?"

"They are my friends and allies," Posey replied. If she was intimidated, her voice betrayed nothing. "We make for Gothyn to request an audience with Lady Ifanna."

"Yes, we know," said the fae, dragging his gaze back to me. His smile was sharp, his teeth sharper. "We have been tracking you since you set foot on our land two days ago."

"Two days?" Danesh blurted. "You lie. We have only been walking since the morning."

Ryder hissed sharply, and the fae raised his silver eyebrows, his smile widening, but I cut him off before he could chastise her or, more likely, send his blade flying at her throat. Accusing a fae of lying was a terrible insult.

"It is her first journey into the fae realm," I lied, making a note to wring Danesh's neck if we made it out of this alive. "You will, I hope, pity her for her ignorance and escort us to the Court of Shadows?"

The fae cocked his head, examining my face, and then lowered his sword. I followed suit.

"Pity a human?" he mused. "A fascinating idea. I shall consider it. And yes, daughter of Kerezen, we will take you to the Queen of the Veil." He offered me his arm with a mocking bow. "We are cousins, after all, you and I. Our veins carry the blood of the same goddess."

It felt dangerous to refuse him, so I took his arm even though my entire body screamed with the urge to run. Instead I recited the old prayer to Kerezen that I'd learned as a child.

"For sight and sound and taste and touch," I said, "for the scent of the wind and the strength of my limbs, thanks be to Kerezen, god of my body, maker of bone and blood—"

"And so it shall ever be," he finished. "Are you surprised that I know the prayers of Edyn? You shouldn't be. We in the Court of Shadows are great admirers of human customs."

I didn't trust anything about him, especially not the false kindness in his voice. "And do you admire the humans who create these customs as well?"

Laughter was his only answer. I regretted asking the question. The forest had grown dark, the only light coming from the snow crunching beneath our feet, which glowed with the same silver sheen as the Mist did. I didn't dare look back at the others. Seeing fear on my sisters' faces would summon my own. I let my escort guide us all into the trees.

⟡

I couldn't say how long it took us to reach Gothyn. One moment we were trudging silently through the snowy forest. The next, the trees seemed to twist and turn around us as if we were looking at them through a rippling mirror. Though I easily kept my balance, I heard some of the others stumble behind me.

Then, suddenly, we were there.

The Court of Shadows, some called it. Others, the Veiled Court.

And it was magnificent.

Our escorts led us through a massive hall of iridescent stone. Mammoth trees cloaked in violet moss rose up on either side of us, their branches twining with the dark wooden rafters overhead. Thousands of lanterns and candles, some hanging from the trees' branches and others hovering in mid-air just over our heads, lit the room with shimmering pools of light. The walls were made of gleaming onyx and tangled trees, their shape and color changing with my every step.

And on either side of us were dozens of fae. Some were tall and lithe with gleaming skin—green, like Posey; purest black, like my escort; stark white, shimmering silver, bright bronze. Others were short and squat, their skin gnarled as if carved from trees. Some were very small, hardly more than orbs of light; others towered, their spangled heads—glittering with dozens of heavy jewels and draped chains—nearly reaching the trees overhead.

They sprawled on couches in glittering finery and dined at tables laden with elaborate dishes in outrageous colors—bright turquoise, vivid pink, every shade of purple imaginable. Several small orchestras were scattered throughout the room, playing several different rollicking tunes. It was a cacophony of melodies, but the fae didn't seem to mind. They danced with unbridled glee, toasted with goblets full of steaming liquor, played elaborate card games with tokens that looked suspiciously like human teeth.

I'd read every book about the fae in Rosewarren's libraries. I knew that they were descendants of twins birthed by Kerezen and fathered by Caiathos. They could craft glamours, they had an affinity for natural magic, and they were gifted with strength and long lives. I had been to fae courts before, and Posey had also briefed us all on what we might see.

But nothing could have prepared me for this.

At the end of the long hall stood three wide, arcing steps carpeted in velvet and moss. They led to a throne of polished bone and glittering onyx that was bolted to the floor by a tangle of flowering tree roots.

And on the throne, draped in silks and furs, sat a fae with gleaming skin the color of sandstone. On her head, atop a nest of coiled loam-dark hair, sat a slender silver crown. Her eyes were as black as the throne upon which she sat, and they narrowed as we approached.

The sight of her nearly rendered me speechless, but I managed to kneel before her on the cold, hard floor and heard the others do the same behind me.

"Lady Ifanna," I began, remembering the greeting Posey had taught us. "Queen of the Veil. Jewel of the Court of Shadows. Your city is a marvel, your court a splendor. We come before you with gifts and request the honor of an audience."

Lady Ifanna smiled, baring her pointed teeth. She crossed one long leg over the other, her bare ankles glittering with elaborate chains. She took a sip from the chalice in her right hand.

"But you have not seen my city," she said smoothly. "How do you know it is a marvel?"

"I have heard tales told across the land by your many admirers, as well as testimony from our friend Posey of the Frinthians."

Lady Ifanna's gaze slid past me. "Yes, I see her there, bowing so prettily. My little cousin. How good of you to bring your friends to me."

"And gifts," Posey added, "if your guards will allow us to open our bags—"

"I will not, and I care nothing for your gifts. None are as interesting as you." Lady Ifanna set down her chalice and glided down the steps, the folds of her gauzy silver gown cascading over her body like a waterfall. "What an interesting group you are," she murmured, walking slowly among us. "I see you, of course, demon. I suppose we are cousins too—you the descendant of Jaetris and Zelphenia, me of Kerezen and Caiathos."

Talan inclined his head. "Indeed. Well met, cousin."

"And the rest of you?" Ifanna returned to her dais and stood on the bottom step. Her gaze flicked to me. "You. Tell me, what powers exist among you?"

"My name is Mara, and I am a sentinel, Your Majesty. And my sisters—"

"I know that one," came a new voice.

I turned to see another fae leaving the revels to join us. His skin gleamed a burnished copper, and his hair trailed behind him in a froth of white, like a ribbon of sea-foam. The silver chains adorning his ears sparkled merrily in the candlelight.

Grinning, he raised one jewel-encrusted arm to point at Gareth. "Him. I know him."

Gareth turned ashen, every muscle in his body pulling taut. "Luthaes," he whispered. There was real fear in his voice, and the sound slicked my bones with dread. Gareth's reaction could mean only one thing: Luthaes had been in Mhorghast during Gareth's imprisonment. I glanced at Posey, a question in my eyes—*Do you know him?*—but her expression was one of utter confusion. When our eyes met, she shook her head at me ever so slightly.

"And him. And her." The fae, Luthaes, pointed to Ryder, then to Farrin. I didn't like his turquoise eyes; they were too bright, too cold. "They stole my prize from me. A wilder woman. Very pretty. Same coloring as you." He considered Ryder, a slow smile spreading across his face. "Are you her brother? How touching."

Ryder's hand twitched as if he wanted to reach for Farrin. But he stayed right where he was, his jaw working.

"They stole from you?" Lady Ifanna regarded us with fresh amusement. "Luthaes, I'm disappointed. They're only human."

"Yes, but that one has a voice like nothing I've ever heard," said Luthaes, nodding at Farrin. "She doesn't look like much, but don't let that fool you."

Farrin's hands were in fists at her sides, her lips pressed together hard.

"And him." Luthaes pointed once more at Gareth with a little chuckle. He drawled his words, very clearly drunk. "He was one of his favorites. So much mind to grab on to."

Gareth recoiled as if Luthaes had struck him. Seeing the bleak look on his face made me boil, and I looked at Lady Ifanna with a hot-footed panic skittering up my spine. A fae who'd had at least some power in Mhorghast was here in the Veiled Court, and given the careless way he had approached the throne, he was no doubt favored by the queen.

He was one of his favorites.

His favorites.

Kilraith.

We had said as much in the Warden's office, Gareth and I, discussing the possibility of Lady Ifanna's great prize being one of the *ytheliad* anchors.

Either Lady Ifanna stole it from him…

Or she is an ally of Kilraith.

Ifanna must have seen the realization dawning on my face, for her grin turned feral.

"You do have one of Kilraith's anchors," I said, my mouth dry and my blood roaring. "And you didn't steal it from Mhorghast. Kilraith gave it to you."

"For safekeeping," Ifanna replied, snapping her fingers. One of the guards flanking her throne brought her the discarded chalice. She took a long, slow sip from it, her eyes never leaving mine. "What a shame. The next time the Order decides to ally with a fae, perhaps you should choose one who isn't a traitor and can actually bring you reliable intelligence."

"*You* are the traitor!" Posey cried, lurching hard against her escort's grip. "That creature endangers both worlds. We must unite against him!"

Her escort released her just long enough to strike her hard across the face. Her knees buckled, and when she looked up, green blood stained her lips.

Beyond her, the entire hall had gone silent. Hundreds of eyes watched us. Even the candles' flames seemed to still.

Ifanna regarded Posey with contempt. "Creature? An ugly word for a magnificent being. But I should've expected nothing less from a Frinthian. He Who Is All was right to destroy your kind. He must have sniffed out the deception brewing in your veins and knew the only way to rid us of it was extermination. Which makes you a novelty, Posey. The only Frinthian left alive. What a trophy you are. I think I shall keep you."

Posey made a choking sound and staggered as if her escort had kicked her in the gut. Stone-faced, his skin white as the moon, he held her up, not letting her fall even as she howled out her grief. Her screams echoed eerily throughout the cold hall.

"Enough of this," Ryder growled. He was practically vibrating with fury. "You knew we were coming, and now we're here. What do you want with us?"

Before she could answer, Gareth, held fast in the grip of his captor, took a small step forward. "If Your Majesty will permit me," he said, his voice strong and clear, "I would like to propose an accord."

A wave of excited whispers hissed through the hall. Lady Ifanna stared at Gareth with a new, eager light in her eyes.

"An accord?" Her voice slithered. "The last resort of the desperate prisoner. Do tell."

Stunned, furious, I watched her slink toward Gareth. The lanterns all around us silvered the lenses of his glasses. He was terribly pale, his brow slick with sweat. I could have killed him. An accord with a fae was no small thing. Even uttering the word was like setting a paper ablaze. Once done, it could not be undone.

"You possess something we want," Gareth said. "The key that serves as one of Kilraith's anchors of the *ytheliad*. And you possess something Kilraith wants: us. Am I correct in what I say?"

I listened with my heart in my throat but didn't dare say anything to stop him. It was a bold gamble to name the key outright. But fae appreciated boldness, and maybe that would be enough to get information out of Ifanna.

After a moment, the fae queen answered, "You are correct." Her black eyes glittered as she beheld Gareth. "And why is it that Kilraith wants *you*?"

A small chill shivered across my nape. So Ifanna did have an anchor, and it was indeed the key. Gareth's gamble had paid off.

Gareth smiled. "You mean he hasn't told you about us? That's odd. I assumed he had taken you into his confidence."

"And you assume correctly," Ifanna snapped. Her hair streamed behind her as if roused by a static charge. "I am one of his favored. I offered my loyalty and my soldiers in exchange for a place at his side in the new world."

"Of course," Gareth said. "My apologies."

I could hardly breathe. Gareth was playing a dangerous game. Toying with a fae's pride was like walking along a cliff's edge with your eyes closed, trusting that you wouldn't take a false step.

"Tell me who you are, then," Ifanna said, "and why Kilraith would want you."

Luthaes huffed out an irritated breath. "Your Majesty, you are allowing this *human* to impair your judgment—"

"Be quiet, Luthaes, or I will cut out your tongue." Ifanna didn't take her eyes off Gareth. "Well?"

"It's the month of your winter games, is it not?"

That caught her by surprise. "And how does a human such as you know about our games?"

He smiled, ignoring the question. "Here, then, are the terms I propose: You begin your games here, tonight, with a hunt. My friends and I will participate as hunters, and you will allow us to use, unimpeded, whatever power and weapons we possess. If we win, you will give us the key Kilraith entrusted to you and allow us to safely leave Gothyn. If we lose, I will tell you who we are and why Kilraith wants us, and let you bring us straight to him." He flashed her one of his dazzling smiles. "I assure you that would win you his favor beyond all others."

I couldn't believe what I was hearing. Fae games were brutal, not meant for humans, and their hunts were the most brutal of all. Violent visions swarmed my mind: my sisters impaled on fae spears, my Roses reduced to bloody shreds by fae hounds. *We should never have come here,* I thought wildly. *I should never have brought them to such a place.*

"And what do winning and losing mean in this game of yours?" Ifanna asked softly. The hall was so deadly quiet that her voice resonated like thunder. "The terms must be clear."

Careful, Gareth. My jaw ached with tension.

"Winning means reaching the target first and claiming it," Gareth replied. "Losing means failing to do so, as is customary for your hunts. And," he added, "there are twelve of us, so you must utilize only twelve of your kind. An even match."

Ifanna's lip curled. She had obviously been hoping he would forget this crucial detail, but now, by the magic of the accord, she was bound by it.

"And what will this target be?" she crooned.

My mind raced. I had to speak, and speak *now*, before any of the fae named a target that would put us at a disadvantage.

Then an idea formed, and a carefully hidden part of me—knotted and cowering, worn thin from exhaustion—thrilled at the sheer danger of it, at how likely it was that I could die because of what I was about to propose. A warm sense of calm fell through my body.

"Me," I said, my voice clear and hard. "The target will be me."

The magic that had been growing between Gareth and Ifanna latched on to me as well, sending a few golden sparks flying. The impact left me reeling, and my ears rang. Only dimly did I hear everyone's protests: Farrin's gasp, Gemma's little sob, angry curses from Danesh and Ryder. The rest of my attention was fixed on Gareth, who looked as if all the life had been sucked out of him at once. I hated him for looking at me like that. It was his rash decision that had forced my hand.

"Mara, gods, *no*," he choked out.

Ifanna ignored all of them. She looked hard at me with her obsidian eyes. "Does that not give your friends an unfair advantage? You would run from us and seek haven with them, make it easier for them to claim you."

"Then let us alter the terms of the accord," I said at once. "If we have an advantage, then so should you. You may use double the number of hunters that we have: twelve of us, twenty-four of you."

I ignored Gareth's rough curse behind me and tensed, my legs tensed to leap and my hands itching to strike. The words had been said, the fight was laid out before me, and I was ready for whatever fate awaited me. All the times I'd snuck away to the Old Country seeking violence suddenly seemed foolish and pale. *This* was the hopeless danger I'd been craving.

"Agreed, Mara the sentinel," Lady Ifanna said at last with a sharp crescent-moon smile. She went to her throne and withdrew from behind it a beautiful bow carved of white bone and a quiver full of arrows. "The accord has been altered and is now complete. I suggest you start running."

Chapter 15

I tore out of Ifanna's court and into the surrounding forest of silver-barked trees, my mind racing to recall everything I knew about fae hunts.

They would let me run for five minutes unimpeded before unleashing their hounds, their antlered war-horses, their trained raptors with feathers like knives. Longing for Freyda pierced my heart, but I was glad we hadn't brought our familiars on this mission. More heartbreaking than watching them die would be seeing them bespelled and turned against us.

The fae would use every trick in their arsenal—glamours, music, their own allure—to try and best us. But we had Gemma, Farrin, Talan, Bette, and Tressa—two demigods, a greater demon, an elemental, and a beholder. I had to hope they would be able to see through every deception.

But beyond their numbers, the fae had an even greater advantage: this was their land, riddled with safeguards and traps and Olden beasts who would certainly side with fae over humans from Edyn.

I leapt over a fallen tree, scattering a thousand glowing white moths. Something fat and fleshy rose up from the frosty undergrowth and snapped at me, hissing, but I kicked it away and kept running. The snow was lighter here, but flakes were beginning to fall, and a chill wind nipped at my heels. I didn't trust these skies; fae were children of Kerezen and of Caiathos, god of the earth. If they wanted to call a sudden blizzard down upon our hunt, they would.

I tore through tangled thickets, ignoring every scratch and bite of pain, and thought back over every word Gareth and I had uttered. I looked for loopholes, mistakes we had made in the accord's terms. But I found nothing; if we had to forge an accord with a fae queen, we'd done a fine job of it.

Fury gave me a burst of extra speed. I leapt across a roaring river swirling with long, darting shapes that glowed like stars. They swarmed along my path as I soared overhead, and a knot of them slithered out onto the opposite bank—eels, or something like them, skittering after me with gnashing teeth—but I was too fast for them. I crashed through the trees and slammed into the ground, which rattled my bones, but I relished the slight pain, the bite of frost on my palms, and kept running.

Fool. Gareth was an unforgivable fool. He wasn't the leader of this mission. I was. That he'd struck such a deadly bargain without consulting me filled my veins with lightning-hot rage.

A scream pierced the air. I darted behind a tree and pressed against it, my pulse pounding, and listened. The scream came again; it was avian. I looked left, following the sound, and saw a cloud of gigantic birds burst out of the trees some distance from me. They rose up in chaos, then slid into an arrowhead formation and dove back down as one unit. In their wake, the faint sound of music met my ears. Farrin's voice—sharp, percussive, swelling in volume. The melody rose fast, then crested. A slight shock wave tore through the forest, whipping my hair across my face.

I closed my eyes, allowing myself a breath of relief. Good. Ryder was wilding; Farrin was singing, and her voice was strong. Hopefully

Gareth, with all that sage brilliance at his disposal, was smart enough to stay glued to their sides.

But I couldn't waste time worrying about him. I listened hard to the surrounding forest. If I was going to pull off the wild plan forming at the back of my mind, I would need to find Gemma without drawing every fae in the forest right to us.

I waited another moment, then darted out of my hiding place. I'd not taken three strides before something slammed into my side, throwing me off my feet. I flew into the trunk of a nearby tree and dropped to the ground, gasping. To my left: movement, sound, getting closer, getting louder.

I shook myself and rolled to safety half a second before a feathered spear flew into the ground right where I'd fallen. I pulled my sword from its sheath and pushed myself to my knees just as another spear came flying at me. I swung my sword hard, knocking the spear out of the air, then jumped to my feet and whirled around to meet my attacker. Our blades crashed together, and for a moment we were caught in each other's grip. Familiar violet eyes glared at me from behind our crossed blades: my captor from before, the fae with white hair and gorgeous obsidian skin.

"Daughter of Kerezen," he said, grinning. "We meet again."

I shoved my sword against his with such force that he staggered back and nearly fell. I pounced immediately, but he was ready for me, and this time, when our swords met, the crash was so brutal that I fell hard on my tailbone and lost my sword.

My body throbbing with pain, I scrambled away, fumbling for my lost weapon. The fae stalked after me, slicing through the bracken with his sword. With each stroke of his blade against the dirt, I imagined it chopping through my leg and tried to push myself back to my feet, but something was holding me down, pinning me to the earth.

When I glanced down, my heart sank. Bright pink vines were

unfurling from the snow-dusted undergrowth, joining those already coiled around my wrists. When I yanked against them, they broke easily, but fresh ones—dozens of them—took their place, winding around my neck, snaking across my cheeks.

The fae sauntered over, triumph blazing on his gorgeous face. He looked down at me, pressed the tip of his blade to my throat, and said, "I claim—"

But before he could finish the sentence, a blade thrust through his chest from behind. He choked on his own voice, looked down at the wound in a daze, and coughed up bright green blood.

His killer yanked the blade free, letting him fall. Behind him, dripping dagger in hand, was Posey. Her eyes blazed with Olden fire. The lines of her face were sharper, her fingers longer. Her silver hair drifted behind her in hissing, restless tendrils.

I kicked free of the vines, which had fallen inert upon the fae's death, and clasped Posey's offered hand. She helped me to my feet with one fluid pull.

"If you'd gotten yourself killed because of a few measly plants," she said solemnly, "I would have ensured that the story of your death traveled far and wide and became the stuff of legend."

I smiled. "So what you're saying is, I shouldn't assume that we're friends again."

She cocked one silver eyebrow. "Hardly. You'll need to come to *my* rescue a few times before we get there."

"Fair enough. And don't claim me just yet," I added, cutting her off before she could speak. "I don't trust that Lady Ifanna will actually fulfill her end of the accord if we win. No one can claim me as their prize until we find the key."

Posey nodded grimly, the hard light of grief in her eyes. "You are wise to doubt her. Breaking accord magic is a great risk, but after what she has done… Clearly she has no honor."

I glanced at her, noting the desolate look in her eyes. All of her kin, every Frinthian, was gone, if Ifanna could be believed. And yet Posey had still found the strength to fight for us.

I clasped her arm gently. The only words I had for her seemed pale. "I'm sorry, Posey."

She looked away, dragging a hand across her face. When she looked back at me, her eyes were bright but hard.

"How do we track down this key?" she said. "A tree that never sleeps? If such a thing actually exists and isn't simply the stuff of rumor."

"It's the best lead we have."

She gestured at the surrounding forest. "Well, finding it might take a while."

"We need Gemma." I strode past her to kneel in a mossy patch of earth that was free of vines. I closed my eyes and placed my palms against the soil.

"What are you doing?" Posey asked.

"Trying to find her."

"You can do that?"

Honestly, I didn't know. But I could still feel the cool embrace of Gemma's glamour against my skin, disguising my true nature from Olden eyes. Not only did that mean she was still alive, it could, I hoped, act as a tether connecting us, much as we Roses were bound to the Warden and could use that link to guide us home from anywhere in either world.

I concentrated on the memory of us at the safe house, when Gemma had encased me in the glamour. It had felt like stepping through a soft sheet of rain, and recalling the memory made it come alive in my mind. I could almost smell the dying embers in the safe house's hearth. I could almost feel my sister's touch—

There. There she was.

My eyes snapped open. "I found her. We'll have to run fast."

"I know of no other way," Posey replied.

"Cover me."

Then, together, we bolted.

I followed the feeling of my sister like a hound stalking a scent. As the snow fell ever more thickly and the trees grew fatter and closer, I heard the twang of shot arrows, the hard strikes of spears impaling bark. I didn't stop to look, trusting Posey to protect me. From a distance came a familiar whooping battle cry—Danesh. Grinning, charged with fresh relief, I scrambled up rocky ridges slick with fresh ice, tore through tangles of sticky ferns that must have been twelve feet tall.

Somewhere behind me, Posey grunted in pain.

"Keep going!" she shouted.

I gritted my teeth and obeyed, and then, finally, I saw her.

Gemma was on her hands and knees in the dirt, huddled behind a shield of uprooted trees. Talan, bow and arrow in hand, stood over her. I ducked to join them just as he let loose a thick black arrow. It zipped through the forest and hit something hard—a fae? A forest creature? A scream rang out, inhuman and furious, and something huge crashed toward us through the trees.

"Don't claim me," I warned them. "Not yet."

"I'm sending out waves of confusion to disorient them," Talan muttered tensely, his body radiating scorching heat as he flooded the forest with empathic power. "But I won't be able to do it for much longer. There are four of them, and they're quite strong."

"Fae?"

"And their hounds," Posey growled, peering past the shield of trees. Her shoulder glistened bright green.

"Gemma?" I took my sister's face in my hands and nearly recoiled. She was burning up, sweat slicked her skin, and her lips had gone white. "Can you hear me?"

"Yes." She offered me a faint smile. "It's just…the magic here, it's everywhere, and it burns. It's hard to focus. I just need a moment."

My heart ached to see her like this, but I swallowed hard against the feeling. I didn't have time for heartache.

"Listen carefully," I told her. "The tree that never sleeps. Remember?"

Gemma nodded, bleary-eyed. "An unlocked door that never opens."

"I need you to find it. Before anyone claims me to end the hunt, we *have* to retrieve the key. Otherwise Ifanna could break the accord and betray us."

"Is that possible?" Gemma whispered.

"Posey seems to think Ifanna might risk it. And," I added, "whatever you do, don't let the glamours fall. That magic is how I found you. It's how I'll find you again. Don't worry about protecting Talan. Posey will go with the two of you."

I glanced over at Posey. She nodded sharply. "I won't let anything happen to them."

"How do I find it?" Gemma murmured.

"Do you remember how you found me that day in the Vilia's woods?" Talan asked from above us. "You followed that ravine and entered my lair."

Gemma smiled a little. "The demon's lair. Yes. The air pressed down on me. There was a fist in my chest, pulling me forward."

"You sensed the great magic hidden there and followed it. You found *me*, darling. Your power showed you the way."

"I did. It did." Gemma leaned against Talan's leg and kissed the back of his knee. Some of the light was coming back to her eyes.

"And this will be easier," I said. "You're not finding a demon's lair, you're finding a tree. That's Mother's magic. *Philippa*'s magic, and yours too."

Gemma, clinging to Talan's leg, drew a shaky breath. "Philippa Wren and her house of ivy." When she looked up at me, her jaw was set. "I can find it. I *will* find it."

I drew her into a quick, fierce embrace. "Good. I'll find Farrin and meet you there. Posey, cover them."

I dashed off into the trees without a backward glance. I hated to leave them, but my legs were feline, fluid, unstoppable, and their stride fortified my resolve. After splashing across a frigid creek, I decided I'd reached a safe enough spot to catch my breath. A sturdy pine loomed nearby. I would climb it, give myself a moment to concentrate, and follow the rope of glamoured power that connected Gemma to me and to Farrin.

Just then, a thunderous noise exploded through the trees to my right. A grove down the creek line snapped and splintered. I ducked to avoid a flying branch and darted out of a falling pine's path just as huge dark shapes tore through the wreckage. My mouth went dry at the sight of them: one was a fae war-horse, cloaked in moss and mud. Its enormous antlers plowed through pines like they were nothing.

Two wolves pursued the war-horse, each of them twice as big as our priory horses. Wild fae cries tore through the air, followed by two familiar sounds—Ryder's crossbow firing and a voice as clear as a bell.

An invisible cord tugged at my navel.

Farrin.

I ran after the war-horse, low and fast to avoid being spotted by the wolves. Getting closer, I saw what I had dreaded: Farrin and Ryder sat astride the monstrous beast. It ran smoothly, even docilely, its hot breath steaming in the air; Ryder must have wilded it. He was loading another arrow into his crossbow, and Farrin—gods, she was beautiful, fearless, her braid come loose and her hair streaming behind her. With Ryder's body shielding her back, she clutched the creature's wild mane, singing a shrill battle hymn against its neck.

Even though the song wasn't for me, my legs pumped faster at the sound of it, and I was so distracted by this new burst of energy that I didn't spot the danger until it was too late.

The war-horse jumped over a snowdrift onto what looked like a flat stretch of ground—but it was a reeking bog covered with fresh snow, and the horse plunged straight into it. The mire wasn't deep, but it was thick and rimmed with ice. The horse lost its footing, and Ryder and Farrin went flying.

I ran to catch my sister before she cracked her head open, the fae's triumphant cries ringing in my ears and my blood roaring with fury. Ryder landed hard not far from us, shook the snow from his hair with an angry growl, and pushed himself to his feet.

Farrin clung to me with a breathy laugh. "Oh, thank the gods. I claim—"

"No! Not yet. We have to find the key. Accord or no, I don't trust Ifanna to keep her promises." I glanced up. "Ryder?"

"Just tell me where to go," he said gruffly, retrieving his crossbow from the muck. Just past him, the war-horse climbed out of the bog, its ears flat and angry, its eyes a brilliant red.

"Take Farrin and go to Gemma. She's due west." I pointed along the invisible cord of magic that pulled at my gut.

"I can feel it too," Farrin said grimly. "It's from the glamours?"

I gave her a smile. "Right in one."

Ryder spat out a few harsh words at the war-horse, wilding it once again, then helped Farrin mount the beast and climbed up behind her. I turned to face the oncoming fae with my sister's war song in my ears—a song for strength, for speed—and the sound of it shot me forward, as if the ground beneath my boots had risen up to launch me.

The fae barely had time to see me coming. I vaulted between them, dagger in hand, and by the time I landed, they were down, their throats slit and their baffled wolves splattered with green blood. Before they could round on me, I pulled a second dagger from the strap at my waist and threw a blade right into each of their throats. They bled out in seconds.

I strode over to them and ripped the weapons from their glistening hides. Standing over them, I allowed myself a moment to catch my breath—a mistake. For as soon as my heartbeat slowed enough that I could think, I realized I hadn't yet seen Gareth.

My stomach dropped, my battle-fevered blood going ice-cold. He wasn't with Gemma or Farrin. Why wasn't he *with* them?

As if he'd heard my thoughts—and maybe he had, maybe some strange bit of fae magic had whispered into his ear at just the right moment—a sudden agonized scream tore through the forest.

I knew that voice. I felt it in my bones, as if it were bound to me by our own kind of magic. Whatever was hurting him, I felt it too.

Gareth.

I followed the sound of his screaming, running so fast it hurt. This could have been a trick, but I didn't care. Nothing mattered but the knowledge that I could help him, and that whoever was hurting him would pay.

Bursting through a thicket of saplings, I saw them: Gareth, running with a limp, clutching his left arm. He looked back over his shoulder, choked out a yelp, and hit the ground. A whistling spear missed his head by mere inches.

And right on its heels came Luthaes, the beautiful fae from Mhorghast. He lifted another spear, ready to strike. His silver eyes gleamed like blades, and his grin grew too wide for his face.

I know that one.

He was one of his favorites.

So much mind to grab on to.

I rammed into him as hard as I could. The blow was like slamming into a wall and knocked us both to the ground. Spitting curses, Luthaes staggered to his feet, trying and failing to find his balance. I leaned over with my hands on my knees, my vision full of stars, and looked around wildly for Gareth. I found him huddling among a cluster of ferns. He was covered in red and green blood, and his clothes were in shreds, but he was alive, he was *alive*. And when our eyes locked, his wide with fear, a surge of primal instinct rushed through me.

Mine.

He was mine, and if I had to, I would tear down this entire forest to save him.

I rounded on Luthaes just in time. He'd lost his spear, but he had knives, and one whipped toward my throat. I ducked, the blade barely nicking my shoulder, and spun around to plunge my dagger into his neck, but he was faster than the others had been, and stronger. He dodged my blow with a grin. Lurching past him, I lost my footing, then whirled around just in time to knock his flying blade from the air with my own.

Then he was on me, slamming me to the ground. My dagger flew off into the trees, and my sword was pinned painfully beneath me. Luthaes climbed atop my chest and grabbed my neck, hard.

He grinned down at me, pressing his thumbs into my throat until I gagged. Gareth was screaming my name, but I could barely hear him over the thrum of my own panicked blood. Luthaes's hands tightened, choking off my air.

"He is your mate, then?" Luthaes crooned. "I'd wondered. How sweet." Then he called out gleefully to Gareth, "How does it feel to see another man claim your mate as his prize?"

I refused to let this creature kill me—not now, not ever. Power rose inside me, roaring like a river flooding its banks. I was not simply a human or a Rose. I was a demigod, a true daughter of Kerezen. I thought of Mother as she might have been before the Unmaking: eyes of golden fire, an entire age of ancient power coursing through her veins. Maybe she had towered over the mountains. Maybe she had sung the first stars into the sky.

Gemma's glamour begin to crack around me, as if it were ice and I a warming spring. Luthaes stared down at me in shock as my true power illuminated him from below. Soon I would be obvious—my hair newly lustrous, my skin suffused with light, specks of gold in my brown eyes.

"What are you?" Luthaes whispered. The pressure of his hands let up ever so slightly, enough for me to throw him off me and roll. Gasping for air, I grappled for something, anything, to use as a weapon. My hand landed on a stone as big as a dinner plate. It would do.

I wrenched it out of the earth, spun around, and threw it hard. It crashed into Luthaes's head with a sickening crunch, killing him immediately, but I didn't stop there. My power was hungry, tired of being trapped behind a glamour, and this fae deserved no peace, even in death. He had tried to kill Gareth. My Gareth.

Feeling wild, I strode over to Luthaes, picked up the rock, and struck him with it again and again. I was battle-hungry, my power lighting me up like a storm, but I knew exactly what I was doing. With each blow, I heard his body crunch and watched his bones shatter. A scream burst out of me, punctuating my final blow. Luthaes was a pulpy ruin beneath me, and the rock in my hands was hot and slick.

I rose and tossed the rock aside, breathing hard and fast. When I wiped my mouth with my sleeve, I tasted copper and salt, and smiled.

"Mara..." Gareth's voice was quiet.

I turned to face him, realizing a second too late how I must have looked to him—half glamoured, covered in blood, grinning like a madwoman. The air rippled hotly around me; this snowy forest was a desert, and I was both the mirage and the true oasis.

But then Gareth's stricken gaze dropped to the ruin of Luthaes, and that single look punched all the air out of me.

Monster. The word spiraled viciously through my mind. I was monstrous. I craved pain and death and rejected love. I belonged here with the fae and their beasts more than I did back in Edyn. And Gareth knew it. I could see it on his face. One of his lenses was cracked, and this small, stupid detail made my eyes burn. His glasses were broken, and he was terrified of me.

I breathed steadily, slowing my heartbeat. I imagined stone flooding my insides, cooling me, settling me. I couldn't let the damaged glamour fall.

"Come on," I said shortly. "We have to go to Gemma. She'll guide us to the key. I hope."

I held out my hand, and he took it in silence, grimacing as the movement jostled his hurt arm. Quickly I inspected his wound—a welcome distraction. It wasn't deep and had already stopped bleeding. But a nasty blue-black bruise surrounded it, and the nearest veins had gone dark.

"Venom," Gareth said through gritted teeth. "A variation of what poisoned Farrin at the ball, I think. Their spears are laced with it. I have an antidote back at Rosewarren."

I glanced up at him. "Can you run?"

He gave me a wry smile. "Not as fast as you."

I didn't believe that smile, not for a second. He hid his revulsion well, but I knew better. My heart twisted as I imagined what he must be thinking.

"I'll slow my pace to match yours," I muttered. "Just try and keep up the best you can."

As we ran, the forest grew quiet. Too quiet. Besides the crunch of our boots in the snow and Gareth's labored panting, there was nothing. My nape tingled with misgiving, but when I scanned the darkness, I saw nothing but more trees. Somehow that made me feel worse. I started doubting my senses; was I following the right trail? Maybe damaging my glamour had muddied my connection to Gemma.

But then, so suddenly and brutally that it was like crashing through a thick sheet of ice, we tore through something cold and sharp—a magical barrier of some kind. Damaged ward magic, I guessed, meant to guard against intruders but no longer intact. We plunged into darkness, and sounds exploded all around us—the clash of swords, battle cries. Shot arrows, rumbling earth. My sister singing.

We tumbled down an icy slope into a sunken clearing. I caught Gareth's arm at the bottom, steadying him, and took a moment to grasp what I was seeing.

A colossal tree stood before us, even bigger than the Heart Tree in the Rosewarren barracks. Its bark was black, its shape gnarled, and it was *thrashing.* A dozen branches snapped through the air like whips. With each movement, the ground beneath us quaked.

"The tree that never sleeps," Gareth whispered.

I looked around, my blood pumping fast. It was dark here, the snow dull and the air thick with shadows, but my sentinel eyes were sharp. Ryder and Posey were engaged in combat against two armored fae. A fierce cry made me whirl around to see Danesh and Edra fighting three fae on the other side of the clearing. Four more fae leapt toward them through the trees, spears in hand.

And amidst all of them, choking the clearing, were huge white flowers as tall as the fae themselves, weaving and rattling like angry snakes. I watched in horror as one of them lunged for Danesh, the dark pistil at its center yawning open.

Danesh dropped and rolled right before the flower's head slammed into the ground. The impact flooded the clearing with a rancid, sour stink. Danesh pushed herself up with an angry roar and slashed her sword through the flower's thick stem. The whole thing collapsed and convulsed, hissing furiously. Watching it made my gorge rise.

"Where in the name of the gods is Bette?" Danesh cried.

Bette—the earth elemental in our ranks. I allowed myself a quick hope that she was alive, then bolted for my sisters, who were at the base of the giant tree. Talan stood guard over them, his face bloodied, chopping down any flower that snaked too close.

And my sisters… Gemma was slumped beside Farrin, her sweaty face tight with pain and her hands clutching the root nearest her. Farrin held her up, singing something so vast and multitonal that its magic rushed toward our friends like water from a broken dam.

I knelt in front of them, and Gareth sank down to my left.

"It's in there," Gemma murmured. She nodded toward the tree, then glanced over at me. "I can feel it. The tree has a tight hold on it. It's lodged deep."

Gareth touched Farrin's arm, gave her an encouraging smile. "Can you get to it?" he asked Gemma.

"I think so, but I'll need all of Farrin's attention to get me through it."

"You mean she has to stop singing for the others?"

Gemma nodded miserably, her eyes bright. "I'm so sorry. There's so much magic here, and I can't… It hurts so much. I can hardly breathe. Her music will keep me conscious."

"You are brilliant and brave," I told her, "and I'm so proud of you."

I glanced up at Talan, whose body flickered right before my eyes. He was Talan, beautiful and raven-haired, and then he was a tangle of thick roots, shielding us from the battle beyond. He ducked the blow of an attacking flower, then reared up and decapitated the awful thing with one smooth hack of his sword. At the same moment, the solid shield of roots stood in the same spot he did. A demonic illusion. He was right there, still guarding my sisters, but to our attackers, he would simply look like more of the tree.

"I won't let anything get to them," he shouted back at me, his voice fierce, battle-hard. "Go. Hurry!"

"Give me your sword," Gareth said to me. "I'll help him."

From somewhere beyond him came a scream of agony—a woman's scream. A Rose's scream.

Wordlessly I gave him the sword and turned away from the sound, shoving past my anger to focus on Gemma. "Tell me how to help you."

"We have to dig," Gemma said. She drew in a shuddering breath. "Follow my lead and keep an eye on the tree. Once it realizes what we're doing..."

It would stop fighting the others and come straight for us.

I nodded. "I'm ready."

Gemma briefly closed her eyes. When she opened them, they were bright as blue fire, and her hand, marked by the scar from the Three-Eyed Crown, glowed just as brilliantly. Her power rose up fast, her body suddenly scorching hot. She pressed her lips together, grabbed the nearest root, and tugged hard.

It came free with a thick, muscly snap. Gemma tossed it to the side and let it writhe, which it did for only a moment before falling still, crisped, slightly smoking.

Gemma smiled a little. Her beauty was astonishing, her hair gilded with inner fire. With her attention divided, our glamours were fading. Through the cracks came the telltale shimmer of her godly light. She worked fast, and with each root she wrenched free of the earth, she grew faster, stronger.

I worked at her side, not even my sentinel strength powerful enough to keep me from straining with effort. I could pry up only one root in the time Gemma took to rip out four, but we were doing it—slowly boring into the tree's heart, creating a tunnel big enough to crawl through.

Ahead of us, something silver glimmered in the thick tangle of roots. The moment my eyes locked on to it, a hot wave of magic rushed past us and raced out into the clearing. Talan let out a sharp cry of pain, confirmation that something belonging to Kilraith was here. The echoes of servitude that still lived in Talan's body could feel it.

Gemma faltered slightly at the sound and paused to recover her breath, and right at that moment, a ball of sizzling magic slammed into the tree over our heads with a deafening crack.

I looked up just in time to see a huge section of the tree fall away. The root Gemma held lashed out, throwing her back toward Farrin. She hit the ground and was still.

My heart in my throat, I hurried over and felt for her pulse—faint but steady. Farrin, still singing, touched my hand. I followed her gaze to the tree, which had gone completely still. The tunnel Gemma and I had made was gone, buried in fallen branches. Whatever had hit the tree—some stray bit of magic from a fae or from one of my Roses—had punched a hole into its gnarled trunk and stunned it silent. I scanned the wreckage, making quick calculations. We'd gotten extraordinarily lucky; that hole was positioned right above the key.

"Keep singing, Farrin," I said, then started to climb.

I hadn't made it three feet before Gareth joined me, carrying my sword in one hand.

"I'm coming with you," he announced breathlessly.

I didn't stop climbing, but I was sorely tempted to, if only so I could punch him. "Get out of here," I snapped, snatching back my sword and returning it to its sheath. "You're supposed to be helping Talan."

"He's fine. Truly a strapping young man. It's more important that I help you."

"And what help will you be to me, exactly?"

The hole was just ahead, yawning like the mouth of a cave. The charred bark around it pulsed with a soft blue light. Beneath us, something shifted with a faint groan. We froze, listening hard and barely daring to breathe, but then the tree fell silent once more. We climbed the last few yards in silence, then crouched at the hole and peered inside.

We saw only a thick and quiet darkness, and at the very bottom, a faint glimmer of silver.

Gareth raised his broken glasses to wipe his face. I caught a glimpse of his wounded arm; the venom's bruise had doubled in size.

"If you die," he answered mildly, "then at least you won't be alone."

His quiet voice shook me. The sounds of battle raged behind us—the crackle of magic, our friends in combat—and Gareth's voice was the thing that nearly made me lose my nerve. I could see the words he didn't say right there on his face: he didn't trust that I wouldn't die doing this thing. More than that, he didn't trust that I would fight to stay alive.

Maybe he was right not to.

"As soon as I have the key in my hands," I said, a little shaky, "you'll need to claim me as your prize and end the hunt. So as long as I'm alive, you'd better be too."

Then I climbed through the hole and began my descent. Gareth followed my path, and despite my best efforts to remain unimpressed, he impressed me. Even with a limp and a poisoned arm, he moved at a decent speed, and he didn't slip once.

A few short minutes later, my boot touched earth. We stood in a vast cavern of roots and stone. The only light came from the hole through which we'd climbed—now some seventy feet above us—and from my own body. The glamour was gone, and my skin glowed softly with power.

"Well, that's handy," Gareth remarked. To his credit, he did not gawk.

I said nothing, scanning the labyrinth around us until a faint glimmer to the right caught my eye.

"There it is," I whispered.

Now that we were this close to it, the similarity to the other anchors was undeniable. Made of the same dark metal as the Three-Eyed Crown and the Mhorghast egg, the key lay in a tangle of feathery roots and bright yellow moss. It was half the length of my forearm and crusted with jewels, and as we approached, it began, quietly, to hum.

I reached for it, then hesitated and glanced at Gareth. The air around the key vibrated with power, making my fingertips tingle, but nothing pushed me back. No ward magic, no barriers at all.

"Too easy?" Gareth suggested, gazing at the key in fascination.

"Let's hope not," I murmured.

Then, as I reached for the key, my hand brushed against the yellow moss.

The pain was so sudden and sharp that I nearly blacked out. Even worse, everything around us abruptly heaved—the roots, the earth itself—like a massive beast gasping for breath. Gareth caught me before I could fall, and I leaned against him for a moment, blinking away the pain. A deep rumble shook my chest as the roots continued to shift.

The tree, it seemed, was waking up.

"It *burned* me," I spat, shaking out my hand. I tried to ignore the angry yellow welts forming on my fingers.

"And now there's more of it," Gareth muttered. "Look."

As the tree stirred, its rumbling groans growing louder by the second, the yellow moss began to spread. Its tendrils snaked everywhere—around the roots, across the floor. As the moss moved, so did the roots, as if it was the thing awakening them. One root lashed across the ground; Gareth jumped out of the way with a curse just as a crash from above made us look up.

The hole was closing—our only way out.

I grabbed my sword and passed it to Gareth. "Cover me. Chop the roots, whack the moss, I don't care. Just strike anything that comes for us and climb as fast as you can."

He took the sword without question, and then, before either of us could talk me out of it, I thrust my hand deep into the moss.

I'd never stuck my hand into a fire before, but I imagined this was how it would feel. The searing pain made me see stars, and I couldn't shake the idea that something in this moss was peeling my skin from my bones. But I kept digging until my fingers finally met metal. I was sobbing, though I didn't realize it until I wrenched the key free of the moss and staggered back.

"Breathe, Mara, and listen to me," Gareth was saying, his voice thick with tears. "Gods, I'm so sorry. It will be all right. We've got to climb now, darling. Can you climb?"

Gasping for breath, I wedged the key into my waistband. The metal bit into the skin of my belly, but that was nothing compared to the pain in my hand. I couldn't look at it. I couldn't, or I would be sick.

I started to climb, tears streaming down my face. Each time I grabbed on to a root with my bare hand, the pain exploded anew. But I had to keep climbing no matter what. If my fingers fell off, I'd do it one-handed.

Gareth was right behind me, his progress inconsistent. Every few seconds he stopped to hack away at something. The chop of the blade against wood was sickening. I felt like we were clawing through the meat of a beast's belly. And the hole above us was closing faster and faster, weaving itself shut. The darkness was terrible. I couldn't see where I was going, and the air hissed with awakening roots, like we were crawling through a pit of snakes. I felt like my body was gone, like it had fallen away and all that was left of me was agony.

For an instant I imagined letting go and dropping to my death, letting the moss eat me alive. That would be it. There would be no more pain, no more dead Roses, no more anything.

"Mara, don't you dare," Gareth shouted from below me. "Keep climbing, or so help me, I'll kill you myself."

That made me laugh through my tears. The hole above us was nearly closed. We'd never fit. Maybe I could punch my way through with my good hand. Then I'd have a matching ruined set.

"Kill me?" I gasped. "You'd never, not before you've had the chance to fuck me."

"And what would *that* be like? Do tell, and please spare me no details."

His voice gave me the push I needed to climb the last few feet, and just as we reached the top and I started to laugh in delirious despair at the sight of the fistsized hole, the entire top of the tree exploded outward. Splintered wood flew everywhere, and the world outside roared with the sounds of battle, but the sight of escape was irresistible.

I climbed fast, screaming through the pain, screaming for Gareth to hurry. Once we were out, I scrambled down the roots with him just behind me. I was clumsy, uncaring. I fell twice, knocked my jaw against a root and tasted blood, but at last we were free, standing on solid ground.

And there was Gemma, haggard and half alive. But even so, her hands were bright with power, and her magic washed over us in hot waves, reassembling our glamours and keeping the thrashing roots at bay. Just behind her was Farrin, still holding her up and singing, her voice as fresh as ever and her song ringing with triumph.

I felt for the key—still there, tucked against my skin—and reached for Gareth with my unhurt hand. He took it gently and pulled me against him, and I closed my eyes and held on to him. His arm was strong around my waist; his heart beat wildly against mine.

"I claim you as my prize," he murmured into my hair, "and thus this hunt is finished."

The relief that swept through me was nearly as powerful as the pain in my hand. I sagged against Gareth in a daze, only dimly noticing our surroundings. Cries of anger, then of fear. Dark shapes darting swiftly through the air. A clash of swords; a sharp fae scream. Golden eyes flying toward me, and the cool brush of dark wings. "*Kill them!*" someone cried.

"Mother?" I whispered.

Then I knew nothing more.

Chapter 16

Pain tore me out of unconsciousness, and I sat up gasping.

Brigid was beside me, her face drawn and white. Her hand was on my left arm; she'd just shaken me awake. I lay on a cot, and beyond Brigid stood the walls of the Rosewarren infirmary. We were alone, with only Freyda for company. She paced from side to side along the perch in the corner of the room, all her feathers flattened against her body as if to make herself look smaller.

"Gemma?" I croaked. "Farrin, Gareth—where are they?"

"They're fine, but your sisters couldn't stay. They took the key south to Fairhaven to keep it out of reach of the fae. The Warden was *not* happy that all three of the anchors you've found so far will now be at Fairhaven, but I think she was too distracted to stop them."

This news punched the air out of me. "They're gone?"

"They left notes for you." Brigid touched her jacket pocket. "I'll give them to you later. But they're all right. Ryder and Talan too. My squadron brought you home from Gothyn maybe two hours ago. The Warden came with us."

"And Gareth?" Only moments ago I'd been in his arms, felt his breath on my skin. His sudden absence left me cold. "Where is he?"

"In a room down the hall, recovering." Brigid looked as if she were steeling herself for something terrible. "Mara, listen—"

Before she could say more, I glanced down and saw my left hand. A bandage hid the damage from view, but it might as well have not been there. In my mind's eye I was suddenly back beneath the tree, trying not to stare at the blistered yellow welts that encased my hand like a glove.

A wave of fresh pain coursed through my body, and I lurched over the side of the mattress and retched. Brigid was ready with a pail and a rag. As I huddled over the pail, shivering and aching, she said quietly, "I'm sorry to do this. You look like shit and probably feel like it too. But you need to come with me at once. The Warden is punishing Posey, and she won't listen to me. She won't listen to anyone."

The dread that dropped through me was like ice. Of course. I should have expected this. Why had I not *thought* of this? Posey's intelligence had brought us to Gothyn, to a fae queen loyal to Kilraith and a hunt that could have killed us all. Posey had assured us that the Cirrinoc clan would never bow to him, but Posey had been wrong. And the Warden had allowed her to stay at Rosewarren in the first place only because I'd convinced her to do so.

She can be useful, I had told her. *A boon to our intelligence efforts*.

I looked up at Brigid. "Did we all come back safely?"

Brigid hesitated before answering. "Bette and Tressa are dead. We burn their bodies tomorrow."

I turned away, squeezing my eyes shut. I wasn't unused to death, but right then I didn't have the strength to protect myself from the grief that came on its heels. Bette, dead. Tressa, dead. On a mission I'd led based on assurances from a fae I'd enlisted to help us. I'd long suspected the Warden was eager for a reason—any reason—to dispatch Posey. It wouldn't matter to her that Posey hadn't been the one to suggest the fae hunt. Roses had died, and in the Warden's eyes, Posey had led them to their deaths.

"It isn't your fault," Brigid began.

"Of course it is." I pushed myself to my feet, a dozen terrible images flashing before my eyes. When Brigid offered her arm, I brushed past her and started up the stairs. Freyda followed me, chirping quietly in distress.

"Are they in the Stillhouse?" I asked.

"The central training yard," Brigid replied, just behind me. "I think the Warden wants everyone to see it happen."

I gritted my teeth so they wouldn't chatter, forcing my shaky legs to carry me upstairs. The main hallways on the first floor were eerily quiet—until a distant scream pierced the air. I stopped short to lean against a wall and catch my breath.

"She has never tortured someone in public before," I said quietly. "Not even prisoners of war."

"The Warden is not herself."

I glanced up at Brigid. "What do you mean?"

"I've never seen her so close to losing control—not like this, not with so many of us watching." Brigid stared down the hallway toward the wooden double doors that opened to the training yards. "It's almost as if she's fighting herself, like part of her wants to spare Posey and the other part, the stronger part, is too angry to see reason and feels not even a flicker of mercy. She won't listen to any of us. She even struck Lorna when she tried to intervene. And she won't *stop*."

Another scream, much closer now, barreled down the corridor. I blew out a sharp breath and strode toward the doors. "She'll listen to me."

"Mara, I'm serious." Brigid caught me by the arm. Her lips were pressed thin, her brow furrowed. Freyda alighted on her shoulder, letting out soft, shrill chirps of agreement. "Something isn't right. *She* isn't right. And if she hurts you—"

"She won't." I pulled free of Brigid, a tingle of warning tapping at my throat, and pushed open the doors.

"Please, Madam, *please*!" Posey's shredded voice echoed through the training yards. "I swear to you, I didn't know, I didn't *know*!"

A sickening crack rang out. My stomach dropped. I knew that sound. It was the smack of wood against bone. And it happened again, and again, and *again*.

I ran out of the shadowed colonnade surrounding the central training yard, noticing little details with automatic precision. Four dozen Roses had gathered to watch, hovering at the edges of the yard with their familiars. The gray sky, swirling with clouds and Mist, was spitting snow. The Warden stood in the center of the yard, the sleeves of her black gown rolled up to her elbows and a practice staff in hand, ready to strike.

Posey was huddled on the ground in front of her, covered in her own green blood—face swollen, teeth missing, her left arm bent at a grotesque angle.

I threw myself between them and caught the Warden's staff as it swung through the air. It hit my unhurt palm with such a hard smack that the Warden lost her balance and nearly fell.

"Let go, Mara," she said, very low. "You can't stop this."

The Warden's skin looked sallow. Strands of sweaty hair had come loose from her normally neat bun and clung to her cheeks. The hard light in her eyes reminded me of Freyda when she was itching to hunt.

"Madam, this is a mistake," I told her, standing firm. "Posey deserves no punishment."

"She led you right into a trap."

"A risk we all take every time we pursue a piece of intelligence." I stepped closer, lowering my voice. "Look at what you're doing. This is the behavior you wish to model for us?"

The Warden glanced to the right, her fierce expression wavering at the sight of two littles hiding their faces in Cira's tunic.

I took a chance and pushed a little. "This isn't you, Madam. You are not yourself. Posey is one of us now and has been for months. She is not our enemy."

Behind me, Posey let out a gurgling cough. "Mara, tell her I didn't know about Kilraith. Tell her!"

The sound of Posey's voice snapped the Warden out of her reverie. With a surprising burst of strength, she pushed me aside, ripped the staff from my hand, and brought it down hard on Posey's broken arm.

Posey howled in pain, her screams wreathed in sobs. I raced to the weapons rack against the wall, grabbed a staff, and made it back to the Warden before she could deal another blow.

Our staffs crashed together and locked in place. I heard Freyda shriek from somewhere behind me and prayed Brigid would manage to restrain her.

"Madam, *stop this,*" I spat out. "Look at me and remember yourself."

But she wouldn't look at me. She pushed hard against my staff, but I was ready and met her with a shove of my own. She stumbled backward, and I kept after her, dealing blow after blow against her staff while she threw up sloppy defenses. Only when I'd cornered her against the wall did I relent.

I backed away slowly, holding my staff across my body and keeping my eyes trained on the Warden's even though looking at her made me feel queasy. Cowering against the wall like that, she looked so much smaller than usual and stared at me in a dazed sort of shock. I had never defied her like this, not even when she'd tortured the harpy, Nerys, for those long weeks.

I would not condemn Posey to the same fate.

"Posey, can you get up?" I said, keeping my voice as calm as I could.

Her breathing was ragged. She could only grunt a garbled assent.

"Get up slowly," I told her, "and walk away. Cira and Brigid will help you to the infirmary."

"No," said the Warden. Her voice was faint, but then she sucked in a breath and said it again: *"No."*

This time the word had teeth. It grabbed on to the binding magic that had lived inside me since my trials—the magic that bound me to the Mist and the Warden and compelled me to obey her—and it bit down hard.

Don't move. The compulsion was irresistible and rang through my head in the Warden's voice. *Don't stop me.*

I had never been compelled like this before. The Warden had never needed to use that power on me. I was a good little Rose, always had been. Rebellion was not in my nature. She seldom used this trick of the binding magic on anyone, even willful Roses like Danesh. She preferred that our eager obedience come naturally.

Nothing could have prepared me for the feeling that swept over me. Cold fire scorched my veins and turned my vision white. I dropped the staff and crashed to my knees, my body frozen in agony, and then I watched, helpless, as the Warden strode toward Posey and withdrew from her pocket a slender glass syringe. Inside it was a single drop of dull purple liquid.

My racing heart kicked into a gallop. It was the Box, the poison I'd seen used only once during my time in the Order. On that occasion, a Rose had betrayed one of our scouting teams to a reader—an eyeless Olden creature of Jaetris gifted with the art of reading and influencing the thoughts of others. To gain safe passage into Edyn, the reader had convinced everyone on the team that it would be wise to throw themselves off a cliff into the sea, and they had agreed and jumped happily to their deaths.

When the traitor Rose had been found out and the Warden had asked her why she had betrayed her sisters, she had answered, dry-eyed, "They aren't my sisters any more than you are my mother." It was the only explanation she had offered.

The Warden had made me stay and watch as she'd injected the traitor with the Box. We'd been in the Stillhouse; even then, at age twelve, I had already been her favorite. I would never forget the sounds the traitor had made as the Box did its work. By the time she was dead, she'd been nothing more than a mess of viscera on the floor.

Imagining Posey convulsing as that Rose had done—imagining the poison snapping each of her bones, and jerking her across the ground, and knotting up her beautiful green limbs like they were nothing more than gummy ropes of clay—gave me the strength to move. The Warden's binding magic was fierce, turning my legs to stone and my blood molten. Its commands circled through my mind—*don't move, don't move*—but I thought of my father, how he would feel fear but not be afraid, and pushed through them.

As I dragged myself across the yard, sound came to me in muffled bursts. I heard Brigid yell something furious before falling abruptly silent. I heard Posey's screams turn animal as the poison took hold of her. What remained of her crystalline fae voice disappeared. Through my hazy vision, I saw someone approach the Warden. Two people. Three. She moved toward them, shouting angrily.

Now was my chance. I willed myself to move faster, calling on all the strength I possessed. My bandaged hand scraped across the cobblestones. When I reached Posey, she gurgled something I couldn't understand. I pulled myself closer, trying not to gag at the sight and sound and *smell* of her. One of her legs snapped in half, exposing muscle and bone. One side of her face collapsed, leaving her jaw dangling. The scents of blood and urine surrounded her like a rancid cloud.

"Please," she rasped, "kill me."

Nerys had said the same, and Petra too. Their voices lived in my memory—one gnarled and ancient, the other that of a trembling child. And now Posey's joined their ranks. I would hear her pleas every day for the rest of my life and remember how completely I had failed her.

"I'm sorry," I whispered. At least I tried to. The Warden's magic slowed my voice. But I think Posey understood. I locked eyes with her, or with the eye I could see—one was buried in the ruined pulp of her face—and grabbed her head, and twisted. Hard. Sharp.

Her neck snapped. Her screams stopped, and her body went still. It wasn't as neat as the Warden's sword slicing through Nerys the harpy's neck, but it was better than the Box. Anything was better than the Box.

There.

Her long suffering has ended.

Am I not merciful?

I wanted to lie down beside her and let the snow cover us both. But once she was dead, the Warden's compulsion died too. There was no need for it now. The object of her wrath, her reason for forcing my obedience, was gone.

Even so, pushing myself to my feet and facing her was the hardest thing I'd ever had to do. She stood in silence not far from me with Brigid and Cira, Glynis and Edra, and even Danesh just beyond her. I didn't dare look at their faces. They would show me the truth of how awful it had been to hear Posey die.

"Get out of my sight," the Warden said hoarsely. Her mouth twisted. She was looking at me as though it were her neck I'd broken. Utter gutting betrayal.

I obeyed, hurrying out of the training yard. Roses parted in silence to let me pass, but no one followed me, not even Freyda; Brigid must have wrangled her inside. I couldn't even feel glad about that. The world was a pulsing blur around me.

I didn't stop until I reached the temple of Kerezen. A circular building of weathered gray stone, the temple had once been a favorite retreat of mine. The faceless statue of Kerezen and the profusion of ivy vines had reminded me of home.

Now I sat on one of the prayer benches at Kerezen's feet and stared up at her featureless stone visage, trying to find Mother's face within it. Depictions of godly faces were considered blasphemous, a tradition that struck me as rather funny. Having now met two gods, I couldn't imagine any of them would actually care about something like that. How fragile and fumbling we humans were. How easily we could fall apart.

Sitting in Kerezen's shadow brought me none of the peace I wanted. The childish urge to flee north to Wardwell and hide away with Mother came and went. She wouldn't be able to help me. Only Jaetris, god of the mind, could scrape memories out of someone's head, and there was no way to know where he'd gone after my sisters and I had killed his human host in Mhorghast. Some godly scrap of him was floating around somewhere, I assumed, waiting to be resurrected. Or maybe without a body, he had lost hold of himself and his memories and drifted away into nothingness like ashes on the wind.

Numbly, I rose to my feet and stared at the pile of half-melted candles perched on Kerezen's dais—old prayers, old hopes. I couldn't drift away like ashes on the wind unless someone burned me, and I didn't particularly want to die in that way if I could help it.

But there were many other ways to die.

I just had to find one before anyone could stop me.

Chapter 17

My legs carried me to the Old Country with little instruction.

I barely noticed the protests of the four Roses standing guard at the rift in the Middlemist that I chose to pass through—the same one I'd approached before, when Gareth's page had interrupted my crossing. I muttered something to them, or maybe even shoved them out of my way. Whatever I did, they chose not to follow me.

I passed through the spells crisscrossing the rift, welcoming their crackling sting. This pain was different from that of my bandaged hand or of watching Posey writhe. This pain was of my own choosing and therefore precious. It reminded me that I was still alive, for now, and gave me a tantalizing taste of what I was walking toward.

The Mist here was thick as cobwebs and darker than its usual filmy silver thanks to the corrupting effect of the nearby rift. According to some, such tears in the Mist's fabric were abominations. They didn't care that the monks at all five Cloisters, who had devoted their lives to studying the gods, had issued statements denouncing this kind of fanatical thinking. In the minds of these zealous faithful, the Mist was a product of the gods and therefore innately perfect. Flaws shouldn't have existed, and the fact that they did—that the Mist was failing, that it was flooding the country, that we were at war with the Oldens—was a sign that we had fallen out of the gods' favor. We deserved punishment, maybe even extermination by invaders, if that was the will of the gods.

No one had ever been able to coherently explain how that would happen, since as far as they knew, the gods were dead and no longer *had* a will. And all of this ignored the fact that if the gods had been as perfect as our holy clerics claimed, the Mist never would have existed in the first place—the seal between our world and the Old Country would have been impenetrable.

Fortunately, I wouldn't be around much longer to debate the issue.

On this night, the Middlemist knew exactly what I wanted. It didn't sing to me about it, nor did it hiss. In solemn silence, it deposited me in a rocky stretch of Olden Country that I recognized at once. Desolate crags stretched from horizon to horizon, their valleys cloaked in fog. The sky was orange, and the slopes were bare. The air was thin and cold. Crashes of thunder echoed across the dreary landscape though there were no clouds in the sky.

Ghorlock, home of the stone titans. That thunder rumbling in my bones was their distant footfalls.

I nearly laughed. The Mist had a dark sense of humor. What a dismal place this was, its beauty stark and cruel. Ghorlock was in the far northern realm of the Old Country, hundreds of miles from the nearest Order-friendly settlement. Though I had left the Mist far behind, I could still feel its presence in the deep corners of my mind.

You want violence, daughter of Kerezen?

You want death?

As you wish.

And here I was. The titans would be only too happy to oblige me. Stone titans weren't as easily provoked as their brethren of fire and wind, but even their patience had limits. Insult them with enough persistence, and they'd flatten you without a word.

It would be quick.

I wouldn't feel it.

I started down the nearest slope, so calm I was almost gliding.

It didn't take me long to find one.

I followed the sound of grinding stone to a mountain path, up which a titan lumbered, churning up dust clouds. He was smallish for his kind but still towered over me by a good fifteen feet. He was human-shaped in the way that wild wolves are dog-shaped: some similarities, but one was clearly more ancient and powerful than the other. He had two legs, two arms, a head, a torso, but instead of flesh, he was made of stone and pebbles and plates of shale. Every time he moved, he rained rocks, and his joints ground against each other like jostling boulders.

He was perfect.

I ran toward him the second I saw him, sprinting across the rocks at breakneck speed. He heard me coming and turned around to look, blinking his small, sunken eyes in confusion. I leapt the last few feet and attacked him with such a hard roundhouse kick that he crashed to his knees with a grunt.

The impact knocked the wind out of me. If a human who wasn't a demigod sentinel had done something as foolish as I just had, she would have shattered every bone in her leg. I slammed to the ground shoulder-first and lay there for a moment, gulping down air, my leg throbbing with pain, before unsteadily climbing back to my feet. The titan was still on his knees, watching me. I couldn't read his expression. His face was a shifting mass of rock, his mouth a thin slit.

"Did you just crawl out of your pit?" I said, speaking haltingly in the harsh Ghorlock tongue. "You're filthy."

He looked down at himself with those unreadable sunken eyes. His limbs were caked in dried mud and frosted with dust. Given that and his size, I wondered if he might in fact be a child, freshly formed in the steaming mud pits where all stone titans were born.

"I thought they didn't let puny newborns like you climb this high," I continued, still in my fighting stance, though my whole body was shaking. I couldn't even tell if I was afraid. I buzzed, I thrummed. I was hot and aching, feverish. I was going to die.

"You'd better hope your elders don't see you," I said, "or else they might throw you down the mountain. You'd fall to pieces, and then you'd have to wait there for someone to wander by and hope they cared enough to stop and help rebuild you. If there was anything left to rebuild, that is. Maybe you'd simply be dust after a drop like that. You certainly don't look strong enough to—"

He moved fast. That had always surprised me—how quickly they could travel given their bulk. One swipe of his arm was all it took. His fist hit my stomach and I went flying. I hit a cliffside so hard that my vision flashed white. And then I was on the ground in a heap, gasping, tasting blood, my ears ringing. The world spun and spun, and the titan began to trudge away.

"Foolish," he rasped in Ghorlock. He waved back at me in disgust. "A human and a fool."

The delirious thought came to me that he was very funny, that I wanted to laugh. Then the world went black.

Rain woke me—a cold, stinging rain. I was floating through the air, which reassured me that I was dead and being transported through channels of *aelum* to the Great Dominion, birthplace of the gods and final resting place of the dead. *Aelum*: the basis of all magical life.

"Yes," came a voice from somewhere above me, "that is indeed the definition. I'm glad to hear that you've still got use of your brain."

The voice jarred me. I forced open my eyes, and a flash of lightning afforded me a glimpse of a familiar spectacled face.

"Gareth?" I croaked.

"At your service," he replied. "Don't worry, we're almost out of the rain. There's a cave not far from where I found you."

His voice was cheerful, as if we were on a pleasant stroll. But his arms shook around me, and he was breathing hard.

"Are you dead too?" I asked.

He choked out a sad burst of laughter. "You're not dead, Mara. You're alive. And I need you to stay with me, all right? I'm not equipped to defend myself against Freyda should you die in my care."

"Freyda's here?"

"She is, and she's very angry and very wet. I told her to wait for us in the cave. We're almost there, darling. Stay with me."

His voice began to fade. My eyes drifted shut.

Do you hear me? His voice floated through the darkness. *Stay with me, Mara. Please.*

When I next awoke, I lay shivering on a blanket. The ground was hard but smooth, and I was in a shallow hollow of stone, like a giant thumbprint. Several yards away from me, the mouth of a cave framed a dark world of wind and rain. My head ached so sharply it felt like someone was screwing knives into my skull. But the world looked a bit more solid, my vision less hazy. I was still alive.

As I lay there, my eyes filled with tears, and I was too tired to keep them from falling.

"Oh, Mara." Gareth moved carefully into my field of vision. He was a mess—his clothes soaked through, streaks of mud all over him, his glasses speckled with raindrops. He cupped my face in his hand and brushed his thumb across my cheek. His touch was cold but so gentle it made my heart twist.

"Please don't cry," he said quietly. "I know it hurts, but—"

"You don't understand," I bit out, staring at the cave ceiling. "I shouldn't be here."

"Well, I suppose that's true. You *should* be at the priory, safe in your bed."

"Safe? At the priory?" I laughed through my tears. "You do tell wonderful jokes."

"Certainly it's safer than Ghorlock."

I glanced at him. "How do you even know about Ghorlock?"

He gave me a look, his mouth quirking into a small smile.

"Oh, right." I rolled my eyes. "You read about it in some obscure text a million years ago and can recall every detail with perfect accuracy."

"Gods, it sounds even better when you say it."

Something moved to my left, and I heard the familiar click of talons. I turned slightly to see Freyda creeping carefully toward me across the cave floor. The sight of her ruffled wet feathers and stern amber glare nearly unstitched me. I held out my wounded hand to her. The bandage was sopping, stained an ugly yellow-brown. She cocked her head and stared at it, then at me.

"Freyda was the one who told me you were gone," Gareth said quietly. "I was up late in the laboratory. Everyone else had gone to bed. And she showed up at the window, fussing like mad. I tried to quiet her, but she was inconsolable. She kept flapping around, trying to push me toward the door. So I finally gave up and let her lead me to you."

"All the way to Ghorlock?"

"All the way to Ghorlock."

I blinked back tears as I met Freyda's eyes. "Our familiars know when we're hurt. She must have panicked when she couldn't find me. I'm sorry, Freyda." I held out my hand to her again. "You're right to be angry, but will you please come here?"

Freyda was not one to forgive easily, especially when I was the transgressor, but I must have looked truly pathetic, because she came to me with only a few soft chirps of irritation. She pressed her beautiful head to my shoulder, and I put my arm around her, scooping her gently against me.

"Does anyone else know I'm here?" I whispered.

"Perhaps the Warden," Gareth replied. "Even I can't claim to know the full breadth of her abilities."

"And you decided to come and fetch me without anyone to help you?"

"I didn't think you'd want anyone else."

"You think very highly of yourself."

"That's true," he said lightly, "but I also can't imagine you'd want the other Roses to see you like this."

"Like what?"

"Half alive and crying, with that horrible dead look in your eyes."

I chuckled softly. "Not dead enough."

Gareth was quiet for a long moment, then shifted a bit closer to me and rummaged around in an oilcloth bag.

"I did bring some supplies," he said. "Food, medicine. As you can see, I haven't built a fire. There's no wood to be found, and I don't much like the idea of attracting the attention of curious titans. But I did bring one of your starstone beacons."

He pulled out a palm-size metal casing and set it carefully on the stone between us. A soft white light shone through its elaborate tracery of roses and briars, casting gentle shadows across the cave walls.

My surprise was faint. I barely felt it. I barely felt anything.

"Did you just march into the supply room and take one off the shelf?" I asked.

"With the approval of Brigid, thank you very much. I told her that I wanted to study the beacon's properties, perhaps adapt some of its design for our tracking stations."

"And she believed that?"

Gareth hesitated, glancing up at me. "Brigid is very astute."

"Meaning she let you, a librarian, venture out into the Old Country to find me on your own?"

"I wasn't alone. I had Freyda."

Freyda chirped in agreement, the sound muffled by my sleeve.

"And maybe Brigid didn't think she could bear what she might find," Gareth added softly.

That took the breath out of me, and I had very little breath as it was. When I closed my eyes, fresh tears rolled down my cheeks.

"Has she come to find you before?" Gareth asked.

Fragments of memories tickled the tired edges of my mind. *Years* of memories.

"No," I whispered. "But she has seen me after. I've never explained myself to her, but I haven't had to. At least she has never told Cira." I dragged a hand across my eyes. "That's a kindness I don't deserve."

After a moment, I heard him move closer to me. "Will you tell me why you came here?"

"I already have."

"Yes, but why *this* time?" He paused. "Brigid told me about Posey."

The sound of her name was a dagger to my heart. "Then you have your answer."

"What happened to her was not your fault."

"It was, but that's not the point."

"What is the point?"

His gentle voice tore something open inside me, something furious and exhausted. "It hurts to be alive," I said, an aching sadness lodged in my throat. "I'm tired of it. Today it's Posey. Tomorrow it will be someone else. And someone else the next day, and on and on. And somehow, I'm never the one who dies. I'm the one who has to watch it happen and keep going. And I'm *tired* of that. I'm tired of having to keep going." I glared at him through my tears. "There. You've dragged it out of me. Are you happy?"

"Happy? No, Mara." Gently he picked up my hand and folded it between his. He looked at me as if I were something rare and precious, something to keep close, to protect. "But I am glad you're still here."

I shook my head slowly. I couldn't seem to stop crying. "You shouldn't have come after me. Why couldn't you just let me be?"

"Because I couldn't imagine having to tell Farrin and Gemma the news and see the heartbreak on their faces," he replied. "Because Cira needs you, and so does Brigid, and so do all the littles who adore you so much it makes them miss their families a bit less. But most of all, because I'm a selfish bastard and I can't bear the thought of losing you."

The hoarse passion in his voice, the way it cut like a serrated knife, quieted me a little. When he leaned closer to wipe my tears, I stared hard at him, examining his face—for what, I didn't know. For confirmation, perhaps, of this thing stretching unsaid between us. For a closer look at his bright green eyes.

"You'd be much better off without me storming around being mad at you for no good reason," I said quietly.

His gaze locked on to mine, and he raised my unhurt hand to his lips and kissed each of my fingers—softly, reverently, each brush of his mouth a quiet prayer. "I would rather you storm around being mad at me for the rest of our lives," he murmured against my skin, "than live in a world without you in it."

My heart pounded an entire symphony against my breastbone. *The rest of our lives* was a terrifying phrase that should have made me rip my hand away from him, but I couldn't bring myself to do it. I watched him lift my other hand to his lips just as tenderly, even though its bandage was soaked and tattered. Freyda scuttled away with an annoyed flutter of feathers and retreated to the shadows to preen.

"I brought medicine for this," Gareth said, cradling my hurt hand in his. "A stronger pain salve than Nanette has been using."

"And where did you get that? Don't tell me you've also taken to robbing apothecary shops."

He released my hand with a smile and turned to his bag. "As fun as *that* sounds, I'm afraid the answer is much less exciting. The Committee of New and Emerging Magics back at the university has been working on stronger variations of the standard medicines the armies stock at their camps. This one is meant for burns." He held up a small tin. "May I?"

I held out my hand to him, and he cut through the bandage with small scissors he took from his bag. As he pulled the fabric away, it tugged at my wounds, and I hissed in pain. He stopped at once, but I nodded at him to keep going, and when the cold air hit my mangled skin, it was like plunging my hand into the moss all over again. I barely managed to stifle my scream.

But then Gareth began smoothing his salve over my fingers, my knuckles, my palm, and wherever his touch went, a tingling coolness bloomed soon afterward. I couldn't look at my hand—feeling his fingers trace the contours of my blisters was nauseating enough—so instead I looked at him. His hair had begun to dry; damp blond tendrils framed his face. His brow was furrowed in concentration, and the starstone beacon painted him silver—his cheekbones, his glasses, his lower lip. The longer I looked at him, the better I felt. The salve was part of that, certainly, but the warmth, the calm that came over me as I watched him work was far more than just that.

When he finished, he sat back to examine the result. Losing his touch made my body ache.

"It's not the prettiest bandage," he said, frowning, "but it'll do what it's supposed to, I think. How do you feel?"

When he looked up at me, I wanted to cry—no longer from pain or desolation, but from the sheer tenderness coursing through me at the sight of his hopeful expression. He looked at me as if I were the first bloom unfurling after a long winter.

The proper words failed me. Instead I reached for him, shivering a little, and said, "Gareth, please come here."

Without another word, he settled beside me and drew me into his arms, and I'd never felt anything as wonderful as this: his body fitted snugly against mine, his hand cupping my head, his arm firmly around me. He trembled with cold, as did I, but I clung to him, my fists full of his coat, and breathed, and breathed, and soon my sentinel blood roared back to life. I rested my cheek against his chest, listened to his racing heartbeat, and imagined pressing all my body's heat into his.

When his trembling ceased, I pulled back to look at him. I didn't realize I was still crying until he took my face in his hands and dried my cheeks. When one of his thumbs brushed against my lips, I took it softly in my mouth and sucked once, gently. His sharp intake of breath warmed me more completely than any fire.

"What do you see when you look at me?" I whispered. I didn't mean to ask the question, but once I said the words, I felt desperate to know the answer. I had beaten the fae Luthaes to a pulp and seen the revulsion on Gareth's face. I had condemned Posey to torture and then killed her with my bare hands, and if he'd witnessed that, I knew he would have stared at me with the same kind of speechless horror.

Daughter of Kerezen.

Monster of Rosewarren.

But in that cave, with the roaring curtain of rain just outside and everyone we loved an entire world away, Gareth looked at me with an expression of such devotion that I lost my breath.

This was not the look of a man beholding a monster. Or maybe I was just the right kind of monster for him. What had Nanette called him? *That man is a menace.* A menace and a monster, I thought sadly. We were well matched.

"I see a brave woman who doesn't deserve the sadness she carries," Gareth replied. "Someone brilliant and powerful and passionate. A leader and a teacher who is so loved." Then he raised a playful eyebrow. "And who, it must be said, is so godsdamned breathtakingly gorgeous that thinking about her keeps me up at night."

This was dangerous, this softness blooming between us. This was everything I'd long ago resolved to reject. But it felt so wonderful to be held by him that pushing him away seemed impossible.

I ignored every ounce of my good sense and smiled up at him. "And what do you do, Professor, when you think of this brave woman while lying awake in your bed?"

"Mara." He pressed his forehead to mine and closed his eyes, as if my words had pained him. "You're hurt and exhausted, and we're lying on the floor of a cave in a land populated by sentient rocks. But when you look at me like that, all I can think about is how desperately I want to kiss you."

I shifted closer to him, feathering my fingers across the line of his jaw. I shouldn't have. This was a terrible idea. Letting it happen could only lead to heartbreak.

But still I whispered, "Then kiss me."

It was like unlocking a door that had been straining to burst open. With a quiet groan, he took my face in his hands as if I were something fragile and remarkable and lowered his mouth to mine. Softly, sweetly, a silent hymn. Heat poured down my body at the touch of his lips, pooling between my legs, and suddenly I wanted more, much more, than a careful kiss. I hadn't kissed someone in a long time, hadn't kissed someone and actually *meant* anything by it for even longer. Kissing

Gareth was like lighting a fire and watching it burn—first quietly, and then with a roar. And with his hands on me, and his tongue gently opening my mouth, and that muffled, shuddering moan he let out against my lips, I didn't care if those flames would simply warm me or rage out of control and destroy me.

When I arched closer to him, his hand glided down my back, and he pulled me hard against him, his fingers digging into my hip. The sudden close contact made me gasp. I slid my unhurt hand into his hair, relishing the smooth softness of every damp curl. The strength in his wiry arms holding me to him and the heat of his arousal between my legs was its own kind of magic. His touch swept away my pain, scorched my sadness to ashes. I circled my hips against him, ready to reach down for his belt, heedless of how fast this was spiraling into an inferno, when suddenly he said breathlessly against my mouth, "Wait, Mara. Wait, hold on."

I froze, though my body was screaming for more—more of this, more of him. "What is it? What's wrong?"

"Nothing's wrong, I just..." He shook his head, taking in the sight of me with a helpless sort of look, like I'd won an unspoken argument by simply existing. "*Gods, look at you,*" he rasped, and then bent to kiss my neck, lightly grazing my skin with his teeth. I moaned, shivering, and canted my hips toward him once more, but after a few blazing seconds of this—his tongue licking a lazy stripe down the column of my throat, my fingers tightening around a fistful of his hair—he pulled away again, with two apologetic kisses to my cheek and brow.

"No, wait," he said roughly. "Gods, I'm sorry. I can hardly think with you looking like that."

"Like what?" I murmured, reaching for the nearest button of his shirt.

He caught my hand with a wry smile, then brushed a soft kiss across my knuckles. "Like you want to let me have you."

That hungry look in his eyes melted something inside me. I touched his cheek, pressed my thumb gently against the corner of his mouth. His lips fell open, his teeth scraped against the pad of my thumb, and I leaned into him, my nipples pebbling beneath my shirt.

"Then have me," I whispered against his skin. "I'm ready, Gareth."

He let out a desperate sound, somewhere between a sob and a laugh. "Darling, there's nothing I want more, but I refuse to do so on a cave floor. You deserve better. And frankly, so do our knees."

"Our knees would recover," I pointed out.

"It's just that I want you in my bed, or in yours," he went on. He pressed his forehead against mine, still catching his breath. "I want you in softness and warmth, and—"

"And I suppose *I* want to be well enough that I won't pass out while I'm on top of you."

That made him laugh, a quick exhale against my lips. "Gods..." he muttered. "There's an image."

"Me passing out?"

"You on top of me. Beneath me. Beside me." He punctuated each phrase with a kiss to my neck, my temple, the hollow of my throat. "The possibilities are endless."

"Or maybe by the time we get home, I'll have recovered enough of my senses to realize this was all some sort of fever dream."

At that he grew quiet. When he pulled away to look at me, his eyes were grave.

"Don't think that we're finished talking about what made you come here today," he said quietly. "You can't just push it aside forever. Not with jokes, not with bravado."

I stared at him, the shift in mood so abrupt that it took me a moment to recover my voice. I put a hand on his chest, making a slight space between us. "*That's* what you want to talk about right now?"

"Ignoring the monster means it will eventually come back for more, and I won't let you hurt yourself again."

The word *monster* stung. I released him and scooted away, feeling cold and damp and strangely abashed. "You won't *let* me?"

"*We* won't let you, I should say."

"What, you'll recruit all of Rosewarren to follow me around and physically restrain me?"

He looked at me with infuriating calm. "If that's what keeps you alive, then yes."

I turned away, my stomach in knots. Whatever madness had swept me up into its grip was gone. That I had kissed this man, that I still ached for more of him, mortified me. Even worse, I understood what he was saying and why he was saying it. But his patient regard made me feel like a fool, like I was a student whose professor was helping her understand where in her equations she had made a crucial mistake.

"I need to rest," I said shortly. "Once I have the strength to take us home, we'll leave."

I lay down with my back to him, my cheeks burning, and offered him nothing more.

Chapter 18

I slept, but only in fits. Once the rain stopped and morning touched the sky, I called to Freyda. The flap of her wings woke Gareth, who gathered his supplies in silence. I didn't look at him; I didn't want to see the hurt on his face or his judgment. Remembering it was awful enough.

I won't let you hurt yourself again, he'd said.

As if he could stop me. As if he had any idea what it was to live my life.

Freyda pricked my arm with one of her talons, and I smeared two fingers through the blood before reaching into my shredded clothes and pressing them to the rose tattoo on my thigh. A physical manifestation of the bond that tied me to the Warden, to my fellow Roses, to the Order, I'd long thought of it as a brand: here stands a Rose, and her body is not her own.

As soon as my blood touched the tattoo, the binding magic bloomed to life and tugged me forward. It was like one end of a hooked chain had been buried deep inside me and the other end of it lived in the Warden's fist. *Come home,* it said. *Come home to me.*

It wasn't a pleasant sensation; the magic was urgent and impatient, and I already felt sick to my stomach. But at least it was a distraction, something to focus on besides the memory of Gareth's kisses and the question of whether my anger was justified or simply embarrassing.

"Follow me," I told him, still refusing to look at him. I held out my hand. "Traveling along the binding magic is faster than taking a greenway, but it's also more violent. You'll have to hold on to me or you won't be able to keep up. The magic will sense a foreign body and reject you."

I hated the cold tone of my voice, hated it even more when Gareth took my hand. I gripped his fingers hard; the last thing I wanted was to lose him somewhere in transit. The thought of never having to look at him again was both horrible and tantalizing. With him gone, the memory of kissing him would fade, and the next time I decided to die, he wouldn't come after me.

Shameful thoughts. I immediately wished I could unthink them.

Hand in hand, we stepped out into the mountains and said nothing else.

The passage back to Rosewarren was a sharp shot through the darkness. One minute we were hiking up a dusty mountainside in Ghorlock, following the binding magic's pull. The next we were stumbling out of a tight nothingness and onto the snowy grounds of Rosewarren.

Gareth lost his footing and caught himself against a tree, gasping for air, but he didn't vomit. Impressive. We rarely allowed anyone outside the Order to travel with us along the binding magic, but when we did, they always got sick immediately afterward. The pressure on your lungs, on your whole body, felt like being squeezed in a giant fist. Traveling through even the harshest greenway couldn't compare.

I watched Gareth long enough to ensure that he wouldn't lose consciousness. When he looked over at me, sweaty but clear-eyed, I turned and trudged through the snow toward the priory's turreted silhouette. Freyda stayed with him, which made me feel a little better about the fact that I couldn't bear to be around him for another second.

But only a little.

My throat ached with regret, but if I lingered, he would speak, and I couldn't bear that. Not now, not when every word trapped inside me was choked with barbs he didn't deserve.

Maybe, I thought, this would be the end of it—a few aborted kisses that I wouldn't have allowed had I been in my right mind, and nothing more. I walked with clenched fists and forced myself to think of Crellin's broken body. Ordinarily, when I recalled my long-ago lover, I preferred to think of her alive and whole. But maybe if I meditated fiercely enough on the memory of her shattered skull, and how the other Roses had to forcibly drag me away from her corpse—maybe if I imagined Gareth's body in place of hers—that would renew my resolve.

That is what happens when a Rose decides to love. I must have said it to myself a hundred times. *Walk away before it's too late.*

The quiet told me it was the middle of the night. Rosewarren's carpeted corridors were quiet; the polished wood-paneled walls gleamed softly in the dim lamplight. Everyone except the night patrol was asleep, and no one bothered me until I reached the barracks, where Danesh sat on a root of the enormous Heart Tree that grew in our common area and supported the roof with its branches. She was reading a book and chewing on the end of her braid. I hadn't seen her do that in years, not since we were children.

I strode past her, hoping my stony silence would deter her, but I should have known better. She jumped up and hurried after me, letting her book fall to the floor.

"Where have you been?" she asked.

"Out."

"Fenwood?"

Why not? "Yes."

"An interesting choice, to take someone to bed right after…" She trailed off.

Posey. Right after you killed Posey.

"Everyone grieves in their own way," I said flatly.

"It must have been a rough one. You look like shit. Did you have sex in a pigsty or something?"

I stopped short and kept my gaze straight ahead. Maybe if I didn't look at her, she would go away. "What do you want, Danesh?"

"I just…" She hesitated, then blew out a sharp breath and came around to face me. "Mara, I'm so sorry."

I wasn't sure I'd ever heard Danesh sound genuinely sad about anything. I was surprised enough that I finally looked right at her. "Sorry for what?"

"I was the one who gave the report to the Warden. I didn't know how to stall her. She was adamant. She wanted every detail. I think she nearly lost her mind when she saw you in Gothyn. You looked half dead. She might have thought you actually *were* dead. And once she heard my report, that was all the justification she needed to target Posey." Danesh looked away, her mouth twisting. "I know we're not the best of friends, but we were inducted together, we endured the trials together, and that means something to me. I didn't like Posey, but for your sake, I never wanted anything to happen to her."

The word *trials* sat between my shoulders like a stone. Petra's auburn hair flickered in the corner of my vision.

"But for her own sake," I said dryly, "you didn't mind so much if it did?"

"Look, I may not trust fae, but that doesn't mean I want them to suffer like that. I don't want anyone to suffer like that." She crossed her arms over her chest, no longer looking at me. "I'm sorry she died.

I'm sorry she died like *that*. And I'm sorry that you had to be the one to do it."

I didn't know what to say. Anger was pointless; when the Warden was set on doing something, there was no deflecting her. And like Gareth, Danesh didn't deserve my anger.

I was starting to think the only person who did was me.

"All right." I touched Danesh's shoulder. "Thank you, Danesh."

When I went to my room, she didn't follow. My exhaustion was so complete that I crawled into bed in my muddy clothes, boots and all, and didn't even stop to light a lamp. The darkness was far preferable anyway; in the darkness, I couldn't see my painted Ivyhill.

But I felt it. I knew every vine winding across my walls, every leaf, the mansion's every meticulously drawn window. My mind whirled with so many thoughts, so many memories—each containing a different hurt—that the weight of them pinned me to the bed. Could a person die of sadness? Could they fall asleep wrapped in grief and longing and never wake up?

I missed my sisters. That was the last thing I remembered thinking before I fell asleep. I missed them so badly that it felt like the distance between us was tearing me in half.

I clutched a pillow to my stomach and willed myself to sleep.

The breach bells woke me a few hours later.

I'd barely opened my eyes when I began transforming, my body snapping and stretching, feathers sprouting down my arms. As my fingers grew talons, my bandage tore open, and I glanced down at my hand with numb curiosity. It was the first time I'd dared to look at it since returning from Gothyn.

Beneath the soft sheen of down, which thickened as my feathers came in, my skin was mottled with blisters. The welts had diminished in size, but there were dozens of them, and they'd blackened, which I distantly registered as an ominous sign. Maybe, I mused numbly, I would lose my hand. And how funny, and fitting, that Gemma's left hand also bore scars, but hers were a net of delicate lines that glittered prettily as an embroidered glove while mine looked like the patchwork hide of a chimaera.

Monster of Rosewarren indeed.

I followed my squadron mates out onto the grounds in a daze. I shouted the commands I was supposed to shout, strapped my weapons to my body as I usually did, and launched into the air alongside my fellow Roses, but it was like my body was doing these things of its own accord. I knew Freyda was flying beside me, but she was a blur. Sounds were muffled, and my mind was a void.

Even when we reached the breach site—Section Twenty; a pack of lycans; a convoy of human refugees headed south—I felt removed from myself, like I was nothing more than a puppet at the mercy of my training instincts. Earthquakes below us; howling winter winds all around us; the snarls and howls of the lycans as we tore through them; and the Mist, a sea of silver loosed from its bindings, flooding it all—I noticed these things as if from a great distance. Unmoved. Unafraid. If my hand hurt from fighting, I didn't feel it.

Only when we returned to Rosewarren—the lycans slaughtered and the surviving refugees shepherded to a nearby settlement—did I start to resurface from the fog I'd fallen into. As we crossed the snowy grounds and approached the priory, all my senses prickled in warning.

Something was wrong.

It was midmorning, the Mist-shrouded sky a churning dull gray, the wintry air so cold it hurt my lungs, and yet no smoke came from the chimneys. The barns were still shut, the training yards were empty, and all the priory's windows were dark.

And we were still in our avian forms. Normally we transformed back to our human selves the moment we touched down at Rosewarren after a mission. But here we all stood with our talons and feathers, which meant that either the Warden had chosen to keep us this way or she was incapacitated.

My horror at the thought was the real first thing I'd felt all day.

Caralind was the first to reach the rear doors.

"Locked," she said, frowning. "That's odd."

"Odd," Brigid agreed grimly, "and ominous."

The sound of quick footsteps crunching through the snow made us turn to see Berthel, one of the human stable hands in our employ, frantically running toward us.

"He has taken control of the littles," she said, tears making her voice thick. "I don't know how, but he's turned them against us!"

Brigid caught her by the arms and held her steady. "Slow down, Berthel. What do you mean, taken control? Who is *he*?"

Berthel shook her head, barely able to speak. Her hair was coming loose from its knot, and her eyes were glazed with horror.

"He has the Warden trapped in her office," she said, "and somehow he's gotten hold of the littles' minds. *All* of them. They're ruthless, and much stronger than they should be. They're chasing the older Roses through the house, they've locked dozens in the barracks, and they've raided the armory." Her voice caught on a sob. "I think they've killed—"

Before she could finish the sentence, a sharp twang rang out, and an arrow hit her right in the neck. She collapsed in Brigid's arms and bled out in seconds.

"There!" Cira pointed to an upper window in one of the priory's turrets. I saw a flutter of motion, a flash of color, then nothing. Imagining any of my sweet littles as deadly snipers made my blood run cold. Our familiars scattered; with a fierce shriek, Freyda soared up to the window and dove inside, undoubtedly determined to track down the perpetrator herself.

I whirled around and kicked down the locked doors, reducing them to splintered shreds. We raced inside, ducking another two arrows shot from above.

"What in the name of the gods did she mean?" Brigid muttered angrily. Her whole front was red with blood. "Who is *he*? Is it Kilraith?"

Cira glared down the corridor, dagger in hand. "But how could he have gotten past the wards?"

"We don't know the full extent of his capabilities," I said quietly, though a terrible idea had begun to form in my mind, even more terrible than the prospect of Kilraith taking over Rosewarren. "He's gotten hold of the littles' minds, whoever he is," I murmured. "A child of Jaetris, then."

"We've got thirty littles living here right now," Brigid said. "A single person couldn't control so many minds."

"No, but if they used another mind—a strong one—as an amplifier and an anchor, they might."

Brigid glanced at me, understanding dawning on her face. "You don't think…"

But I did, and somehow I knew I was right.

He wasn't Kilraith.

He was Gareth.

So much mind to grab on to, Luthaes had said.

And someone was using it to wreak havoc among us.

"Secure the house," I said, pushing hard against my rising panic. "Disable any littles you find, but for gods' sake, try not to hurt them. Brigid, Cira, cover me."

As the others ran off down the shadowed corridors, the three of us flew upstairs toward the Warden's office. I kept my eyes straight ahead, but Brigid and Cira fought off what had to be ten different attackers, all of them with the light, quick footfalls of little girls. Every thud of a small body against the carpet—every soft grunt of pain—lit me up with a brighter fire.

When we reached the Warden's office, I rammed the door down with such force that it flew off its hinges and crashed through the windows on the opposite wall. Quickly I took in the scene. The Warden was unconscious on the floor, blood pooling beneath her head. Three littles, bound in ropes, cowered in front of the desk. Two of them cried silently; one wept into her hands.

And seated at the desk was Gareth.

His green eyes had an unnatural sheen. At our entrance, he sat back in his chair with an indolent smile.

"I was wondering when you'd get here," he said. "Took you long enough. But that's all right, we've had an excellent time all on our own."

His voice was his own, but sweat beaded at his hairline, and the tendons in his neck stood out as if he were straining against something I couldn't see.

"Who are you?" I demanded.

He put a hand to his heart. "You wound me, Mara. Or are you simply being playful? It's so hard to read you."

"We can play if you want. I like games." I scanned the room, my mind racing, my sentinel senses and godly power stretching out to find the truth. If Gareth was the puppet, where was the master?

"Oh, I know." Gareth leaned forward, chin in his hands. "He told me about how well you played in Mhorghast. You and the Vilia. Nesset, right?"

"Mara," Brigid muttered. She held her bow, a nocked arrow at the ready. I felt the anger radiating off of her and waved her quiet with a flick of my hand.

"Nesset, that's right," I said. "What a good memory you have."

"Tell me, did your trials really happen that way?" Gareth's eyes sparkled behind his glasses. The sight of something so familiar turned so evil made my bile rise. "Did you really win every single one of the Warden's games?"

Something tugged at my fingers, a resonance, like feeling the weight of someone's eyes upon you in the dark. I was close.

"I did, easily," I answered.

"And the girl, Petra. Did you really kill her? She was your friend, wasn't she?" His voice slid around its words like a snake. "Funny, that. Even we demons don't—"

He froze, but it was too late. I'd found the source of the magic sizzling at my fingertips, and with a white-hot rage, I sliced through the ropes binding the littles. The girls immediately scrambled away, but I caught one of them by her collar—the one who had been crying into her hands—and lifted her into the air with one hand. With the other, my bandaged one, I pressed the point of my dagger into her neck.

"Show yourself," I hissed.

The image of the girl flickered like a sputtering flame. A slow smile spread across her tearstained face.

"Kilraith says hello," she whispered, "and sends his compliments." Then she thrust herself onto my blade, pushing it hard into her throat.

I dropped her to the floor, watching in disgust as she choked on the rug. With her last gurgling breath, the illusion vanished, and in its place lay a woman as gorgeous and pale as Talan, with shining ash-brown curls and cunning blue eyes now frozen in death.

"A figment?" Cira asked, coming up slowly beside me.

"A demon," Brigid replied, her lip curling. She nudged the dead woman with her boot. "A greater demon, I'd say, just like Talan. A child of Zelphenia and Jaetris, blessed with an empathic mind and the power of illusion. The perfect conduit for Kilraith, especially with Gareth's mind to augment her abilities."

I hardly heard them as I slowly approached Gareth, my heart in my throat. He sat frozen at the desk, and his eyes were his own again, but he looked pale and drawn, and he gripped the edge of the wood with white-knuckled fingers.

"Hello, Gareth." I set down my weapons. "Can you hear me?"

He said nothing, not until I stepped closer to the desk and reached for him. Then it was like something inside him exploded.

He lurched to his feet and stumbled away from me, knocking over his chair. "No," he whispered. *"No!"*

"It's all right," I said, keeping my voice calm. "You're safe now."

"No, no, no." He put his head in his hands. His voice shook, full of tears and terror. "Not safe, not— *Gods*, no. Please. *Please.*"

"Gareth—"

"Don't touch me!" He staggered back, crashed into a table, and fell hard to the floor. His eyes were wild. "Don't touch me. Don't make me touch them. *Don't make me!*"

I knelt a few paces away from him, my throat aching with sadness. "I won't make you do anything. Your mind is your own."

That made him laugh. Tears leaked from his eyes. "My mind is his. It will always be his. He found me. He'll always find me." He struck his head with the heel of his hand—hard, fast, over and over. "Get out," he shouted, "get out, get *out*!"

I'd seen this before. Living as a soldier, it was inevitable. But seeing Gareth caught in the grip of this awful panic—consumed by the animal urge to fight or flee—broke my heart wide open.

"Gareth, please look at me," I said gently. I moved a step closer to him. "It's me, Mara. You trust me, don't you?"

He didn't answer me. He was too far gone, his breaths coming hard and fast. If he didn't slow them down, he would faint.

I moved closer still. "I know you trust me. I know you—" I stopped just short of saying a word I wouldn't have been able to take back. "I know you. And I know you'll believe me when I tell you that you're safe, and that I will do everything in my power to ensure that this doesn't happen to you again." I paused, then moved within reach of him. It was agony not to touch him. "Gareth?"

He clapped a hand over his mouth, sobbing so hard that he nearly choked on his own breath. He reached out to me with shaking fingers. When he found my feathered arm, he fumbled to grab hold and tugged me toward him.

"Mara, oh gods," he choked out. "What they did to me. What they did. And now again, they've done it *again*."

Holding back my own tears, I took him in my arms and folded him into the soft brown cocoon of my wings, letting him cry against the down of my breastbone. He held on to me with a grip that would leave bruises, like I was the only thing standing between him and certain death.

I rocked him gently, my cheek pressed against the hot golden crown of his head. On the other side of the room, Brigid helped the Warden sit up. Cira was herding the two hysterical littles out of the room. Distant cries of grief and screams of horror rose up the stairs to greet us, and I gently pressed my hand against Gareth's ear to shield him from the worst of it.

"I'm here," I whispered into his hair over and over. "I'm here, and I've got you. You're safe. You're *safe*. Gareth, I'm here. I'm here. I won't let them hurt you."

It was then, as he clung to me and I to him, his heart full of nightmares and my own breaking at the sight of his tears, that I knew. The certainty of it crashed down through my body and stole my breath.

I didn't want to. I knew I shouldn't. This road could only lead to sadness.

But I did.

I loved this man.

I *loved* him.

I closed my eyes, letting him keen. Witnessing this grief felt like something sacred—like it belonged to the gods of my childhood, the gods I'd once worshipped with my whole heart.

I loved Gareth Fontaine, and I didn't know what that would mean for me, for us. Once the horror of this moment passed, maybe I would manage to talk myself out of it. I hoped I would even as I prayed I wouldn't.

But I knew this much: Whatever came next, whatever evil came to find us, I would die before letting anything hurt him like this ever again.

Chapter 19

Once I'd ensured that Brigid would see to the Warden and Gareth had calmed enough to walk, I helped him to his room.

No one tried to stop me, though I felt the Warden's eyes on us as we left her office. Now that she was conscious, we had begun shifting back to our human forms. Stray feathers and fluffy bits of down littered the corridors, and the cold air raised goose bumps on my naked body. I grabbed a long gray tunic from one of our many hallway closets—at Rosewarren, fresh clothes were never very far away—and shrugged it on.

The soldier in me felt that I should be downstairs, assessing the damage and comforting the littles, all of whom had hopefully survived. But I couldn't leave Gareth's side. He walked unsteadily, and though he was no longer crying, the dead look in his eyes was somehow worse. Shattered glass glittered among the molted feathers on the floor. I walked carefully, guiding him through the wreckage and hoping we wouldn't see anything worse. Freyda joined us, hopping alongside us using any perch she could find and berating us with a constant stream of sharp chirps, clearly impatient with our progress. But I was so happy to see her alive and well that I couldn't bring myself to scold her.

The librarians' rooms were on the third floor near the servants' wing. Gareth's was small and untidy. Books and papers covered his desk and the top of his dresser. He'd left the one small window open, and a light dusting of snow coated the floor.

I helped him to his bed and then bustled about the room, stacking all the books and papers neatly in one corner, draping clothes over the back of his desk chair, pouring a fresh glass of water from the pitcher on the washbasin. When I brought it to him, he was still sitting in the exact same position on the edge of his unmade bed and staring at nothing. He took the water without looking at me, sipped it quietly for a moment, and then put it on the bedside table with a small grimace of distaste.

"If I drink any more, I'll throw up," he announced.

"That's fine," I told him. "It'll be there when you want it."

"My room is a mess. I'm sorry."

"Why? I'm not the one who has to live in it."

A small smile touched the corner of his mouth. "Fair enough."

Perhaps I should have left him then, but I was so glad to see even a hint of expression on his face that I hated the idea of walking away. I stood there awkwardly, telling myself that it was practical to stay with him. Though unlikely, some trace of the demon's influence *could* still be inside him. Leaving would be irresponsible.

"What would be most helpful to you right now?" I asked. "Food? Solitude?"

He sat there for a long moment, hands on his knees, and then at last he said quietly, "In Mhorghast, I was a plaything. Did I tell you that?"

He said it so matter-of-factly that I felt a little sick. With a sharp look and a silent gesture toward the door, I ordered Freyda to wait outside and then sat down beside him. "Not in so many words, no."

"One moment I was in the basement of the Citadel with Farrin and the others. The next, I was swept up in shadows, and when I came to, I was in a pen with dozens of other humans from across the continent. Oldens inspected us—fae, demons, a furiant, a titan, all loyal to Kilraith. One of them was Luthaes." He blew out a shaky breath. "He came for me specifically. Kilraith had sent him."

"He wanted your mind."

Gareth nodded. "The abductions weren't random. He took those he found most entertaining, or those whose absence would hurt the people he wanted to hurt."

"Like Farrin," I said quietly.

"And Ryder. Though I never saw Alastrina while I was there. I'm sure that was intentional." He stood and began pacing the little room. "Sometimes Kilraith simply wanted fodder. He took those people indiscriminately. They could have been anyone—magic, no magic, it didn't matter as long as they were warm bodies for his followers to torment. He also took *requests*."

The venom with which he spat the word gave me chills. "From his followers?"

"Whatever struck their fancy, whatever type of person they felt like hurting, whatever magic they wished to abuse and turn on others. That was their favorite pastime: turning us against each other."

He stopped at the window, his back to me. "That's where I came in."

I waited for him to continue, my body so tense it ached.

"So much mind to grab on to," murmured Gareth. "That's what Luthaes said, remember? And he was right. The body hosting Jaetris was old and weak, which weakened Jaetris himself even further. He was trapped inside his human host, a prisoner like the rest of us. But with my help, he grew stronger."

"Your mind amplified his power," I said quietly.

"And steadied his grip on the world, made it easier for him and Kilraith to play." Gareth folded his arms across his middle, still facing away from me. His voice was tired, thin. "I don't blame Jaetris. From what I gathered, he'd only recently been reborn. He hadn't had years to orient himself, as your mother had. He was vulnerable. Easy prey for Kilraith."

Gareth was quiet for a long time. His breathing quickened, and his whole body stiffened with tension.

I wanted so badly to go to him, but I stayed where I was. "Gareth, you don't have to tell me any more if—"

"But I do. I haven't told anyone, and it's killing me. I can't look at you, though. I'm sorry, I just can't bear it."

"That's fine. There's nothing to be sorry for."

He laughed. "Oh, but you're wrong. There's *so much* for me to be sorry for, but so many of the people who deserve to hear that the most are dead. And those who still live..." He shuddered. "I can't even be sure they remember what happened. Maybe hearing my apology would help them, but I won't risk unearthing memories that should stay deeply buried just for the sake of my own peace."

Finally he turned back to me. Tears ran silently down his face.

"I remember each and every one of them," he said. "Of course I do. My *fucking* brain. I remember every single person who screamed and cried and begged me for mercy. There were dozens. I cut them and made them cut each other. I beat them, I strangled them, I even forced myself on them while his followers watched and applauded."

As he spoke, my blood burned with fury. I was a soldier; I was no stranger to violence. But seeing Gareth like this, hearing his confession and trying not to imagine the terrible things he'd witnessed—that he'd *done*—was a new kind of horror.

"Sometimes Kilraith wanted me to be their tormentor," he said. "Other times he preferred to simply use me as a conduit. An amplifier, as you put it. I would sit there, held immobile, watching situations unfold as my mind gave Jaetris strength and his tendrils invaded the minds of everyone around me. I was part of the *audience*. I'd be at

Jaetris's feet while he sat on his throne, just as frozen as I was, both of us caught in the same mental prison. Sometimes Kilraith was there, and sometimes he wasn't. But thanks to the *ytheliad*, his will was just as present either way, just as irresistible."

He dragged a shaking hand roughly through his hair. "And I couldn't stop any of it," he whispered. "I tried with everything in me. But I couldn't break their hold on me. I wasn't strong enough. I was the puppet of monsters."

"That's exactly right," I said, trying to keep my voice calm. "You were the puppet of a weak resurrected god and his malevolent creation. What happened was not your fault."

Gareth shook his head, laughing a little. Fresh tears coursed down his cheeks. He ripped off his glasses and rubbed his face.

"You don't know how many times I've told myself that," he said, "but it doesn't help. Their faces are still there when I close my eyes. My hands are still the hands that hurt them." He drew in a choked breath and struck his chest with his fist. "*I* hurt them. I made them hurt each other. Kilraith and Jaetris were the puppet masters, certainly, but when those people close their eyes at night, it's my face they see. It's my violence they remember."

His voice shattered around those last few words, and he sank to his knees.

"And the same thing happened today," he whispered. "He found me. He got through your wards and found me and used me to commit more violence, and he'll do it again." He let out a single harsh sob. "I can't do this anymore. I can't, I *can't*—"

"Yes, you can," I told him, joining him on the floor. I gripped his arms and held him up. "Look at me, Gareth. Please look at me."

He did, a tear shivering on the tip of his nose. "I understand, you see, what drove you to Ghorlock. I would have been furious if you'd managed to kill yourself out there. But I would have understood."

My throat tightened, but I willed myself to remain dry-eyed, steady-voiced. "Do you remember what you told me in that cave?"

"I remember something about you being brave and beautiful and me wanting to kiss you."

That familiar twist of humor in his voice, however faint, made me smile. I ducked down to meet his eyes. "You told me Posey's death wasn't my fault."

"That's not the same thing."

"But it *is*." And I realized as I said the words that I actually believed them. Sitting here with Gareth, being his voice of reason just as he had been mine in that cave, loosened the fist of grief around my heart. It was still there, and it always would be—because of Posey, because of uncountable other losses—but with Gareth beside me, it hurt just a little less.

"No." He pushed me gently away. "You killed Posey to save her from a crueler death. What you did was an act of mercy. What I did—"

"What you did," I said firmly, "was violence against you just as surely as it was violence against those you were forced to hurt."

He slumped and sat back on his heels, staring at his hands. The only sound in the room was the soft patter of snowflakes against the window.

Finally he whispered, "How have you gone on living all this time with such memories in your head?"

"I don't know," I said honestly. "But it's been easier with you here."

My answer surprised me. With a racing heart, I watched him look up at me. He was calmer, his breathing softer. Gently he touched my cheek.

"Now is perhaps not the time," he said slowly, "to point out that you've tried to kill yourself twice since I've been here."

He was right. One attempt, quite abbreviated, interrupted by his page; the other, nearly successful, interrupted by him. Realizing this made me laugh. I couldn't help it; the sound burst out of me. None of this was funny, and yet the next thing I knew, we were both slumped back against his bed, laughing deliriously through our tears.

"All right, maybe it hasn't been *easier*," I said after a moment, wiping my face. "But I do like that you're here. I like it very much."

Gently, he took my hurt hand and rubbed soft, slow circles across my wrist. "I think that's the nicest thing you've ever said to me."

"It was bound to happen sooner or later."

"You finally succumbing to my charms, you mean?"

My heart twisted. *If only I could, Gareth.* "I'll allow you to say that only this once."

"Duly noted."

We sat in a strange, easy silence for a few moments, my hand in his and my bare legs prickling with cold. Then I said quietly, "Thank you for sharing all of that with me. You didn't have to."

He leaned his head back against the mattress and closed his eyes. "Maybe I shouldn't have. You have enough violence in your memory without me piling on my own. Gods." He rubbed his forehead, frowning. "I really shouldn't have put all of this on you. What an *ass* I am."

The idea came to me quietly and brought with it the cold echoes of my first few weeks at Rosewarren: Petra's hair, Petra's laugh. The black lake under the full moon, and my ten-year-old hand holding a blood-soaked dagger.

"Would it help if I told you about my trials?" I asked slowly. "An exchange: memories for memories, violence for violence. It would make us even."

Gareth opened his eyes to stare, as if I'd proposed something extraordinary. "Are you sure?"

I nodded, though beneath my outer calm, I was a buzzing hive of nerves. "It seems only fair." I stood and held out my hand. "Do you mind taking a short trip?"

"I'll go anywhere if you're with me." He took my hand and stood. "But shouldn't we help downstairs?"

I tried to ignore how the simple sweetness of his words made my heart race. "You shouldn't be seen for a while," I said, "not until things have calmed. You're safer with me. And they can do without me for an hour. And—"

"And you don't want to see it just yet," Gareth finished quietly.

It. The wrecked priory, the possibility of yet more death.

"Not particularly," I said.

"I don't either." He gave me a strained smile. "Do you think the Warden will send me away after this?"

I wish she would.

I pray she won't.

"She can try." I tugged lightly on his hand. "Come on. We'll take the back stairs."

The network of greenways that led us to the lake was well traveled and smooth, and the lake itself shone black and still at the heart of a secluded forest.

"The moon is always full here," I told Gareth. We stood on the shore as he took a moment to recover from the journey. "No matter where you go, as long as the lake is in sight, you can look up and see a huge white moon. But the second you lose sight of the lake, the moon snaps back into its proper phase."

"Fascinating," Gareth said quietly. "That reminds me of Wardwell. It's almost as if they exist in their own worlds—like pockets, separate from their surroundings, with their own seasons and their own configuration of time."

I understood the urge to whisper even though we were alone. It was a somber place, and despite the wind whispering through the nearby pines, the lake remained smooth as glass.

"The Warden guards this place well," I agreed. "Not once has an Olden set foot here without permission."

Gareth turned around slowly, his tired green eyes cataloging everything. "It looks exactly like the images we've constructed from our studies of the crown and the egg. I'm baffled that your searches here haven't turned up any signs of an anchor."

"Your team should conduct a search, confirm it for yourselves. I suppose it's possible we've missed something during the twenty times we've scoured this place from treetop to lake bed."

"But unlikely."

"Unlikely," I agreed.

"Does it have a name? The lake?"

"Voroth. But we never call it that. It's only ever 'the lake.'"

"And your trials were here, in this very spot?"

"Twelve years ago."

"Ten-year-old Mara." He smiled sadly. "I wish I'd known you when we were children. By the time I met Farrin, you were gone."

Over the years, I'd gotten very good at ignoring the twinge in my heart that came with remembering my childhood. But here on the shores of this lake, everything hurt more than it should have. I breathed long and slow, smoothing over the sharp ache.

"Older Roses woke us in the middle of the night and brought us here," I began, walking slowly along the shore. "We were still in our nightgowns. The Warden was waiting, and there was a bonfire, and many other Roses, all of them in masks. The games began immediately."

Gareth walked quietly beside me. "Were you afraid?"

"I felt fear, but I wasn't afraid." My chest tightened at the old memory. I'd thought of it so many times over the years that returning to it felt like settling under a familiar blanket. "Father taught me that long ago, that it was possible to feel fear and not let it make you afraid. Fear keeps you sharp, but being afraid can paralyze you."

"That sounds like Gideon Ashbourne, all right. What happened then?"

Hearing the fondness in his voice was like pressing hard on a bruise. How many days had he spent at Ivyhill over the years, attending Father's balls, pulling pranks with Gemma, swapping secrets with Farrin late into the night? Things I wished I could have enjoyed along with them. Things I would never do again—not without this sadness, this awareness of lost years looming over me.

"I had one friend among the new recruits, and I killed her," I said bluntly, my fingers trembling at my sides. Thinking of my past was always dangerous; this time it had ripped away my composure altogether. "Her name was Petra. She was unfailingly kind to me in the days before our trials. Life would have been unbearable without her. But in the end, that didn't matter. The Warden told me to kill her, and I did."

I came to a stop at the water's edge, my eyes burning as I stared across the lake at the old wooden pier. I nodded sharply at it.

"Petra didn't have magic," I said. "I told her and the others like her to wait on that pier while the rest of us distracted the hostiles—a water titan the Warden had roped into the festivities, a dozen Roses in masks. Though at first we didn't know they were Roses."

"My brave Mara," Gareth said softly.

"No. Not brave." Suddenly I didn't have the will to tell the story nicely; was it even possible for such a tale to be nice? "Petra rowed away from the pier, abandoning the others. She was terrified, I'm sure, and she made a break for it. I don't know what she thought she would do—get to the opposite shore and run? Run where? A tiny human girl alone in the Old Country?"

My voice was fraying at the edges. I blinked hard, set my jaw. "The

Warden took me up into a tree and bade me to watch. I was her favorite even then. She told me that allowing Petra to join our ranks would corrupt the Order. That she was a coward, and cowards were dangerous. She told me that I should be the one to get rid of her, that the binding magic would honor my sacrifice, strengthen the bonds between me and my fellow recruits. So during the hunting games, I did. I stabbed her in the heart and watched her die."

I laughed bitterly into the night. "I didn't want to kill her. Gods, I didn't want to. But after I did it, the Warden was so *pleased*. She told me she was proud of me, and that made everything feel a bit better. What sort of monstrous person does such a thing?"

"You weren't monstrous, Mara," Gareth said. "You were a frightened, manipulated child."

Then he touched my arm so gently that it made me unreasonably furious. Now that I'd said it aloud, my story seemed pale beside Gareth's confession, and the realization left me feeling broken with shame.

I jerked away from him and took a step back. "I'm sorry. This was a terrible idea. I don't know why I thought you needed to hear this."

"But Mara—"

"It's insulting to compare this to what you've gone through. Memories for memories, violence for violence?" I let out a harsh laugh. "I killed a girl when I didn't have to—I could have saved her and chose not to—and you had your autonomy stripped from you entirely. This is far from a fair exchange."

I started walking away, but he caught me by the arm before I could get very far.

"You know how I told you I'd be happy with you storming around being angry at me for the rest of our lives?" he said ruefully. "This is not one of those times. You can't walk away from me like this right now, not after what we've just shared."

"It's insulting to you," I muttered, staring at my dirty bare feet.

"This may seem like a radical concept, but in fact *I* get to decide what I do and do not consider an insult."

"I'm so sorry for what they did to you."

"Mara—"

"You didn't deserve it. No one does, but especially not you."

Gareth took my face gently in his hands. He was always taking my face gently in his hands, as if I were a treasure to be revered; part of me hoped he would never stop.

"You say that as if I'm some paragon of goodness," he said gently.

I looked up at him through a veil of tears. "In fact, you're a menace."

He smiled, smoothing his thumb across my jawline. "That's more like it."

Then he kissed me—so soft and sweet that it left me breathless—and for that brief, precious time in his arms, on that moonlit black beach, I let it happen. I wouldn't ever again, I told myself. But I could allow it this one last time. I could almost trick myself into some kind of happiness.

The feeling lingered all the way back to Rosewarren. A quiet heat thrummed between us, his eyes blazed every time he looked at me, and my body felt so primed to devour him that the longing was like physical pain. I knew there was work to be done; I hadn't completely lost hold of my senses. Returning to Rosewarren would mean fresh grief, which I would push aside to tend to everyone else's.

But right then, all I could think about was him—how much I wanted him, how *good* it would feel to be with him, and how I would have to somehow find it in me to turn him away forever.

Then we came within sight of the priory, and my whole body went cold with dread.

The Warden stood at the top of the snowy slope, watching our approach. And even from so far away, with her face hidden in shadow, I could feel the sting of her fury.

Chapter 20

The Warden said not a word to me until Gareth was safely back in his room—guarded by Brigid, at my request—and we were alone in her office. Once the door was closed behind us, she wasted no time getting to the point.

"How dare you," she snapped, rounding on me. "After what's just happened, you run off without telling anyone? And with the man whose mind was overtaken by a demon only three hours ago?"

At first I was too shocked to respond. I'd seen her angry many times, but I'd never—not *once*—seen her cry. And now her dark eyes shone with tears.

"I thought it best to keep him away from the others," I managed to say. "Until things settle, he's at risk."

"And, perhaps, a threat."

"The demon is dead," I said, bristling at the implication in her voice. "Gareth is no longer a danger and should be left in peace to recover."

"I didn't realize you were an expert on the subject of demonic possession."

"And I didn't realize that your vaunted wards were so deeply flawed that they would allow a demon working for the enemy to enter Rosewarren."

I took advantage of her stunned silence to press on, all the angry grief that had been brewing inside me since Posey's death bubbling to the surface. "You direct your ire at Gareth and at me when in fact it's *you* who are to blame for what's happened."

She recovered quickly, touching the fresh bandage on her forehead with shaking fingers. "Insolent child. The vast majority of demons are not like your friend Talan. They are cunning and sadistic and have very little regard for humans."

"Yes, Madam, but that does not invalidate my point."

"And I cannot be expected to stand against Kilraith's operatives all on my own."

I ignored the twinge of sympathy in my heart. "You are not on your own. You have all of us, and you have an entire team of the university's best and brightest at your disposal. But whenever anyone comes to you with a suggestion about modifying or fortifying the wards, you turn them away."

She shook her head as I spoke and finally let out a stifled harsh sob. "What if something had happened to you?"

The question was sharp, furious. And though she held her mouth in a thin line, it trembled nonetheless as she glared at me, as if she were fighting against some great simmering emotion.

Once again I was speechless. I knew how to handle an angry Warden; I knew how to argue with her. I didn't know how to stand against her tears.

"What would we all do if you were killed?" she went on. "What would *I* do without you, Mara?"

Her voice broke on that last question, and I got the terrible feeling that she was going to truly cry right there in front of me.

I cleared my throat and reached for calm. "I'm sorry for speaking so harshly. I know that you're tired and that you try your best—"

"Do you think I'm oblivious to your many reckless ventures?"

That was a blow. The boldness that had spurred me to challenge her fled, and in its place, a sick, cold feeling trickled down my body.

The Warden smiled tightly. "Yes, I can see that you did." She moved to stand behind her desk. "I've not said anything until now, though perhaps I should have. I trusted you to know your limits and to remember your duty before you went too far. But that has always been the risk of loving you: that my affection would blind me to your faults." She sighed and placed her hands flat on the desktop. "I suppose it can happen to any devoted mother."

And that—that was the thing that nearly kicked my legs out from under me.

Since the night of my trials, I'd known I was her favorite. But never had she been this candid with me, and never had she said the words I'd long ago given up hope of hearing. I wanted to be angry at her. I *was* angry at her, and more than a little afraid of her—her erratic behavior, her volatile temper, the cruelty she could so deftly deal.

But standing there before her, helpless in the grip of an embarrassing, desperate need, all I could do was whisper, "Do you love me, Madam?"

She glanced up at me irritably. "Well, of course I do, Mara. Someday I'll birth a daughter of my own blood, and I won't love her half as much as I do you. Unfortunate child. But she'll learn to live with it."

Somehow my scrambling thoughts managed to hold on to that piece of information: the Warden did not, in fact, have a secret daughter. Whether that was cause for relief or urgent worry, I couldn't decide, and I didn't care to try. My stupid, confused heart had no capacity for it.

"But the feelings of my future child are not important right now," the Warden said briskly. She sat in her chair, opened a leather packet of paper, and began writing. "What's important is giving you time and space to consider your actions and hopefully find the resolve to make better decisions in the future. And you weren't wrong tonight, even if you shouldn't have acted without consulting me: Professor Fontaine should indeed be kept out of harm's way while we tend to our dead. He'll accompany you."

"Our dead?" I said faintly.

"Three littles and five members of our household staff. No grown Roses, thank the gods." She tore out the paper she'd been writing on and folded it into crisp thirds.

Three littles. Five members of our staff. I clasped my hands behind my back so hard that my healing palm screamed with pain. But I had to hold on to *something.* My head was a mess, and my heart felt even worse. I wasn't sure whether to celebrate being sent away with Gareth or protest on behalf of my sanity.

"Where will you send us?" I asked.

"North." She sealed the letter, first with wax, then with a wordless binding spell that made my eyes water. "The Falkeron Cloisters. I've received intelligence that the monks there have been conducting their own search for Zelphenia and may have stumbled upon a lead. Here." She held out the letter. "This is for the Blessed Abbot. He's a curmudgeon obsessed with etiquette and appreciates a proper note of introduction upon receiving visitors."

But I was still stuck on the fact that the Falkeron monks had possibly found a clue as to Zelphenia's whereabouts. That they had been searching for their patron goddess didn't surprise me; after Mhorghast's destruction, word of the gods' return had spread quickly.

What *did* surprise me was that the Warden had learned about their efforts only through the Order's intelligence network.

Normally I wouldn't have hesitated to voice these thoughts to her, but after everything that had happened, it took me a moment to recover my courage. "Why didn't they share their findings with you voluntarily?"

The Warden's mouth turned down irritably at the corners. "Pride? Caution? An overblown commitment to honoring Zelphenia's secretive nature by being secretive themselves? The Blessed Abbot's deranged sense of humor? I haven't the slightest idea."

"Have they told anyone else what they've found?"

"That would be incredibly foolish of them, wouldn't it? Here." She waved the letter at me. "Leave as soon as you can. I'm sure the professor will want to bring all manner of devices so he can search for the remaining anchors during your journey, but I trust you'll be able to rein him in? You'll need to travel light and fast. It's a bad winter already up there."

I took the letter from her, an uneasy feeling niggling at the back of my mind. So many things about what had happened here today didn't feel right, and my instinct told me that if I correctly assembled them I would uncover some crucial truth. But doing so felt impossible; I didn't even know how to begin.

The Warden noticed my hesitation and looked up from her papers. Her eyes were dry, and her countenance had smoothed out to its usual impeccable state. Even her posture had improved. "You can leave now, Mara."

I picked one worry out of the dozens fighting for dominance in my mind. "With all due respect, Madam, five minutes ago you said Gareth could be dangerous and scolded me for being near him. Now you're sending us on a mission together? I don't understand."

She sighed, returning her gaze to her paper-strewn desk. "You've noticed, I'm sure, that I've not been myself of late. That incident with the fae was regrettable behavior on my part. I know it upset you, and for that I'm sorriest of all."

I went very still at the mention of Posey. Her death had *upset* me?

"Yes, Madam," I replied, my fingers clammy around the sealed letter.

"The stresses of war are wearing on me more than I'd care to admit," she continued. "I find myself to be full of contradictions these days. Rash decisions, bad judgments. I may have to rely on you more heavily, Mara, in the days to come. All of that is to say, I know very well that Professor Fontaine is no danger. I was afraid for you, and I let that fear run away with my temper and my reason. If the touch of the demon were still upon him, I'd feel it, as I feel everything that happens within these walls." She smiled sadly, her gaze distant. "I suppose I must have that baby sooner rather than later. Does that frighten you? The idea of a new Warden?"

"No, Madam," I answered honestly. "It will be an enormous change for everyone, but we will adapt, as we always do."

I felt that there was more to say, something important that crowded the back of my mouth. But I couldn't find the right words, and then the Warden was waving me away.

"Dismissed," she said, returning her attention to her papers. I knew that tone and didn't dare risk defying her when I'd already dared so much.

It wasn't until I was packing supplies in my room later that night that I understood what they'd been, those throat-crowding words. The realization crept in slowly until suddenly I had to sit down, boots in hand, stomach in knots, and let the feeling fill me.

No, the idea of a new Warden doesn't frighten me.

What frightens me is you.

And what I become, what I'm reduced to, when I'm around you.

Chapter 21

For our journey north, the Warden gave us permission to use her own private greenways, which I'd never set foot in before. They were strong and smooth; traveling through them was like sliding into a warm, easy sleep.

But they only went as far as Alderfeld, a small town that hardly deserved the designation. Comprising a smattering of cabins and an admittedly excellent inn, it stood in the northernmost reaches of the Spine of Caiathos, a mountain range that spanned the entire length of the continent. From there, we would have to travel the rest of the way to the Falkeron Cloisters by horseback, on a path well-trodden by the faithful. If we followed this same path to the southwest, we would eventually reach Vallenvoren, the town where we had all stayed on the way to Wardwell—though of course at the time, we'd had no idea what we were walking toward.

Thinking of those first moments in Wardwell was always bittersweet. My sisters and I had followed a strange voice through the snowy northern forest until we'd emerged into a much sweeter and greener wood near a cottage surrounded by flowers.

And there Mother had stood, her arms open, as if welcoming us home at last. Upon seeing her for the first time in twelve years, I'd at first felt only incredible relief. It was like I was ten years old all over again. My mother was alive after all, and somehow she would mend everything.

Then Farrin had struck her with a staff, and we'd all watched in horror as her shattered face had knitted itself back together. After that, after hearing her wild story, everything had changed, for all of us.

"It seems to me," Gareth said beside me, kicking his snowy boots against the doorframe, "that the Warden should have a greenway that leads directly to the Cloisters, yes? So we could avoid all this wintry trudging?"

His wry voice brought me back to the present, where the mountain winds howled. Even though I wore fur-trimmed sealskin boots, I could barely feel my feet. I shook off the memory of Mother and the ache of missing her—an ache that had been my constant companion for twelve years and showed no signs of abating—and followed Gareth inside the Order safe house where we would spend the night.

It was small, meant to house only the Warden and not an entire squadron of Roses. But it was well made and well stocked and stood strong against the elements. The snowstorm had come upon us quickly, chasing us past the alluring sight of Alderfeld's cheerfully lit windows and into the dark pine forest beyond, where we used a starstone beacon to light our way. I wondered if this was an ordinary winter storm or the result of some Mistland breach hundreds of miles south. But this far north, and in the roaring darkness of the night, it was impossible to tell.

I tried not to imagine what was happening down there—in the Mistlands, and at Rosewarren. Who was on patrol? What was the mood in the barracks after yesterday's slaughter?

And would it happen again? Our fortress had been breached for the first time since I'd arrived there, and at the moment my overstuffed mind couldn't recall one bit of Order history. Had Rosewarren *ever* been breached before? Was this the beginning of the end?

I startled at the gentle weight of Gareth's hand on my arm.

"Are you all right?" he asked quietly. "I feel like you went somewhere far away just now."

I reached into my pocket for matches and moved away from him. Since leaving the Warden's office, I'd felt raw and unsettled, and the bitter cold made everything feel worse. I longed for Freyda, who had obeyed my order to remain at Rosewarren only after giving me a sharp mutinous bite on my right thumb. After everything that had happened, I refused to risk her life on such a hard journey. And she was exceptionally gentle with children; the grieving littles would appreciate her company.

"I'm fine," I replied. "Just tired. And she used to have one, actually." I crouched before the cast-iron stove, which was full of fresh wood. "A greenway that led straight to Falkeron, I mean. There were five, one for each of the Cloisters. But the most recent Council of Abbots made her dismantle them."

"Claiming that no one, not even the Warden, was entitled to travel to and from the Cloisters at their leisure?"

"Something like that." I shook out a match and stood, watching the wood catch fire. "It's a small room. It should warm up quickly."

For a long time I gazed at the snapping flames, listening to Gareth unpack our supplies behind me. I heard the exact moment he noticed the room's only bed; the sounds of his industrious bustling fell abruptly silent.

"Don't worry," I said without turning around. "I'm perfectly happy to sleep on the floor. I'm more used to sleeping in strange places than you are. And it's warmer by the stove anyway."

"Ah. I see." He stepped toward me, then hesitated, then took another step, then hesitated again before clearing his throat. "Well, at the risk of seeming indelicate, or perhaps simply far too bold—"

"I can't," I whispered, my eyes watering from the heat of the growing fire. Or so I told myself. "We *can't*, Gareth."

"Darling, trust me, after the past couple of days, there is nothing I want more in this world than a good night's sleep. I promise I won't keep you awake with chatter or snoring or other untoward behavior."

"Don't do that." I finally tore my gaze away from the fire and looked at him. "Stop calling me *darling*."

He blinked at me behind his glasses, looking owlishly charming in his snowy furs and the flickering golden light. "All right. I will. I'm sorry, I didn't think—"

"No. You didn't."

He scratched the back of his head and looked away, frowning. "I'm sorry, Mara. I didn't mean to overstep. It's only that I—"

"Fine. Good." I found a blanket in the corner cupboard and began setting it up near the fire. My fingers shook as I worked; I felt like I was going to burst. Focusing on each small step of the task helped me keep ahold of myself: unfold the blanket, shake it out, fold it neatly in front of the fire, take off your boots, don't cry, keep breathing.

The whole time, Gareth watched me. When I heard him start moving about again, I thought maybe he'd given up and would go to sleep without another word.

But instead he came over and crouched beside me. "What's happening here? Are you angry at me?"

"I should think the answer is obvious," I snapped.

"Well, it isn't."

"Surely you and your brilliant brain can figure it out."

"This may come as a shock to you, but when it comes to matters of the heart, my brilliant brain is decidedly less so."

I tossed my boots aside. "Is everything a joke to you?"

"Oh, yes. For example, my imprisonment and captivity were loads of fun."

"Don't try to shame me like that. You know that's not what I mean."

"No, quite frankly, I don't know *what* you mean, about anything." He stood and walked away, dragging his hands through his hair. "This keeps happening. We share something—a moment, a tragedy, a look, a kiss—and I think maybe, just maybe, you feel even the barest hint of what I feel for you. And then you completely close yourself off to me. You treat me like I've done something wrong when I know I haven't. Why?"

Listening to him, I could hardly breathe. All I could do was sit there on the floor and search for words that wouldn't come.

He watched me, waiting, until finally his shoulders sagged and the light went out of his eyes. He nodded to himself and made for the bed, shrugging off his coat. Something about the way he held himself, like all the hope had been torn out of him, made me panic. If we fell asleep like this, I would lose him. The thought terrified me. And yet I *wanted* to lose him, didn't I?

"I'm trying to do what's best," I blurted out.

He sat on the edge of the bed, elbows on his knees, and regarded me evenly. "I don't know what that means."

"It means..." I shook my head and pressed my lips together, looking around the room as if I'd find the answer somewhere on the walls. But there was no answer. Whatever choice I made, there would be only heartbreak.

"I'm too afraid to tell you," I whispered.

"Well, we can't go on like this, can we?"

"Can't we?"

"I can't. My heart can't bear it."

The resigned sadness in his voice shattered my resolve. The whole wild world had narrowed down to this single room, this single man, and the tidy fire burning steadily at my back. I was too close to it; I felt like I was boiling and would soon spill over. I could no longer pretend nothing was wrong. *Everything* was wrong.

"And neither can mine!" The words burst out of me. "No matter what I do here, it will hurt me, and I'm tired of hurting, Gareth."

I drew in a ragged breath. My throat was so tight that it was hard to speak.

"With the exception of the few living people left whom I truly love," I said, "I have lost everything dear to me. My home, my family. Lovers, friends. My freedom. And then you saunter into my life with your books and your glasses, and that godsdamned arrogant smile, and that hair that you're forever running your hands through."

I couldn't properly see him anymore. Through the shimmer of my tears, I could make out only the blurry shape of his body amongst the warm shadows.

"And your brilliant brain," I went on, wiping my face, "and how kind you are to me, and to my sister. How good and patient and diligent you are with your colleagues, and how brave you are, how completely heedless of your own safety."

He returned to the fire and knelt beside me, gently taking my hands in his. "That sounds an awful lot like someone else I know."

"And you make me laugh. I'll never forget that feeling of dancing with you at the ball. I'd not laughed in so long. I'm not very good at it."

He touched my face with the backs of his fingers. "You're good at everything, and I won't hear any different."

I shook my head and reached up to cover his hand with my own—my hurt one, still bandaged, still tender. For the rest of my life, I would see my scarred hand and remember the fae tree, and how he'd shouted up at me as we climbed, refusing to let me give up.

"I'm not good at this," I said desperately.

"Neither am I." He sat back on his heels with a smile. "What a splendid match we are."

"A monster," I whispered, "and a menace."

"A menace I most certainly am, but you are *not* a monster."

"You thought I was when I killed Luthaes." I looked up at him, steeling myself against the memory. "I saw your face after I bludgeoned him."

"Well, I'd just nearly been killed, and yes, it startled me, but—"

My heart sank. I started to move away. "You see?"

"*But,*" he continued quickly, turning me back to him, "he deserved it. And you saved me. I just don't have a strong stomach, I'm afraid." He smiled, his expression as tender as a spring morning. "Although it's gotten stronger, these last few weeks. So much of me has grown stronger, and that's all because of you."

I laughed sadly. "Because you've had to adapt to survive around me."

"No—godsdamn it, Mara. It's because everything about you makes me want to be better than I am." He cupped my face in his hands, then shifted to his knees and drew me up along with him. "You make me want to work harder, fight harder, love harder than I ever have before. You're so full of goodness that you lift up everyone around you simply by existing."

"It's too dangerous."

"What is? Love?"

I nodded miserably into the cradle of his hands, working so hard to stifle my rising sadness that my whole body ached.

"Isn't it fitting, then," he said gently, "in this world of horrors, to push back against all that danger with some of our own?"

That strange, perfect logic was my undoing. I leaned into him and pressed my forehead against his. His skin was so warm and smooth that I could barely resist nuzzling him.

"I can't lose anything else," I whispered.

"And I can't promise you won't lose me to something neither of us can control," he said back to me, his voice quiet and grave, only a slight tremble belying his outward calm. "But what I can promise you is that however many days are left to me, I will love you for all of them."

For a moment, all I could do was look at him—his eyes, so close to mine, green and fierce and earnest; the lone blond curl kissing the corner of his glasses. Just outside the door, the snowstorm raged on, and any day—tomorrow, next week, next year—could bring the end. For us, for everyone. But in this house, the air was warm and quiet, the fire crackled steadily, and we were safe. For at least this night, we were safe, and as I beheld the gorgeous, brilliant, infuriating man before me, the last stubborn barrier inside me gave way.

"Gareth," I whispered with a little sob, and then I leaned in and kissed him—softly, inelegantly, trying and failing to gather some semblance of composure. Tears rolled silently down my cheeks and onto his fingers, and after a moment I had to pull back from him and catch my breath.

As I rested my head against his shoulder, he stroked my hair in its messy bun, tenderly smoothing back the loose, tangled strands. He kissed the skin behind my ear, then worked his way down my neck—softly, carefully—until I'd fully melted into his embrace. He cupped the back of my head with one hand and held my waist with the other, and I leaned back and let him explore.

His kisses were long and slow, luxurious, unhurried, so light and sweet against my skin that each new caress left me more desperate for the next one. He kissed the hollow of my throat, his breath hot against my collarbone. He brushed his lips against my cheeks and the corners of my mouth, then gently pulled my lower lip between his teeth.

The tender little bite made me cry out softly and raised goose bumps all down my body, which delighted him. He hummed a low, satisfied sound and worked his way down my neck with softer and softer kisses while deftly undoing the ties of my coat. I slid my hands into his hair and wound my fingers through it, holding him to me, and when he could go no farther, he said roughly against my skin, "Mara, the idea of unraveling you slowly, taking you apart piece by piece, drives me wild. I've dreamt of nothing else for weeks, but..."

I bowed my head over his and murmured into his hair, "But you want me now."

He pressed a kiss to the exposed skin right above my collar. His hands tightened around me. "Yes," he said. "*Gods*, yes."

The sheer rasping *want* in his voice made me shudder in his arms. I closed my eyes, smiling a little, and whispered, "Then have me."

Suddenly the fire that had been kindling between us blazed eagerly to life. I brought him back to me with a sharp tug of his hair, and he laughed breathlessly against my mouth and kissed me with such hunger that I felt dizzy. When he pulled me to my feet, I swayed a little, which for a moment embarrassed me. I wasn't used to clumsiness, had barely fumbled even a single step in my entire life.

But then Gareth caught me, and I felt the hard length of him against my thigh, and that was the last time I thought about anything beyond my aching need for him to touch me.

I tugged off my coat and let it fall to the floor. He started unbuttoning his shirt, but he wasn't fast enough. I helped him, leaning into him, laughing a little against his cheek as he cursed breathlessly, something about the uselessness of buttons. Together we slid off his shirt, and then I dragged my hands down his torso. He shuddered at my touch and took a staggering step back toward the bed. I followed him, tugging his undershirt out of his trousers.

"I don't know what's worse," I said, "buttons or winter layers."

"It's all terrible," he agreed, and then my fingers touched the warm bare skin of his abdomen, and he jerked against my touch and let out a groan that nearly brought me to my knees. Before I lost all control of my shaking legs, I stepped back from him to peel off my trousers, my tights, my socks. Once my legs were completely bare, he sank onto the edge of the bed and pulled me back to him.

"Look at you," he whispered, his hands on my naked hips. "Look at how exquisite you are." He pulled me even closer, nuzzled beneath my tunic, nudged up my undershirt, and kissed the trembling skin below my navel. His hands drifted down my legs and then back up, tracing the shape of my rose tattoo. Just when I thought I would scream from impatience, he kissed my stomach once more, his breath shaky against my skin, and gently pushed open my trembling thighs to circle his thumb against the hottest, wettest part of me. I cried out and arched my hips toward him, clutching at his shoulders to hold myself up.

"*Gods*, you're..." His voice broke on the words. "You're perfect. You're a vision, Mara. You're more beautiful than the moon." With each sentence, he pressed a kiss against the crease of my thigh, and then he looked up at me. His lips were swollen from our kisses, his cheeks were flushed, and his hair was already an absolute disaster.

I'd never wanted anything as desperately as I wanted him—more of him, all of him. Again and again.

"I think," he said slowly, with a little grin, "that you might perhaps be ready for me. Possibly. Though confirming it might take more investigation."

"You idiot," I gasped out, bracing myself against him as he slid a finger inside me, then another. "If you don't have your way with me in the next five seconds—"

"You'll explode?" He laughed, holding my hips firmly in place as he worked me expertly with his fingers. "That *is* the general idea, darling."

He started moving faster, deeper, fisting my tunic in his other hand to pull me even closer. When he found just the right spot inside me, my knees nearly gave out, and my breath hitched around a little sob.

"Gareth, *please*—"

"Agreed," he said breathlessly, with a choked little laugh. He rose shakily to his feet, fumbling at his belt as I tugged off my tunic and undershirt, and when he pulled me back toward him and my bare skin finally met his, I nearly lost myself right then and there. I slid my arms around his neck and kissed him, opening my mouth to his tongue. He moved back toward the bed until he hit the mattress, tore off his glasses and tossed them onto his forgotten clothes, then sank down upon the bed and pulled me on top of him.

I clung to him, my arms tight around his neck, and started moving slowly, sliding up and down against his hard length—not letting him enter just yet, tormenting both of us. Each time I moved, his arousal pressed against me in just the right spot and brought me a little closer to the edge.

"You," he murmured against my breasts, "are going to kill me."

I smiled and started to reply—to tease him, to make him all the more ravenous for me—but then he flicked his tongue across one of my nipples and took it in his mouth, sucking gently, and my mind went blank.

"Keep doing that," I whispered, and then I reached down to take hold of him—hot, eager, hard as iron and soft as velvet—and slowly sank onto him. Once I'd settled fully against him, he stilled and clutched my hips hard.

"Just a moment," he said, his voice muffled against me.

I traced the line of his jaw and lifted his chin so I could see his eyes.

"Has the rogue librarian, master of sex and seducer of women, finally met his match?" I crooned.

"Absolutely," he replied at once, fervently, "in every possible way." His eyes, still locked on me, were dark with desire. I slid my arms back around his neck, my heart fluttering with anticipation, and started to move.

At first I was slow, deliberate, concentrating on memorizing every detail of this moment, of him, of us. His kisses on my breasts, tender one moment and ravenous the next. His hands on my thighs, the soft scrape of his teeth. The maddening drag of pleasure every time I lifted myself up his length and then sank slowly back down, letting him fill me.

"Gods, you feel good," he whispered hoarsely. "You feel like all the light that exists in the world, and none of the shadows."

His trembling voice melted me. I curled my fingers into his hair, kissed the nearest smooth lock of it. Then he slid one of his hands up to circle the back of my neck—insistent, questing, profoundly gentle—and that slight pressure left me completely undone. This was not enough—not fast enough, not hard enough. The ache between my legs was almost unbearable; I needed more.

I started moving faster, and immediately he tightened his grip on me, his fingers digging into me, helping me ride him. His skin was slick under my palms and blazingly hot, and with each wet slap of my hips against his, I felt like I was going a little more mad. His body ground against me in just the right spot, and gods, he was strong, tireless. Soon I barely had to move; it was all him, pulling me down again and again, slamming our hips together.

I wrapped my arms around his neck and tucked my head against his, bearing down on him as much as I could, desperate for more. I murmured it against his ear—*more, more*. I was rising, everything inside me was rising, building toward completion. I clenched around him, gasping, every inch of my body prickling, gathering, trembling. My sense of rhythm had disappeared. I was helpless in his arms, my hips spasming against his.

"Yes, Mara," he groaned against my neck, "that's it, darling. Move on me. Let it come. I'm right behind you."

I began to shake, and he held me even more tightly to him, not letting me ease up on the breathless, blinding pleasure breaking open inside me. His thrusts grew erratic—sharper, harder. He murmured over and over, each word rougher than the last, "Beautiful, you're so beautiful, yes, Mara, *yes*, that's it," and when I finally came, the pleasure, the euphoric relief, was so overwhelming that I nearly blacked out. I held on to him and cried out into his hair, gasping for breath, and not long after, he buried his face in my neck and finished inside me with a groan, my name on his lips—an incantation, a prayer.

He was right: he couldn't promise I wouldn't lose him, nor could I promise him the same.

But this—this passion between us, this instinctive understanding, the glory of finding happiness and clinging to it, no matter the danger—that was a promise we both could make. Unspoken and unbreakable.

We held each other for so long that my soaked skin cooled and I started to shiver, but even then I didn't want to let go of him.

"Lie down with me, Mara," he said at last, tenderly. "Let me hold you." Then he helped me off of his lap and guided me into bed beside him, and once we were settled and snug, I finally felt like it was safe enough to look at him—that he wouldn't disappear, or be ripped away from me by some unnamed disaster waiting in the shadows.

I smoothed my thumb against his jaw. His stubble was coming in. I'd never seen it before. The last few days, I supposed, hadn't allowed him the chance to shave. The sensation of it scraping against the pad of my thumb was unbearably sweet.

"What?" He smiled at me, soft and sleepy, his eyes shining as his gaze moved across my face. Then he turned his face to my palm and kissed it. "Gods, you're an absolute love-mussed mess," he murmured against my skin. "I've never seen anything so utterly beguiling in my entire life."

"You and your clever tongue," I whispered. "What can I say after that? After any of this?" I trailed my fingers softly through his hair, pressed a soft kiss to his lips, and lingered there, nuzzling my cheek against his.

"That, right there," he said, drawing me gently against him. "That's more than enough."

He was deliciously warm, and he smelled of me, of us, of sex and sweat. I nestled against his chest, feeling small and safe in his arms, quiet in heart and mind for the first time in as long as I could remember. While the fire crackled on, I listened to the rise and fall of his breathing, basked in the caress of his fingers drawing lazy circles on my back—softly, softer, slowing—and let myself drift into sleep.

Chapter 22

When I woke, the fire was nothing but embers, and though snow and sleet still pattered lightly against the roof and the windows, the howling wind had died down. Through the shutters I could see only inky darkness: not yet morning. I'd never felt such relief in my life.

I lay there for a long time in Gareth's arms, listening to him breathe. We'd hardly moved as we slept. I wished I never had to move again. His chest underneath my cheek, his thigh resting between my legs, his arm draped loosely across my back—every bit of him was solid and warm. I felt like a sated cat, curled up with a belly full of cream.

But if we awakened to a frigid room in the morning, leaving our little sanctuary would be even more unbearable. I carefully slipped out of his embrace and padded naked to the stove to rekindle the fire. The floor was like ice under my feet, but I waited until the flames had caught and were crackling steadily before I turned back to the bed.

Gareth was watching me with the dearest, dreamiest smile on his face. "I can't see you that well without my glasses," he said softly, "but even as a blur, you take my breath away. A very shapely blur, I should say."

I retrieved his glasses from where they'd fallen and climbed back into bed. Straddling him, I slid his glasses on, then sat back a little and grinned. "What about now?"

"Hmm. Well, let me see." He put his hands behind his head and adopted an undeniably professorial expression. "This requires serious consideration."

"You take your job very seriously, it seems."

"Impossible not to when the subject at hand is so enticing."

His gaze raked down my body with unabashed desire. I circled my hips gently against his, relishing how hard he was.

"Well, Professor?" I murmured. "Do I pass muster?"

"In fact, you're exemplary."

I wrinkled my nose. "That's far too academic a word."

"What about resplendent?" He shifted me slightly and sat up, his arm hooked around my waist, and started pressing soft kisses to my wrist, my forearm, the crook of my elbow.

"Ravishing?" he suggested. "Irresistible?"

The low murmur of his voice against my skin made me shiver. "An improvement, certainly, but I think you can do even better."

I'd barely said the words before he cupped the back of my neck with his hand and brought my lips down to his with a hungry little growl. The air was freezing, but wherever he touched my chilled skin felt like a warm kiss of sunshine: his mouth on mine, his thighs hard and lean beneath me. Then he palmed one of my breasts and gently pinched my nipple, and a searing jolt of pleasure made me break away from him, gasping, and reach down for the blankets that separated us. I was soaked and aching, ready to pull him free and ride him until I saw stars.

But he stopped me with a hand on my wrist and pulled back, breathing hard, with a bashful smile.

"As much as I want you to do exactly what you were about to do," he said, his voice low and rough, "I have a request to make. It may sound silly, but I fell asleep thinking about it, and I did tell you I've dreamt about loving you slowly."

His words conjured images that made me even more desperate for him, but somehow I managed to control myself and keep my hands above the blankets. "I do recall something about you wanting to worship me."

"For hours," he added. "An important detail."

"Well, then? I'm listening." I canted my hips forward just enough to make him a little bit sorry for the delay. He groaned sharply and leaned into me with a breathy laugh.

"You don't play fair," he said, kissing my shoulder.

"Make your request before I get tired of you and go back to sleep."

At that, he slid one hand down my abdomen to dip his fingers between my legs. I cried out sharply at his touch—fire kissing fire—and grabbed on to him, and he looked up at me with a smug grin.

"Tired of me?" he said. "Somehow I don't think that will happen."

"Such arrogance."

"But is it really arrogance if it's true?"

I pressed my forehead against his, leaning into him. "*Gareth*, either ask me your question or lay me back on this bed and—"

"Do you have a comb?"

I pulled back a little, blinking at him. "A comb."

"I forgot mine, and I'd like to..." He gave me a rueful smile. "I'd like to brush your hair."

"You're joking."

"I am entirely serious. Your hair is beautiful, Mara, and there are so many ways I'd like to love you. This is one of them."

My instinct was to tease him for that, but the sincerity on his face made me bite my tongue. I climbed off him, went to my bag, and brought him one of the wooden combs I always carried with me while traveling, small enough to fit in a pocket.

I handed it to him, feeling suddenly shy. I knew how to have sex. I wasn't sure I knew how to do whatever this was.

"Where do you want me?" I asked.

He shifted back on the bed and patted the mattress in front of him. "Right here, with your back to me."

I obeyed with a frown I couldn't quite hide. "You're very eager."

"I want to spoil you," he replied. "Is that such a terrible thing?"

I didn't know how to answer him. My parents had spoiled me when I was a child, I supposed, but my memories of them from Ivyhill were patchy, hazy, and the thought of the Warden ever spoiling any of us Roses was laughable.

"No, I suppose not," I answered, but I felt stupidly tense sitting there before him, waiting for him to begin, and when he first touched my hair, I actually flinched.

He stopped at once. "Are you all right? If you're uncomfortable, I don't have to do this."

"I'm not uncomfortable," I lied. "Just a little cold. Keep going."

I steeled myself, determined to be the most unflappable person ever to have been spoiled by a librarian with a comb. Slowly, Gareth began untying my hair from its sloppy bun. After our long day of travel, then making love with him and sleeping smashed up against him, it was an absolute mess.

But Gareth was patient, and exceedingly gentle, and by the time my tangled hair hung loose down my back, I felt a little less like a cornered animal.

He pressed a kiss to my bare shoulder. "Can I keep going?"

I nodded, forcing myself to at least try and relax, which at first felt impossible. Even the soft strokes of the comb through the less tangled parts of my hair jarred me.

But then he encountered trickier knots, and instead of just yanking the comb through them until they cooperated—my personal strategy of choice—he grew even gentler. When the comb hit a knot that needed extra care, he tried instead to untangle it with his fingers.

It was then that I started wondering if somewhere in Gareth's gods-blessed brain he possessed a trace of empathic powers and was using them to placate me, because surely no one could have such a delicate touch as this. He worked through every last one of my tangles with careful focus. Whenever his fingers brushed against my nape, he followed the caress with a soft kiss between my shoulder blades.

Soon I closed my eyes and let my chin droop. Once he saw to every tangle, he started drawing the comb down through my hair in long, slow strokes. I shivered, goose bumps erupting all over my body.

He kissed the crown of my head, a low sound of satisfaction rumbling in his chest. "I can't describe how delighted I am to see you enjoying this."

I mumbled some kind of agreement, which made him laugh, and once my hair felt like a smooth waterfall cascading down my back, he threaded his fingers through it and started massaging my scalp.

I let out a mortifyingly erotic cry, like he'd just put his head between my legs, not his fingers into my hair. But my embarrassment disappeared immediately, and all I could do was tilt my head back and lean into his touch. The slow circling pressure of his fingers completely unspooled me, melting away every bit of tension in my body. By the time he moved his hands down to my shoulders and started gently kneading them, I felt certain I was about to start crying.

"Are you all right?" Gareth murmured.

I shook my head helplessly. "I've never felt anything like this before. Nobody has ever..."

I couldn't finish the sentence. It felt too sad for such a moment. Instead I gave myself up to the bliss of his hands until I could no longer bear the thought of keeping my back to him for even one more second.

When I turned around and took his face in my hands, he frowned a little and brought his hands up to cover mine.

"You're crying," he said. "Do you want to talk—"

"No." I smoothed my thumbs across his stubbled cheeks. He looked so dear in the firelight, so handsome and golden, and suddenly I needed him—on me, in me, beside me, all of it. All of *him*.

"I want *you*," I whispered. Then I kissed him, and he slid his arms around me with a groan, and when he laid me back against the bed, I felt giddy, drunk, as warm and soft as I'd ever been. He kissed his way down my body and settled between my legs with a deep, contented sigh. The sound nearly finished me before he'd even begun. Then he buried his face between my thighs and put his mouth on me, slow and soft, as tender and thorough as he'd been with my hair. My eyelids fluttered shut. I threaded my fingers through his messy golden curls, arched up against him, and let him have me.

⟡

The Falkeron Cloisters sat atop seaside cliffs on the smallest of the Northern Isles. Every other settlement on these islands was a ramble of cozy stone cottages, weather-beaten piers, and crooked cobblestone roads strewn with sand and bits of seashells, but the Cloisters were all straight lines and orderly paths, not a stray weed or pebble to be found. Constructed of the dark gray stone native to the northern coastlines, the holy buildings loomed forbiddingly over the crashing waves below.

And even though it was entirely irrational, as the oar strokes of our hired sailor brought us closer and closer to the island and the severe square turrets of the Cloisters grew larger, I felt a twinge of unease deep in my gut.

There was no need for nerves. The Order enjoyed a comfortable relationship with the continent's five monasteries. The Warden visited each of them at least once a year and called upon the Falkeron Cloisters much more frequently than that.

The joke among us Roses was that the frigid, unfriendly climate of these harsh northern islands suited the Warden's personality better than any other place in the world. Brigid's and my private theory was that she had chosen the Blessed Abbot to father her child—the future leader of the Order—and that she frequented the Cloisters because of her and the abbot's salacious trysts.

Besides all of that, the monks here at Falkeron were renowned for their hospitality. Those intrepid faithful who made the trek here to pay tribute to the gods or to learn from the monks were welcomed, housed, and fed without question.

And yet a chill kissed my nape as our little boat approached the rocky, snow-dusted shore.

"Why do I feel like I'm being frowned at by an especially stern teacher?" Gareth murmured, gazing up at the monastery's towers.

"Oh, not to worry, sir," our hired sailor replied happily. She was a hardy, ruddy-cheeked woman who seemed more at home on the water than most people did on land. "The Cloisters cut a mean figure there—as they should, I would say, so as to remind us of the mighty power we come from—but the holy fellowship is always happy to receive the faithful. In fact, the Blessed Abbot is quite famous up here for his beef stew. Warms you up fierce on these winter nights."

"I do love a good stew," Gareth replied.

"As does anyone with a pulse and a brain, I would think, sir."

"Indeed."

As they continued their conversation about stews—which was their favorite, and why, and what ideal "stew weather" was, and various notable stews they'd each consumed—I resisted the urge to reach over and wipe Gareth's glasses clean. It had taken us all day to reach our destination, and we'd been lucky; only now was it beginning to snow. Fresh, fat flakes dotted his fur-trimmed hood, and melted ones spattered his lenses, but he didn't seem to mind.

I both envied and resented his ability to act as though nothing had changed, as if the world we occupied today was the same as it had been yesterday.

Yesterday, I'd been determined to quash any and all feelings of love for Gareth Fontaine.

Today, no matter how diligently I tried to steer my thoughts elsewhere, I couldn't stop thinking about his hands on my body, his lips on mine, how his voice had fractured around my name as he'd finished inside me. *However many days are left to me, I will love you for all of them.*

That memory, more than anything else, was the one that made my chest quietly seize up every time I came back to it. I closed my eyes, the harsh sea wind nipping at my cheeks.

What would this mean for us?

Would the days ahead now become even more difficult to bear?

I knew how Gareth would answer that question: *What if loving each other makes the days to come* easier *to bear?*

Maybe my years in the Order had made me too cynical, but trying to wrap my mind around that idea felt like trying to grab hold of a wriggling fish. Last night, wrapped up in the haze of my desire, I'd relented in the face of his hopeful logic.

But now, in the harsh light of day, miles away from that cozy little cabin, it was taking all my strength not to let my thoughts tumble somewhere dark and cruel.

I was a fool for letting this happen.

If he really loved me, he would have abandoned the idea forever upon seeing my hesitation.

I was a fool.

We're at war, and I cannot let anything distract me from my duty.

Someone will kill him, or me, and the one left alive will never recover.

I am a fool.

And so is he.

Our boat softly knocking against the wooden dock wrenched my thoughts back to the present. Gareth was already standing a few paces down the pier, looking back at me curiously.

I hefted my bag over my shoulder, offered the sailor a pouch of extra coin, and lightly jumped up onto the dock with a barely courteous good-bye. The sailor stared after me in wonder; I suspected not many of her passengers chose to eschew the ladder.

"I shouldn't have done that," I muttered, joining Gareth. "She'll remember us now."

"Given our gorgeous faces, she would have anyway," Gareth said lightly. "And besides, why does it matter? As far as I understand it, our mission isn't covert. Unless you've neglected to tell me something?"

I bit back a curt reply. "I've kept nothing from you. I suppose I'm just not used to traveling like this."

"With the man you love?"

The words jolted me, but I kept staring straight ahead at the path before us—a tidy switchback that climbed up the grassy slope. *With the man I love.* I held the words in my mouth but couldn't imagine actually saying them. The very idea of them felt dangerous, even as part of me warmed to hear the easy affection in Gareth's voice—the foolish part of me, the part I'd carefully paved over with years of stone, the part that it seemed I could no longer ignore.

"Without any Roses," I replied. "Solo missions are rare. Too dangerous."

For a moment, Gareth walked beside me in silence. Then he said quietly, "Don't do that, Mara."

"Do what?" I said, even though I knew very well what.

"Push me away."

"All I did was answer your question."

He came around to stand in front of me. His jaw was square, and his eyes were bright with green fire. "I'm not letting you walk away from this, from us. Not after what we shared."

I moved past him and continued up the path, my heart in knots. "I'm not walking away from anything. I'm answering your question."

"You're being deliberately obtuse, and it's insulting and unkind."

"I'm just trying to focus on our mission."

He blew out a sharp breath. "You're afraid. And you're letting it control you. You're letting it *win*."

I stopped abruptly on a square landing of stone and hard-packed sand, upon which stood a simple stone bench.

"Those are my father's words," I said, glaring at him.

Gareth cocked an eyebrow. "And I'm not allowed to repeat them?"

"That's not what I meant."

"What *do* you mean?"

My frustration left me boiling, and I couldn't decide where to direct it—at him, or at myself. "I told you this yesterday. I *told* you this is too dangerous."

"What's too dangerous?" Gareth spread his arms wide, as if to encompass the entire island. "This path we're climbing? The northern seas? The Mist? The war?"

He was baiting me. A challenge glinted in his eyes, and the word he wanted to say hung in the air between us, buzzing against my skin. But I couldn't say it; all my instincts screamed with panic.

And yet my body swayed toward him, pulled by the echo of his hands on my skin, by how easy it would be to let him—let this overwhelming, relentless yearning—take me somewhere I'd never been. The ache in my chest felt like the pain that accompanied my daydreams of Ivyhill—the home I had lost, the life I'd never had the chance to live. It was the same desperate, hopeful, hopeless feeling: *This is a thing I want. This is a thing I can never have.*

I drew in a shaky breath, fighting for control of my tongue. The slopes of Falkeron were not the place for this conversation. "Gareth, I know you think this is all very simple and obvious, and that it's absurd of me to be afraid, but—"

"Not absurd." He came to me and took my gloved hands in his. "Just unnecessary. Yesterday I promised I would love you for the rest of my days. Yesterday you agreed to love me too. I know you didn't say it with your words, but you did with your body, with your every touch."

"Yesterday I was weak," I said helplessly. "And I can't enter the Cloisters, or protect my sisters, or fight a war with all of this whirling about in my head. Which is the *problem*, Gareth, can't you see that?"

"No, that's not the problem."

I ripped my hands out of his and stepped back. The *nerve* he had to stand there and dictate what we were, what I felt, what I should and shouldn't be afraid of.

"You spend one night with me," I said tightly, "and think you understand my feelings better than I do?"

He gave me an unhappy little smile. "I didn't say that. But I think I understand you better than you give me credit for."

"You couldn't possibly." It was as though someone was yanking the words out of my gut; I couldn't stop them, even though I knew they were unfair. "You haven't been through what I have. You had parents, a home, a life."

Gareth's face shuttered. "A home I hated and a life I couldn't wait to escape."

I pounced on that, desperate to regain my footing. It seemed that I only ever lost my footing around him—a warning sign I'd ignored for weeks and weeks. No longer.

"Just like every young person itching to get out on their own," I replied.

"No, not like every young person. My mother—"

"Were you taken from your home when you were still a child?"

He stared at me. "You aren't seriously doing this."

The disappointment in his voice chilled me, but I pushed on. "If one day you decided to go back home, you could, couldn't you?"

"Suffering is not a competition," he said, very low. "No, I can't fully understand what you've been through, nor can you understand what I've endured. But I want to learn every bit of you—your story, your body, your mind. *Everything,* Mara. As much as one person can absorb another's life and pain and hopes, that's what I want to do for you. And I want you to learn me and my life in return. And the problem here"—he raised his voice a little, cutting me off before I could speak—"the problem isn't that you can't focus on fighting a war and having a lover at the same time, so don't pretend that. Give me at least that much honesty. The problem is that you're so afraid of heartbreak that you deny yourself happiness for fear of someday losing it."

That tore a sharp laugh out of me. I hated how sad it sounded, how fragile and exposed on this lonely, windswept hill. "And what I if I am? I've been shattered so many times, I've put myself back together so many times. Too many times. What if I don't want to do that again? What if I *can't* do it again?"

"But darling, that's what I'm telling you," he said, gentler now. His smile deserved none of my ire, and yet I couldn't stand the sight of it. I wished he would yell instead of treating me so softly; I deserved to be yelled at.

"You won't have to put yourself back together on your own ever again," he continued. "We'll do it together. I'll help you."

"And what if you can't?" I felt like I was careening toward a cliff's edge and could find nothing to grab on to, nothing to break my fall. But that was the point, wasn't it? I would only drag Gareth down along with me.

"What if you can't put me back together?" I asked. "What if you try again and again—because I *will* keep breaking, I promise you that—and it's impossible? You'll get tired of me and walk away, or you'll stay with me out of stubbornness and I'll ruin you, or you'll die, and that will ruin *me*." I shrugged, laughing a little. "Is loving me for a little while worth all of that? Is loving *you* worth it to me?"

Now he was the one to step away. Roughly, he rubbed the back of his head, his mouth twisting. All the passionate light was gone from his eyes. I'd snuffed him out.

"Is loving you worth all of that?" He laughed quietly. "I've already told you my answer in every way I know how. What you find worth the trouble and risk, I'm still not sure. And if you won't tell me, or can't, then…"

I hardly breathed, waiting for him to finish, not sure how I wanted him to finish. The possibilities made me sick with sadness, with relief. *Then I can't do this. Then this is a waste of time. Then you're cruel, and I'm a fool for thinking I could ever really love you.*

But before he could say another word, and as the air pulled taut and sour between us, a delicate cough drew our attention to the stone bench. A pale man sat there, with shaggy gray hair that fell around his face in windblown waves. He wore dark brown robes and sat with his hands in his lap. Once we noticed him, his placid expression warmed into a smile that deepened the lines of age carved into his face.

"Welcome to Falkeron, my fellow children of the gods," he said. "Have you come to us in tribute, in need, or with curiosity?"

I recovered quickly, so thankful for the interruption that I couldn't bring myself to care about how much this man might have overheard. I even ignored the strange fact that he'd somehow appeared on the bench without a sound. We were on Falkeron, after all; the monks here worshipped Zelphenia, Goddess of the Unknowable. It was impossible to know what sorts of spells or other obscure enchantments they might practice.

"We come in friendship, Brother," I answered, only a little shaky. "My name is Mara Ashbourne, and this—"

"Ah, the Rose and the librarian!" Immediately the man's face lit up. "Mara Ashbourne and Gareth Fontaine. Of course. I should have guessed it at once. The Blessed Abbot told us you were coming. You have traveled far, yes? All the way from Rosewarren."

Hearing our names together like that made me flinch. "Yes, Brother. With a message and a request from our Warden."

The man gave us a knowing smile. "Yes, always up to something, that one, isn't she?" He rose to his feet and gestured up the path to the monastery at its peak. "Please, come with me. I'll show you to your rooms so you can refresh yourselves before supper. It's not often that we receive such distinguished guests. You'll forgive any unbecoming excitement you might see from us tonight, I hope."

Gareth brushed past me and greeted the man with a hearty handshake. "If you'll forgive *my* excitement, Brother, at the chance to peruse your archives."

"Normally we do not permit visitors to enter the archives," the man said, amusement coloring his voice.

"But you will allow me, won't you?" Gareth flashed him one of his notorious grins. "Since I'm a special envoy of the Warden and all?"

The man chuckled and placed a hand on Gareth's arm, gently guiding him back toward the path. "Do not worry, Professor," he said pleasantly. "You are indeed honored guests here at Falkeron, and we plan to celebrate your arrival accordingly."

They proceeded up the path without me, Gareth peppering the monk with questions about the archives and doing it loudly enough that his cheery voice drifted back to me on the wind at a grating volume. He meant to irritate me, I assumed, and to prove that I couldn't dampen his spirits no matter how hard I tried.

I let them get a ways ahead of me before following them up the hill. Neither of them looked back, and I tried to tell myself that this was perfectly fine, that the best thing for both Gareth and me at this moment was space. Being apart would give him a chance to realize what a mistake he'd made to love me. And it would allow me to truly harden myself against him at last.

Surely we would both realize that what we'd done, what we'd thought we felt, could be attributed to lust and a brief lack of judgment, nothing more.

I recited these lies to myself all the way up the hill, my scarred hand in a hard fist.

Nothing more.

Nothing more.

Nothing more.

This is a thing I want.

This is a thing I can never have.

Chapter 23

After Errik, the monk who'd greeted us on the hill, showed us to our rooms, I immediately bathed in the hottest water I could stand. I scrubbed until I felt some semblance of calm, then dressed in a thick woolen sweater and clean trousers and bound my hair into a tight braided bun. By the time I entered the dining hall for supper with Gareth beside me, my mind was quiet. I even managed to control my breathing, which always seemed to quicken around him.

But as we crossed the threshold into the great hall, where dozens of monks sat at two long tables, all the murmured conversations buzzing through the torchlit room fell silent.

I froze, my skin crawling with sudden foreboding as every eye in the room turned toward us. Instinctively I put out an arm to block Gareth's path.

Errik gently touched shoulder. "Forgive them, Mara," he said with a rueful smile. "With the weather so harsh of late, we haven't had many visitors at all, let alone ones so distinguished. And I do hope you'll pardon the Blessed Abbot's absence from our supper tonight."

"He's busy?" I said sharply. "Doing what?"

Gareth's eyebrows shot up, but Errik seemed wholly unbothered by my rudeness. "Oh, I'm afraid not even I am privy to every detail of the Blessed Abbot's schedule," he said mildly. "Rest assured, he will join us later this evening."

Then he glided toward the long table at the front of the room, which stood on a raised platform. The central chair, taller and grander than the others, sat empty. Errik clapped his hands once and gestured at the room as if shooing everyone away.

"Surely we haven't lost all sense of decorum?" he called out. "Stop gawking, my friends, and return to your supper."

The seated monks obeyed, digging back into their meals. A low rumble of voices returned to the room, and someone laughed. It was a perfectly ordinary laugh, and the scents of buttered bread and the Blessed Abbot's famous beef stew filled the air, and the candles lining the tables and flickering in great iron chandeliers overhead cast a warm glow over everything—and yet I felt uneasy. The discomfiture I'd felt in the Warden's office returned, along with my unanswered questions.

Why hadn't the Falkeron monks shared their findings with the Order? Why weren't we working with them to track down Zelphenia and protect her from Kilraith? Why had the Warden found out about their progress only through spy work?

And why did it bother me so immensely that the Blessed Abbot was absent? Surely there was nothing extraordinary about someone of his stature having a full docket of tasks.

Beside me, Gareth quietly cleared his throat. "Is everything all right?"

The sudden sound of his voice made me even more tense. I hadn't realized he was so close to me. His arm was only a hair's breadth from mine; the heat of his body pulled at me like a hook in my skin.

"Ignore me," I muttered. "I'm fine. Everything is fine. I just need some food."

I strode toward the high table before Gareth could say anything else, and before I could say the words that hovered on the tip of my tongue: *Nothing is fine. It's your fault I'm on edge for no good reason. You've left me undone.*

Errik waited between two empty chairs, a pleasant smile on his face. If he sensed the tension between Gareth and me, he didn't comment on it.

"Please sit, and enjoy your meal," he said. "We hope it warms both your bodies and your spirits after such a long journey."

I sat stiffly in the offered chair and dug into my steaming bowl of stew without another word. The broth burned my tongue, but even that was better than talking to Gareth—not that he was paying much attention to me anyway. He and Errik immediately launched into a conversation about a recent archaeological expedition to the Unmade Lands that had unearthed ruins of a city destroyed upon the gods' Unmaking. I ate with furious relish, half listening to their annoyingly enthusiastic chatter, half listening to the noise of the dining hall, and trying desperately to ignore Gareth's leg under the table, and how close it was to mine.

Other than the unsettling silence upon our arrival, the dinner proceeded without incident and was even rather boring, unless one was interested in discussing Olden arcana with Gareth and Errik, which I certainly was not. My sentinel hearing caught snatches of conversation from the monks nearest me—a debate over various interpretations of an obscure text about the goddess Zelphenia, someone bemoaning the chore assignments they'd drawn for the next week, laughter at a surprisingly vulgar joke.

And yet as I sat there, scarfing down stew I barely tasted, my skin prickled with a warning I couldn't shake. Even the sight of the long tables bothered me; too many chairs were empty.

Suddenly I couldn't see the value in waiting any longer to remind Errik of the reason for our visit. I cleared my throat, cutting Gareth off mid-sentence.

"I'm looking forward to learning more about your efforts to find Zelphenia, Brother Errik," I said carefully, lifting a spoonful of broth to my lips.

A hush fell over our table—only a beat of quiet before conversation returned, but it was like something had dropped into a still pond, sending ripples blooming outward. Errik went very still. The other monks seated near us continued eating, but I sensed they were listening hard.

Beside me, Gareth tensed. I pressed my heel against his foot in warning.

"Professor Fontaine and I are among many who have recently been dedicating our time to finding the gods," I continued, keeping my voice light, still eating my stew. "I assume you've heard from the Warden about our efforts in the Order? I know she and the Blessed Abbot have been corresponding frequently, especially during these unprecedented times."

I glanced up at Errik, who still wore a friendly smile. "Yes, old friends, those two."

"The Warden believes that cooperation between the Order and the five Cloisters is essential in order to protect the realm from those who would defy the gods' will. Olden hostiles. Human traitors."

Errik inclined his head. "The Blessed Abbot greatly values the Warden's opinions on such matters."

I swallowed my last bite of food and set down my spoon. "Funny, then, that he has not kept her apprised of your progress, that indeed he didn't tell her about your search at all until quite recently." I looked at him steadily. "I trust the Blessed Abbot has a good reason for such an insult?"

Normally I wouldn't have been so combative. But danger was nearby. I could almost smell it. My senses were tingling, sharp as knives. And if I couldn't fight something with my fists, I would do it with my words. Father had taught me that when I was small. *A wise sentinel knows when to use her strength and when not to.* The memory of his voice came unbidden, making me even more eager to move, to defend myself and Gareth—but against *what*?

Gareth, blessedly quiet, took a careful sip of wine from his goblet. I barely resisted the urge to knock the drink from his hands, my mind automatically running through a list of every poison I could think of, and their antidotes.

"The Blessed Abbot has a good reason for everything he chooses to do," Errik said, rising smoothly to his feet, "and everything he chooses not to." He gestured at the door with that same bland smile. "Shall we join him? I believe that by now he should have finished his daily tasks and retired to his chambers."

Two of the other monks at the high table rose with him and escorted us out of the dining hall. The other three monks remained seated. One looked after us once, quickly, before his gaze darted back to his food; one stared bleakly at the table, the other out at the dining hall as if in a daze.

I followed Errik with my hands in fists, resisting the urge to grab Gareth and run. The air crackled against my skin as I struggled to keep my power hidden but at the ready. It was possible the Warden hadn't told them I was a sentinel, and they certainly wouldn't know I was a demigod. I wanted to keep it that way for as long as I could.

Behind us, the dining hall once again fell quiet. The cavernous silence followed us down the dimly lit stone corridors. I focused on extending my power into the shadows as far as I could without alerting any of our hosts, stretching my enhanced sentinel senses to gather scents, sounds, and shadow-cloaked details normal humans wouldn't be able to detect.

The effort focused my mind. The hallway to our left held faint scents of manure, straw, and animal hide; it must have led outside to the monastery's barns. From the right, down one of the corridors we quickly moved past, came the distant sound of someone sobbing. *Pleading.* A monk in passionate prayer? Or something more sinister? Either way, the sound curdled my stomach.

Gareth's knuckles brushed against mine, tugging on my focus. I glanced at him, saw the question in his eyes. If only I'd had time to teach him the Order's hand signals. Nevertheless I signed a quick warning against my thigh. *Something is wrong. Eyes open.*

He nodded once, his expression grim. In another situation, I would've laughed. Of *course* Gareth and his sage mind knew our hand signals. He'd probably seen them only once but would still remember them forever.

"Tell me, Mara Ashbourne," Errik said, walking just ahead of us, his voice as smooth and untroubled as his gliding gait, "is it true that you have met the creature Ankaret?"

Of all the questions he might have asked me, that was a particularly unexpected one. I thought quickly, keeping my face blank. What was the point of such a query? It didn't feel like simple curiosity.

"No, I'm afraid I haven't," I said, trying to sound bored, "though I've heard tales. She must have been quite splendid."

"But you were in the city called Mhorghast, were you not?"

My awareness of Gareth pinged sharply at the word, but his stride didn't falter for even a second.

"Unfortunately, yes, I was."

"Then surely you must have seen her? She died there, I've been told. Kilraith killed her."

"So people have said. I was rather occupied at the time."

Errik stopped at a set of great wooden doors and looked back at me keenly. Torchlight flickered in his eyes. "Yes. You and your sisters have been busy indeed. You killed the god Jaetris. You looked into his eyes and tore open the body that held him." He tilted his head to the side. "Do you think you could do that again?"

All the fine hairs on my nape stood up. How did this monk know the details of what we'd done? Gareth moved a bit closer to me, his body radiating heat. I swore I could feel the drum of his racing heartbeat echoing my own.

"You've certainly heard some wild stories, Brother," I said flatly. "I'm sure many would take pride in shocking a holy man such as yourself."

Errik smiled. "You have studied the Olden arcana for years, Mara. You've studied human history, the Unmaking, the gods." His gaze slid to Gareth, his smile widening. "And so have you, Professor. You've dedicated your life to the acquisition of knowledge. And yet nothing either of you had learned properly prepared you for meeting him, did it?"

A shiver skipped down my spine.

"You're talking about Kilraith," Gareth said quietly.

"He Who Is All," Errik replied.

"He Who Is All," intoned other voices. I looked back over my shoulder; a dozen monks had joined us from nearby corridors, forming columns at our backs. Inwardly, I cursed. Somehow I'd missed the sound of their approach. I needed to *focus*.

"Tell me," Errik said, unlatching the two great doors, "what is more powerful than a god?"

"Nothing," Gareth answered immediately.

"Once, I would have agreed with you. Not anymore."

Errik led us through the doors into a huge sunken room, and the other monks flooded in around us. Tapestries depicting legends of the goddess Zelphenia lined the walls, muffling every sound.

A heavy wooden table sat at the room's center, bordered by polished blue tiles. In front of the table was a large stone basin. It must have once been a fountain; a faceless statue of Zelphenia stood in the middle of it, her arms draped in delicately sculpted veils. Faint dark paths streaked down her body where water had once flowed, like the echoes of tears.

But the water she had once stood in was gone.

In its place was a crimson pool of blood.

I froze. One of the monks nearest me tried to pull me forward, but I wouldn't budge, didn't move even an inch. The monk lost his footing and stumbled back.

"Where is the Blessed Abbot?" I said, very low.

Errik stopped at the fountain of blood and turned to face us, his hands clasped at his waist. He still wore that same mild smile plastered across his face, only now I saw clearly that it held nothing but malice.

"I tried to convince him of the truth," Errik replied, "but he would not listen. Now his blood—and the blood of those loyal to him—will serve a greater purpose. You are familiar with the unknowable arts, I assume? The art of divining truth from natural objects? The goddess Zelphenia was particularly fond of scrying pools, and we do not reject her teachings entirely, false god though she may be."

Suddenly the source of that basin of blood was perfectly, horribly clear.

The mocking regret in Errik's voice made me want to tear out his throat. "What truth are you talking about? Of what madness have you convinced yourself?"

"That the gods mustn't be found and protected," Gareth said, his own voice hard as flint. "They must be found and destroyed. Just as Kilraith wishes."

Errik's face lit up with delight. "Exactly right, Professor. And there is your answer. Nothing is more powerful than our fraudulent gods. Nothing except for He Who Is All."

"He Who Is All," echoed the other monks.

Kilraith.

"The one true god," Errik murmured, his eyelids fluttering closed.

"The one true god," responded the others.

Errik's earlier words returned to me like a blow to the temple. *You killed the god Jaetris. You looked into his eyes and tore open the body that held him.*

Do you think you could do that again?

"If you think I'll help you destroy the gods," I muttered, so furious I could hardly see straight, "then you're an even bigger fool than I thought."

Errik smiled sadly at me. "I understand, Mara. Unlearning years of holy teachings is difficult. But you will manage it soon, I think."

As the doors thudded closed behind us, I spun around, fists raised, every muscle in my body taut as a bowstring and ready to fight—but then Errik intoned something under his breath, and acrid spellwork crackled through the air, stealing my breath. I spat out a curse; Errik was a beguiler. My eyes instinctively closed against the sting of magic, and when I opened them again, Gareth was no longer beside me.

He lay on the fountain's stone ledge, kept immobile by Errik's spellwork, and Errik himself held a knife to Gareth's throat. The tip of the blade pressed into his neck, drawing bright drops of blood.

"Agree to help us, and I'll spare his life," Errik said patiently, looking back at me. "I hope you can appreciate the sacrifice I'd be making by letting him live. The blood of a sage would considerably enhance the power of our scrying pool."

He barely got the words out before I lunged at him. My restrained power burst through me like an explosion, and in three seconds I had him pinned flat to the floor. A quick jab to his throat, and he was helpless beneath me, voiceless and gasping for breath.

My head snapped up at the metallic scrape of blades being drawn. The other monks surged toward me, withdrawing daggers from the pockets of their voluminous robes.

Daggers. I faced them all with a grin, my muscles blazing and ready. As if a few knives were enough to best me.

I flew at them lightning fast, my feet barely touching the floor. It felt so good to let loose my strength after everything that had happened—my night with Gareth, the tension between us, the strange supper in the dining hall—that laughter bubbled up in my throat from sheer relieved joy.

A monk came at me with a hard swipe of his blade, and I kicked it from his hand. It went flying, and the monk crashed to his knees, cradling his shattered fingers and howling in pain. Another monk threw spellwork at me; I recognized the murky, rotten odor of magic meant to stun my senses and leave me slow and befuddled. But I was ready for that. I ducked the spell—a shimmer of arcing light cutting through the air like a scythe—and then ran at my attacker, rammed my head into his stomach, and sent him flying. He slammed into a wall and slumped to the floor, unmoving.

More monks entered from side doors—another three, then an additional seven—but as more and more of them flooded the room, I only grew stronger, my power rising gleefully to meet the challenge. I spun and kicked, threw punches and flung dropped blades, and I was so fast and liquid, my senses so sharp, that the world boomed and flashed around me. Each small sound was amplified, each slight change in the air alerted me to a dagger flying at my head or a punch coming for my throat.

Suddenly the floor bucked beneath me, throwing me off my feet. I rolled to cushion my landing and looked up just in time to see a crack in the polished stone racing toward me. *Elemental.* One of the monks was an elemental.

I leapt out of the way just in time, then barely dodged a slab of stone dropping from the ceiling. It crashed to the floor in a cloud of dust. Fragments of stone skidded across the ruined tile.

A cry of despair tore through the room.

"What have you *done?*" came Errik's rasping voice. "No, *no*!"

I whirled around and saw chaos.

Five fresh chasms had cleaved the room into pieces. One of them ran through the fountain, splitting it in two. The statue of Zelphenia toppled over before my eyes; her head smashed into the fountain's rim and shattered. Blood spilled out of the ruined fountain, painting the splintered floor red. I refused to let myself wonder how many people had been murdered to make that scrying pool.

And what Errik and his followers might have used the pool *for*.

What had Kilraith promised them? And what would anyone who survived this night report to him once the dust settled?

But then I saw Gareth, and the sight of him wiped my mind clean of everything else.

He lay amid the ruins of the fountain, his body bent awkwardly over a slab of broken stone. The fountain's spilled blood pooled around him, and he clutched at his throat with frantic red hands. Beside him, clinging to a shattered slab of stone, was Errik, brandishing his knife triumphantly. He grinned at me, wild-eyed and blood-splattered, then drew a rasping breath to speak, but before he could utter a sound, I was on him. One sharp kick to his temple, and he collapsed against the ruins of his beloved fountain, his skull shattered.

I hurried to Gareth and assessed his condition with a sinking heart. He'd lost his glasses somewhere, so nothing blocked my view of his eyes—glassy, terrified. Blood bubbled up between his fingers from a bright red gash on his throat. Not a fatal wound, not yet, but it would become one soon. He was losing too much blood.

"It's all right," I muttered, trying to keep my voice calm even as fear pounded a death knell along my spine. "You're going to be all right. It's not too bad. We just have to stop the bleeding."

I grabbed Errik's knife and used it to cut a strip of cloth from the part of his robes that wasn't soaked in blood. With shaking fingers I tied the cloth around Gareth's neck, as tight as I could make it while still allowing him to breathe. Blood seeped through the cloth immediately. He was pale, gleaming with sweat, and his every breath rattled.

I picked him up as gingerly as I could, trying not to panic at how light he felt in my arms. I knew his body, knew how solid and strong it was, and how it felt to be held by him, loved by him. He felt so insubstantial only because my sentinel strength was at its peak, I told myself. I didn't look at him again; I couldn't, or I'd fall to my knees.

A noise behind me—someone stumbling through the mess of blood and stone. I whirled, rage painting my vision as red as the floor under my feet. I didn't know how I would kill whoever attacked me next; I just knew that I would destroy them so completely that no one would be able to recover even a small piece of their body. I would kill everyone within these sacred walls if I had to.

"Wait! Mercy, please!" A young monk with dark brown skin stood there, her hands raised to ward me off. "I don't want to hurt you!"

"You have three seconds to convince me not to kill you," I said, fury making my voice tremble.

She glanced over my shoulder, then darted to the side and flicked her wrists downward. The floor split open at her feet, and the crack raced behind me, widening as it sped toward its target—another monk, dagger in hand, eyes bright with anger and lip swollen from the impact of my fist. But before he could make another move, the growing chasm reached him, opening up beneath his feet. He fell into it with a scream, and soon nothing was left of him but faint sounds of agony from somewhere below.

I turned back to the young monk—clearly the elemental who'd destroyed the fountain—and gave her a brisk nod. "Fine. I won't kill you. Yet."

"Follow me," she said breathlessly, hurrying past me. "I'll show you the way out."

I obeyed; what choice did I have? Gareth was wheezing in my arms, and I couldn't hold him and keep him alive and fight off more monks at the same time. We needed help; we needed a healer, or at least a quiet, clean room where I could try to stitch his wound closed.

I followed the monk silently through twisting dark corridors, my eyes burning and my throat tight with tears I refused to let fall. We entered a dank passage with stone walls and an earthen floor. The monk took a torch from a bracket on the wall, lit it, and finally spoke again.

"No apology I could offer is enough for what's happened here tonight," she murmured. Her voice was thick with anger. "But I am sorry nevertheless, my lady. I am so sorry."

"Not a lady," I replied automatically. *I'm a Rose.* I said the words over and over to myself like a prayer. *I'm a Rose, and I can save him.*

"A radical sect of the fellowship led by Errik has been secretly serving Kilraith for several weeks now," the monk went on. "I was one of them for a time. But now I see how foolish I was, and I'm doing everything I can to stop them."

"They killed the Blessed Abbot."

"Yes, and twelve others. Including my sister."

Her voice was hard, flat. My chest twisted painfully. Gemma's and Farrin's faces flashed before my eyes.

We reached a heavy wooden door, which the monk unlatched and pushed open with no small effort. I soon saw why: a snowstorm had descended upon the island. Several inches had piled up against the door, and past the glow of our torch, I could see nothing but sheets of snow swirling through the thick black night.

The monk's face fell.

"Don't worry," I told her briskly. "I'll manage."

She glanced up at me. "I hope you'll tell the Warden what's happened here. Errik may be dead, but others will rise to take his place. And after tonight…"

She didn't have to finish. I saw the hollow acceptance right there on her face. If anyone had seen her help me, she was finished. Someone would kill her that very night.

"I'll tell her. You have my word." I paused. It seemed cruel to leave her, but Gareth's breathing was growing shallower by the minute. I couldn't linger.

"What is your name?" I asked her.

"Serra." She smiled a little. "Serralin, but my sister called me Serra."

"Serra." I touched her arm, gave it a slight squeeze. "Thank you for what you've done tonight."

Then I gathered Gareth as close as I could and plunged into the storm.

Chapter 24

The cold slammed into me like a giant frigid fist, but the wind was worse—so strong and howling that if I'd been anyone else, it would have blown both Gareth and me off the cliffs and into the sea. Not even my father could have kept his footing.

I plowed through the snow, which reached just past my knees, and kept a close watch on the ground. My eyes quickly adjusted to the darkness, but even my keen sentinel vision kept taking us too close to the cliffs. The shrieking wind tried to push me off course, and the shivering weight of Gareth in my arms made me cold with terror. I couldn't look down at him. I couldn't, or I would see the blood darkening his neck and lose my nerve.

Finally I came to a creaking wooden dock piled high with snow. I thought it was the same one we'd arrived at before, but I couldn't be certain. The snow hid everything except for my ragged tracks and the vague looming shape of the Cloisters up on the hill, far behind us. Squinting across the water, I thought the dark island in the distance looked familiar, but in truth it could have been any other island in the world.

There was no time for doubt. Gently I lay Gareth in the snow, still not looking at him. He'd gone deathly still, a fact I chose to ignore as I kicked through the drifts around the dock, looking for a boat. Any boat, even if it had holes in the hull. I could row fast enough to get us to that island before it sank.

My foot hit something hard and hollow-sounding. I dug through the snow with my bare hands, heedless of the stinging cold, and unearthed a rickety dinghy. I didn't even take the time to sound it; oars lay inside it, and that was enough. I tromped back through the snow to retrieve Gareth—still not looking at him, I *would not* look at him—and put him in the boat, wrenched it out of its snowbank, grabbed the frozen oars with my frozen hands, and rowed.

The wind was worse out on the water, but my power warmed me, and I pushed through the gale as fast as I could move the oars through the rough black sea. Waves sloshed over my feet and sprayed me in the face, and by the time we reached the island I'd been aiming for, I was breathing hard, every muscle in my body screaming in pain. I drove the boat hard into the shore, jumped out into the freezing water, and gathered Gareth into my arms once more. My traitor eyes glanced down at him, saw his white face, the ice crusting his wet hair, the blood soaking my makeshift bandage.

I gritted my teeth, turned into the wind, and began to pray—angry prayers in an angry rhythm. *He will not die. Do not let him die. If he dies, I will hate you forever. He will not die.*

As I prayed, my mother's face came into my mind. The image made me even angrier, gave me a boost of energy. *If he dies, I will hate you forever.*

There was a little town on this island, far off to my right through the whirling snow—a cluster of dark buildings and a few warmly lit windows—but I didn't trust it. Someone there might be loyal to Errik or to Kilraith. They might have helped murder the Blessed Abbot.

I turned away from the town and kept pushing through the snow until I found another dock on the far side of the island and several fishing boats laden with nets and crates. I chose the sturdiest-looking one and threw its gear into the water to lighten the load, then settled Gareth against the hull's shallow wall, climbed in, and started rowing.

With each pull of the oars through the water, I repeated my angry prayers, but the distance between this island and the next one was longer, the water choppier. By the time we reached the shore, my fingers and toes were burning from the cold and my prayers had become wordless bursts of desperate feeling. When I lifted Gareth's still body into my arms, I bent to kiss his frozen head, a sob trapped in my throat.

I began to lose all sense of where I was, how many islands I'd rowed to and trudged across and rowed away from. I could no longer feel my burning fingers and toes, which frightened me—I'd seen frostbite before, and I already had one maimed hand—but I couldn't allow myself to think of that. I had to get us to the mainland and then find shelter, a fire, a healer. I had to save Gareth. I *would* save Gareth. That was all I knew. And even when I finally lost my footing and pitched forward, my mind was calm, and my thoughts came slowly. *You're going to fall. Then you're going to get back up and keep going.*

But I didn't fall; something warm and solid caught me. Golden eyes flashed at me from beneath a furred hood, and a voice I knew said, "Give him to me." Then another voice—deeper, also familiar—said, "Mara, my girl," and I saw my father's face through the snow.

I clutched Gareth to my chest and stumbled backward. I was hallucinating. "Who are you?" I demanded. My tired mind made quick calculations. I'd have to drop Gareth into the snow, hope the landing was soft enough, then dispatch whoever this was with a roundhouse kick and a swift blow to the head. I wouldn't hold back. I drew myself up, summoning every scrap of power I could find.

"He'll die if we don't hurry," said the first voice. "Only revenants can resurrect the dead. And if it comes to that, he will not be the same man he is now. He will be like your friend Nesset—half alive, half rotten. A walking corpse."

I blinked hard, willing my vision to clear. But the woman was still there.

"Mother?" I said sharply.

She came closer and touched my arm. Her hands were so warm I wanted to cry. I caught her scent—mint and rosemary, one of the few lingering scent memories from my childhood—and nearly relented. But I had to be sure.

I stepped back from her. "What did I whisper to you on that day the Warden took me to Rosewarren?"

"That you had taken my emerald brooch, not Gemma. It was hidden on your shelf behind your favorite book, *The Secret of the Willow Tree*." She hesitated, gave me a sad smile. "That you weren't angry with me. That what was happening wasn't my fault."

It was one of the clearest memories I had of home: putting my lips to my mother's ear and comforting her as she wept.

"I lied," I told her. My voice was hoarse, exhausted. "I *was* angry with you. With both of you. You especially. You cried, but I didn't. I stayed strong. You didn't."

"I know," she said, holding out her arms. Her blue-and-gold eyes were full of sorrow. Blue like Gemma's. Gold like a god's. "Let me carry him now. We must hurry."

If there was still a chance to save Gareth, I had to take it. I placed him gently in her arms, and without his weight against me, reassuring me that I hadn't lost him, I felt untethered. My knees buckled. I couldn't feel my fingers.

Before I could fall, strong arms came around me, and someone lifted me off the ground. I glimpsed a hood, a beard, brown eyes like Farrin's. Like mine.

"Hold on to me," said my father, his voice steely and his grip like iron. "You're safe now."

And for a moment, I *did* feel safe. Like I was a child again, and I'd had a nightmare, and my parents were going to soothe me back to sleep. Whatever monsters I'd dreamed up were not real, and they couldn't hurt me.

I slumped against my father's chest, and as he ran, his long sentinel strides carrying me quickly through the snow, I found my earlier prayer and recited it under my breath, too exhausted to pray but too terrified not to. Gareth would not die. I would not let him. He would not die. He would live. My mother would save him. If she couldn't, I would kill her. It was her fault we were all in this mess in the first place. If she and the other gods had been more careful, if they hadn't destroyed themselves to create the Middlemist, if they'd built a *better* Middlemist, none of this would have happened.

I pressed my fists into my father's chest, willing away my exhaustion. We traveled like lightning, the dark snowy world peeling away at the touch of my mother's gliding footfalls until everything turned white, and so cold that the air burned my skin. I could no longer feel my father's arms or see where we were going, but a great force was pulling at me, like I was being swept away down a river. I sensed that we were still moving, faster now than my eyes could comprehend. Through the brilliant glare I caught a glimpse of a golden-eyed woman wearing platinum armor. Her dark hair shone with jewels.

Kerezen.

My mother.

Suddenly the river stopped, and I blinked like a shocked newborn as Father gently deposited me onto my feet. The world around us was soft and green, and warm with sunlight: Wardwell. My mother's private sanctuary, hidden deep in the northern forests of Gallinor and protected by layers of godly magic. No one could enter unless she allowed it. They could walk right past it or even through it and not see what was truly here. The world we had left behind was a blizzard; here, it was mild summer.

This made me irrationally angry. That Mother could hide up here in her endless peaceful summer while the rest of the world stormed and fought and died felt so unfair that I saw red.

I pushed away my father's offered hand and forced myself to move, following Mother through the flowering clover and into her little house with its thatched roof and smoking chimney. My legs were jelly, my whole body burned from cold and shock, and the remnants of whatever power had gripped us left me queasy.

But all I could focus on was Gareth.

Here in Wardwell, he looked even worse than he had in the storm. The only real color left to him was the blood staining his neck and torso. He looked naked and vulnerable without his glasses; absurdly, that frightened me most of all.

"How did you find us?" I managed to say, my teeth still chattering.

"I heard your prayers," Mother replied wryly. "They were quite loud."

"Really?"

"And we were already en route to Falkeron," she added. "While at Rosewarren, I learned where you were."

"Rosewarren?" Alarm bells clamored in my mind. "Why were you there? Please tell me you didn't reveal yourself to anyone."

"You think so little of me. Rest assured, daughter, that my visit was completely covert. Clear the table," Mother commanded, her voice sharpening, and only then did I realize we were not alone in the house. Gemma and Farrin were there, and Talan, and Ryder, and they all moved quickly to make space for Gareth on the small kitchen table. He was too tall for it—when Mother laid him down, his legs dangled off the side—but then Talan dragged over a small sideboard, and Gemma gently laid Gareth's legs atop it.

Mother sat in a chair by Gareth's head and took his face in her hands. Her expression was grim but resolute. "Ryder, boil a pot of water," she said. "Gideon, bring my kit. It's in the cabinet under the stairs. Farrin, take Mara to a bedroom upstairs and check her fingers and toes for frostbite. Gemma, get her warm. Make sure she eats and rests."

I stood beside the table, staring down at Gareth's face. I couldn't tell if he was breathing. I felt like I was drifting through a world I did not know, no longer attached to my body. Not even the surprise of seeing my sisters could rattle me.

"I'm not going anywhere," I said.

"You can't help him," Mother replied. "Only I can. And you don't want to see what I have to do."

Farrin touched my arm; I jerked away from her. "I won't leave him."

"Don't make me drag you upstairs." Mother glanced up at me, the air around her shimmering with heat and light. She was my mother, but she was also Kerezen, goddess of the body, and she would not suffer defiance. "You're strong, but I'm stronger. And the longer you delay me, the more likely it is that he'll die."

I held her gaze for only a moment before I had to look away, blinking back furious tears. Gemma murmured my name, and I turned toward her and let her and Farrin lead me upstairs. They gave me food and drink, which I forced myself to consume even though every bite made me want to retch. They moved me about like a doll who had no will of her own, checking me for injuries, massaging my hands and feet with an acrid balm. Farrin built a fire; Gemma helped me into a fresh linen shirt and trousers and then crawled into bed beside me.

I observed them as if from a great distance, cataloging their movements with a soldier's precision. But beyond the instincts of my training, my mind was numb, my blood cold and quiet.

It wasn't until I lay sandwiched between my sisters, warmed by their bodies and the heavy quilts they'd pulled around us, that Gareth began to scream. The sound broke through my stupor and stabbed me between the ribs. I drew in a shuddering breath and squeezed my eyes shut and buried my face in Gemma's neck. She held me to her, and Farrin scooted closer to my back, singing softly into my hair.

But not even Farrin's power could drive the sound of Gareth's screams from my mind. I burrowed between my sisters, counting my breaths—three beats in, six beats out—and hoping that whatever horrible godly thing my mother was doing downstairs would be enough to save him.

Chapter 25

I clung to Gemma and Farrin until everything downstairs fell quiet. The light outside had dimmed, and so had the fire; soft shadows painted the room.

I listened to my sisters breathing in the dark. Both of them were still awake. Other than Farrin singing her song, neither of them had said a word. I was glad; I wouldn't have been able to respond.

"Why are you all here?" I said at last. My voice was hoarse, as if I'd not used it for days.

"Philippa summoned us," Farrin replied quietly. "She hasn't yet told us why. She said she wouldn't until you arrived."

"Summoned? How did she summon you?"

"Do you remember when we first found Wardwell? We heard that voice in the forest calling to us through the snow, but we didn't yet know that the voice was hers, and none of the others could hear it."

The others. Talan, Ryder.

Gareth.

I swallowed hard. "I remember."

"It was like that," Gemma said, "except an image instead of a sound. One moment, I was kissing Talan. The next, I opened my eyes and saw Mother shimmering just beyond him." Her voice turned wry. "I nearly jumped out of my skin, which made her laugh. For a moment, until he realized what was happening, I think Talan was terrified I'd lost my mind. To him, it was like I was talking to the air. But I could see her as clearly as I see you now."

I pulled back from her in alarm. "Where were you when this happened? Was anyone else nearby?"

She shook her head. "We'd just returned to Gallinor after two weeks in Vauzanne and were in our room at Ramble House, that inn near Brightbell Vale?"

"And I was in my office at the Citadel," Farrin added. "Not even Ryder was with me."

"She said she needed to speak with all of us urgently, and then she was gone."

I cursed under my breath. "And then she went looking for me at Rosewarren. If anyone besides us could somehow manage to see her, it would be the Warden. We'll have to hope Mother's visit was as covert as she claims." I sat up and pushed gently past Gemma to climb out of bed. "I've got to go see Gareth."

"You need rest," Farrin protested. "Your feet—"

"Have already begun to heal, thanks to your excellent care." It was true. Even though they were tender to walk on, I could feel all of my toes.

I gripped the banisters hard with both hands as I hobbled downstairs in my socked feet, but when I reached the kitchen, Gareth wasn't there. Only my parents sat at the table, talking quietly. A plate of sandwiches sat between them. Once I would have marveled at the sight of them together like this, looking just like any other husband and wife.

But now a fist of panic grabbed my throat. I strode toward them unsteadily, forcing my wobbly legs to move faster. "Where is he?"

Mother looked up at me. "He's in the back room next to mine, resting and recovering." She raised an eyebrow. "As you should be."

"He'll live?" I clutched the back of an empty chair. The wood creaked in my grip. "He'll be all right?"

"Indeed he will be. He's stronger than he looks, that one."

Before she'd even finished speaking, I was hurrying down the hallway toward the back of the house. It was obvious which bedroom was my mother's—ivy vines framed the door—and just past it was another smaller room with a bed, a fireplace, a curtained window, a thick rug. And in the bed was Gareth.

He was sleeping, so I sank quietly into the chair at his bedside, drinking in the sight of his mussed blond hair, the slight flush of color in his cheeks, the steady rise and fall of his chest. He was in fresh clothes, his face held no pain, and his throat was smooth. Only a faint silver scar marked where Errik had slashed him.

I longed to bury my face in that precious curve of his neck and breathe him in, feel the pulse of his heartbeat against my cheek. But something rooted me to my chair, and I sat there stiffly, my muscles aching with tension, until at last Gareth's eyelids fluttered open and he looked at me.

Tears sprang to my eyes. There was so much to say to him—how good it was to see the bright green of his eyes instead of that glassy film of death; how sorry I was for how I'd behaved after our night together.

How awful it had felt to hold him in my arms as he bled and wonder if I'd ever again hear him say my name.

"Hello," I whispered instead. It was the only word I could manage.

He smiled and reached for me. "You look like you're about to burst. Come here, darling."

The sound of his voice unraveled me. I climbed into the bed and burrowed against him, and when his arms came around me and I felt his hand in my hair, the sob I'd been holding in my throat finally spilled out. I cried into his neck, pressed a kiss to his scar.

"I'm so sorry, Gareth." I could barely speak, but it was important that he knew that *I* knew how foolish I'd been. "I'm sorry for all the cruel things I said to you."

"Mara, there's no need—"

"Of course suffering is not a competition. I'm sorry your mother was awful to you. And loving you *is* worth it to me. I do love you." My breath hitched on the words. "I love you, I love you."

I had his quilt's hem in a death grip. Gently he uncurled my scarred hand and brought it to his lips.

"I'd go through all of this again," he murmured against my skin, "if it meant I could wake up and hear you say that."

"Don't make jokes. You'll *never* have to go through something like this again, not as long as I have breath in my body. I'll destroy anyone who tries to hurt you. I'll tear them apart. I'll shatter them."

He hummed deep in his chest. "Again, it's not that I have a death wish, particularly, but the image of you coming to my defense in a vengeful battle fever is a truly glorious one."

I pulled back to look at him. He touched my face, his expression crumpling.

"Please don't cry," he said. "It breaks my heart to see you cry."

"I was awful to you."

"No, you were afraid, and I don't blame you. I shouldn't have been so…"

"Annoying? Insistent? Blithe?"

Grinning, he wiped away my tears with his thumb. "Yes, yes, and yes. Blame it on the afterglow, but I know that doesn't excuse my behavior." He softened. "You've known such loss, more than anyone should ever have to endure. And I do understand that. I'm not so madly in love that I've lost *all* my common sense."

"I still think this is a terrible idea."

He smiled softly. "Loving me?"

"And you loving me."

"Oh, do I love you? Hmm, let me think. Yes, I do seem to recall saying something along those lines."

I let out a shaky laugh against his chest. "You're ruining a nice moment."

"Well, we can't have that." He shifted slightly, which helped me settle even more closely against him. Then he put two gentle fingers beneath my chin, brought my mouth to his, and murmured, "Let me make it up to you."

At first I stiffened, afraid I would hurt him. I should stop this, I thought. I should insist that he rest. But his kisses were slow, tender, and with each soft brush of his lips—against the corners of my mouth, the curve of my cheekbones, the dip of my chin—I felt the tension throughout my body unspool until all thoughts of caution bled from my mind. I needed more. I needed to confirm with touch and heat and rhythm that he was alive, that he was mine, that I was his.

I hooked a leg over his thigh and pulled myself as close to him as I could, slid my hands into his hair and held him still so I could kiss him properly. No more of these light caresses, these whispers of skin to skin. I deepened my kisses, slid my tongue against his, shivered when he groaned beneath me and grabbed my hips. The air between us turned urgent and hungry.

He tore his lips from mine, fisted his hand in my hair, and tugged my head back to expose my throat. He buried his face there and kissed every tender bit of skin, sucking and nibbling until I softly cried out in his arms. Then he ran his hand down my body, slid his fingers beneath my waistband, and found me bare and hot, slick with wanting.

"Gods, Mara," he groaned into my hair, "you know how to drive a man to his knees."

"You're not on your knees," I pointed out, grinning.

"Not yet, but the night is young." He slid two fingers inside me, and as I arched against him, my mouth open in a silent cry, he murmured, "Are you comfortable with me ravishing you in the room next to your mother's?"

"If they have any sense at all, she and Father will plug their ears and stay in the kitchen for the rest of the night," I replied breathlessly, circling against his hand.

He laughed quietly, a sweet, joyful sound that had me smiling into his kisses. Then his fingers curled just right inside me, and I clamped my thighs around his arm and grabbed his hair, gasping against him. My legs were shaking, my blood roaring.

"Gareth—" I let out a little sob.

"You need me inside you," he said hoarsely, his breath hot against my ear. "Is that it? You need to feel just how much I want you. You need me to help you come."

The low rumble of his voice, so rough with desire, painted my skin with goose bumps. I was close to finishing right there against his hand, my body flushed all over and trembling, and neither of us had even bothered to take off our clothes.

"Hurry," I whispered. I kissed his temple, tasted sweat and skin. "Need you now. *Gareth*."

He moved quickly, twisting so that his body was half on top of mine, pinning me to the mattress. I reached down to draw him out of his pants, and when my fingers closed around him—gods, he was hard, and scorching hot—his hips jerked against me, and he tugged my pants down to my knees, and then he was inside me, and the sensation of him filling me so completely, the shaky heat of his breath twining with mine, was like the feeling of coming home that had always haunted my dreams.

I touched my brow to his and closed my eyes, focusing on his warmth, his scent, the simple goodness of his hands on my body.

"I thought I'd lost you," I whispered, fresh tears thick in my voice.

"And yet you're still here," he said gently. "That threat of loss didn't scare you away."

"Not this time."

"Not ever?"

Not ever. The words were right there on my tongue, but I couldn't quite say them. "I'll try," I whispered. "That's all I can promise right now."

He tilted up my chin, prompting me to open my eyes. His smile was so sweet that I could hardly breathe. "I thank you for that promise, Mara Ashbourne," he said quietly, "and I will do everything I can to honor it."

Then he bent low and kissed me, and as I held on to him, meeting each of his kisses with one of my own, he began to move, slowly, deeply. With each delicious thrust, he drew himself completely out of me, then waited for the slightest beat, hovering at my entrance, before sliding back into me, inch by aching inch, until I was full and complete once more.

My body hummed from head to toe. I wrapped my arms around him and held on tight, my fingers digging into the muscles of his back as his thrusts grew faster, driving me closer and closer to the edge with each press of his hips. A hot wave of pleasure was building inside me, spilling like sunlight down my arms and legs, and when it crested, sharp and sudden, it took my breath away.

I cried out, not caring who heard me, and clung to him, and as my body clenched around him, he moved in me again and again, his breath coming in hard bursts against my neck until suddenly he choked out my name and shuddered against me.

We lay like that for what felt like a lifetime—a long, slow, golden lifetime in a world made only for us. He nestled against me; I stroked his hair. His slowing heartbeat drummed against mine, and when we were calm, we finally moved apart and lay among the scattered blankets in drowsy silence. He lightly dragged his fingers down my arm, watching my goose bumps with wonder. I traced the shape of his face until I knew every line of it by heart.

"I'm so glad you're here with me," I said at last. I couldn't look at him after that, too embarrassed by the words I hadn't said.

You've come back to me.

I'm so glad you're alive.

He seemed to understand anyway. He pulled me close and kissed my forehead, and I fell asleep listening to the precious sound of his breathing—steady, sure, and warm.

Chapter 26

The next morning, we all gathered in the cabin's front room after breakfast to hear what Mother had to tell us.

I could hardly bring myself to care.

My night with Gareth held me in a golden haze. We'd spent hours in each other's arms, loving each other to pieces and then back whole. And now I was expected to move through the world and think of anything else? Truly absurd.

As Gareth settled into the chair beside me, I tried not to let my thoughts veer toward darkness. But they dipped their toes into it nevertheless:

This is why love is a bad idea—this distraction, this restlessness.

Every time Gareth moved, every time he spoke, my body leaned toward his.

You've made a terrible mistake.

He glanced over at me, bumped his knuckles against mine with a smile.

How could you let this happen?

I smiled back at Gareth and pushed my scolding thoughts into the furthest corner of my mind.

And then shot an exasperated glare at Gemma, who sat across from us on a velvet divan, her eyes sparkling as she glanced back and forth between us. Farrin elbowed her gently in the ribs, not quite managing to stifle her own smile.

I rolled my eyes, heat rising to my cheeks. Later I would have a serious talk with my sisters about the importance of discretion.

And maybe, I thought, with a little flutter of excitement in my belly, I would tell them what they already knew. I would say the words aloud to someone besides Gareth.

I love him.

"I'm sure you're all wondering why I've summoned you here," Mother began. She sat in an armchair with faded floral upholstery, looking grave and troubled. Father stood beside her, leaning against the wall with his arms crossed over his chest.

The sight of them standing there together rankled me. They looked so natural, as if they hadn't been estranged for years, as if Mother hadn't let us all believe she was dead. If Talan hadn't stumbled across Wardwell and brought us north to investigate it, would she ever have revealed herself to us?

I suspected not. The thought left a sour taste in my mouth.

"I'll be brief," Mother said, "because time is of the essence. From the safety of Wardwell, I have been slowly and carefully honing my godly powers. As you know, it has taken me many years to emerge from within myself, understand and accept that I am both a human woman and a god reborn, and begin to move through the world as such. I am capable of many things, such as traveling great distances very quickly, as I did when rescuing Farrin, Ryder, and Alastrina from Mhorghast, and as I did yesterday when Gideon and I found Mara and Gareth."

She looked at each of us in turn as she said our names with a serenity I found both infuriating and enviable. I'd worked hard over the years to cultivate that kind of calm, but over the past few weeks, I'd been slowly losing my grip on it.

"I can heal even those who are mortally wounded," Mother went on, her eyes gliding back to Gareth. She gave him a small warm smile.

Gareth shifted in his seat, looking a little embarrassed. "And I thank you for that, er..."

"Kerezen. Philippa. Call me whatever you wish. And there is no need to thank me. Using my abilities to help humans whenever I can is not enough to make up for what my brothers and sisters and I have doomed you to, but it is something."

"Doom?" Ryder said, leaning on the back of the divan, just behind Farrin. As ever, he seemed to loom over her slight form—a dark protector, hawkish and fearsome. "You speak as if the ending we're moving toward is a certain one."

"It is not certain," Father said gravely, "but it is a possibility."

"Doom is always a possibility," Farrin said. "That's nothing new." She fixed her keen brown eyes on Mother. "You were going to say something more. What else can you do?"

"I can attack with the kind of power your father can only dream of," Mother said with a sly glance up at him. "I can pinpoint sickness inside a body, and while I cannot yet eradicate it, I will be able to someday, and I can already lessen the suffering it causes." She now looked at me. "And I can sense the presence of others like me."

A faint chill swept across my body. "You've found one of the other gods."

She nodded. "You'll recall that while I was in Mhorghast, I sensed that *something* was there—something like kin. At first I couldn't describe it any better than that. It wasn't until I touched the Bask girl, Alastrina," she nodded at Ryder, "and saw echoes of what she had experienced in Mhorghast, that I understood that what I sensed was my brother Jaetris, and that he was Kilraith's captive."

The talk of Mhorghast made me even more keenly aware of Gareth beside me. He sat very still, hands rigid on his thighs. I placed my scarred left hand over his right one, squeezed his fingers gently. He drew in a soft breath, turned his palm up, grabbed on to me, and held on tight. His thumb brushed across my fingers, and the small gesture made me light up inside. I wanted to raise his hand to my mouth and kiss it. I wanted to lead him back to our little room and press my whole body against his.

Sensing Gemma watching us from across the room, I got hold of myself and resolutely ignored her.

"And now you're experiencing that same feeling?" Talan asked, looking thoughtfully at Mother.

She nodded. "And now that I'm stronger, the feeling is too. I can almost *taste* it. It's like a fuzz on my tongue, a scent I can't shake." She looked fiercely at Farrin, then at me. "It is my sister Neave. She is across the Gloaming Sea in Vauzanne. And I believe she is a captive, just as my brother was."

Gemma sat up straight. She and Talan exchanged a meaningful look.

"A captive of Kilraith?" Ryder asked sharply.

"I do not know who is holding her," Mother replied. "I can sense only *her*—her fear, how lonely she is, and how confused." Her face crumpled. "And I know her voice. I remember the sound of her breathing."

I tried not to feel annoyed at the sadness in my mother's voice. What reason could I possibly have for feeling annoyed at someone's sadness? Especially when it seemed warranted.

Then I realized the truth: since the day I'd been taken from Ivyhill, not once had I heard Mother speak with such sadness about *me*.

"This confirms what we've been hearing," Talan murmured, his brow furrowed.

"Hearing?" Farrin asked.

"There are rumors in Vauzanne. During my years of traveling under Kilraith's command, I did manage to make some true friends, scattered across the continent. They housed me, fed me, let me hide out for a while before I moved on. Several of them, merchants and innkeepers, have ears to the ground." He glanced at Gemma. "We were just in Westry, south of the Knotwood. My friend Kirsa is a fur trader and hosted us after a long stretch on the road."

"And you trust this person?" Father asked sharply.

"I do," Talan answered without hesitation. "She is my oldest human friend. Long ago, I saved her life and the lives of her children. She would not betray us."

"We didn't expect the Falkeron monks to turn on their leader and try to murder Gareth," Father continued. "Anyone outside this room is someone we must guard ourselves against, for the safety of ourselves and of the realm."

"We won't get very far with that philosophy," Gemma said, throwing Father a look. "Talan and I both trust Kirsa. We were safe with her. And she corroborated rumors we'd been hearing for week: that the Lemaire family has come into possession of a great weapon. That's what we were coming home to tell all of you."

Farrin's eyebrows shot up. "The Lemaires? If there's one family in Vauzanne that I'd prefer not have a great weapon in its possession, it's that one."

"Who are the Lemaires?" Gareth asked.

"An extremely influential Anointed family," Farrin replied, "one of the oldest and most powerful in Vauzanne. Famous for their wealth, their connections, their lavish estate on the southern border of the Knotwood…"

"Their ruthlessness," Ryder added darkly.

"And the fact that every Lemaire who has ever lived, without a single exception, has been an elemental." Farrin glanced at our mother. "*Botanical* elementals."

"Ah!" Mother looked pleased. "I would very much like to meet them, then."

"Absolutely not," I said at once. "If it's true that they have Neave, and have somehow been able to *keep* Neave, they'd sniff you out in a second."

"A great weapon," Gareth said quietly, scratching his chin. "The Knotwood's been growing, hasn't it?"

"It's become as unstable as the Middlemist," Talan replied. "The forest has consumed all of the settlements at its borders. All except one."

"The Lemaire estate," I finished, a pit forming in my stomach.

Talan nodded grimly. "It's called Briarcourt. It, the surrounding land, and the road leading south out of the Knotwood have all remained untouched."

"As you might imagine," Gemma added, "hundreds of civilians are fleeing the shrinking south to request shelter on the Lemaire estate."

"And I assume they're welcoming all of them with open arms," Father muttered.

"Hardly. They accept only a few at a time, though they have more than enough space and resources to house thousands." Gemma's blue eyes sparked with anger. "Every fortnight they host a spectacular ball, which select families are allowed to attend. If they adequately impress the Lemaires during the party, they're allowed to stay and enjoy their protection. If not..."

"They're driven out," Ryder guessed.

Gemma nodded. "And sent back to the terrified masses who gather along the southern road, hoping they'll be the next lucky ones."

Her words made my blood boil. "And the crown has done nothing about this?" I asked Farrin. "Surely you knew about this and could have sent—"

"Send who?" Farrin interrupted. "The Upper Army? The Lower? I have no more soldiers to send, Mara. They've already been deployed—all across our continent, out onto the oceans, to Aidurra, and yes, to Vauzanne. Soldiers are already there, spread thin as they combat Olden invaders and try to evacuate civilians from the Knotwood's path. And every resource I can scrape together goes toward feeding them, housing them, supplying them, taking care of the refugees pouring into Fairhaven, and preparing for whatever will happen next. Another sinkhole in the Citadel? Seafaring Oldens who have found another way into Edyn through the ocean floor and are crawling out of the waves onto our shores?"

She breathed in and out twice, then squared her shoulders. "The crown is already doing everything it can. If anyone should be urged to help southern Vauzanne, it's their Warden, Joseline."

"And you think *she* has personnel to spare?" I clamped down on the urge to voice my own list of grievances. "Whatever their Order can do, it's already doing, I can assure you of that."

I held Farrin's tired eyes for a moment, hoping she understood that I wasn't angry at her and wishing that Yvaine hadn't left her such responsibilities. My sister was formidable, but becoming the steward of an entire realm overnight was too great a burden for any one person to bear.

"So the only option left to us," said Talan quietly after a moment, "is to let the armies and the Order do what they do best, and help them by ending this war as quickly as possible."

Ryder nodded and pushed off the back of Farrin's divan, bristling and ready. "We'll go to Vauzanne, then. If the Lemaires have Neave, we'll need all three of you to free her."

He looked at me when he said it, his expression alight with conviction.

I couldn't help but smile at him. "You believe in us Ashbournes so fiercely."

He raised an eyebrow. "As anyone with a scrap of sense should."

"Wait a moment," Gareth said, holding up a hand. "The Lemaire estate is clearly being protected by something—something strong enough to deflect the Knotwood, which suggests elemental abilities. And that power belongs to Caiathos, not Neave."

"No," Mother said, quiet but firm. "The presence tugging my heart toward Vauzanne is my sister. I would bet my life on it."

And our lives too? I very nearly said. For wasn't that what she and all the other gods had done, in their carelessness and arrogance, all those thousands of years ago? They had Unmade themselves to create our imperfect world, left us open to eventual invasion, and created Kilraith and Ankaret. And for what? To bask in their own splendor? Or had their acts been as thoughtless and automatic as breathing?

My body grew hot with anger. I released Gareth's hand and clasped my own firmly in my lap until the feeling passed.

"Keeping the Knotwood away from Briarcourt like that," Gareth began thoughtfully. "Philippa... Kerezen..." He shook his head a little. "Is that something you would be able to do?"

She looked at him, amused. "Perhaps."

"Even though you are the goddess of the body, not of the earth?"

"I truly do not know. I've not yet tried such a thing."

"And you shouldn't," Father said quickly. "You've risked enough as it is."

Farrin bristled, glaring at both of them. "*She* has risked enough?"

Father blinked at her, abashed.

"He's right," Ryder said. He gently put one of his huge hands on the cushion beside Farrin's shoulder, not quite touching her. "Kilraith hasn't found her yet. She should remain here and live as quietly as possible. Clearly this is the safest place for her."

Gareth was staring at the floor, distractedly scratching the back of his head. "If it isn't Neave protecting Briarcourt, then it's obviously something else...another god. We don't know where Jaetris is, or even if any scrap of him is left intact after Mhorghast."

"So, if not them, then it would be either Caiathos or Zelphenia," Gemma said.

"Or Kilraith," I muttered, thinking quickly. "Either by himself or with another god he's controlling, as he did Jaetris. Maybe the Lemaires have allied with him. They're one of the most powerful families in the world, yes? What if in exchange for protection from the Knotwood, they've offered to hide Neave for him?"

Talan looked grim. "Their house guards number in the hundreds, and by all accounts, their arsenal rivals the Lower Army's."

"I can't think of a better place to hide a god," I agreed.

"While opening their home to strangers for these balls?" Father mused. "I can't imagine Kilraith would allow that."

"He's rather busy elsewhere, I expect," Gemma said dryly.

"And he'd no doubt be delighted by such parties," Talan said. A shadow of memory flitted across his face. "Humans prancing and preening in front of each other, every dance and conversation a potential key to their survival. I'm surprised he can manage to tear himself away."

The longer the conversation went on, the more restless I became. I rose from my chair. "Whatever is there, we have to investigate it. If it's not Neave—"

"It is," Mother said patiently.

The tone of her voice made me want to punch something. "If it isn't Neave," I said, ignoring her, "it could be another god or an anchor. No matter what it is, we can't leave it with the Lemaires."

"It will take weeks to reach Briarcourt," Farrin said. "I can't in good conscience be away from Fairhaven for that long."

"That reminds me," said Gareth. "Have you made any progress in your search for Ankaret?"

A shadow of sadness flickered across Farrin's face. "No. I can't devote many resources to it at this point, but I've got three spies surveying the continent inch by inch. They come back every week with reports of misery and ruin, Mistfires and Miststorms, but nothing about Ankaret. I'm starting to think General Haldrin was right, that her last words were simply those of a dying creature. Don't people say all manner of absurd things on their deathbeds?"

Farrin's voice was flat, careful, like she was trying to quash any tremor of emotion. For a long moment, everyone was silent.

Then Mother, looking sorrowfully at Farrin, said, "I think I can get all of you there, at least across the ocean and to Westry. I probably shouldn't venture closer to Briarcourt than that."

Ryder stared at her. "Are you mad?"

She grinned. "When you were a boy, Ryder Bask, dutifully muttering your prayers, did you ever imagine that you would someday meet a god and question her sanity out loud?"

"You assume that there was anything dutiful about the prayers I muttered."

I looked hard at my mother. "You mean you could transport us—all of us—like you did Gareth and me yesterday?"

"And as you took Ryder, Alastrina, and me out of Mhorghast?" Farrin added.

Mother nodded serenely. "It's really quite easy. I've never tried carrying anyone, not even myself, over such great a distance, but I know I can manage it. Goddess of the senses, goddess of the body." She picked up her pipe, discarded on the table beside her, and tapped it against her teeth. "I can do it and return in only a few moments, I think."

"And what if that is enough to alert Kilraith to your presence?" Father said, irritation plain in his voice. "What if he comes for you and then we lose the only god we've got?"

"Gideon, try not to be so romantic in front of the children," Mother said, glancing up at him with a smile. "They don't want to hear their parents flirt."

Hearing that coy note in her voice made me flinch, a physical reaction that sparked deep in my gut and took me completely by surprise. I covered it by moving quickly to the kitchen, where I grabbed a bright red apple from a bowl on the counter and took a loud, crunchy bite. It was a perfectly fine apple, but its taste was sour on my tongue. I could barely bring myself to chew it.

"And how would you get us back?" Ryder said. "There's no point in whisking us to Vauzanne to investigate the Lemaires if we don't have an equally fast exit ready."

"*A second crossing* is certainly too dangerous," Father said tightly.

"He's right," added Talan. "If Kilraith detects her on our first passage, he'll watch obsessively for her second."

"Whatever we find...god, anchor...I'll take it and run," I said, forcing myself to swallow the chunk of apple. "I can run fast. Not as fast as whatever it is you do," I said, cutting a quick look at my mother, "but faster than anything else. I'll get to the coast, find a boat, and go straight to Fairhaven. The more quickly we can get whatever the Lemaires have to the safety of the Citadel, the better. The rest of you can catch up with me later."

I didn't dare look at Gareth, but I could feel him watching me.

"And what if something intercepts you during this mad dash to the coast?" Father said at once. "You might not be able to defend your quarry and yourself at the same time."

I laughed a little without really meaning to. "How would you know what I'm capable of? It's been a long time since we had our lessons, Father."

I couldn't bear to be in the same room with them after that—my mother and my father, standing so close to each other, as if they were any other husband and wife talking with their daughters over breakfast.

As if all the years I'd been away from home had never happened. As if they had decided all that grief and loss could be swept away.

My stomach churned. The apple was a mistake. Nevertheless, I took another bite from it and strode out of the house.

Chapter 27

Mother told us that Gareth needed at least another day to fully regain his strength. Given how thoroughly he'd loved me the previous night, I thought his strength was perfectly sufficient, but I didn't protest.

Instead, I kept to myself: a long, brisk run through the woods, training with a heavy branch that made a serviceable practice staff, and then a quick dive into a nearby pond to cool down.

I lay naked on a flat rock to dry in the sun, trying in vain to silence my roiling thoughts, until I lost hope that Gareth would wander this far into the woods, stumble upon me, and proceed to distract me with those deft hands of his.

I dressed and walked back to the house, and by the time I arrived, my stomach was growling and I had a headache from sheer irritation. The beauty of Wardwell grated on my every nerve. Rationally I knew that Mother staying hidden up here and strengthening her powers in secret was the safest thing for all of us. Parading around Gallinor to reinforce Order patrols or search for the *ytheliad* anchors alongside Gemma and Talan would be like presenting a slab of fresh meat to a hungry wolf and expecting it not to bite.

Kilraith would certainly bite.

I couldn't bring myself to go into the house. The sunlight felt too nice on my skin, even as enchanted and false as it was. I picked an armful of fruit and vegetables from the gardens behind the cottage, then found a soft patch of grass under an ancient-looking oak tree and sat and ate. *Snacking and sulking,* I thought to myself. Not my finest moment. Especially when there were so many more pressing things to ruminate on than all the old sadnesses swimming around in my mind.

From the tree's shadows I could see everyone coming and going from the cottage: Father and Gemma walking arm in arm, deep in quiet conversation; Mother humming to herself around the stem of her pipe while Talan dutifully handed her one wet garment after another to hang on the clothesline; and, to my delight, Ryder and Gareth having a sparring session on the lawn.

I heard Farrin's footsteps behind me long before she spoke.

"Ryder wanted to give Gareth a chance to test his muscles," she said, sitting down beside me.

I nodded. "Ryder is a smart man. We'll all need to be able to fight." I popped three blueberries into my mouth and munched angrily. "I should have been the one to think of that."

"You needed some time to yourself," Farrin said. "I certainly understand that. I've just been on a long walk myself."

We sat in silence for a time, and then Farrin cleared her throat delicately. "So. You and Gareth."

My cheeks burned. I grabbed five blueberries this time, enough that I had a moment to chew and think.

"Me and Gareth," I replied at last. A profound response, to be sure.

"If he hurts you, I'll kill him."

"He won't." The confidence with which I said the words surprised me, but they were true. I felt in my bones that they were true. "And if he does," I added lightly, "I'll kill him long before you get the chance to."

She laughed once, softly, then drew her knees up to her chest and wrapped her arms around her legs. "For all the years I've known him, I've never seen him like this."

A sudden lump in my throat made it difficult to swallow. "Seen him like what?"

"Happy. Strong. Settled. It's like he's finally grown up. Several years too late," she added dryly.

"We've been here for only a few hours, during several of which he was unconscious... Or otherwise occupied," Farrin added slyly.

I blushed. "...and you've already managed to see all of that?"

"He's my best friend. I can tell."

Finally I found the courage to look at her, a question on my lips, one that had been stirring in the back of my mind for weeks. "Farrin, do you mind at all?"

She smiled. Wisps of golden-brown hair had fallen loose from her braid. Her eyes were just as soft. "In fact, I'm delighted. Just surprised."

That made me laugh. "No one's more surprised than I am."

"When we were all in Vallenvoren in the fall, and he kept pestering you and mooning over you..."

"I'm used to that sort of thing. Usually people aren't so earnest about it though."

"Earnest. Yes." Farrin watched Ryder and Gareth with a thoughtful look on her face. "He *is* earnest, though I don't think many people know that. He makes jokes, he flashes that smile, he beds his latest paramour and then breaks her heart when she inevitably falls in love with him, and everyone thinks they know exactly who he is. But they don't. He's brave, and he doesn't love easily—not *real* love—but when he does, it's with his entire heart."

I followed her gaze to the lawn just as Ryder swung his practice sword and caught Gareth behind his knees, making him stumble. Ryder let out a hearty laugh that broke off quickly as Gareth caught himself and spun around to strike. Ryder just barely managed to block Gareth's sword before it smacked him on the shoulder.

Gareth crowed in triumph and pushed his sweaty hair back from his forehead, his smile as bright as the sun. Looking at him, I felt the knots of tension in my shoulders begin to melt away.

"Who is he to you?" Farrin asked quietly.

When I turned once more to look at her, she kept her eyes trained on the men, a small but fierce furrow between her eyebrows. The guarded note in her voice was obvious: *If you hurt him, I'll kill you.*

The thought made me feel so tender toward her—my angry, tired sister with her golden voice and her heart of steel—that I had to move closer to her, hook my arm through hers, and take one of her hands in mine.

"He hurts like I do," I said at last, choosing my words carefully... not for her, but for myself. "And he isn't afraid of me." I hesitated, thinking of that lonesome mountain in Ghorlock where I'd lain down to die. "I've done things that would frighten most people away. They'd run and never return. But he sees them—sees *me*—and he keeps coming back."

As I spoke, Ryder knocked Gareth to the ground with the butt of his sword, and Gareth lay there, gasping with laughter. "Peace, you bearded brute!" he cried. "Let me catch my breath!"

Ryder relented, lowered his sword, and offered his hand to help Gareth to his feet. But after Gareth grabbed hold of him, he pulled hard and brought Ryder crashing to the ground.

"Talan!" Gareth shouted, scrambling atop Ryder to pin him in place. "Talan, get your beautiful, gallant ass over here! I've got him! Grab a weapon and come to my aid before he recovers!"

But Ryder, it seemed, was in no danger of recovering anytime soon. He was flat on the ground, shaking with laughter—big booming laughs that left him completely incapacitated.

Gareth rose to his feet, tossed away his sword, and raised his hands in triumph. "The mighty house of Bask, bested by a librarian! A banner day for academics everywhere!"

He barely got the words out before Ryder rolled over and kicked his legs out from under him. Gareth fell as gracelessly as it was possible for a person to fall, and then they were both howling with laughter in the dirt. Talan, grinning, abandoned his post at Mother's side and hurried to retrieve the two fallen swords, which made Gareth cry out in alarm through his laughter, "The demon's coming for us, Ryder! We must cast aside our petty differences and ally against him to save the realm!"

"Don't you dare go over there with those two idiots," Mother called out after Talan, to no avail. "You'll get dirt all over this clean laundry!"

I watched the chaos with a smile on my face. Farrin did too, for a time, but then I felt her looking at me instead.

"I've never seen you smile like that," she said quietly.

"He makes me smile," I replied, "and laugh, which astonishes me every time. I don't laugh much anymore. But when I do, it's because of him. His wit is as sharp as mine, if not sharper. He infuriates me. He challenges me. He's so good with his team at Rosewarren. He leads them effortlessly and never hesitates to encourage them. He's not a warrior, but that doesn't stop him from throwing himself into battle with as much courage as any Rose. If it wasn't for him, I'm not sure I would have survived Gothyn. I think I would have given up and stopped climbing that tree. I would have let it consume me and the key too."

I blinked back a sudden rush of tears. "But he doesn't let me give up, even when giving up is all I want to do. Even when it's the only option I feel is left to me."

Farrin squeezed my hand gently. "You love him."

"I do." I looked at my sister, let my tears spill over. "I love him, and it terrifies me. Look at me." I gestured helplessly at my face. "This isn't me."

"But maybe it is." Farrin wiped my cheeks with the backs of her fingers. "Maybe you've just had to hide this part of yourself for so long that you don't remember it. Brave Mara. I'm so sorry for everything. If I could go back to that day, I would take your place in an instant. I would insist that the Warden—"

"I'm glad you didn't." I swiped a hand across my face and looked away. "We all have our places in the world. Rosewarren is mine. Ivyhill is yours, and it wouldn't have survived without you. Father wouldn't have survived without you."

After that, we were quiet for a long time. All three men were now wrestling like schoolboys on the lawn, covered in mud and grass stains, but I felt as though they were very far away. My world was only as large as my sister and me. She nestled against me, and I held on to her, and the leaves above us rustled softly in the wind.

When I recovered my voice and my calm, I remembered a question I'd thought of while lying in Gareth's arms early that morning, all the worries of my own life wiped away by his touch.

"Gareth has told me that his parents were cruel," I said quietly, "especially his mother. But he hasn't said more than that. I assume you know the story?"

"I do, but it's not my story to tell. Please be patient with him when you ask him about it. Those are old wounds, and humiliating ones."

"I know a thing or two about old wounds."

Farrin blew out a quick, sad breath. "I wish I could take all of that away from both of you."

I moved closer to her, relishing the feeling of her warm body next to mine. Memories of my childhood at Ivyhill were so often muddled, but this I remembered perfectly—this closeness, the warmth of my sisters' bodies. I remembered whispering to Farrin under the covers after a bad dream and chasing a squealing Gemma through our mother's ivy-crowned hallways.

I remembered little, but I remembered the most important things.

"This helps," I said to Farrin. "This helps more than you know."

⟡

Later that night, after supper, I sorted through Mother's bountiful supplies to gather what we might need in Vauzanne.

Everything Gareth and I had brought from Rosewarren remained at the Falkeron monastery, including his glasses; while I didn't expect to miraculously find a spare pair at Wardwell, I was nevertheless disappointed not to. We would have to watch him carefully in Vauzanne. His eyesight wasn't dreadful close up, but he could still confuse things from a distance.

I sat on the floor of Mother's storeroom, thinking through logistics—what we would take from Wardwell; what we could borrow from Talan's friend Kirsa, at whose house we would stay in the Vauzanian town of Westry; what food I should eat over the next twenty-four hours to ensure that I could run all the way from Briarcourt to Vauzanne's southeastern coast, if it came to that. My body was strong and fast, but it was still a body and needed fuel. I'd have to eat like a horse between now and then.

Suddenly a cry of terror shattered the storeroom's quiet, followed by the sound of something crashing to pieces. I bolted to my feet and made it to the kitchen a few seconds before Father did.

Mother stood beside the kitchen table, shards of plates at her feet and her face white, frozen. Her mouth was open in a silent scream, and she held her head in her hands. Everything in the cottage rattled quietly, as if some great beast were thundering closer and closer.

I hurried to Mother, pried her hands loose, and shook her a little. "What is it? Speak. Are we in danger?"

When she blinked, silent tears spilled down her cheeks. "It's

Neave," she whispered. "She's in terrible pain. Someone is hurting her. Someone is making her bleed."

I heard the others hurrying into the front room but kept my eyes fixed on my mother.

"We need more information," I told her. "Think hard. What can you see? Who is hurting her? Where is she?"

"A house," she whispered after a moment. "A grand house in a dark wood."

"Briarcourt," Ryder muttered behind me.

"What else?" I demanded. "Every detail is helpful."

Mother's wide-eyed gaze was far away. "A towering staircase. A pretty room and a pretty bed. A man with rings. And music." Her gaze shifted, and she found Farrin, who stood stiffly at Ryder's side. "I hear music. A piano, and it's making such a racket."

Her dazed expression crumpled, and her hands flew up to cover her ears. "It's so loud. He thinks no one can hear her over the sound of it, but they *can*."

Father moved past me and helped her sit, murmuring to her in his low, gruff voice. Mother blinked and looked at him. She leaned her forehead against his.

I turned away from them, my throat closing with anger. The thought of them here, together and safe in this beautiful house, while the rest of us ran straight into certain danger, made my skin crawl. Suddenly I understood why the first thing Farrin had done upon seeing our mother after all those years without her was to break her jaw.

"As soon as Mother gets hold of herself and has the strength to transport us," I told the others, "we'll leave. I've made a list of supplies to take with us. Talan and Gareth, if you'll gather the food items, Ryder and I will handle the weapons. Farrin and Gemma, you should train as much as you can in the time we have left. Use your powers and make sure they're ready, but don't overtax yourself. The three of us especially will need to be at our best."

I looked at each of them in turn, saving Gareth for last. His bright, ready gaze made me feel a bit stronger. He believed that I could do this, and he was right. I was a Rose, and I'd led soldiers into far more dire situations than this.

I squared my shoulders and marched past my parents into the kitchen. Before anything else happened, I needed something to eat. Already my body was humming, preparing itself. It wanted to run. It wanted to fight. And soon it would get its chance.

Chapter 28

A demon, an Anointed wilder, three demigods, and an Anointed sage. Our group of six certainly didn't lack power.

Still, it was easier than I'd thought it would be to sneak into the Lemaire estate of Briarcourt—an ease that pushed my nerves to their limit.

Hundreds of hopeful refugees crowded the narrow dirt road that led south from the estate, out of the Knotwood, and into open country. Tangled trees flanked the road, thick-trunked and monstrously tall. High above us, their branches met in a dark canopy that blocked out the wintry night sky. And they *hissed*. It wasn't loud, but I could hear it underneath the road's clamor: a low, malevolent thread of sound that turned my blood cold.

I'd never been to the Knotwood, or to Vauzanne, but I certainly knew how to read giant magical barriers, and I got the distinct feeling that the Knotwood wasn't happy about being held back from this road. Whatever bargain the Lemaire family had struck to make this happen, I felt in my gut that it wouldn't last forever. Someday the Knotwood would lose its patience and consume this road, and Briarcourt, and everyone who lived there.

I just hoped that day would not be today.

We pushed our way up the road, a task made monumentally easier by Talan and Farrin. Every time eyes fell upon us, Talan sent the owner a feeling of contentment, and they looked away, languid and happy, utterly uninterested in us. And since the moment we'd left Kirsa's house in our borrowed finery, Farrin had been singing a song of disguise and stealth under her breath.

When I glanced at her, noting the thin sheen of sweat on her forehead, doubt crept into my mind. Our passage across the Gloaming Sea, cradled in the shell of Mother's power, had been swift but staggering. We'd arrived at Kirsa's house in Westry wrung out and dripping with sweat, and Mother hadn't lingered to help us recover. One moment she'd been there, shimmering in her platinum armor, fully resplendent and golden-eyed—Philippa's humanity completely overshadowed by Kerezen's godliness—and the next she'd been gone. The only sign that she'd been there at all was a dark circle of flattened grass, faintly steaming.

Traveling across such a great distance in the grip of such powerful magic could have done more to drain us of strength than I'd realized. If Farrin used up all her energy simply getting us through the doors, getting us back out again would be infinitely more difficult.

I glanced at Ryder, a question in my eyes. He shook his head slightly, the corner of his mouth quirked into a smile. He looked fierce with pride. Farrin, that look told me, would be just fine.

As we followed Talan up the road, I scanned the crowd for signs of trouble. But not even my demigod senses could make sense of the commotion. There were too many sweating, squirming bodies trying to reach Briarcourt's doors, too many voices crying out desperately in case the Lemaires heard their pleas and took pity on them. Everyone wore gowns and suits, coattails and stoles; some were clean and understated like the ones we'd borrowed from Kirsa, others as flashy as peacocks, still others threadbare patchwork.

And though Talan and Farrin carved us a path through the chaos, the roaring crowd pressed in on us from all sides, and as we pushed deeper and deeper into the Knotwood, the trees became enormous, some twice as tall as Rosewarren's highest tower.

By the time we slipped past Lemaire's guards and into the house, every hair on the back of my neck was standing up. In a few quick seconds, I surveyed the room: 316 guests; thirty-four guards carrying weapons I could see; another thirty who were not obviously armed. The main ballroom was three stories high; the railings on the upper floors were festooned with silver ribbons, golden bells, frosted winter foliage. Tables piled with food and drink lined the room. Three enormous chandeliers hung from the ceiling, dripping with hundreds of flickering candles. Each tall, gilt-framed window boasted a view of the great black wood outside, which dwarfed the grounds and made the Lemaires' mansion feel like a dollhouse. On a low stage in the northeastern corner of the room, a ten-piece orchestra played a cheery waltz.

And perched by the grand staircase were Lord and Lady Lemaire. Glamorous and glittering—he in a suit of light green and silver brocade, she in a matching gown—they presided over the room amidst a crowd of fluttering admirers. A line of guests waited at the foot of their dais, arms laden with gifts. A young woman in a modest gray gown knelt before them and offered their guard a small velvet pouch—full of coin she couldn't afford to lose, no doubt.

Fury rose in me as we circled the room. These people made refugees compete for shelter, forced them to go through this mockery of a ball, and still had the nerve to accept tributes. Perhaps they even required them.

If this mission ended up affording me even a few minutes of spare time, I'd use every second of it to terrify the Lemaires so completely that they'd have nightmares for weeks.

As planned, Talan and Farrin began slowly easing back on their power, and by the time their protections lifted and Farrin stopped singing at last, we'd split into three groups of two: Gemma and Talan, Farrin and Ryder, Gareth and me. Being in pairs would make it easier to blend in.

Gareth took my hand, grabbed a goblet of wine from a nearby table, and led me to a velvet chaise pushed against the wall. He lounged on it with ease, sipped his wine, wrapped his arm around my shoulders. I leaned into him, put my hand on his thigh. To the other guests, I hoped, we'd look like nothing more than a lucky couple enjoying the party.

"In five minutes," I murmured close to Gareth's ear, a sly smile on my face, "we'll move toward that tapestry to your left. The lounges just past it are full of gambling tables. Everyone's loud and drunk. We'll be able to slip through them without anyone noticing."

Gareth turned his head toward me and laughed a little, as if I'd told a wonderful joke. "I understand," he said quietly. "How many guards?"

"Three, and they're distracted."

"And drunk too, I hope."

"One of them certainly is. He can't quite keep his balance."

A passel of giggling girls hurried past us, their hands full of lace-trimmed fans and sloshing goblets. I recognized the leader by her hair. Kirsa, Talan, and Gemma had briefed us on the Lemaire family—three girls and a young man of twenty, all of them with their father's unmissable locks, icy-blond and striking. All of them were botanical elementals like my mother had been before the goddess living inside her had awakened.

As the girls passed, Gareth leaned in to kiss me. His mouth tasted of wine, and when his hand slid around my waist to pull me closer to him, my stomach tightened and heat gathered between my legs. He held me to him until not even my sensitive hearing could detect the girls' chatter over the noise of the party.

When I pulled back from him, he smiled, his green eyes sparkling. "I know this is a deadly mission and all, but I have to say, I'm having a marvelous time so far."

The low tone of his voice sent a frisson of desire through my body. "Stay focused, Professor."

"What were they talking about? Anything helpful?"

"Aralinda Lemaire is angry with her parents. Something to do with her brother and a woman named Lily. She doesn't think Lily is suitable for her brother, but her parents won't do anything to discourage him from pursuing her. And she's annoyed with her sister too. The youngest, Griselda. She has a weak stomach, apparently."

"Family gossip."

"But not the useful kind."

Gareth frowned. "I'm not sure why someone having a weak stomach is grounds for annoyance."

I glanced past him at the crowded ballroom, quickly noting my sisters' locations. The gowns we'd borrowed from Kirsa were sturdy but unremarkable, the fabric in need of a good laundering: dusty blue for Farrin, dull olive green for Gemma, faded lavender for me. We'd chosen them in order to blend in, but even in plain gowns that didn't fit quite right, my sisters stood out more than I was comfortable with. Gemma and Talan had settled themselves at one of many high tables, a plate of food between them; Farrin and Ryder danced in a throng of others. But my eyes went to them immediately.

Was it simply because they were my sisters? Or was it because my sharp eyes couldn't help but notice the trace of Kerezen's power that lingered upon us?

"What's wrong?" Gareth murmured, leaning back to sip from his goblet. "You're restless."

"I don't like waiting. I like moving."

"And you move most excellently, in all manner of scenarios."

"Please don't make jokes right now."

He glanced at me. "Something is wrong," he said quietly. "Tell me."

"My sisters are too obvious. They have a glow about them, and they don't look frightened enough."

Gareth shifted on the chaise and lazily surveyed the ballroom over the rim of his goblet. I allowed myself a brief moment to admire how his borrowed coat, vest, and trousers hugged his long, lean body.

"I see no glow," he said. "And isn't the point of this party to convince the Lemaires that you're having a good time so they'll keep you around? If Gemma and Farrin were cowering in the corner, they'd draw much more attention, I think, and not the good kind."

He was right, of course. But I couldn't shake my unease, and Aralinda Lemaire's laughter echoed through my mind, raising alarm bells I couldn't explain. The sooner we completed this mission, the better.

"I sense you're about to tell me that we should get started," Gareth added, "even though it hasn't yet been five minutes."

"You sense correctly."

"Before we do, I must tell you one very important thing."

I bit back an impatient curse. "Go on, then."

He put down his goblet and turned to kiss my hair, his arm still loosely about my shoulders. "Even in your borrowed dress," he murmured, "you look beautiful. If this were an ordinary party, I'd dance all night with you, stopping only occasionally to pull you into some shadowy corner and kiss you senseless. Then, after we got back home, I'd take you upstairs and—"

"Home?"

"Come now, you stopped me at the best part," he said, gently teasing.

"What home, Gareth?" I didn't know why the word had pierced me so deeply, but it had, and for a moment I couldn't quite catch my breath.

"Our home," he said simply, and then pulled back to look at me, his smile wavering. "It was only a daydream. I wanted to fill your head with nice imagery before we dashed off to spy and murder. I'm sorry."

Our home. I took Gareth's hand and kissed it, my heart thudding against my ribs. I wasn't sure if what I felt was terror or terrible happiness.

"There's nothing to be sorry for," I said, standing, not quite looking at him. "Let's go. I can't bear to sit here any longer."

"Easy, Mara." He tugged gently on my fingers. "We're meant to look like partygoers, not assassins."

He was right, of course. I forced my muscles to relax and looped my arm through his. As we wandered toward the gambling rooms, his words flitted through my mind with every heartbeat, like starlight scattered across a dark sea: *Our home. Our home. Our home.*

CHAPTER 29

An hour later, we'd found no leads, I'd knocked six house guards unconscious and left them slumped in various dark corners, and even Gareth was beginning to look worried.

As we hurried down yet another quiet, carpeted hallway lined with portraits of dead Lemaires and elaborate wooden carvings of the Knotwood, I thought over Mother's words for the hundredth time: *A towering staircase. A pretty room and a pretty bed. A man with rings. A piano, and it's making such a racket.*

Evocative words, but the only towering staircase I'd seen since entering this wretched house was the one in the ballroom, and that part of the mansion was Gemma and Talan's territory. No matter how far I stretched my senses, I couldn't take in the whole house at once, and all I could really hear anyway was a faint din from the party.

And footsteps against the carpet, approaching steadily from around the corner up ahead.

I held out an arm, warning Gareth away. He fell back and stood flat against the wall. His hand hovered over the knife strapped to his hip, hidden under his coat. He gave me a sharp nod, and quick as a cat I raced ahead down the hallway and darted around the left corner. The footsteps belonged to a house guard on patrol—tall, broad-shouldered, quite obviously bored. I delivered one sharp blow to a spot between her shoulder blades, and she collapsed to the floor before she even got a chance to see me coming.

I carried her to a linen closet we'd passed, tucked her inside, and returned to Gareth.

"Another guard," I muttered. "Let's keep going."

"That makes seven," he said, joining me as we hurried down the now empty hallway. "Someone might start noticing something's wrong if we dispose of too many more."

"If it were just me, I could probably slip past them with no need for incapacitation."

"If you're implying that it might have been better to leave me safely at Kirsa's house," he said wryly, "I can't say I disagree with you."

In fact, I *was* starting to think this very thing. The longer the night crept on, the more I worried about him, and the more I worried, the more distracted I became. Normally, my mind was clear and sharp as crystal during missions. No agitation, only calculations.

Tonight, however, I felt as though I was laden with precious, vulnerable cargo. Gareth could fight, certainly, but would he be able to see well enough to do so?

"I do wish you had your glasses," I admitted.

"That makes two of us."

More footsteps. I held out my arm and waited for Gareth to flatten himself against the wall, then hurried down the corridor, turned right at the next junction, and knocked the patrolling guard unconscious with a swift kick to his head.

And that makes eight, I thought grimly, hurrying back to Gareth. But he wasn't where I'd left him. He was moving slowly back down the hallway, running his fingers over the wall with his head slightly bent as if listening hard to something.

I hurried to him, fighting the urge to scold him for wandering off. "What are you doing?"

"These wall carvings," he murmured. "I've been pressed up against several of them now while you dispatched our guard friends, and they all look the same: twisting branches, leaves, the occasional animal. A lovely tribute to the Knotwood. But every ten feet is a random nonsense word tucked into the carvings. The letters are scrambled. But right here"—he touched a particular gnarl of wood—"this is an *actual* word. It says *enter*."

I squinted at it. "All I see are leaves."

"It's well hidden unless you can read Zelophar. Then it leaps out like a beacon."

"Good thing you're a brilliant Anointed sage with a mind like a steel trap who memorizes and files away everything he's ever seen."

"Yes, that helps too," he said pleasantly.

Zelophar. The word sounded familiar. "Is that an Olden language?"

He nodded. "Believed to be the favored tongue of the gods. Various sites all over the world are marked with these characters—high mountain cliffs, excavated caves, the land where the five Cloisters now stand. Old places, places scholars agree were marked by the gods themselves."

"How many people can read Zelophar?"

"Besides me? Two of my colleagues at the university. Certainly the five abbots." He paused. "The *four* abbots, now."

"And when were you going to tell me about all these hidden words you've been fondling?"

"When I found something worth reporting," he replied. "Is your eyesight good enough to determine whether this wood is newer than what surrounds it?"

I bent down to examine the letters, which looked to me more like pictures drawn with harsh lines. Scanning the minuscule whorls in the wood, I caught the faint sheen of oil from recent fingerprints—and older, fainter fingerprints beneath that.

"It's certainly *different* from the rest," I said slowly. "It's a slight shade darker and less worn. And someone besides you has touched it many times. But the wood surrounding it is clean."

"What are the chances someone would touch this one specific spot on the wall and ignore all the rest?"

I straightened. "It says *enter*?"

"Yes, but if there *is* a secret door hidden in the wall, it won't budge." He glanced at me sheepishly. "I was too curious to wait for you."

"A curious librarian," I muttered. "Now, that's a shock." I scanned the wall once more, then glanced at him. "Stand back. There is a door. I can see the seams. I'm going to kick it open as quietly as I can. Then we'll wait to see if anyone comes to investigate the noise."

He stared at me. "You can kick open a door *quietly*?"

In answer, I spun around and struck the wall with my right foot. At the last second, I pulled back the slightest bit, and my foot made contact with only a slight thud. But the seething power coiled in my leg muscles did its job anyway. The door flew open, and we hurried into the stone passage behind it, which was dimly lit by a single flickering torch in an iron sconce.

I pulled the door mostly closed, leaving only a sliver of the hallway visible. For five excruciating minutes, I listened hard, stretching my senses down every corridor I could find. Nothing. Silence. Satisfied, I pulled the door all the way shut. It clicked into place with barely a sound.

"Have I ever mentioned," Gareth murmured, his eyes merry in the torchlight, "how devastatingly beautiful you are when you're kicking down doors and knocking out guards?"

I shot him a small smile and grabbed the torch. "Let's see where this goes."

"Ah, let me carry that," he said, gesturing for it. "It matters much less if one of my hands is occupied."

He had a point. I gave it to him, and we crept down the passage in silence, shadows flickering all around us, until suddenly a faint noise made me freeze. I grabbed Gareth's arm, my heart pounding.

Music. I was hearing music.

Someone was playing a piano.

A piano, and it's making such a racket.

A small chill skipped down my arms. Gareth was tense beside me, not daring to say a word. I pressed on along the passage, and I knew the moment Gareth started to hear the music too. He drew in a quick breath, and the faint murmur of his heartbeat grew faster, louder.

The passage ended at a wooden door set into the stone wall, lit by a second torch. I paused beside it, listening past the cheerful music for any sign that someone besides our mysterious pianist waited on the other side of the door. But gods, the piano *was* making a racket; the music was frenetic and gratingly loud. Skillful, but inelegant. I immediately thought of Farrin, how much better this music would sound if played by her dexterous fingers. A little flare of worry sparked in my mind: Where was my sister at this moment? Was she safe? Was Gemma?

I shoved the thought aside and glanced at Gareth. "Stay here until I signal for you."

He didn't look happy about that, but he nodded and stepped back, and I opened the door as quietly and slowly as I'd ever done anything in my life. It opened into a small but grand ballroom, lit only by a few glimmers of candlelight. The parquet floor gleamed softly; flowering vines wound through the white rafters. A girl with white-blond hair sat at a piano in the center of the room, wearing a prim, lace-trimmed dress. Beyond her, a spiral of iron stairs climbed nearly all the way to the ceiling. At the top was a small landing and a door set into the wall.

My blood ran cold. I wished passionately that I could shove Gareth into a safe cupboard somewhere; the frantic music rattling around the room and the lone girl and the lone staircase told me something terrible was about to happen. The staircase was so odd, standing out harshly against the room's pastel finery. And where did that door at the top lead?

I went to Gareth and said against his ear, very calmly, "Take off your coat and douse the torch with it, but keep it with you to use as a club if you have to. Head for the staircase, but keep to the edges of the room. The shadows might hide us."

He nodded, his expression grim, and followed me into the ballroom. My mind raced through every possibility I could think of. The girl was clearly Griselda Lemaire, for Aralinda was the second of the three sisters, and this girl playing the piano was smaller than she was. The moment she saw us, she might use her elemental magic to send the ceiling vines whipping down toward us. Or she might call for help, or press a secret mechanism that would alert the house guard and bring them rushing in.

Or she might cower at the sight of us and run off to cry in a corner. *The little brat has a weak stomach*, Aralinda had said to her friends.

We crept along the left side of the room while Griselda hammered away at her piano. The music was deafening, and I started to think we might make it all the way to the staircase, and maybe even up it, without the girl noticing a thing.

But then came a break in the music, and without turning around on her bench, she said quietly, "Have you come to save her?"

Her voice was small, thin. A pause, her fingers hovering above the keyboard, and then she resumed playing.

I gestured sharply at Gareth to stay where he was, then went to the girl. My body thrummed with restrained force; my skin was scorching hot. I'd knock her straight through her piano if I had to.

But then came three quick, triumphant chords, and the music stopped. The piece was over. And Griselda Lemaire turned to me with tears streaming down her face. Her face was thin, her lips chapped and raw, as if she'd been biting them all through her little recital.

"I've been hoping someone would come," she whispered. "It's gone on for far too long. He's up there right now. I won't call the guards. I'll keep playing and hide the noise. Just please get her out."

I watched Griselda closely. "Who are you talking about?"

Her face fell. She turned back to the piano, riffled through a pile of sheet music. "I have to start playing again," she said quickly, "or else he'll come yell at me."

I grabbed her thin wrist with one hand and clamped my other over her mouth, holding her tightly enough to hurt.

"When I let go," I said quietly, "you'll tell me what's happening here, and you'll do it fast, or I'll break your wrists so you can't play at all. Do you understand?"

She nodded, and when I released her, she wasted no time. "They keep Lily in the room at the top of the stairs," she whispered frantically. "I don't know why. She's just some farmer's daughter. Mama brought her to us months ago, right when the Knotwood started growing. And Papa put her up in the room, and he left Eldric in charge of her. He goes to her often, and when he does, I'm to play down here until he's had his fill of her and leaves."

She drew in a shuddering breath. "I'm to play as loud as I can so no one will hear her. Eldric doesn't want to upset our staff. And he hates me," she added, her eyes filling with fresh tears. "He always has. He likes to terrify me. *Mouse,* he calls me. If I don't do this, he'll punish me, and he likes few things more than that." Her mouth trembled. "So you see, I have to do this." She selected a piece of music with shaking fingers.

My mouth tasted sour with fury. "Is it just the two of them up there? Eldric and Lily?"

Griselda nodded.

"No guards?"

She shook her head.

"And the stairs are the only way in or out?"

She nodded again. Tears plopped onto her fingers.

I gritted my teeth and placed a gentle hand on Griselda's shoulder. This single kindness was all I could offer her, and even my light touch made her flinch. A moment later, she was playing again, her fingers crashing onto the keys with such vigor that I could barely hear myself think.

I hurried back to Gareth. "Did you hear all of that?"

"I wish I hadn't," he said, his voice hard and angry. He glanced up the stairs. "Do you think this Lily is unaware of her true nature?"

"Yes, like Mother was, and Yvaine too." I quickly looked around the room one more time, but no guards burst in, and Griselda was completely immersed in her own frenzied performance. The ceiling's canopy of vines suddenly seemed ominous. "We'll have to act fast, before Eldric can use his magic against us."

Gareth glanced up at the vines. "Yes, if we can avoid it, I'd prefer not to be strangled by greenery today."

I hurried to the stairs and climbed them, Gareth on my heels. At the top, I turned back to scan the room, but we were still alone with Griselda.

I tried the door, but it was locked, and as I stepped back to kick it open, a woman's scream rang out from inside the room. The music cloaked it, but not well enough. Gareth flinched and held the torch higher. Griselda faltered at her piano, the music breaking off for an instant before resuming, louder and sharper than before.

My body lit up with rage. Whether that was Neave in there or truly just a farmer's daughter named Lily, this demented arrangement had gone on long enough.

I kicked down the door and sent it flying across the room, where it crashed through a window and sailed out into the night. A young man scrambled out of a canopy bed: Eldric Lemaire. He had icy-blond hair that fell in waves to his shoulders, and he wore a loose white tunic and rumpled trousers of fine gold brocade. He was sweaty, wild-eyed. His mad gaze darted to the shattered window, which was framed by quivering vines. The whole *room* teemed with greenery; hundreds of vines, maybe even thousands, stretched across the ceiling. The walls were thick with them. And in this house, vines might as well have been swords.

I tore across the room and rammed Eldric in the chest with my shoulder. The impact cracked his ribs and left him crumpled against the wall, gasping for breath.

I went to the bed at once, where a woman who looked to be about my age lay curled up in a mess of silk sheets. She wore a white nightgown, and she stared at nothing, her eyes puffy and red. Her pale skin was a tapestry of cuts and scars, and the blood glistening at each wound was both red and gold. Red, the blood of her human host; gold, the blood of her true godly self.

For a brief moment, it felt like all the breath left my body.

Mother had been right.

Neave.

I knew it was her as surely as I felt the floor under my feet. All of my senses whirled in alarmed recognition. This was Neave, in the body of a farmer's daughter named Lily, who might not even know what—*who*—she carried inside her.

"Mara," Gareth said sharply, a warning in his voice. At the same moment, a bolt of magic shot through the room, raising all the hairs on my arms.

I whirled around. Eldric, huddled against the wall and cradling his ribs, had summoned the vines. They moved fast, slithering like snakes. Some of them came for me, others for Gareth. And still others went straight for Eldric, wrapping him in a hissing green cocoon several layers thick. Not even I would be able to get Neave and Gareth to safety *and* give this disgusting worm of a man the grisly fate he deserved. Not before the vines consumed us.

I scooped Neave into my arms and ran for the door, shouting Gareth's name. But when I glanced back to find him, he wasn't running after me. He'd found a candelabra on a side table with four lit candles, and as I watched, he tossed aside his burned jacket and thrust the darkened, oil-soaked torch into the flames.

As soon as the torch burst back to life, Gareth flung it toward Eldric and his shield of vines. The spinning flames ignited the bed's canopy and then crashed into the spot where Eldric hid. The rest of the bed caught fire immediately, and the vines not long after, but Gareth was already racing toward the door. We ran down the stairs to the sound of Eldric's screams.

I'd never loved Gareth more fiercely than I did in that moment.

The ballroom was empty; Griselda had abandoned her piano, but the door to the passage stood open. A wave of gratitude tore through me. She could have easily locked us in here if she'd wanted to.

Back in the main house, the hallways were quiet and empty, just as we'd left them, but the party had erupted into chaos. I heard it long before Gareth could—Aralinda Lemaire sobbing, her father calling for the doors to be locked, house guards shouting for everyone to present themselves for inspection. Someone had set fire to the house; someone had murdered Eldric Lemaire.

Griselda. I bit back a curse. This was a big house; the only way anyone could already know about the fire was if she had reported it to her parents. I stopped a few paces from the now-empty gambling rooms to listen more closely.

"She could have told them exactly where to find us," muttered Gareth, who had obviously come to the same conclusion I had. "But she didn't. They could've come for us, and no one at the party would have been the wiser."

I nodded. "This chaos will be a welcome distraction."

"Thank you, Griselda," he said lightly. "As long as we can still get out, that is."

I glanced down at the girl in my arms. Lily. *Neave.* I had to think of her as a god, not as a human girl, or else the horror of what had happened to her would fell me. She felt weightless in my arms, so still and quiet that if my senses hadn't told me she was indeed breathing, that her tired heart still beat, I would have thought she was dead.

Suddenly the sound of breaking glass exploded from inside the ballroom—one crash after another, and then another, followed by shrieks both human and beastly.

I smiled. My hearing was so sharp that I could see the scene unfurling as clearly as I would with my eyes.

"Ryder has wilded creatures from the Knotwood," I told Gareth. "Birds, raptors, stags, wolves. Hundreds of them. They've broken the windows. They've burst in through the doors. It's havoc. Even the guards are running."

"What an excellent whiskered ruffian he is," Gareth said. Then he looked at me and added gravely, "You know what this means."

I did, and I hated it. "I've got to take Neave and run."

"And the rest of us will regroup outside and head for Kirsa's house. And..." He trailed off.

"And I'll meet all of you in Fairhaven," I finished firmly. "In two weeks or less, I hope. If only you all weren't such slowpokes."

Gareth looked as wretched as I felt. I shifted Neave into one arm, tugged him close with my free hand, and kissed him hard. Then I held him to me and pressed my forehead against his.

"If you let yourself get hurt," I said, "I'll kill you. Right there in the Citadel before hundreds of witnesses."

He smiled faintly. "Stay safe, darling," he whispered, and then he kissed my cheek, and I turned with my heart in my throat and started to run.

CHAPTER 30

I'd run long distances before. I'd run so fast that to anyone I passed, I appeared as little more than a blur. And I'd done both at the same time on countless occasions while on missions for the Order.

But until the night I fled Briarcourt with a half-dead god in my arms, I'd never had to run so hard and so fast for so long. It was a good two hundred miles from the Knotwood's mouth to Rithia, a port city on Vauzanne's southeastern shore. I had Order contacts there; I would secure passage on the fastest ship I could find and hopefully make it across the Gloaming Sea to Fairhaven before anyone could catch up to me.

Kilraith, my mind whispered in Talan's voice, then in my sisters'. *Before* Kilraith *catches up to you.*

He knows.

He's coming.

No one tried to stop me as I raced out of Briarcourt. They were too busy flooding outside themselves, evading Ryder's mad wilded beasts. Just as I ducked under a flowered arbor and into the Briarcourt gardens, an arrow whizzed past me and pierced the flank of a bounding stag. I dodged the poor bleating creature, leapt over a hedge, and tore through the rest of the gardens—a sea of guests and guards, wolves and bears and hawks, sweaty finery and polished armor bearing the crest of the House of Lemaire.

The cry of a falcon pierced the chaos and made my heart seize. I wished desperately that I hadn't ordered Freyda to stay at Rosewarren. The long road ahead would have felt much shorter if I'd had her with me. And with her tireless amber eyes overhead, scanning the horizon for Kilraith, I wouldn't have had to worry quite so much about being ambushed.

"You run so fast," murmured Neave, dreamy and half-awake in my arms. The sound of her voice startled me.

"Just stay put and relax," I told her. "I've got you."

Suddenly a deep groan rumbled behind me, followed by a fresh wave of screams. I looked back just in time to see darkness spilling from one of the gigantic trees nearest the house. Roots sprang free from the earth, spitting mud and stone, and as I watched in horror, long black tendrils latched onto the corner of Briarcourt and began climbing up its walls.

Whatever had held back the Knotwood was gone, and now this wild, gods-crafted forest was waking up.

I turned away and bolted down the road. My stomach turned at the sounds I heard. Each one painted a vivid picture of crumbling stone, collapsing towers, shrieking people, and a hungry forest knitting itself closed around the Briarcourt grounds.

I knew what happened when the Middlemist broke past its boundaries, as it had done a little more every day over the past few months. The land it consumed became Mistland—gray and sunless, unpredictable, and vulnerable to Olden invasion. Those who didn't make it out of Briarcourt in time could end up facing unimaginable horrors in the depths of those woods.

Neave peered past my arm. "They're helping," she murmured. Her eyes were cloudy, her lips white. "Your friends are helping. How do I know that?"

"You're dreaming," I told her. "Go back to sleep."

But her words made my throat tighten. *They're helping.* My sisters, my friends.

My Gareth.

Neave could have been delirious, but I knew in my heart that she was right. Of *course* they were trying to help as many people escape as they could. I might have done the same if I were them. The Warden would have scolded me for it. *Unnecessary heroics* was what she called that sort of thing. Our lives, she always told us, were too precious for us to take needless risks. *Keep to the mission. You cannot save everyone.*

And she was right. Nevertheless, it was torment to run away from the others. Part of me wanted to toss this girl I neither knew nor loved into the bracken and tear back up the road to make sure all five of them survived. I would carry them on my back if I had to. I would blaze a new fiery road through the trees and stun the Knotwood in its tracks.

But instead I gritted my teeth and kept running. The trees on either side of me shrank from monstrous to simply tall. Soon they were gone, and it was just Neave and me alone on the road, with Briarcourt behind us and open country ahead. The horizon was white, the sky thick and gray. It had begun to snow.

⟡

Neave was light, but she didn't weigh nothing, and as far as I could tell, no one was following us.

So, forty miles into my run, I stopped beside a small creek to stretch my legs and dunk my head into the icy water. Even though the air was cold and the snow came thickly, my muscles were warm, limber, and happy, and the exercise had cleared my mind.

I considered Neave while I wrung out my hair and twisted it into a tight knot. She was a pitiful sight, hardly more than a bundle of knobby elbows and scarred legs. I wished I'd thought to snatch someone's coat before fleeing Briarcourt. My body was hot enough to warm her as we ran, but she deserved to wear something more dignified than the nightgown of her imprisonment.

I squatted beside her and brushed the dark hair off her face. It was chin length and jaggedly cut, most likely hacked to pieces by Eldric Lemaire's knife. She reminded me of Alastrina Bask. After her time in Mhorghast, Alastrina had looked like this—as if all the good, strong pieces of who she'd been had been cut away. According to Ryder, her time recuperating at the estate of Gemma's friend Illaria Farrow was the only thing that had brought some life back into her eyes.

"Lily?" I said. "I need you to listen to me." When she didn't respond, I lightly pushed her. "Wake up, Lily. This is important."

Her eyelids fluttered open. "That's not my name."

"What is your name, then?"

I waited, but all she could do was frown at me.

"I don't know," she mumbled. "It's far away."

"Excellent. I'm Mara. Nice to meet you, Faraway."

A flutter of irritation crossed her face. "That's not my name."

"It will have to do. Listen carefully. We're going to start running again, and we won't stop for a long time. Do you remember when you told me that my friends were helping?"

She stared at me, but it was obvious she wasn't really seeing me. Her pale hazel eyes swam with specks of bright gold.

"I do," she replied, her voice quiet but steady. "Your sisters and their lovers. *Your* lover." She touched my cheek. Realization dawned in her eyes. "Kerezen."

I grabbed on to her wrist, as if that would somehow keep her with me. "Neave? Can you hear me?"

The shadow of another face flickered across her features. "You are my sister's daughter."

Her solemn proclamation chilled me. "I am, and I need you to stay with me, all right? I need you to keep watch as I run. I'm going to run faster now, and I'll need to put all my energy into that. It's possible someone might come after us on the road. If you sense anyone coming toward us with ill intent, tell me at once. Do you understand?"

"Ill intent?"

She was fading. Neave was fading. The gold in her eyes dimmed; her voice wavered.

"Ill intent means that someone wants to hurt us," I said.

She nodded, her gaze distant. "And he does. He wants to very much."

My blood turned to ice, then fire. "Who does?"

"Him."

I was loath to say his name. "I need more than that."

"He Who Is All," she replied. Her unseeing gaze lifted to mine. "Kilraith. He seeks with many arms, and many eyes, and all of them are cruel."

"What do you see? Is he coming after us?"

"He comes," she said, her voice lowering, "with ill intent."

"How far away is he?"

"Faraway. That is my name, not his."

I nearly slapped her. The clouded look in her eyes was terrible. "How close is he?"

But as soon as I asked the question, I felt the answer myself. The ground began to shake, a faint tremor that neither of my sisters would have noticed. A sour charge filled the air, like the scent of lightning. And then, from perhaps a few miles behind us, came sounds I knew well: a glottal roar, an avian shriek, and the hard, swift gallop of paws and hooves.

Chimaera. Ten of them. I cocked my head, listening. Three avian, two ursine, four lupine, one feline. And they weren't alone. From somewhere behind them came a deep, slow rumble like a rolling wave, and suddenly Kilraith's voice slithered out of my memories.

You are certainly interesting, he'd told me. On that night in Mhorghast, when my sisters and I had retrieved the egg anchor, when Ankaret had come at Farrin's call and destroyed it—and herself—we'd first had to play Kilraith's cruel games of illusion. Farrin had navigated a replica of Ivyhill; Gemma and Talan had once again fought through the dark hallways of Talan's childhood home, Brimgard.

And I, with Nesset at my side, had faced the trials of my childhood. On the shores of a false Lake Voroth, I'd endured dozens of trials, stabbed Kilraith's illusion of Petra dozens of times. Everything I'd done to try and change her fate had failed. And when I'd stood over her dead body for the final time, stone paving my insides cold, Petra's eyes had opened, and a smile that was not the one I remembered had spread across her face.

"You are certainly interesting," she'd said in Kilraith's smooth voice. "I'm not sure I've ever encountered a creature who despises herself so completely."

Then her smile had widened. "Except perhaps myself. Kindred spirits, you and I."

I'd lunged at him then and plunged my dagger into Petra's ruined chest, but all that had done was make Kilraith laugh. I'd watched Petra's body disintegrate into ashes at the touch of my blade, and as Kilraith's laughter filled the air, the illusion of Lake Voroth had disappeared. In its place had been the god Jaetris trapped in an old man's human body—and my sisters, and our father, and Ryder, and Gareth, all of them bound in Kilraith's shadows.

The memories teemed in my mind, frightened, furious. And as

if my thoughts had uprooted something terrible, the ground heaved under my feet, and a whooping howl split the cold night air.

I scooped Neave into my arms and ran.

I never once looked back, but I could hear the chimaera crashing through the trees behind us, and soon they weren't even two miles away. The sounds painted an awful picture: ten darting dark shapes forming a hungry V behind me. Surrounding me. Preparing for the kill.

Even though I'd never fought ten chimaera on my own before, my instinct was to stop and try anyway—but I didn't dare. If I lost Neave in battle, all of this would be for nothing.

I leapt across a frozen ravine, hit the ground on the other side, kept running. I hoped there wouldn't be too many more of those. Every jump cost me. My lungs were burning, and it was still fifty miles to the port of Rithia. Veering sharply to the right, I charged into a woodland I'd seen a few miles ago from higher ground. It wasn't ideal—I ran much faster in open country—but we needed the cover.

Suddenly the ground in front of us erupted. Thick black roots burst into the air, then whipped across our path and flattened dozens of trees in an instant.

Kilraith.

He was a child of all five gods, unwittingly created at the moment of their deaths. He carried pieces of all their powers inside him. And clearly he was strong enough to use elemental magic from wherever he was and turn this forest against me.

I couldn't decide which would be worse: his power being this effective even while he was far way, halfway across the world in Aidurra or gathering followers in the Old Country, or him being here in the flesh, tearing across the country toward me and drawing ever closer.

My blood turned to ice at the thought of facing him all alone, but then my father's voice echoed through my mind: *You can feel fear, but you cannot be afraid.*

I tucked Neave close to my chest and jumped over the flying roots, ducked under them, wove through them—until one caught my shin and sent me tumbling. Neave flew out of my arms and into the underbrush. I scrambled after her, yanked her back into my arms, and tore off through the ruin of trees just as the earth split open right where I'd been standing.

And then, only a few hundred yards later, the first of my pursuers finally attacked.

One of the avian chimaera—with mottled naked flesh and great batlike wings—dove down from the canopy and slashed open my back with its claws.

The pain was like fire. I lost my footing and fell—blinded, gasping—but when the beast circled back to make another dive at me, I was ready. I spun around and kicked it right in its soft underbelly, but I was in such furious pain that my kick was wild, my balance off. When my boot hit the creature, knocking it hard against a nearby tree, the impact cracked my leg.

I collapsed with a sharp cry, pain shooting through my body like a knife, but I held tight to Neave, gritted my teeth, and pushed myself back up. The avian chimaera was a dead heap in the dirt, but others were right behind it: a bearlike beast with paws the size of my head; a monstrous lupine creature with scales mottling its coat and plates of bone protruding from its back.

The latter bounded toward me through the trees and reached me first. I held Neave tight to my chest, bowed my head over her, and ran toward the beast, turning at the last moment to ram my right shoulder into its ribs. It yelped in pain and collapsed, its chest caved in, but not before one of its paws caught me across the back, right over my fresh wound.

I fell to my knees once more, stars bursting across my vision and the pain nearly making me lose consciousness. But the bear chimaera was nearly on us, and I had to move. I couldn't kick it, couldn't ram into it. I didn't think my battered body would be able to withstand another hard impact so soon.

The only thing to do was turn and run—through the writhing trees, toward the distant shore. Each time I put weight on my broken leg, blinding pain surged up my body. But I couldn't stop. If I did, Neave would die or fall back into Kilraith's hands. If I stopped, I'd never start again.

All I could do was keep breathing, though even that was painful. Each breath I sucked in burned my lungs. Muscles all over my body throbbed, teetering on the edge of seizing up. And each second brought my attackers closer. I could feel their hot snarling breaths against my nape. I could hear the furious roaring of their blood.

"Child, you are in such pain," Neave murmured, tucked safely against my chest. Her voice was odd. It seemed split in two. "Soon your bones will shatter. Do not fear. Come and find her. Come and find me. I will find you."

I couldn't spare the breath to shut her up. The woodland was denser now, slowing me down. And with my strength so sapped, I couldn't simply break a new path through the trees. All around me, their branches hissed and snapped, lashing my skin and Neave's, though I tried my best to shield her from it.

Please, help me. My prayer was a frantic, automatic compulsion, my mind scrambling for some sense of hope. I'd prayed to Mother before, and she'd come for me and Gareth. She could do it again. I didn't care about how dangerous it would be for her; I wanted nothing except relief. I prayed to her, to my father, to Gareth, to the gods as I'd imagined them in childhood, to the ruined trees splintering on either side of me. Cold sweat poured down my body. There were maybe thirty miles left to the shore. I'd never make it. That, too, became my prayer. *Please, help me. I'll never make it. Please. I won't make it. They'll kill me. I'll lose Neave. I'll lose everything. Please. Please help.*

Tears streaming down my face, I focused on the fading light of my power; it was the only thing keeping me moving. I could barely feel my own body. I was no longer legs and sinew and flesh; I was a firestorm of pain. Something cracked, but I was too far gone to name it. All I knew was it slowed me down; my gait stuttered, my knees close to buckling. I had a faint sense that something was protruding from me that shouldn't have been.

And then, the most remarkable thing: to my left, through the trees, a white brilliance burst into life like a star come down from the sky. Even more remarkably, it kept pace with me.

What new menace was this? I glanced over at it, watching it race through the tangled trees. It grew brighter as I watched, and then came a low humming sound like a sigh, like a song.

At the thought of Farrin, I nearly fell apart. Memories spun through my mind: Gemma's baby fist squeezing my finger. Farrin's voice singing us both to sleep. Little Gemma, deft with blooms, teaching us how to braid flower crowns. Farrin, holding me fiercely to her the night before the Warden came to take me. Gemma had curled up against my back that night, trying valiantly not to cry. *We will always love you,* Farrin had whispered into my hair. *Always, always, always.*

I clung to the images of my sisters with a desperation that felt like hanging onto a crumbling ledge. The world around me was fading; my vision sparkled, turning the trees and Neave and the brilliant racing star into a blur of spinning light.

Do not fear, came a voice—an odd voice that I could barely understand. It was human, it was avian, it was like nothing I'd ever heard.

"Do not fear," Neave echoed in my arms.

Come and find me.

"She will find you," Neave answered. Then she drew in a shocked, shuddering breath, went stiff in my arms, and said something in a language I didn't know.

Gareth would know it. That was the only thought left to me, the only one I could hold on to. He *would* know it—he held dozens of languages in his mind—and he would hate this. He would hate what was happening to me; it would kill him to see it. I was glad he wouldn't.

Distantly I heard roars of pain behind me. Cracks like lightning zipped through the air, sizzling against my skin.

Then, at last, only a few miles from the port city of Rithia, my body gave out. My leg shattered. The burning pain of my ruined back swallowed me whole.

I fell hard and waited for the end, for darkness to take me, but it didn't come.

Instead, a great light shone behind my closed eyelids, forcing them open. At first all I could see was brilliant white tinged with gold. My soldier's instincts still had some life left; I imagined pushing myself to my feet, clenching my fists, turning my body into a battering ram. If this was death, I would meet it with one last burst of defiance.

But I couldn't move. Instead, the light came to me.

"Do not be afraid," it said, in a voice I was starting to recognize. A musical voice like Farrin's but also odd, inhuman. A voice that belonged to something ancient and Olden.

I squinted through the light and caught a glimpse of two brilliant blue eyes, then a fall of hair like cascading fire. Violet and gold, brilliant white and fiery orange. A flash of wings; a woman's regal, benevolent smile. Familiar. Incandescent.

Impossible.

I clutched Neave to my chest with all the strength I had left.

"Yvaine?" I choked out. "Is it you?"

She cocked her head, blinking. "What is this name? I have never heard it, and yet somehow it rings true."

Her figure flickered—woman to bird to woman once more. The low, smooth sound of her voice drew fresh tears from my eyes.

"Ankaret," I said instead, which made her smile in delight, as if she'd heard something wondrous for the very first time.

"You found her," she said, and then she bent low to look at me with two brilliant eyes of fire. Something about her countenance shifted; she looked suddenly stern. "Listen, now. This will hurt, and when you wake, I will be small, hidden, but not gone. It will take me some time to come back to myself, for I will be newly reborn. But do not be afraid. I will not leave you again. Do you understand?"

I didn't. Maybe this wasn't truly happening. Maybe this was a delusion overtaking my mind as I slipped into the Great Dominion.

But I nodded anyway, my arms still wrapped like iron around Neave's shivering frame.

Ankaret, real or not, smiled, and in the next moment, warmth surrounded me, as if I'd crawled from darkness into sunlight. The relief was so profound that it was hard to breathe. But then that gentle warmth turned scorching, a blazing fire I couldn't escape. The pain tore a scream from my throat. Suddenly I couldn't open my eyes. An enormous pressure kept them closed. Only once did I manage to crack them open for a moment. I saw swirling flashes of color, felt the burn of lightning. That same low hum I'd heard in the forest murmured all around me. I had the sense of moving very fast—too fast, faster than I could ever possibly run.

Then, abruptly, everything stopped. The overwhelming heat vanished; silence dropped over me. I blinked, trying to make sense of the world around me. I was in a place I knew. The floor shone; the looming walls sparkled with windows. Everything was soft, painted in pearlescent shades: coral, sunrise, palest lavender.

The Citadel. The words came to me slowly. *I am in the Citadel.*

"Lady Mara!" A surprised voice floated to me from far away. "This is a surprise. We thought you were still up north."

"And what good timing!" another voice said, this one bursting with excitement and coming closer. "Our team has found the goblet. The *goblet*, my lady. Another anchor! Where is Professor Fontaine? Has he—? Oh, gods. My lady— Someone help! We need help here!"

I became aware of a rush of sound: overlapping voices, footsteps hurrying toward me. Someone cried out in horror. Someone called for a healer.

"Her name is Lily," I managed to say, my words thick and slurred. I presented Neave to the blurry world, my arms still locked around her. "Treat her wounds immediately."

It took some doing for them to pry her away from me. Once they did, I lost all sense of the world and fell forward. My last thought was of Farrin in Mhorghast, thrusting that brilliant feather into the air, her brave voice ringing out into the darkness: *Ankaret!*

The image brought me comfort. I slid toward it into oblivion.

CHAPTER 31

When I woke, it was to soft darkness. I felt a light breeze against my skin. The bitter scent of medicine stung my nose. I tried to move my body, but I couldn't feel it.

Panic drummed through me. Logic suggested that the scent of medicine meant I was being treated by a healer, that I couldn't feel my body because I'd been given poppy's tears to numb the pain.

But my own tears came anyway, slipping silently down my cheeks. My body was my greatest tool; not being able to move it or assess its damage made me feel like I was back in that writhing woodland, fleeing danger that I couldn't stop to fight. Instead I had to run. Running, running, I had to keep running.

"Sleep," came a small voice, followed by a slight press of warmth against my chest. When I glanced down, I saw a soft light shining at the hem of my quilt. It reminded me of fire, but it didn't burn. A memory tickled the edge of my mind, but the poppy's tears must have been potent, for I couldn't grasp it. A heaviness pulled my eyelids closed.

I slept.

⸻◆◇◆⸻

The next time I woke, pale morning light greeted me. The room was still quiet, but beyond its walls I could hear the soft bustle of activity: people talking in low voices, bodies moving and shifting. Footsteps. A dull clink of glass that evoked an image of the tidy jars in Nanette's infirmary.

Thinking of Rosewarren made my panic return. How many days had it been since I'd left with Gareth for Falkeron? Too many. I had lost count. The Warden, I knew, must have been out of her mind with worry. She would be furious. The thought turned me cold.

Brigid. Cira. Nesset. Freyda. The littles. Names floated up from the abyss of my drugged mind like ashes disturbed by the wind.

Talan. Ryder.

Gemma. Farrin.

Wardwell.

Briarcourt.

Gareth.

My breath caught in the back of my throat. I imagined the warmth of his touch, his smooth skin, the silky waves of his messy golden hair. I remembered how it felt to be held by him: like the snug circle of his arms around my body marked the edge of all things, and within that sacred place there was only goodness. When I recalled the brush of his lips against my thighs, the sturdy anchor of his forehead pressed to mine, my heart clenched, and for the first time in what felt like an age, the lines of my body began coming back into focus.

"Do not cry," said the small voice from before. "You will heal, and your power will return. You used so much of it. A little more, and there would have been nothing left."

Something about the odd, halting way the voice spoke struck a chord in my chest. I looked around, elated that I could now move my head, and found a tiny creature made of light perched at the foot of my bed. Its brilliant corona masked its form, but my keen sentinel eyes nevertheless found recognizable shapes within its glow: a trembling wing, a bare leg.

All at once I vividly remembered our exchange in the woodland. She hadn't known the name then, but maybe something in her mind had shifted since then.

"Yvaine?" I asked carefully. My mind felt sharper, calmer; it was easier to speak.

The small voice hummed. "Again, this name I know and yet do not."

A pinch of worry twisted inside me. Either this wasn't Ankaret but a creature pretending to be her, or this *was* Ankaret and she remembered nothing of her previous life as Queen Yvaine Ballantere of Edyn.

"Tell me who you are, then," I said.

"Yvaine," the creature murmured, as if she hadn't heard me. "Yvaine, Yvaine. I do know this name. Every time she says it, the shape of it becomes stronger."

Then she looked up at me. Two pinpricks of bright blue light marked her eyes.

"Yvaine," she said again, a note of astonishment in her voice. "That was once my name. She was queen. She lived here. She was I, and I was she. There were gardens, and so many lost days. One eye of violet and one of gold. She *remembers*."

As the creature spoke, her light grew stronger, her shape larger and better defined. A face crystallized amidst the shimmering white gold, and two legs with feet of flame brought her quickly to my side.

"Farrin," she said, her voice now thick with longing. "Where is Farrin?"

I blinked back tears, trying to hold myself together. "You are Ankaret. You died."

"She died, and now she lives," she said with an irritated flick of her fiery wings. "She understands now. Pieces come back, and then they fly away, but I am catching more and more of them. My hands are strong."

"How is this possible?" I whispered. "Your last words to Farrin were *come and find me*. But we didn't. We tried, and we couldn't. Farrin has been searching for weeks and weeks."

"When you ran, your power raced across the world in search of salvation and awakened me. I found you at the brink of death and pulled you back into the world of the living." She said all of this quickly, as if it was nothing, as if I should have known it already, then placed her two small hot hands on my arm. "Where is Farrin? Please tell me."

Trying to wrap my mind around everything she'd said was like chasing the memory of a dream. "I awakened you with my power? But how? I didn't know such a thing was possible."

"Possible, yes. Difficult, yes. Your power was desperate. It touched the living world with one hand and death with the other. The power of a man and the power of a goddess. Red and gold. Human and not."

Inside her crown of flames, her face softened—and what a face it was. White hair lined with fire, a delicate chin, eyes like blue lightning.

When she next spoke, her voice was gentler, more human. "There is still so much inside you that remains untouched. So much that you do not understand. But you will. And she will grow stronger, and her words more upright, easier to hold. She promises."

I felt myself slipping back into unconsciousness. My joints ached, and a dull pain was blooming behind my eyes, but before I let myself fade, I managed to say, "Farrin is in Vauzanne with the others. I ran ahead to keep Neave safe. They'll be here as soon as they can. Neave…" Her name plucked a taut string in my mind. I tried to sit up and failed. "Where is Neave?"

Sleep pulled me under before Ankaret could answer.

⟡

When I woke a third time, I could hardly think for the pain.

I understood that I was on my stomach, that something cool and smooth was being administered to my back. But my skin was on fire, and the cool thing was doing very little to diminish the burn. *Balm,* my mind offered. *Medicine.*

I tried to say Ankaret's name but couldn't form the word, and when I searched for her, all I could see was a red cloud of pain. I could barely lift my head. Someone with a kind voice told me I would be all right, that it wouldn't hurt for much longer. *You heal quickly, my lady.*

That was true. I did. I could endure this. I'd endured worse, I told myself.

But I knew very well that was a lie. A tear slipped down my nose. A memory surfaced—Gareth, sipping wine beside me at Briarcourt. *Our home,* he had said. *I'm sorry. It was only a daydream.* I fell asleep thinking of his face.

⟡

For days I drifted in and out of the world. When the healers came to change my bandages and administer medicine, Ankaret hid somewhere in the room, or else flitted out the window onto the roof, but only during the day, when the sun was bright enough to hide her fire.

But once my nurses left, Ankaret stayed with me. We spoke very little; I didn't have the strength for it. But the simple fact of her presence was a comfort. She was warm and patient, content to sit for hours beside me. And every time I woke, she was a little larger, a little more defined.

One day, nearly two weeks into my recovery, I opened my eyes to see a young woman pacing the room. She was small and pale, thin as a reed, but her jaw was square with determination, and she held her fists clenched at her sides. As she turned briskly for another circuit, her long white hair came into view, and fire snapped at her heels.

A chill raced down my arms. I knew that fire and that hair.

"Ankaret?" I whispered.

"She has— *I* have been practicing," she said at once, fiercely. "It requires much concentration, and it is both tiring and tiresome. But it will be easier for everyone if I appear as Yvaine as often as I can. Ankaret stalking the halls would frighten the advisors."

"And we can't have that."

She smiled grimly. "You are feeling better. Good."

"Am I?" I pushed myself up onto my elbows, wincing. "I suppose we could call it that, if we're being generous."

Ankaret paused to look at me. "Can you walk?"

"I think so," I replied, gingerly touching my toes to the floor. I hesitated, then slowly started putting weight on my feet. My joints ached in protest, and by the time I stood fully upright, a light sheen of sweat had broken out on my forehead. But I still managed to take a few halting steps, and with each one I felt a bit stronger.

I reached the table at the foot of my bed, leaned heavily on it, and turned back to Ankaret with a triumphant grin. But she wasn't looking at me; she was staring at the closed door, worrying her hands together.

"They're coming," she said quietly. "They're here. Forgive me, I cannot show myself yet. Later I will do it. Later, when I can bear it."

"What? Who's coming?"

She glanced at me with a small smile. "Your loves, Mara."

My chest clenched around my heart. For a moment I couldn't move, couldn't breathe. Then one of the healers burst in—Welma, a robust woman with sharp eyes and strong hands. She was my favorite out of all of them, and as she hurried toward me, she was beaming.

"Come, my lady," she said, gently taking my arm. "Your sisters have arrived. You can lean on me. One step at a time, and then straight back to bed as soon as I say so."

I glanced over my shoulder, but Ankaret was gone, and Welma showed no signs of having seen her. Still, I felt fluttery with nerves as we left the room. My sisters had arrived, and thank the gods for that, but what about the others?

"Gareth." His name escaped my lips on a single shaky breath.

There he was—there they *all* were, all five of them. They looked travel-worn and exhausted, and they wore borrowed clothes stained with mud and salt, but they were *alive.*

They turned to look at me, as did the dozen of others in the room—advisors from the royal council, healers, palace staff—and for a moment I feared my knees would give out, even with Welma holding me up.

But then Gareth was striding toward me, and everyone between us moved to make way for him. He was filthy, his hair was horribly mussed, as if he'd been raking his hands through it for hours, and his eyes were bright and a little wild, and he still didn't have any glasses—and he was the most beautiful thing I'd ever seen.

He came to me and cradled my face in his hands. Welma scooted away with an irritated huff.

"Mara," he said, his voice breaking. He smoothed his thumbs over my cheeks, and then he let out a shuddering breath and pulled me to him so gently that I wanted to cry. Instead I pressed my face into his collar and melted into him, my throat burning with trapped tears. He smelled like sweat, the sea, warm skin. He smelled like *him.*

Slowly he wrapped his arms around me and buried his face in my hair. He drew in a breath that sounded like pain.

"Don't ever do that to me again," he said. "Do you hear me?"

Somehow I managed to find my voice. "You mean running far away from you into certain danger to save the world?"

I felt his smile against my cheek. "Yes. That. I'm afraid I can't support such a thing. My heart can't bear it."

Then he brought one of his hands up to cup the back of my head. The soft press of his fingers against my scalp made me feel alive again. I clutched the front of his jacket and pulled him as close to me as I could.

"Mara, Mara," he said quietly, roughly, brushing his lips against my temple. "Please, darling. I'm begging you. Never again. Not without me."

I pressed a kiss to the triangle of skin above his ragged collar. "Not without you," I whispered back. "Never again."

CHAPTER 32

Welma didn't much like the idea of Gareth taking up residence in my room.

"You need to *rest*, my lady," she said rather grumpily, "not spend your energy—"

She fell abruptly silent and gestured to Gareth, who stood at my side. I leaned heavily against him, my cheek pressed to his sleeve. With each moment that passed, I felt a little less capable of standing.

"Not spend her energy doing *what*, Welma?" Gareth asked, a smile in his voice. "I'm afraid you'll have to be more specific."

Welma drew herself up indignantly, her cheeks flushing. "You know very well what I mean, Professor, and feigning ignorance just to poke fun at me is not as charming as you think it is."

Gareth inclined his head and took my hand gently in his. "I assure you," he said quietly, "nothing is more important to me than Mara's recovery. I will not—and would never—do anything to hurt her. I simply wish to be near her."

"Please, Welma," I said, fighting to keep my eyes from drifting shut. I was so *tired*, and after only a few minutes out of bed. "Having him beside me will be a great comfort."

Welma pressed her lips together and considered us. "Very well," she said after a moment. "Before you settle, I'll change the bed linens and find an extra pillow. And gods unmade, Professor, will you help her *sit down*?"

Gareth obeyed, guiding me carefully onto a cushioned bench outside my room. I teetered at the edge of wakefulness, and through my exhaustion I sensed pieces of everyone around me—my sisters, my friends. Gemma's curls pressed against my cheek as she embraced me; Talan gently kissed my forehead. Ryder placed his hand on my shoulder; Farrin curled her fingers around mine and held them against her chest, right over her heart.

"Rest, Mara," she whispered. "We're here now."

Her words were like a lullaby. I followed it gratefully into the softness of sleep.

Gareth was sitting beside my bed when I woke, a book with a faded green cover open in his lap. He was distractedly biting his thumbnail as he read, his brow furrowed with fierce concentration, and he wore a new pair of wire-rimmed glasses. Their gold frames glinted in the soft candlelight. My heart swelled at the sight of them. Such a little thing, and so familiar, so dear.

For a moment I watched him in contented silence. Then I realized he wasn't actually reading; minutes had passed, and he hadn't turned the page.

"Hello, Professor," I said, my voice hoarse and tired.

He looked up at the sound, all the worry on his face melting away. He placed the book on the bedside table and then leaned forward to gather my hand in his—my left hand, rough with scars. He kissed my fingers, then my palm, and looked up at me. The softness in his eyes made me ache.

"Hello there," he said quietly. A small smile passed over his face, and then he shook his head and looked away, blinking hard.

To distract him, I voiced a question to which I desperately wanted an answer. "Where is Neave?"

"Down the hall," Gareth answered at once. He cleared his throat and then spoke more steadily. "The healers have been tending to Lily's injuries. She isn't conscious very often, and when she is, it's Neave speaking, not Lily. Welma told me that sometimes she thinks she sees Lily there behind her eyes, but then Neave takes over, and then they're both unconscious again. It's a terrible mess."

"We have to help her," I said. Each word hurt my dry throat. "Neave, certainly, but Lily too. We can't just discard the poor girl."

"We certainly will not," Gareth said firmly. "I've already begun searching for her family. We haven't dared to probe her for information, she's too fragile for that, but I've got a whole team of clerks at the university scouring our census records for anyone that age named Lily. Not just in Vauzanne, but in Aidurra, and here in Gallinor too. We'll find her family. We'll see to it that she heals. And," he added grimly, "I personally will not rest until any surviving Lemaires are brought to Fairhaven to be sentenced for their crimes by the royal courts. It will have to wait until after the war is over, when things are safer, but I swear to you, Mara, I will not let them escape justice for what they did to her, and to Griselda too, whether it was under Kilraith's influence or not."

I watched him for a moment—how heavily he leaned on his elbows, how tightly he clasped his hands together, the desolate anger on his face.

I reached for him gently. "Come here, Gareth."

He took off his glasses and dashed a hand across his eyes. "I suppose, though," he added, laughing bitterly, "that if the Lemaire family is punished for their actions, so should I be for mine."

"In Mhorghast you were a prisoner, controlled by the god of the mind himself. It was different."

“I don’t see how.”

“Clearly the Lemaires made a bargain with Kilraith to protect their land from the Knotwood,” I said, wincing a little at the effort it took to reach for him. “They had a choice. You didn’t.”

He must have heard the strain in my voice, for he turned to me and took my hands in his and kissed them, squeezing his eyes shut. “I’m sorry,” he whispered against my fingers. “Don’t listen to me.”

“But I like listening to you, and I’m glad you’re helping Lily. Of course you’re helping her. My Gareth.” I struggled toward him, wanting to kiss him but unable to find the strength for it. “Please come closer, won’t you?”

“The healers told us that you nearly exhausted yourself to death,” Gareth said, hiding his face against my hands. His jaw clenched. “You were drawing on your power so fiercely and for so long that it almost ran out entirely, and with it your life. They’d never seen anything like that before. They didn’t know if they would be able to save you. Mara, I’ve never…” He blew out a sad, choked little laugh. “When they said that, I couldn’t breathe for a moment. Darling, you came so close to dying.”

“But I didn’t,” I said, my eyes hot with tears, “and now you know how I felt when I carried you away from that godsforsaken island. I suppose in a way this makes us even, doesn’t it?”

“No.” He shook his head. “No, that’s not true. Don’t shrug off what happened to you. That may work on other people, but it doesn’t work on me. And anyway, I wasn’t alone when I was injured. I had you. You had no one.”

Of course, that wasn’t entirely true, but I didn’t yet know how to break the news about Ankaret, and I’d never seen such raw despair on Gareth’s face. I tugged gently on his hands, offered him a small smile. “Gareth Fontaine, I won’t ask you again: Why aren’t you in this bed with me?”

He looked helplessly at me. “Gods, Mara, I’m the clumsiest ass to have ever lived. I don't want to jostle you. I don't know what might hurt you."

"You're not clumsy. In fact, you're quick and brave and good."

"None of that negates clumsiness," he said, a familiar wry note in his voice.

"Come here." I tugged on his hands again, and this time, at last, he relented. He took off his shoes and then crawled into the bed so carefully that if he weren't so obviously distressed, I might have laughed. Instead I kissed the tear trembling on the tip of his nose and drew him down to me. He shook in my arms, pressed a kiss to the hollow of my throat.

"What did you call me once? A menace?" He laughed quietly, the sound catching on a sob. "A menace indeed, crawling into your sickbed just to cry all over you."

A monster and a menace. Suddenly, the word *monster* didn't bother me as it once had. If I was indeed a monster, at least I was *his* monster. I closed my eyes and drew my fingers slowly through his hair.

"You honor me with your tears, Gareth Fontaine," I said softly, and then added, "Besides, it's nice to have someone besides me crying in this bed for once."

"Oh gods," he said roughly. "Mara, the thought of you crying here all by yourself, and in such pain—"

"No, forget I said that. It was a bad joke. I just don't quite know what to do with myself, seeing you this sad." I turned to kiss his hair. He'd bathed while I slept, and his soap smelled of sage and sandalwood. He was fresh and warm; I wanted to sink into the heat of him and never leave.

"I'm here, Gareth," I whispered against his brow. "I'm right here, and I love you."

⟡

I hated letting Gareth leave my sight, but there were things to discuss, and I wasn't yet in a fit state to leave my bed—a fact that grated on me terribly. He and the others had been in conference with the royal councils all morning, and not knowing what they were talking about was driving me mad. When I couldn't bear the stillness any longer, I forced myself out of bed and started to hobble around the room.

"You are anxious," Ankaret remarked, sitting quietly in the corner. I'd given her one of the sleeping gowns Welma had provided for me. Somehow she made the humble cloth look regal.

"What gave me away?"

"You have been frowning and pacing for the last fifteen minutes. I do not think Welma would approve."

Apparently dry humor was lost on this reborn Ankaret. I stopped to brace myself against the back of a chair and regarded her. "When will you show yourself to them? You've been able to maintain this form all morning."

She shifted uneasily. As she did, flames sputtered at her fingertips. "I have not yet mastered control of my fire."

"And what if you never do? Will you hide away forever?"

That made her bristle. I was glad of it; with her shoulders square and her jaw set, and her hair gathered up into a tidy knot, she looked like the queen I remembered. The only differences were the occasional erratic flames that crackled down her body and the color of her eyes. Yvaine's eyes had been violet and gold; both of Ankaret's eyes were a brilliant blue, as if they carried whole storms inside them.

Right now they flashed at me. She drew herself up as tall as she could. "You cannot understand what it feels like to die, to be reborn, to come back to the world as yourself and yet not."

I sighed and rubbed my temple. My body longed to return to bed even as my heart revolted against the idea.

"No, I suppose I can't understand that," I admitted. "I'm sorry. I just don't like being kept in this room. I feel like a caged animal."

"You know that everyone only wishes for you to heal."

I shot her a look. "Just as you know that Farrin won't care whether you look exactly the same as you did. She'll be overjoyed to see you. Besides, we have a war to fight, and your presence would be helpful."

For a moment, Ankaret stared hard at me. Then her shoulders relaxed, and she inclined her head.

"When you are healthy enough to join them in their meetings," she said quietly, "I will come with you."

That seemed fair. I nodded at her and resumed my pacing. Moving was painful, but it felt good too. Useful. I'd just begun to consider marching out of the room and demanding that Welma bring me to the council meeting when the door opened.

Gareth entered looking grave and contemplative, but when he glanced past me, his eyes widened. He drew in a sharp breath and quickly shut the door behind him.

"Ankaret?" he whispered. His eyes cut to me, then back to her. "She's— You're *alive*."

She returned his stare proudly. "Mara found me. She called to me, and her power pulled me back from where I had gone."

He looked astonished. "And where was that?"

"A place beyond life and death. A place without time."

"The Great Dominion," Gareth whispered.

"As it is called here, yes."

Gareth's eyes sparkled with curiosity, but he drew a long breath and visibly reined himself in. "I should very much like to discuss this with you someday," he said evenly.

"Yes, I am certain you would," Ankaret said, amused.

"But..." Gareth looked between us once more. "Why have you not shown yourself to us? You've been here with Mara all this time?"

"She wanted to wait for the right moment," I said carefully, glancing at Ankaret. "It will be a startling revelation, as you might imagine."

"And the right moment is now." Ankaret held her arms stiffly at her sides, her hands in fists. "Mara's heartbeat is steady, her gait uneven but strong. She is ready, and so am I."

Welma turned white at the sight of Ankaret, but she got hold of herself quickly and led us all to the council room through hallways used by the household staff. They were blessedly empty, except for a young kitchen boy who burst into tears at the sight of his late queen, but a stern word from Welma and Ankaret's gentle hand on his shoulder quieted him. He swore passionately that he would not speak a word to anyone about what he had seen. The look he gave Ankaret as we moved past him was one of pure, proud adoration.

Still, the incident made me nervy. As we neared the council room, I braced myself for an outcry. Gareth had gone ahead of us to warn Talan and Ryder that something extraordinary was about to happen and that should the council members or the generals or the guards standing outside the main doors react poorly, they were to promptly set them straight by whatever means necessary.

But I needn't have worried. The moment we stepped past Welma through the servant's door, a stunned silence swept through the room. Farrin's chief advisor, Thirsk, put a hand to his heart. Gemma sat frozen at Talan's side, struck speechless for perhaps only the fourth time in her life.

And Farrin, who had been standing near a window, fiddling with the end of her braid and looking troubled, turned to us with a look of slight annoyance on her face—that is, until she saw Ankaret, and then she let out a sound so anguished that I felt compelled to banish everyone else from the room. She rushed toward us, her face crumpling, and didn't hesitate for an instant before pulling Ankaret into a fierce embrace.

"I searched for you," she said, sobbing. "I was starting to think it was hopeless, that I'd imagined what you said, or that there was a secret somewhere that I wasn't clever enough to see, or—"

She broke off, no longer able to speak, and shook her head.

Ankaret put her arms around Farrin with excruciating care, as if afraid that moving too quickly might undo all of this, or in disbelief that it was happening at all.

"My dearest friend," she said at last, her voice clear and low, like some huge gentle bell. Fire flickered in her hair, and the love on her face was so overwhelming that I had to look away.

"Back to your notes, everyone," Gareth said briskly, shooing his hands at the others in the room. He sat in an empty chair and began straightening a messy stack of papers. "There's much to discuss, and I believe lunch will be here soon."

For a moment I could only stare at him, frozen with gratitude. Then he took off his glasses and quickly wiped his eyes with his sleeve, and I felt suddenly and unbearably fond of him—his glasses, his quick thinking, his love for my sister. I took the empty chair beside him, found his hand under the table, and gently pressed my thumb into his palm. *Thank you.*

Chapter 33

After lunch, Ankaret requested the room, and though her advisors and generals were reluctant to leave, they could hardly disobey. Her return was miraculous, a sign that perhaps the tides of war would shift in our favor.

Soon the seven of us were alone. I faced the others, relieved and almost giddy. *Finally* my body was allowing me to do something besides lie abed in pain.

"Tell me everything," I said. "Everything I've missed. Where is Neave? And the goblet—someone from Gareth's team told me they'd found the goblet."

Gemma drew in a deep breath and leaned forward. "Well, first of all—"

"Wait, no, I'm sorry." Ryder held up a hand. He was sitting back in his chair, his posture deceptively relaxed. "Gemma, love, we all adore you, but time is of the essence, and you have a tendency to digress."

"Oh, thank you," she said, slumping a little. "I could already tell I was going to ramble. I blame Talan for waking me up so early."

Talan looked at her fondly, an amused smile toying at his lips. "I was only following Farrin's instructions, my love."

"I know, I know. The meeting started at eight o'clock, and it's wartime. I'll never be able to sleep in again at this rate." Gemma snatched up one of the last remaining sandwiches and waved it at Ryder before taking a hearty bite. "Go on, then."

Ryder stifled his smile and sat forward in his chair. "Gareth's team did find the goblet. It's now in safekeeping with the crown and the key. A team at the university is ready to begin dismantling all of them, which we think is essential to slowing down Kilraith's army." He cocked an eyebrow. "Assuming, that is, that it's *possible* to dismantle them. Gareth believes it is, and that we've learned all we can from them."

I glanced at Gareth, who nodded reassuringly at me. "More on that later," he said.

"Once this is done," Ryder continued, "and since Ankaret destroyed the egg in Mhorghast, there will be only one anchor left—of course, we still don't know where or what that is."

"No leads, then?" I asked.

"Not a one."

"We should send teams back to Lake Voroth. It *has* to be there. The visions you gleaned from studying the anchors, the image of the black lake under a full moon...the details are identical."

"Already done," Ryder said. "Joint squadrons of Roses and Gareth's trackers are searching there as we speak. So far, nothing."

I sat back uneasily, pushing thoughts of Rosewarren to the back of my mind. But I felt the presence of the Warden nevertheless, as keenly as if she were standing over my shoulder, glaring disapprovingly at us all.

"The sooner we can begin dismantling the anchors we do have," Ryder said, "the better. With Kilraith's power diminished—which we hope it will be—the spread of the Mist might slow. It has now flooded so far south that its border is only ten miles from Ivyhill."

"It's taken Derryndell, then?" I said, stunned.

"Nearly," Farrin replied. She looked back worriedly at Ankaret, who was pacing by the window. "Father left Wardwell to evacuate Ivyhill. I received a letter from him before we left for Vauzanne. The household staff, the refugees they've been housing—they're all fleeing to Fairhaven."

I couldn't help but imagine the Mist creeping across Ivyhill's grounds, consuming every fountain, every stable, every room of the house. The thought turned my stomach. I could barely bring myself to look at my sisters.

"General Pallien has moved the Lower Army to this southern front," Ryder went on, with a quick glance at Farrin. When their eyes locked, he gave her a grim smile, and she returned it bravely. He reached out for her hand; she took hold of it at once, and his touch seemed to settle her.

"But their numbers are diminishing, and there aren't enough soldiers to maintain a presence from coast to coast," Ryder said. "And the Olden hostiles who attack the front aren't strays accidentally tumbling out of the Old Country. They're organized. They constantly probe for weaknesses. General Haldrin has had to reassign Upper Army squadrons to reinforce the southern front, which leaves the northern front even more vulnerable." He paused, his jaw tightening. "But more people live south of the Mist. I can't blame them for resorting to triage."

A terrible thought occurred to me. "Has the northern front reached Wardwell?"

"Not yet," Ryder said, "but it's only a matter of time."

"Soon we'll have to get Philippa to safety," Farrin said. "Fairhaven would be ideal, though I hate the idea of having her, Neave, and the anchors all in one place."

Gareth shifted in his seat, his knee bouncing restlessly. In his hand was the green book he'd been holding the day prior. He was thinking hard about something, his brow furrowed and his gaze distant, but he said nothing.

"There have been no sightings of Kilraith himself?" I asked.

Ryder shook his head. "The last definitive report we received was from our informants in Aidurra. They claimed he and an Olden army of hundreds had fought their way out of the Crescent of Storms and were advancing on the capital." He looked grim and angry. "That was the last we heard. All communication from Aidurra has ceased. We assume the capital has been overtaken."

"As has Vauzanne," Talan added quietly. "The Knotwood consumed Briarcourt and didn't stop there. As we sailed away from Rithia, we could see it roiling on the horizon. This morning we heard from Kirsa, who escaped with her household on one of her merchant ships. They barely got out in time. Oldens have completely overtaken the city."

I absorbed everything he said with a quietly mounting horror. "We've waited too long to destroy the anchors," I said. "We should have dismantled them immediately, cut Kilraith off at the knees."

"But we had to study the crown to find the others," Gemma argued, "and then the key after that. Without the information we gleaned from them, Gareth's team could never have found the goblet."

She was right, of course, but that didn't make any of this easier to bear. I looked at Ryder. "What else?"

He leaned forward, resting his forearms against the table's edge. "The body housing Neave—Lily's body—is failing. We can't treat Lily properly while Neave is still within her. And if we don't find Neave another stronger host—and soon—we'll lose her, either to oblivion or to Kilraith. Which, I think you'll agree, would be extremely unfortunate. In the end, having at least two gods on our side might make all the difference."

His bluntness struck me like a fist. "And where is Caiathos in all of this? We still have no leads on him?"

Talan spoke grimly. "If those last reports from Aidurra were accurate, it's very possible that Kilraith already has Caiathos under his control. They spoke of entire sections of the coast falling into the ocean."

"Which means it's even more important for us to secure Neave," Farrin said quietly.

My eyes flew back to Gareth. "The transference procedure that you and your team at the university were working on. Are you prepared to begin it?"

"In every way but one," Gareth replied. He dropped the green book onto the table and dragged a hand through his hair in frustration. "I've spent the last several days going over my team's notes and reading and rereading the volumes they pulled from the royal archives, but everything indicates the same conclusion: there *is* no power source great enough to fuel such a procedure. We'd have to, I don't know…" He gestured irritably at the window. "Capture the power of the Mist somehow, or find an endless supply of Anointed magicians willing to sacrifice themselves, or harness the heat of the sun. Name any ludicrous idea you can think of, and it'll be as good as anything we've got."

"You've found an artificer, then?" I asked, remembering back to when Gareth had first spoken of transference—weeks and weeks ago, in this very room.

"We have," Gareth replied. "Or rather, General Haldrin has. An artificer requested asylum during a recent battle on the southern front." His expression turned grim. "She has been *thoroughly* questioned, per the general's rigorous standards."

Talan cleared his throat, looking grave. "And even if she agrees to cooperate, it won't matter if we don't have a strong enough power source."

"Correct," Gareth said, "which means—"

Then he fell silent, and his eyes flew to mine. I saw on his face the same idea that had started brewing in my own mind.

"Wait," he whispered. "Of course. Do you think that would work?"

Farrin sat up straight, clearly reaching the same conclusion as we had. "Absolutely not," she said. "It's out of the question."

"But it is the only way," Ankaret said, speaking for the first time since the others had left the room. She sounded pleasant, even cheerful, and stopped pacing to face us all. "I have been contemplating every other possibility. They are outlandish. I must fuel the transference. Neave will live, and so will Lily, and Kilraith"—her voice wavered slightly; shadows flitted across her face—"will sense what is happening, and he will come to me." She tilted her head, looked at Gareth. "A *lure*, yes? That is the word?"

Ryder rubbed a hand over his face. "Gods unmade. Could this actually work?"

"We can't do it here," Gemma said. "Not in Fairhaven."

I agreed, thinking of the thousands of refugees currently safe inside the city walls. "No, we'll need to go somewhere more remote." I looked at Gareth. "Is it possible to relocate all of your equipment?"

"I should think so," Gareth muttered distractedly, rubbing his chin.

Farrin shot to her feet—face ashen, eyes blazing. "I won't let you do this. I won't let any of you do this."

"Dearest Farrin," Ankaret said, taking her hands with a fond smile, "I am the child of gods. I contain an abundance of their power. If I wish to do something, I will do it." She touched Farrin's face. "No matter how fiercely you might wish otherwise."

"But you've only just come back," Farrin whispered miserably. "What if this destroys you all over again?"

"Then I will come back again, and again, until I no longer have to." Ankaret looked around at all of us, fire skipping down her arms. "Well? Shall we begin? I am ready. I have always been ready."

I could hardly believe what was happening. Suddenly it seemed that everything was unfolding at lightning speed.

"We need Kerezen," Talan said, "and reinforcements from at least the Upper Army."

I nodded. "And from the Order. I'll handle that. The Warden can't possibly refuse."

My voice sounded much more confident than I felt. I'd left the Roses in such a state, the violence of Gareth's possession still fresh and raw. And the Warden, I knew, could very well refuse our request. The memory of my last moments in her office tore through me. I heard her voice as clearly as I had that night:

Do you think I'm oblivious to your many reckless ventures?

My stomach clenched uneasily. Fleeing Falkeron for Wardwell, then for Vauzanne, and finally for Fairhaven, all while sending her no word of my whereabouts? Certainly she would consider that reckless.

"I know where we can go," Gareth said, bringing me back to the present. His voice was strange, carefully flat. I hadn't heard this tone from him in ages, and it immediately put me on guard.

He raised his eyes to mine, then looked quickly away.

"Big Deep," he muttered. "My home there. The house is big enough to shelter all of us, and well situated—easy to defend, difficult to attack. And I know those canyons like the back of my hand."

Gemma pulled one of the many maps on the table closer to her. Talan peered over her shoulder.

"The southern front is a good deal north of there," he pointed out. "At least we wouldn't have to worry about fighting that battle as well."

"How will we even fight *this* battle?" Gemma said. "Both times we've faced Kilraith, he's managed to survive."

Ankaret plopped down in a chair beside Farrin with a soft puff of flame and started scribbling eagerly on a piece of paper. "She has— *I* have some ideas about that very thing."

I couldn't take my eyes off Gareth. His face was completely closed off to me. While everyone else buzzed around him, looking over maps and papers, their voices overlapping, he sat very still, staring blankly at the table. I longed to go to him. Returning to his hated childhood home was a brilliant idea from a strategic perspective and a terrible one otherwise. My mind raced, searching for an alternative, desperate to spare him this. But I could think of nowhere safer.

"So the question remains," Talan said, pushing back from the table with a frown, "how in the name of the gods will we find someone willing to undergo the transference and be Neave's new host?"

"Do not worry," Ankaret said, still writing furiously on her paper. "I have thought of everything. She is nearly here. I sent for her just a little while ago."

An instant later, the doors flew open, and Alastrina Bask strode in, wearing a long, loose black tunic, unlaced boots, and a highly annoyed expression. Even in her disarray, she was as formidable a sight as ever—pale as winter, raven-black hair swinging over her shoulders, blue eyes bright and furious. Just behind her was Gemma's best friend, Illaria Farrow, who wore a more than slightly rumpled dressing gown and was trying unsuccessfully to stifle a smile. Her warm brown skin glistened with a delicate sheen of sweat.

"This had better be good," Alastrina muttered, glaring around at us all. "Your message interrupted a *very* pleasant lunch."

Chapter 34

For the next three days, everyone prepared to move our *base of operations*—as Talan called it quite seriously and Gareth referred to it with a glint of dark humor—to the Fontaine estate in the network of canyons known as Big Deep.

Alastrina and Ankaret spent the time holed up in the university laboratories with Gareth's team, preparing for the transference of Neave into Alastrina's body. Ryder, furious about this part of our plan, stayed at Alastrina's side in a futile attempt to dissuade her from participating—which, predictably, seemed only to solidify her decision even more.

"Once this is done," she told Ryder, grinning mischievously after a particularly loud shouting match at a particularly awkward dinner, "you'll never again be able to pretend that you're better at wilding than I am."

Smiling grimly at the memory, I spun around on my left leg and kicked out with my right. My foot made clean, hard contact with the leather punching bag hanging from the ceiling. I bounced back, ducking cleanly under an imaginary attacker's sword. Then I darted forward, leapt up, and pounded the punching bag once more, this time with my fists—one, two, one-two—until I had to step back, catch my breath, and wipe the sweat from my eyes. The sensation of *moving* again, finally being able to make use of my body instead of being trapped in a bed, felt almost as good as sex.

Gemma had taken it upon herself to find training equipment for me and an unused space large enough to accommodate my routine, and she had succeeded beautifully. Now I spent every moment I could in an empty ballroom conditioning my body, interrupted in two-hour intervals by Welma and her team of healers for quick examinations. They were astonished by the rate of my recovery.

"I've treated many sentinels, my lady," Welma had murmured to me during her most recent assessment. She'd rested my leg in her lap and run her fingers over it as if searching for any sign that it had recently been shattered. "But never once have I seen one heal from such extreme injuries so quickly."

Well, you've never treated a demigod before. Outwardly I managed a modest smile. "They train us well in the Order. Easier to heal when your body is in peak condition."

But it seemed that no amount of training could quiet my mind.

I'd been working for an hour straight with only fleeting seconds of rest. Several rounds with the punching bag, aerobic exercises that got my blood pumping, agility work, sparring sessions with phantom hostiles—through all of this, my body perfectly obeyed my commands, but still I couldn't shake the thousand worst-case scenarios brewing in the back of my head.

What if, during the transference, something terrible happened to Lily? Or to Ankaret, or to Alastrina? The former would destroy Farrin, the latter Ryder. What if Ankaret's power was not enough to fuel the procedure? She had only just been reborn, and though she seemed stronger and more lucid every day, none of us knew what would happen once the transference began. And if it didn't work and anyone was hurt—or, gods forbid, *killed*—Gareth would take the blame.

What if all of our powers and those of the soldiers at our command weren't enough to destroy Kilraith—*truly* destroy him? And what would happen to the Mist, the Knotwood, the Crescent of Storms if we *did* succeed?

And when I returned to Rosewarren, what would I find? I was set to depart the next day and plead our case to the Warden for Order reinforcements. I couldn't stop thinking about the demon who had possessed Gareth there. Had other Oldens managed to breach the priory's protections? What did Brigid and Cira think of me being gone for so long?

What did the Warden think?

Her face floated through my thoughts like a nightmare I couldn't quite forget. That I'd heard nothing from her during my prolonged absence felt more and more like a warning.

I tossed aside my gloves and knee pads, which I'd worn only to appease Welma, stripped off the tunic I wore over my sleeveless undershirt, and began a series of slow stretches on the floor. As I shifted through each position, I tried to focus solely on my breathing. If rigorous movement couldn't soothe my nerves, maybe this would.

Just as I lowered myself parallel to the floor, supporting my weight on my arms alone, footsteps sounded outside in the hallway. I knew their quick rhythm at once and smiled as the door opened.

Gareth entered in a huff, his sleeves rolled up to his elbows and his professor's tie hanging loose about his neck. But once he caught sight of me in the middle of the room, his breath caught, and my senses, stoked by my training, allowed me to hear his heartbeat roar into a gallop. He deposited his armful of books on the table by the door with airy indifference.

"I was going to find somewhere to enjoy a stiff drink," he said, "but I think I'll just watch you instead."

I looked up with a grin to see him leaning against the doorframe and watching me with obvious, unabashed desire. The look in his eyes made me shiver with want. Even seeing him just standing there, so reverently focused on me, cleared my mind more effectively than any of my exercises had—cleared it of everything but him.

"Has it been a long day, Professor?" I asked innocently, arching my back as I lowered my belly to the floor. "You look haggard."

His eyes followed my every movement, branding me with heat that I felt all the way down to my toes.

"You wound me, my lady. Not all of us were lucky enough to be born with a face like yours."

Serenely I crossed my legs and swiveled around to face him. "A face like what? Do elaborate."

"Hm. Perhaps later, once the sting of that 'haggard' comment has faded."

"You fiend. You know very well you've got what Gemma's romance novels might call dashing good looks."

Unable to resist teasing him, I pushed myself to my feet, stretched up onto my toes with a contented sigh—offering him a splendid view of my body while doing so—and began collecting my equipment neatly in one corner of the room.

He laughed, a low, throaty sound that made me shiver. "You're right, of course. And it's unbecoming to pretend modesty." Then he put his hands in his pockets and came toward me, suddenly more interested in looking at the floor than at me.

"Welma told me you were down here," he said quietly. "She looked quite sour about it. Now I see why."

Bristling, I lowered one of my practice staffs to the floor and turned to face him. "And here I thought you were just here to admire me and make me feel pretty."

The corner of his mouth twitched, his gaze flicking up and down my body. "I can do that and scold you at the same time."

"I know my body better than Welma does. If she had her way, I'd be convalescing until June."

"I'll accept that," he said, stopping a few feet from me, "if you promise me that this isn't your way of fighting a stone titan without actually fighting a stone titan."

The implication was clear, and I couldn't even blame him for it. "No, this isn't that," I said, walking past him toward the door. "We're preparing for what promises to be a terrific battle, and I need to get in shape for it, and fast. And I can't show up to Rosewarren looking ragged. The Warden will be furious enough as it is."

"She won't hurt you, will she?"

Not even my sweaty, humming body could ward off the chill that came over me. I turned back to him, hiding my shiver with a smirk. "If she tries, she'll regret it."

"I'm serious, Mara."

"And so am I. If everyone could stop fussing over me, and acting like they know my mind and body better than I do, I'd be much happier. It's extremely tiresome to be lectured at and hovered over."

He came toward me, raising one sardonic eyebrow. "Oh yes, it's truly awful, isn't it, to have people who care about you?"

"You know that isn't what I meant," I snapped, glaring at him as he approached.

For a moment neither of us said another word. He was close now, looking down at me with his hands still in his pockets and a soft, adoring light in his eyes that I did everything in my power to resist.

"You look soppy and ridiculous," I declared. "You can't just make me angry and then pretend nothing has happened."

"And would it be terribly trite of me to observe that you're beautiful when you're angry?"

"It most certainly would."

He smiled, smoothing a damp tendril of hair back from my face. "Then trite I shall be, for you are magnificent, darling."

His touch was too delicious; I couldn't help but lean into it. When he bent to kiss my neck, running his hands lightly down the curve of my back, my eyes drifted closed, and I took a step toward him, into him. His body burned against mine.

"I assume," he murmured against my skin, "that since you've been training so vigorously, you're also well enough for all kinds of other activities?"

I tilted my head back, allowing him access to the hollow of my throat, my breastbone, the hem of my shirt. His lips brushed against the swell of my breasts, and my entire body broke out in goose bumps.

"What a brilliant deductive mind you have, Professor," I said breathlessly.

"Is that a yes?"

I ran my fingers through his hair and tugged him back up to me. His pupils were blown wide with wanting, and as I leaned in to take his bottom lip gently between my teeth, I circled against him, aching for him, begging for him. Even through our clothes, I could feel how hard he was, how desperately he wanted me, and with my body primed and humming from my hours of training, I nearly finished right then and there, simply from the friction of his hips against mine.

"Gareth," I gasped out, "either take me right now or let me be so I can do it myself."

He groaned, tugging down one of the straps of my undershirt with shaking fingers. "Oh gods, what an image. Can't we do both?"

"Later. First, I need you inside me. Fast."

"Absolutely," he agreed, his breath hot against my mouth, and when we kissed, it was wild and hungry, like we'd never done it before and had been bursting to, or maybe like we'd never do it again. His hands were in my hair, and then they were tugging off my shirt, and I was bare before him, flushed and panting, and he bent to kiss my breasts like a man undone. I fumbled with the buckle of his trousers, my vision a cloud of color, my fingers clumsy and trembling, and a spectacular want like nothing I'd ever felt before shooting through my body like stars.

We parted only once—to slide off my trousers, to tug his down over his hips—and then he dragged his hands down my body to cup my ass and hoist me up. I opened my legs for him, holding onto him with one hand and gripping the nearby table with the other, and when he pushed inside me it was with a rough, masculine groan, almost animal with need.

The sound made me dizzy. I tugged on his hair, his tie, the tails of his shirt—anything to bring him deeper inside me. Every hard thrust pushed me back against the wall, and each one left me a little more out of my mind. Waves of pleasure pulsed through me, golden and shimmering; I needed more. I fisted my hand in Gareth's hair, pressed my lips to his ear, and whispered hotly, "Harder, Gareth. Give me everything you have. I'm almost there."

"*Yes*," he rasped, the word catching in his throat. "Mara, *Mara*. Anything for you, darling. *Anything*."

He held me flush against him as he shifted me onto the little table by the door, and I'd never felt as safe as I did during those few seconds in his arms, so treasured, so desired. Once my hips settled on the edge, he held the back of my neck with one hand, grabbed the table with the other, and drove back into me at just the right angle to make me cry out, sharp and wanton and not caring if anyone heard.

I hooked my legs around his thighs and pressed my forehead against his. Our gazes locked as we moved together, frantic and fast, the table knocking sharply against the wall with each thrust. Gareth's books fell to the floor, forgotten. Our rhythm was growing erratic, desperate, our breathing ragged. The wet slap of our hips echoed obscenely in the grand, quiet room, and it was this—the raw, uninhibited sound of our passion—that lifted me up and over the edge. I finished suddenly and hard, trembling all around him, tears springing to my eyes from the sheer stunning pleasure of it all.

"Beautiful," he gasped out. "Mara, you're perfect, you're everything. *Gods*, you feel incredible. I…I can't…" He dropped his head helplessly onto my shoulder.

I wrapped my arms around him, still shaking, still coming quietly around him. "That's it, Gareth," I murmured, kissing his hair, his temple, the sweet shell of his ear. "You're close. I can feel it. Let go, let me have you. I'm right here."

He pressed his face against my neck, his mouth hot and wet and his teeth lightly grazing my skin, and when he came, with a few final sharp thrusts and a cry so deep and primal that it almost sounded like pain, I closed my eyes and held him to me as tight as I could. I listened to his breathing, felt his blood roar under my palms, and imagined that I could somehow sink into him, and him into me. That there was no war, no danger, no uncertain tomorrow. That we could live the rest of our lives in an unbreakable embrace.

⟡

Later that night, we lay together in silence as a parade of thin clouds drifted across the moon. I absently traced the lines of Gareth's bare chest, mulling over the questions that had been hovering on the tip of my tongue for days.

"I'm leaving tomorrow," I said slowly.

He pulled me closer, his arms warm and solid around me, and kissed my brow. "The worst sentence ever to be uttered."

"And I won't see you again until we gather at Big Deep."

As soon as I said the name, he went very still. Even his breathing grew quieter. Then, a beat later, he began toying gently with the ends of my hair.

I propped myself up on my elbow so I could see his eyes. "Is there anything you want to talk to me about before then? I haven't wanted to push you, and there's been so much to do, but I saw your face when you proposed the idea at our meeting. You looked like you'd had all the life punched out of you."

He smiled grimly, staring at the ceiling. "It certainly felt something like that."

"Will you tell me about your past? What it was like growing up at Big Deep?"

"Oh, what's to tell? I was an adorable child and a rebellious teenager. Very ordinary, really."

His careless tone didn't fool me for a second. I touched his cheek and turned his face toward mine. "Don't do that, don't push me away," I murmured, echoing what he'd said at my bedside. "That may work with other people, but it doesn't with me."

He softened at the memory. "You'll never let me forget that one, will you?"

"As if you won't be using it on me as often as you can."

"Well, that's true." He drew in a breath and resumed playing with my hair, concentrating on the slip of each lock through his fingers. "It was a great disappointment to both my parents when I decided to pursue academia instead of following in their footsteps and enlisting. My father was a strategist in the Lower Army and was far more interested in that than in being a father. I hardly knew him. Hardly saw him, really. And my mother…"

His mouth thinned. "She started drinking during her service in the Upper Army, and she never stopped. It's killing her, especially now that Father's gone. She's not a kind woman at the best of times, and the drink makes it worse. I've never been happier than I was the day I realized I'd grown too strong for her to hurt me anymore. Until the day I met you, that is." He looked back up at me, the shadows on his face vanishing the moment his eyes locked with mine. "And every day I've spent with you since then has brought me more joy than the last."

My whole body warmed at his words. "Even when I'm angry with you?"

"Angry, coy, blissfully euphoric in the wake of fantastic sex. I love it all. Every day." He kissed my fingers, his gaze soft on my face. "Every moment."

I longed to melt into him, to love him so thoroughly that all his old sadnesses would simply float away. But first he had to know that I understood what it meant for memories of home to leave wounds in their wake.

"I'm so sorry we're taking you back there," I whispered. "If you want to tell me more about them, if there's anything I can do—"

He silenced me with two fingers against my lips. "Being with you here, tonight, is the best comfort I could ask for."

Before I could say another word, he pulled me gently down against him and kissed me—softly at first, and then, as if we hadn't already been making love all night, with a growing passion that made my toes curl in anticipation. I hooked one of my legs over his, tangling the sheets around us like spider silk, and shifted closer. He held my head in one hand and slid his other hand down my belly to gently open my thighs. I shivered at his touch, already slick and ready.

"Gods, there you are," he moaned against my cheek. "There you are, sweet Mara. The most beautiful creature to have ever lived."

Then he pressed two fingers inside me, and then three, working me with such focused care, and breathing such a passionate litany into my hair, that by the time he entered me fully, I was gone. My mind was quiet, my body sang with happiness, and sleep, when it came at last, was so serene and complete that not even the most stubborn dreams could find me.

Chapter 35

The next morning, my passage through the greenway to Rosewarren knocked a constellation of fresh bruises into my skin. I'd been expecting this violence. With the unstable Mist pushing farther south every day, all the southern greenways were being pounded with turbulence that the wayfarers who'd designed them never could have anticipated.

Still, I felt unduly shaken in both body and mind when the greenway deposited me onto the grounds of Rosewarren. True winter had descended onto the priory; a thick blanket of snow cast an eerie hush over the nearby woods. I heard no birdsong, no rustling bare branches, not even the whispers of the Mist roiling just outside the priory walls. The wards had held, I was glad to see. The air around Rosewarren was crisp and clear, a stark contrast to the hissing gray world beyond it.

I took the long way around, through the stables and training yards and across the vast sloping lawn. I told myself it was because I wanted to make a quick inspection of the grounds before going inside, but my bones knew the truth: I was afraid.

The house was quiet, warm, entirely ordinary. A soft bustle of noise floated up from the kitchens; it was nearly breakfast time. From the direction of the barracks came the faintest sounds of girls laughing, chatting, bathing, snoring. The night patrols would have just settled in for a few hours of sleep, the morning patrols were already gone, and everyone else was likely preparing for their daily assignments: training, feeding their familiars, grooming the horses, cleaning weapons.

If I didn't know better, I would have never guessed that chaos had so recently flooded these halls.

All morning, since I'd woken at Gareth's side and slipped quietly out of bed, memories of that day had been tearing through my mind: all the littles possessed by the violence of a demon; the arrow that had pierced Berthel's neck; Gareth reigning over the horrific scene in the Warden's office with a smile that was not his own.

But that wasn't so very recent, was it? I heard the Warden's voice in my head; I'd been hearing it all morning. And it was right. The truth was that I'd been gone for three long weeks.

For the first time since I'd arrived at Rosewarren as a ten-year-old child, I felt like a stranger in my own home.

Footsteps were coming down the barrack stairs, and I turned toward them with a jolt of happiness. I knew that gait; the sound of it loosened the knot in my stomach.

A few seconds later, Brigid emerged from the stairwell, yawning and sleep-rumpled, her cropped blond hair only haphazardly brushed. She looked in dire need of her favorite breakfast: coffee and a sausage roll. Recalling that silly, small detail lifted my spirits. I hadn't forgotten *everything*.

But as soon as she saw me, Brigid's eyes went wide and her face paled, and suddenly that knot in my stomach pulled even tighter.

She hurried toward me, not for an embrace but to grip my arms hard in both hands.

"Whatever you've been doing," she said in a rush, "wherever you've been, go back. She'll *kill* you, Mara."

Her words turned me so cold that I could hardly breathe. "What?" I said, stupid with shock. "Who?"

My answer came with an icy rush of air, a swirl of darkness, and a sharp knock to the back of my head. I gasped for breath, my vision flickering. Someone was dragging me by my collar; the fabric bunched tightly under my chin.

Then whoever it was dropped me onto the floor. There was a rug under me, cold and stiff, caked with mud. Our rugs always needed cleaning in the winter, with so many feet tracking snow inside. I knew this particular rug, those dark swirls of midnight blue and brick red—I'd walked across them every day. I was in the entrance hall.

And I knew who it was looming above me too, though my mind refused to believe it, scrambling for some other possibility it couldn't find.

I forced myself to look up and meet her eyes.

The Warden stared back at me, fury etched into the new lines of exhaustion on her face. I'd never seen her look so haggard. She prided herself on meticulous discipline even when it came to her looks, seldom letting us see her with even a hair out of place.

Haggard. Only yesterday I'd teased Gareth with that very word. The thought made me want to cry.

"How dare you," the Warden said. Normally her voice was smooth, unreadable. Now it vibrated with anger so thick I could taste it. "I sent you away with him to keep him safe, to keep you happy, to give us all a chance to recover in peace from the violence he allowed into our home. And instead of returning once your mission was complete, you left. For *weeks*. No word from you, no request for aid. You could have been dead, for all we knew. But you weren't, were you?" She took a step closer, pinning me in place with her eyes. "You were with him."

I tried to find the right words, my heart pounding at the back of my throat. "Madam, we weren't alone, we were working with my sisters to—"

Her hand met my face like a lash of fire. She struck me again and again, each blow harder than the last, until I could no longer hold myself up. I lay trembling on the rug, the world spinning and full of stars.

"It is not your decision where you go and what you do," the Warden hissed. "*I* decide that. You go where I tell you to go. You undertake the missions *I* assign."

I swallowed, tasting blood, and made myself look back up at her. It was then that I saw we weren't alone. Dozens of Roses peered at us from the shadows of the room, the mouths of nearby hallways, the mezzanines of the upper floors. Cira was tearfully trying to usher away a passel of gaping littles. Danesh, Caralind, and two others whose faces I couldn't see were holding Brigid back at the edge of the room, trying to cover her mouth. Rage twisted Brigid's face; if she managed to get free, she would launch herself at us, and the Warden would kill her.

I knew this with bone-chilling certainty: in this state, the Warden would not shy away from murder.

My horrified mind searched in vain for the right thing to say. But I'd seen her like this only once before: when she had beaten Posey nearly to death. And the only thing that had stopped her that day was me. Killing Posey myself had shocked the Warden back into sanity.

Now I was the sole object of her ire, and in my terror, I couldn't think of how to stop her.

"Madam," I began, "our mission to Falkeron was an abject failure. The Blessed Abbot—"

"I know all about what happened to the Blessed Abbot, and I know about that traitorous fool Errik and his deranged followers. I know *everything*, Mara."

She didn't know everything; she couldn't. She didn't know about Mother or Wardwell. She didn't know what I was, what my sisters were.

And yet that mocking glint in her eyes cut me like a blade.

"There was a girl at Falkeron," I said, desperate to change the subject. "Serra. She helped us escape. If she's still alive—"

"Do you truly think I allowed any of them to live after what they did to you?"

An icy silence followed her words, and grief for this girl I barely knew flared up inside me. "You kill innocent people to avenge me, and yet you strike me with such cruelty, as if you hate me." I drew in a painful breath. "As if you'd like to kill me yourself."

"Oh, Mara." Then she smiled, mockingly tender. She crouched beside me and stroked my hair. The drag of her cold fingers reduced me to the child I'd once been, shivering alone on an unfamiliar cot.

"You're so wrong," she crooned. "I don't want to kill you. I want you to understand how completely and irrevocably you are mine. And until I'm convinced that I've corrected your misguided thinking…"

She stood slowly, her gaze never leaving mine, and for a moment everything grew still—the crawl of time, the panic buzzing through my body. Then she sighed, cocked her head slightly to one side, and held her hand out to me, palm to the ceiling.

"Until then, I'm afraid I've no choice but to punish you."

I nearly reached for her hand, some stupid part of me still believing that this was a mistake, that she would help me to my feet with a smile and apologize for frightening me.

But then she clenched that open palm into a fist, and with it came a feeling I knew well—the feeling of transformation. Only this time, when my body stretched and my bones snapped into their new positions, pain like I'd never known ripped through my body, stealing my breath, my voice, my mind—worse than the brutal cold of Falkeron, worse than my flight across Vauzanne.

No Rose remembered her binding, which always took place on the last night of our trials. The older girls had told me this was a gift from the Warden. The binding was so painful, they said, that remembering it would shatter the mind. But the Warden had softened the experience for all of us. She softened everything, even our normal transformations. She protected us from the worst of her magic, and she did it out of love.

Even so, transformation was inherently brutal; the first few times had left me sobbing, not only from the pain but also from the disturbing realization that my body was no longer my own. It could change according to someone else's will. To my child's mind, this was an attack. But, as had happened with so many kinds of violence over the years, I'd grown used to it.

This, though—*this* was different. It was agony. It was the world tearing itself to pieces, and I was the world. *I* was the thing being destroyed. A thousand feathers burst out of my skin, drawing blood as they cascaded down my arms. Wings broke through my back with a crack like splitting bone. My shredded clothes floated to the floor, and when it was finished, I was left naked and alone in the silent hall, choking on my own sobs.

Had this been what my ten-year-old self had felt during her binding all those years ago? I wept for that child, for the pain she had endured. All she had wanted was to go home. Instead she had killed and suffered, and now she suffered again, and she always would. My head reeled with sadness. I could hardly breathe through it.

The Warden knelt beside me, watching me shiver. When I retched, she glided out of the way so I wouldn't soil her clothes. Then she leaned close and kissed my downy cheek.

"You are bound to me," she whispered, almost lovingly. "Your blood, your thoughts, the power that you carry—it all belongs to me. Remember that as you fly back to your lover." She stood and began walking away, only to pause and add with mocking concern, "I wonder what he'll think once he realizes this is now the only form of you he can have."

Then she left me. They all did, all the Roses hovering in horror at the edges of my awareness. I couldn't be angry at them. If they protested, she would kill them. Even comforting me could be dangerous.

I curled into myself on the rug, my wings limp and bloody, and waited for the strength to stand.

Chapter 36

Normally the down covering me in my avian form felt like velvet. When I was younger, I liked to rub my own arm against my face, catlike, just to savor its softness.

Now, in the wake of the Warden's punishment, that same silken fuzz itched and burned, as if insects were swarming my skin. I felt like clawing myself to pieces.

But I uttered no protest, allowed not even a whimper to pass my lips. I wouldn't give the Warden the satisfaction. Instead I cleaned the blood off of my body as best I could, then went down to the infirmary, where Nanette applied a balm so gently that my determination not to cry nearly broke.

The hours stretched by in agony; at some point during that torment Freyda found me, and after five minutes of huddling against me, chirping mournfully into my feathers, she hopped onto the cot's edge, putting her small body in front of me like a shield, and watched Nanette's every movement with murderous golden eyes.

Before I left the infirmary, Nanette folded two jars of the balm into my hands, her knuckles brushing against my talons.

"Apply it every few hours if you can," she said, her chin trembling ever so slightly. "Get someone to help you. In a day or two, it will hurt much less."

I thanked her, the words dropping like stones, and tried to recall a time I'd seen Nanette look so obviously near tears. I couldn't think of a single one.

After my public humiliation, the Warden was all too happy to send me to Big Deep with a detachment of Roses at my side. She gave us permission to use one of her private greenways, which would deposit us only a few miles from the Fontaine estate. I could see it in her eyes as she dismissed us, feel it in the way her gaze burned into my back: she wouldn't trigger the other Roses' transformations yet. She wanted me to arrive at Big Deep in disgrace, surrounded by ordinary women.

I resolved to disappoint her. I would not be disgraced by this form; I would wear it proudly. She wanted me to cower in shame, hide myself from everyone who loved me. But I would stride into Big Deep with my head held high.

Despite the turmoil of the Mist, our passage was smooth and quick. The Warden's greenways were always impeccable, no matter the state of the world beyond them. By the time we arrived in the south, I had paved over my every thought and feeling. Cool stone, impervious, all the way down.

Brigid touched my arm. She was part of our detachment, of course. All of my friends were: Cira, Danesh, Caralind, Nesset, plus five recruits, freshly bound and eager for battle. The Warden had chosen wisely. The Roses who cared about me most would have to witness my mortification and feel my pain themselves, and to the recruits I would be a warning: defy the Warden and suffer. Not even her favorites were immune to her fury.

"You can go ahead if you'd like," Brigid said quietly, nodding south.

She handed me the little pouch that contained the jars of Nanette's balm. She had insisted upon carrying them; anything, she'd said, eyes bright, to make my passage even a little bit easier. "You'll be much faster flying."

She tried to sound sunny about it, but I knew better. She'd been miserable for three days, ever since the Warden's punishment. She'd slept outside my door in the barracks with Cira every night, just in case I decided to let them in. And this—this offer to let me arrive alone so I could slink into Big Deep unnoticed, like a coward—this was pity and a plea for forgiveness. For not somehow stopping the Warden, for not insisting on being part of that torture right along with me. Part of me wanted to reject it on principle. If I couldn't be comfortable, then no one else would either.

But in the end I couldn't resist. The thought of how Gareth would look at me was like a knife driving into my heart. It would be better for both of us if he saw me alone.

"You shouldn't feel sorry for me," I told Brigid, not looking at her, "nor should you be sorry. Find me when you arrive, and I'll show everyone to their rooms."

"Mara," she began, her voice heavy with sorrow.

Cira, on my other side, approached with light, careful footsteps. She would probably try to embrace me. The girl loved touch; fierce as she was, she often crept into my room at Rosewarren and snuggled up to me when she couldn't sleep. She said I reminded her of her mother.

"Freyda, stay with them," I ordered, without a glance at my familiar. Then I took the pouch from Brigid, launched myself into the air, and flew away before any of them could reach for me, or say another word.

⸻

Before leaving Fairhaven, during those three days of preparations, Gareth had drawn an elaborate map of Big Deep for us to study.

The town itself was two miles away from the Fontaine estate. In addition to five guest cottages, the stables, and the extensive grounds, there was a great house that boasted fifty rooms. The estate sat on a tract of high, flat land at the canyon's heart with ridges and cliffs all around and a drop to the canyon floor only half a mile from the eastern lawn.

During my flight, as I scanned the canyon and its rivers, I ran through the map in my mind twenty times without pause. The Lower and Upper Army detachments, which would arrive in waves over the next few days, would set up camp on the woodsy back lawn. At the back of the lawn, after a sudden sharp slope, was a narrow but deep river that would serve nicely as a natural line of defense. Father had returned to Wardwell with Gemma and Talan; when they arrived at Big Deep with Mother, she would stay in the house's disused west wing and erect protective wards to hide her presence. In the east wing, Gareth and his team, including Ankaret, would begin the transference process to move Neave from Lily's body into Alastrina's, and a detachment of Roses and Upper Army soldiers would guard them in rotating shifts. Underground tunnels connected the house's basement to a cavern underneath Lady Fontaine's shooting range, where they would all shelter with my mother, if need be.

And in the attic—which took up the entire top floor of the house and was, according to Gareth, depressingly empty because his mother had once burned all their family memorabilia in a drunken rage—my sisters and I would destroy the goblet, the key, and the crown. Ankaret seemed to think that we were perfectly capable of doing so and promised her guidance, if not her power. We had to conserve that as much as possible; she would need it all for the transference.

Reciting the plan and envisioning the map soothed me. This would be a battle, and I'd fought in hundreds of those. My body knew how to fight, I told myself, both in this form and my human one. Nothing else mattered. Nothing but the fight, my friends, and my sisters and all the ways in which I could help them.

And Gareth.

When Big Deep appeared, I focused on matching up my view of the estate to the memory of Gareth's map. There were the guest cottages and lawns, there was the river, and there, at the heart of it all, stood the house. My heart sank at the sight of it. Vines covered every inch of the brickwork, but they were nothing like the manicured green leaves of Ivyhill. They were wild, tangled, and gave the house the look of a hairy creature that had recently crawled up from the mud. The windows were filthy, the lawns overgrown.

The house's appearance in and of itself didn't bother me. The structure, Gareth had reassured us, was sound, and from a tactical perspective, the estate was ideally located. To reach us, Kilraith and his forces would have to contend with the canyon's deep chasms and unfamiliar terrain.

But thinking of Gareth here—as a lonely child, and now as a man returning to a place that held nothing but bad memories—was enough to make me forget my own shame for a while and imagine his. I still had much to learn about his home and his parents, but I knew enough. He would hate for us to see this, even though coming here had been his idea.

He would hate for *me* to see it.

I landed by the river to splash cold water on my face and then started trudging up the great rear lawn, which buzzed with activity. Gareth had hired groundskeepers to trim the grass, and the soldiers Generals Haldrin and Pallien had promised us were already setting up camp by the dozens.

I felt their eyes on me as I strode toward the house, my pouch of balm in hand. I'd thought the walk would be a good idea, that it would grant me a last few minutes of peace before I had to face anyone. But even though the soldiers' glances were quick and unbothered—they knew Order reinforcements were coming, and they'd seen Roses all their lives—I nevertheless felt cracks beginning to form in the stone of my calm. My heart started to race; my talons left a path of small divots in the newly shorn lawn. Something about the harsh winter sunlight beaming down on me left me feeling exposed, even ridiculous.

A bead of sweat rolled down my neck and into the downy fuzz covering my bare breasts. I was hardly embarrassed about my nakedness. Whenever we transformed, the process shredded our clothes; we hardly ever wore armor or even simple garments into battle. There usually wasn't time to don them; clothes were impractical. And some stubborn part of me thought that choosing not to cover myself was a gesture of defiance toward the Warden, even though she wasn't here to see it. She would have expected me to hide this body however I could, for as long as I could. So, then, I would refuse to.

And yet I felt myself shrinking as I neared the house, as if I could will myself small and disappear into the overgrown weeds. The thought was so ludicrously appealing that I got lost in it and didn't notice the small woman glaring at me from the terrace until I'd nearly run into her.

I stepped back, the musky smell of wine suddenly flooding my nose. The woman wore her gray hair in an untidy knot, and the shadows under her eyes spoke of too many unhappy nights. She wore a pristine Upper Army uniform, and something about the shape of her nose, the lines of her mouth, looked familiar.

My mouth went dry. This was Gareth's mother.

"Gareth told me a whole passel of you creatures would be joining us," she said, her words slightly slurred. The smell of drink on her breath was rancid. She looked me up and down with quick gray eyes. "But I see only you."

I nodded once in greeting, my heart pounding so hard I could feel it in the barb of every feather. "Lady Fontaine. I'm honored to meet you."

"Why? Who am I to you?" Then the hard mask of her face shifted into disbelief. "You're Mara, aren't you? *You* are the one my son has chosen."

I didn't know how to respond to that, but I didn't need to. She barreled on, her voice clipped and harsh.

"Why do you look like this?" she demanded. "I thought Roses turned into beasts only during battle."

Her words bludgeoned me, shattering my calm, my resolve, and the remaining shreds of my courage with one fell blow. The stone I'd used to pave over my heart crumbled into dust, leaving me raw and bleeding all over again.

A beast.

A *monster*.

This woman had never seen me before, and the first thing that had come to her mind upon meeting me was *monster*.

"I can no longer transform like the others," I replied, screaming at myself to shut my mouth even as the words tumbled out of me. "I…" I gestured helplessly at my body. "This is me now."

It was like I'd fallen victim to some awful spellwork. I knew I shouldn't care about Lady Fontaine's opinion. She was a drunk, she was unkind, and Gareth hated her. And yet my body burned with shame under her incredulous gaze. I felt clumsy, stupid, absurd.

"Really?" she asked. She sounded almost *gleeful*. "Why? Is this a punishment?"

Suddenly I was back there in the entrance hall of Rosewarren, screaming my throat raw as the Warden's will ripped through my body, the binding magic that tethered me to her obeying her commands without mercy. The memory made my skin crawl. Soon I would need to apply Nanette's balm.

"Yes," I whispered. "A punishment."

"Does Gareth know?" She peered closely at me. "I think not. Not even *my* son would willingly fuck you when you look like this. How would that even happen? Is your cunt the same as it was? Or does it now have teeth?"

I could hardly breathe. My eyes burned with tears, but I couldn't let them fall, I *couldn't,* or I felt sure that I would die.

"Well?" She stepped a bit closer, her mouth twitching with a smile. "Does he know?"

The look on my face must have given her the answer. She burst out laughing.

"Everyone!" she crowed, calling to the soldiers setting up their tents. "Come and listen to this! Come see! My son, the vaunted professor, has been bedding a *bird* woman. A *beast.*" She looked at me impatiently. "What do you even call yourself?"

The soldiers nearest us had fallen utterly silent. Some of them looked so distressed that I thought they might come forward at any moment and help me get away from Lady Fontaine. I even thought I glimpsed a shape that looked very much like General Haldrin striding angrily toward us from one of the officers' tents, but my tears made everything blurry, and I could no longer feel my arms and legs. This was all happening so quickly, and yet it seemed it would never end.

Then, before anyone could say another word, rapid footsteps approached from inside the house, and Gareth burst out into the sunshine. The sight of him left my knees weak. He wore a plain shirt with the sleeves rolled up to his elbows, and there were ink smudges on his fingers, and his glasses needed a good cleaning, and I'd never been so happy to see someone and simultaneously so full of dread in my entire life.

He stormed over to his mother, stopping right in front of her with such a dark look on his face that she staggered back in astonishment.

"Walk away from her," he said, very low, his voice tight with anger.

"Right now. And if you say even one more hateful word to her or about her, if you don't treat her with the respect she deserves, if you even for a *moment* consider cruelty again, I will have you removed from this house and make sure that you can *never* come back to it. Do you understand me?"

Lady Fontaine nodded slowly, apparently shocked into silence.

I didn't wait there for another second. I hurried past Gareth and made straight for the kitchen stairs. I knew this house; I knew Gareth's map and the gentle hands that had drawn it. I fled to the silence of the attic.

It was a huge room and just as empty as Gareth had said it would be. Sunlight streamed through four dirty windows; the floor's wide wooden planks were coated with dust. Here my sisters and I would destroy three anchors of the *ytheliad* curse and eliminate one of Kilraith's greatest advantages.

But as I sank to my knees in the corner of the room, where the sunlight couldn't quite touch me, I could hardly imagine doing such a thing. My tired mind could no longer wrap itself around the concepts of facing my sisters, or calling upon my power, or putting my tired body through yet more punishment.

I hugged myself and shivered there in the shadows until I remembered Nanette's balm. Applying that, at least, was something I could do. An easy thing. I slipped the pouch's strap off my wrist, talking myself through each motion like I was learning how to move through the world for the very first time.

Grip the jar with one hand and the lid with the other.

Twist open the lid.

Coat your fingers in the balm.

Rub it into your grotesque, inhuman skin.

The laugh that burst out of me turned quickly into tears. Soon I couldn't see what I was doing, how much balm I was using, if it was absorbing properly. I would run out if I wasn't careful. I wouldn't be able to help my sisters destroy the anchors because I'd be too busy scratching my skin off.

What would the Warden think, I wondered, if she saw me like this? Hunched pathetically in the corner of a dusty room, rubbing medicine into my abused body with trembling, taloned hands.

A small part of me hoped she would feel remorse, and that vain hope made me cry even harder. My fingers were shaking; I could no longer hold the jar. Someone took it away from me, set it safely on the floor. Someone's hands gently took hold of my own; their thumbs brushed my talons tenderly. I knew those hands.

I looked up to see Gareth crouching before me, looking at me just as he always had—like I was marvelous, and full of goodness. Like he would be happy looking at me and only me, for the rest of his life.

"I'm so sorry, Mara," he said. I'd never heard such sadness in a man's voice. "I could kill her for saying those things. They meant nothing. She's a miserable, sour person whose only pleasure comes from shooting, drinking, and hurting those around her who dare to be happy. Especially me."

"But she was right, Gareth. Look at me."

He did, unflinchingly, his eyes soft. "I'm looking, and I'm delighted to. You are beautiful, Mara, in this form and every other."

"Didn't you hear what I told her? I can no longer transform. I'm *stuck* like this."

"It's hurting you, isn't it?" He picked up the jar of balm. "Nanette gave this to you?"

I nodded, fresh tears slipping down my cheeks. Their warmth stung my sensitive skin. "It's meant to help the pain. Every few hours until it's gone, she said."

"Can I help you apply it? If it becomes too much, you can tell me to back off. But until then—"

"Gods, Gareth, just *stop*," I blurted out, squeezing my eyes shut. "Don't you understand what I'm telling you? Unless she decides to grant me relief, if she ever does, this is me. *This*, forever. I'm hers, forever."

"No." He was on his knees now, so close that my body prickled from the heat of his. "You are not hers. Binding magic, Order duty, I don't care. That doesn't matter. You are not hers. You belong only to yourself."

"No, no, you don't understand—"

"But I *do* understand. Look at me, darling." His voice broke on the familiar endearment. "Gods, I want to touch you, but I don't want to hurt you. Will you please look at me?"

I did, and immediately wished I hadn't. That fierce conviction in his eyes, the passion painting color on his cheeks—he was too beautiful, too dear. I couldn't bear it.

"There you are," he whispered, smiling. "Did you know that I first fell in love with you because of your eyes?"

I let out a sob. "Gareth—"

"It's true. All your power and grace, and it was your eyes that first ensnared me. They're warm and kind, and when you're angry, they're keen as knives, and when you're happy, they light up like stars. And the wild, wonderful thing is, they're only a small part of you. There's so much else to love. Your strength, your heart, your wit. The care you have for others. The way you look at me when I'm being an ass. The way you look at me when you *want* my ass."

It was such an unexpected, perfectly *Gareth* comment that I laughed despite myself. His face lit up at the sound.

"Please, darling," he said, gently brushing his fingers against my cheek. "Let me help you."

I was too tired to argue anymore, and some fragile, frightened part of me still dared to hope. This was Gareth; he loved me. He wanted a life with me. *Our home.* With a slight nod, I relented.

He began with my legs, applying the balm with long, gentle strokes. I held myself stiffly, bracing myself for disaster: I would flinch from pain, and he would never be able to bring himself to touch me again. He would suddenly realize what was happening, the true horror of what I was, and leave me, repulsed.

But I should have never doubted him. He worked in silence, a look of earnest concentration on his face, and not once as his hands smoothed the balm across my changed body did he recoil. In fact, he seemed entranced. I let my eyes drift shut, shifting whenever he murmured for me to do so. He ran his hands down my arms, between my fingers, across my back and—reverently, carefully—between my thighs. The way he touched me was like praying. I was the god, and he was the man on his knees in worship.

When he finished, I opened my eyes to find that my wings had come around to encircle him. He gazed at me, flushed and adoring, from within a nimbus of brown-and-gray feathers.

"Did that hurt you?" he whispered.

I shook my head, feeling suddenly shy.

"Good. Now, you listen to me. Your heart is your own. Your mind is your own. You belong only to yourself and not to her, *never* to her. But gods help me, Mara, you're also *mine*."

He brought my hands to his lips and kissed the hard curves of my talons. "You're mine to love, mine to cherish, in this form and in every other. I wanted to have you as you were in Fairhaven, and I want to have you now. Don't you see how lovely you are?" He bent to kiss me, a soft sigh escaping him. "The lines of your body, the feathers in your hair, the power in your muscles, the breadth of your wings. Darling, you feel like silk in my hands. And I will want you and love you—*all* of you, every part of you—for the rest of my life."

I closed my eyes, the last of my tears spilling over. "I love you," I whispered, sliding my feathered arms around his neck and pulling him into the curve of my body. "I love you, I love you."

He kissed my hair, my brow, the curve of my chin. When he palmed my breast, I arched quietly against him, natural as breathing.

"Mara, I need to ask you something," he said quietly, "and you must promise to answer me truthfully."

"Of course I will."

"You're certain my touch doesn't hurt you? You're not just saying that to reassure me?"

"It doesn't hurt me," I replied. "The balm helps. And, I think, it doesn't hurt because it's you."

"Oh, Mara." He bent to kiss me, soft and slow, and then dragged his lips down to the hollow of my throat. "Let me take you downstairs to my bed. Let me love you properly. You'll never doubt your beauty again."

I tilted my head back to let him explore, ran my talons through his hair. The soft scrape of my claws across his scalp tore a moan from his throat, and he shivered against me. The familiar heat of his body was glorious; I was suddenly ravenous for it.

One last jolt of uncertainty gave me pause. "Gareth, I…I've never made love like this before."

He pulled back from me, held out his hand, and helped me rise. His eyes were soft, his smile gentle. "Then let's find out what it's like together."

CHAPTER 37

Two days later, I stood near the back of the library in Big Deep's east wing, watching the scene before me with chills running up and down my body. Part of me wanted to look away; it was too huge, this magic, too volatile. The air was hard to breathe, like it had taken on a physicality the room couldn't quite contain.

But I couldn't possibly look away. Not yet. The impossible was unfolding right before my eyes, and my Gareth was the one orchestrating it all.

Lily and Alastrina lay on two heavy tables parallel to one another. Surrounding them in two concentric circles were twelve Anointed magicians from Gareth's university team—six elementals in the inner circle, and six beguilers in the outer one. They murmured spells and prayers, but not in unison; each magician's litany was highly personal and uttered at their own pace. For the most part they remained stationary, but every now and then someone would shift or exchange places with another.

Outside the circles, eight more Anointed drifted slowly around the room, following a strange pattern that reminded me of dancers cycling through an excruciatingly slow waltz. I recognized several members of

Gareth's Rosewarren team among them, including his friends Tarek, Loudon, and Blaise, the librarians Marvyn and Fiacra, and Gareth's scowling assistant from the university, Heldine.

And in the center of it all, between Lily and Alastrina, stood two figures with bowed heads. The first was Ankaret, one hand touching each woman's forehead. Her white hair streamed out behind her like a banner, and as I watched, the tiny flames outlining her body shifted, expanding to cloak her entire form in fire. Wings unfolded from her back, spread wide, then retracted. An instant later, the flames resumed their previous tame form.

The other figure was Mhyll, the artificer to whom General Haldrin had granted asylum in exchange for her services. She looked entirely human—light brown skin like Cira's, a soft cap of black hair, an elegant bearing—but her arms were not made of flesh. They were made of undulating, blue-tinged light, and they were *inside* Lily's chest, and Alastrina's too—probing, cutting, siphoning. Artificers were surgeons, only they didn't cut bone and organs; they cut magic, manipulated it, transformed it into something new.

As I watched her, I tried not to think of five-year-old Gemma trapped in a room with such a being, screaming her poor little heart out as she was cut open and remade at our parents' command. I understood why they'd done it; her magic was conflicted, torn between the botanical magic she'd inherited from Philippa Wren and the power of the goddess Kerezen, who in those days had only just begun to awaken inside the body of our mother.

I understood, but I wasn't sure their decision had been the right one. And the sound of Gemma's screams echoing through the house was one of the few clear memories I'd retained from my years at Ivyhill. No amount of Farrin clamping her hands over my ears could truly block out such a sound.

I shifted my attention to the iridescent cords of magic streaming through the room. They were delicate and coiled, like curls of smoke, connecting the magicians to Ankaret and her to them, amplifying their magic and fueling their spellwork, which in turn allowed the artificer to carry out her own work. Gareth had explained the whole thing to me the day before, but even with his careful, confident descriptions in my mind, I couldn't quite believe that what I saw was real.

The most important factor, he'd told me, was Ankaret. Her power made all of this possible. And rather than draining her, reducing her to the tiny creature she'd been on my sickbed in the Citadel, the effort made her look stronger and more resplendent than ever. After only a few minutes, she'd grown too bright to look at comfortably.

Gareth was in constant motion, overseeing everything with a patient watchfulness that reminded me of Brigid. He traveled slowly from person to person, providing them with water and food, assessing their comfort, observing their magic and offering suggestions on how to adjust the rhythm of their incantations, the angles at which they raised their arms.

I tried not to worry about the shadows under his eyes or the fact that they'd been at this for twenty-one hours straight. What if it didn't work? What if they exhausted themselves to death first? Thinking back to Vauzanne and my own brush with that particular danger made me want to yank Gareth away from this room and tuck him away somewhere safe, somewhere far away from this humming, crackling magic that both smelled and tasted like burning.

But worrying would help neither of us, and I had my own work to do. I left the crates of fresh sandwiches I'd brought from the kitchen near Gareth's paper-strewn desk. Then I quietly left the room, residual magic sticking to my taloned feet like wet snow.

Brigid met me in the entrance hall for our morning patrol. She glanced at my feet with mild curiosity. "You're buzzing."

"Stray magic sloughed off during the transference. It will fade." I gestured to the front doors. It was quiet, still dark. Dawn had not yet come. "Shall we?"

She fell into step beside me. Freyda circled overhead, Brigid's hawk familiar not far from her.

"Well?" Brigid said. "Are they making progress with the transference?"

"Everything looks the same to me as it did when they started yesterday morning, only now they're clearly exhausted. I'm trying not to read anything into that."

"Since you don't really know what you're looking at?"

"Exactly."

We nodded in greeting to three Lower Army soldiers en route to their lookout posts, freshly cleaned rifles strapped to their backs. Once we were past them, Brigid cleared her throat.

"And how is Gareth?"

I glanced at her. "I don't think I like your tone."

"Oh, it's not that much of a tone. I've just observed that you look much more comfortable than you did three days ago."

"Nanette's balm has worked wonders."

"Ah, Nanette's balm," she said gravely. "Yes, of course."

I swallowed a smile. I'd missed this. I'd missed Brigid. If I ignored the tidy battlefield all around us—the barricades and trenches, the watchtowers and soldiers, the hum of ward magic surrounding the grounds—I could almost imagine that we were on patrol in the Mistlands, years ago, when things were easier.

Except back then, I'd known Gareth only through Farrin's letters.

And now I couldn't imagine living even a day without him.

"He's behaving himself, then?" Brigid asked after a comfortable silence. "He doesn't need any sort of talking-to?"

"Brigid," I began.

"Because I have several on hand."

We stopped on a ridge overlooking the long, rocky slope down to the northern perimeter. A slight breeze slid between my feathers. Beyond us stretched the network of canyons, still black and blue with night, and beyond even that lay the southern front—and the encroaching Mistline, which grew closer every day. It now hovered on the horizon like a thin line of smoke, illuminated by the distant lightning strikes of storms and Mistfires.

"You don't need to worry about Gareth," I told Brigid. It was peaceful here on this ridge. Even the Mist, at this distance, was beautiful.

"I'm not worried about Gareth," Brigid replied. "I'm worried about you. I want you to be happy, as impossible as that might be given your propensity for self-destruction. Though there does seem to be a bit less of that now that he's in your life. As your friend, however, I must remain skeptical."

"Of course."

"It's my solemn duty, and I expect you to do the same for me, should I ever find someone I can tolerate sharing a bed with for longer than an hour or two."

The slight disgust in her voice made me smile. "I understand, and you know that I will."

Another peaceful silence fell. Then Brigid cleared her throat again, this time more delicately. "As your friend," she said, "it's also my solemn duty to ask for details about how well that gorgeous man satisfies you, and in what particular ways he does so."

My smile became a grin. Gareth's hands gliding through my feathers, the kisses he stamped into my downy skin, my talons encircling his wrists as I rode him on his childhood bed—the memories made my heart soar and my legs weak.

"I love him, Brigid." I looked right at her so she could see the truth on my face. "I love him so much."

She smiled at me, just as she had as a younger woman on the day of my trials—a little proud and terribly fond. "I know you do."

Then, to my left, a quick flash of brilliant light came and went.

I whipped my head around to find the source—not lightning, not an Upper Army soldier running drills. Something else. With my mother's help, the Upper Army's beguiler teams had erected a shell of protective wards around the Fontaine estate. Now, as we watched, that shell thrummed, shimmering with watery blue light, before falling silent and dark once more.

That could mean only one thing: something had breached the wards, or at least tried to.

The next instant, I was in the air, Brigid transforming just behind me. The swift eruption of her familiar gray-and-white feathers turned my stomach a little. It had happened so *quickly*. I knew very well, of course, that the Warden had the ability to surveil far beyond the priory. Whenever a Rose in her human form encountered danger, she transformed not long after.

But suddenly I couldn't shake the disturbing thought that the Warden was watching us far more closely than I'd realized. Was it possible she'd even spied on Gareth and me? A wild part of me hoped she had. *Let her see how little we care about what she did to me. Let her witness our joy and seethe.*

I shoved thoughts of the Warden aside as Brigid and I landed at the perimeter a few seconds later.

"What's happened?" I demanded.

A group of six Lower Army soldiers were struggling to get hold of something writhing in the dirt. One of them looked over his shoulder in panic.

"It's a man, my lady!" he cried. "Somehow he broke through the wards!"

"Somehow?" The man on the ground was tall, well built. He

laughed through hysterical tears. "*Somehow?* Can't you see what's happening right before your eyes?"

The sound of his voice unnerved me. One moment it seemed entirely human; the next, it was like two different voices had folded messily into one.

I crouched beside him and easily pinned his flailing arms to the ground. At my touch, something flickered in his wide, wet eyes, and he fell still.

"Who are you?" he whispered.

I inspected him quickly. Lacerations marred his dark brown skin. He had recently been bound; open sores encircled his wrists, ankles, and neck.

And the blood that glimmered there had a golden sheen.

My heart pounding, I kept my face impassive. "You first," I told him.

He blinked up at me, eerily calm. Then his face shifted, and a flicker of amber light flared to life in his eyes.

"I am Caiathos," he said, in a deep, steady voice that seemed too grand even for his impressive stature. It carried the weight of ages. It reminded me of my mother when she'd come to Gareth and me during our flight from Falkeron—armor and bone, brilliant jewels and gliding footsteps that spanned miles.

"Kilraith is coming," the man claiming to be Caiathos continued. "In fact, he's right behind me."

Chapter 38

Icy dread ripped through my body, throwing all my senses into high alert. Brigid tensed beside me, and one of the Lower Army guards hovering nearby muttered shakily, "Gods unmade…"

I stared hard at Caiathos. His calm face was beginning to twitch. That godly light in his eyes was gone, but when I looked at his wounds more closely, I saw the telltale glimmer of gold once more.

"I'm going to need more information," I told him. "Has he been holding you captive? How did you escape him?"

He stared at me for another beat, his gaze darting across my face, and then his body jerked violently, his expression fell to pieces, and he began to scream.

"He's coming from the trees!" he cried, thrashing anew. "He's coming from the sky! You're not ready, you don't *understand*!"

Suddenly, with a thunderous crash, angry orange light burst across the sky. We all looked up. My skin prickled from the air's sudden volcanic charge.

Lightning slashed through the woodlands a few hundred yards beyond our perimeter. Every single one of the trees exploded in a quick chain reaction, and a dozen sizzling rings of light opened among the ruins like fiery mouths. The same thing was happening above the nearest canyon cliffs—lightning tearing holes in the sky. *Portals,* I realized with horror. Like greenways, but anchored to the air instead of foliage.

And out of them poured Kilraith's army.

A vanguard of avian chimaera cascaded out of the sky. From the destroyed woodlands hurtled a line of terrestrial ones—dozens of them, *hundreds*. Wave after wave, letting out a cacophony of bestial sound, all of them charging straight for us.

I threw the screaming Caiathos over my shoulder, ordered Freyda to stay with Brigid, to keep her safe, and then shouted at Brigid herself, "Tell them to reinforce the wards!"

With that, I launched into the air and flew up the lawn toward the house. Our defenses surged into action; within seconds, the grounds teemed with officers shouting commands, soldiers scrambling for their weapons. Something crashed behind me with a thunderous boom. The entire shell of ward magic juddered, its light shifting rapidly between cool blue and seething orange.

I landed on the house's front steps and looked back.

The chimaera were hurling themselves at the wards. One wave crashed against the shield of light and immediately fell back, repelled and momentarily stunned, only for the next wave to attack right after them. The wards would hold; they had to. The magic of so many Anointed beguilers *and* my mother couldn't possibly fail just because a few beasts were pounding on it. Kilraith would have to do better than that.

The problem was, I knew he would. But how, and when, and from where? My sisters and I hadn't even begun to dismantle the anchors, which suddenly seemed like the worst kind of arrogance. We'd thought we had time, that Kilraith would obey the tidiness of our plan: first transfer Neave into Alastrina, *then* work on the anchors. Too much complex magic happening at once, we'd thought, might endanger both procedures.

Now, it seemed, we had no choice but to risk it.

I raced into the house, soldiers streaming out on either side of me. Mother hurried into the entrance hall, Father at her heels. She'd been sheltering in the west wing behind even more layers of ward magic, conserving her energy. Our plan was for her to remain in the house and from there extend her power across the grounds like a trawler's net, boosting the strength and speed of as many soldiers as she could.

But now things had changed. I shoved Caiathos at her. The man was convulsing; his eyes shifted between dark and gold, human and god.

"Deal with him," I snapped. "Calm him down, make him understand what's happening, and help him get ahold of himself. I think his host body is unstable, but we'll need him before the end of this."

Mother stared at him in astonishment. "Brother…" she whispered, touching his face.

I couldn't wait around to help them. I glanced at Father, saw that sentinel fire in his eyes. Much like mine, his body was clearly buzzing with the fever of battle.

He nodded fiercely at me. "I won't let anything touch them."

"And don't let yourself get distracted. The battle outside—"

"Trust me, daughter—now that I'm back at your mother's side, nothing in either world could tear me away from her."

A sweet sentiment, I supposed, but it left a bitter taste in my mouth. The question of why he so consistently seemed to favor devotion to my mother over devotion to his daughters was one I couldn't answer. I wasn't sure I wanted to, or cared enough even to try.

"Lady Mara!"

I turned to see three librarians from Gareth's team hurrying toward me. Each of them carried a padlocked iron box that hummed with protective spellwork.

The anchors.

My heart sank as I realized that *this* was my task now—not

bolstering our defenses or standing by with my fellow Roses, ready to rip out the throats of any chimaera that might slither through the wards.

First I had to dismantle these anchors. Doing so was essential.

But my body itched to fight, and my heart longed for Gareth.

I glanced past the librarians at the shuttered east wing. "Are they making progress?"

"We can't say, my lady," one of the librarians answered. I couldn't remember her name; my battle-focused brain couldn't spare the energy. "There's been no word from Professor Fontaine, and we don't have clearance to enter the room. But we've no reason to suspect that there's a problem. Everything's been nice and quiet in that wing." She paused. "Until now, at least."

I swallowed a sick feeling. Certainly Ankaret would be able to sense what was happening outside, even if no one else could. Would the battle distract her? Would the clash of magic nearby disrupt the delicate balance of Gareth's procedure?

And would I have a chance to speak to him again before this was over?

I shook away those desolate thoughts as my sisters hurried over, Talan and Ryder armed and grim at their sides. Gemma's eyes, which always showed exactly how she was feeling, were wide and wild with panic. But when she spoke, her voice was calm.

"Will destroying the anchors interfere with the transference?" she asked. "Is there any way we can wait a bit, or at least ask Gareth's team what they suggest?"

"We shouldn't interrupt them, my lady," one of the librarians said urgently.

"Agreed," Talan said, resolutely not looking at the box that contained the crown. "With all this chaos, any disruption might be disastrous."

"And we can't wait," Farrin said quietly. She hadn't spoken for days, conserving her voice for our practice sessions. "We don't know how long this will take."

"Or how well the wards will hold," Ryder added darkly.

"They'll hold," I said at once. I headed for the stairs, refusing to look back at the east wing. I would have to trust Gareth; I *did* trust Gareth. "We have to begin now."

As we hurried toward the stairs, we passed Lady Fontaine. She stood near the wall, watching the activity in the entrance hall with wide eyes. The sizzling crash of the chimaera's onslaught outside shook the house. The cobwebbed glass lamp on the table beside her rattled in its casing. She looked a bit lost standing there in her outdated Upper Army uniform, and more than a little pathetic. I felt her gaze on me as we passed but paid her no mind. She had said nothing to me since the day of my arrival. I'd hardly even seen the woman. Gareth's anger must have truly shaken her.

Good, I thought. *I hope all of this makes her realize how unimportant she is, and how utterly her drink and cruelty have ruined her.*

I did not think of her again.

Chapter 39

The attic was empty except for the three anchors, my sisters, and me. Talan and Ryder stood guard outside the door, and a small detachment of Lower Army soldiers patrolled the floor below.

We arranged the anchors into a triangle, then sat around them in one of our own.

"Shapes are very helpful to me," Ankaret had said before the transference began. We'd spoken with her for well over an hour about how she had destroyed the egg anchor in Mhorghast. "Think of shapes, and make them, both in your minds and with your bodies, as often as you can. Magic becomes more pliable when it's tidy. It enjoys being organized."

I thought of her voice now, how pleasant and confident it had sounded—a welcome alternative to the thunder outside. The onslaught of chimaera hadn't paused for a second. Constant vibrations shook the house, thrumming like discordant music in my bones. But there was still no sign of Kilraith.

I couldn't decide if that was comforting or terrifying.

"Remember what Ankaret said," Farrin murmured, a lilt to her words. "She is a child of the gods, and so are we. If she can destroy these anchors, we can too."

I caught Gemma's eye, saw the same doubt I felt flicker over her face. I didn't much like that reasoning now, and I hadn't when Ankaret had said it either. We were merely demigods; Ankaret was a creature that defied classification.

But neither of us voiced our fears, instead waiting for Farrin to begin.

Her song started slowly, softly, a mere hum in the back of her throat. She sounded content, even a bit distracted, like she was absently singing to herself while lounging in bed and we weren't being attacked from all sides by an angry Olden army.

Then a melody began to take shape. At first it sounded like the kind of rudimentary tune a child might practice when learning to play an instrument. But then the simple song started growing, just as Farrin had said it would during our practice sessions. She sang a little louder with each passing note, her voice clear and sweet. The straightforward progression of melody remained essentially the same, but each repetition was a more complex variation of the previous one. A little predictable, but with slight embellishments here and there—a trill, a modulation. Tidy shapes.

I held my breath until Farrin gave a single serene nod. Our cue.

As one, we reached for the key. The scarred skin of my taloned left hand shivered a little. I would never forget the shape of this thing, the weight of it in my fingers as I'd ripped it out of that poisonous yellow moss. We'd decided unanimously to begin with this anchor. Gareth's theory was that I'd already weakened it when I'd extracted it from the fae tree; his team had found it much easier to examine than both the crown and goblet. They could manipulate its elaborate engravings, which all the *ytheliad* anchors had in common, as easily as sifting through a pile of stones.

The second our fingers touched the dull metal, the key flared to life. Brilliant blue light outlined every shape carved into its surface, and it grew hot to the touch. The cords of my sisters' powers twined with my own, each of us tugging the key in a different direction. I tempered my strength to match theirs, and soon we reached a perfect equilibrium, held immobile by the opposing forces of each other's power.

As Farrin's cheerful song continued, filling the room and my body with a balmy feeling that was almost peaceful, I focused on the image I wished to make real: the key coming apart neatly in our hands. Three sisters, three clean pieces.

I couldn't measure the time, too absorbed by my task. Perhaps five minutes passed, maybe ten. I imagined my power as a roaring fire within me, one that would never burn out, and then I imagined drawing upon that fire, channeling its heat and light through my fingers and into the key. I thought of little Farrin building a tower of blocks on a blanket, how easily and softly they would clatter to the floor. I thought of little Gemma carefully lifting a wedge of pie from its dish, determined not to dislodge a single crumb. My body felt warm and supple, perfectly aligned with my sisters.

And then, without warning, the key softly came apart in our hands. Three sisters, three tidy pieces. We froze, hardly daring to breathe, as they dissolved, coating our palms with cold glittering ash.

"We did it," Gemma whispered. Her eyes shone as she looked between Farrin and me. "We *did* it, my darlings. And I feel fine, don't you?"

"I do, though I'm also a bit baffled," Farrin replied. She examined her hands, the ash glinting softly on her palms. "That was too easy. It shouldn't have been that easy."

"And why not? We're stronger than we've ever been, and we knew this one would be easy after what Mara did to it."

"We *hoped* it would," I said. I glanced at the goblet, which still stood innocuously where we'd placed it. One of Gareth's tracking teams had found it in the woods just outside the northern Mistlands, which had struck me as oddly convenient. But when nothing terrible had happened and no hostiles had tracked the goblet to Fairhaven and invaded, I'd eventually moved past my suspicions.

But now there was the matter of this unexpected ease.

It all made me think that someone had *wanted* us to find the goblet, and that maybe whoever it was wanted us to do exactly what we were doing now.

I shook myself a little. Such thoughts were of no help to anyone.

"Maybe Ankaret's presence has weakened their structural integrity," I mused.

"And the excess of magic bleeding out from the transference," Gemma added, "*and* all the work the librarians have already done. Gareth said this might happen."

He had, and all of this did make logical sense. Still, I felt uneasy.

"Yes," Farrin said, "that must be it." Her worried gaze flicked up to mine.

I took a moment to stretch my senses past the attic—to Talan and Ryder standing guard, to the soldiers patrolling beneath us, to the lawn and our soldiers and the chimaera still throwing themselves tirelessly against the wards. The portals still hovered in the air, casting an orange glow over the canyon, but nothing more emerged from them. Another lucky thing that made my feathers bristle with warning.

"We should keep going," I decided. Maybe the answer really was as simple as Ankaret's nearness enfeebling the anchors' metal. Maybe she was even consciously helping us somehow.

My sisters agreed, and Farrin began her song. It was identical to the first one in both melody and rhythm—pleasantly predictable, pleasantly ordered. As it moved over us and through us, the air thrumming with our joined power, I thought of the same images of tumbling blocks, a tidy wedge of pie, and my sisters, small and careful, content. *Simplicity,* urged the sweet timbre of Farrin's song. *Softness. Unlatch. Unmake.*

Gemma gasped softly, and a second later, the goblet cracked in three. The light outlining its carvings disappeared, the hot metal went cold, and soon another layer of ashes coated our hands.

We stared at each other in bewildered silence. Even Gemma, with all her cheerful optimism, looked surprised.

"All right, then," she said, a little uncertainly. She glanced at the crown, which now sat alone in the center of our triangle. It had always been the most fearsome-looking anchor, with those sharp spikes and the three jewels like eyes. *The Man with the Three-Eyed Crown*. It seemed like ages since we'd been to Brimgard, where Gemma had torn the crown from Talan's head and broken his bondage to Kilraith.

I took a deep breath. There was no sense in delaying this, no logic in fearing this dead metal thing. "Farrin—"

Her name disappeared in an explosion of sound and a burst of brilliant light. The house jolted around us; the light outside was suddenly a sinister flood of orange.

I hurried toward the windows, dread high in my throat, already knowing what I would see. What met my eyes was even worse than I expected: the shell of ward magic still stood in place around Big Deep, but the surface of it had shattered like thin ice. And the chimaera were no longer alone. Titans, fae, furiants with their flashing fists, nymphs wielding spirals of fire and water, griffins with wingspans twice as large as mine—Kilraith's army had in its ranks every kind of Olden being I'd ever faced. I watched them pour out of the portals hovering in the sky only long enough to see a wind titan dive straight for the wards. Tall, thin, and pale, with eyes like lightning and fists swirling with cyclones, it rammed into the wall of magic so hard that a dozen fresh cracks appeared in its surface.

I watched our armies hurry into formation with a pit in my stomach. We'd prepared for this. We'd known it would happen. And yet our soldiers seemed suddenly pitiful in the face of all this Olden glory. We needed Caiathos. We needed Neave.

We needed Mother.

And we needed my sisters.

And me.

I hurried back to them, my blood roaring with the desire to leap out the window and tear across the lawn into battle. I said nothing; they could see everything they needed to know on my face and hear it in the din from outside. Either Kilraith remained strong enough to control that army even with only two anchors left to him, or all those Oldens were just as determined to crush us even with Kilraith's will weakened.

Or Kilraiths' will hadn't been weakened at all.

Our plan was in shambles. Every decision that had led us here seemed suddenly, fatally foolish.

I looked fiercely at Farrin. *Begin.*

She obeyed at once, pale but resolute. Her song uncoiled from her throat just as sweetly as it had twice before. But when our fingers touched the crown, there was nothing tidy or easy about its magic; it flared brilliantly to life, bucking wildly against our power. So much for an equilibrium of strength; I had to use all my energy to grip the godsdamned thing and keep it from flinging my sisters across the room. Holding on to it made me feel like the whole house was tilting around me.

With our triangle unbalanced, Farrin's song faltered, but she recovered quickly and shifted into the most complicated variation yet. Her voice was strong, her rhythm sure, but I could barely find the original melody anymore. I could barely hear myself *think*.

Blue lightning so bright it rivaled the brilliance of Ankaret's eyes poured out of the crown's carvings and wrapped around our bodies, weaving a knot around our hands. Soon we were completely wreathed inside it, and the cursed power tugging on us, trying to pry open our fingers, made it hard to breathe. A high vibrating whine rang in my ears, buzzing around my head like a wasp, and for a moment I thought maybe I'd lost my hearing. Then the whine became a shriek, and I realized with horror that it was coming from the crown. But I could still hear Farrin's song and see the glimmer of Gemma's scarred hand, which the crown's anger had turned incandescent.

Anger—that was the right word. The crown was *angry*. I had the wild thought that maybe it had absorbed all the might of the goblet and key to use for itself.

Or maybe this was why Kilraith hadn't yet appeared with his army; maybe he was *in here*, fighting us from inside the crown.

Past the sound of that shrieking fury came the sound of Talan screaming in pain outside on the landing. I looked quickly at Gemma, but she was utterly focused on holding on to the crown, her cheeks red from the effort.

"*Farrin!*" Ryder roared from beyond the door. Some kind of racket was clattering up the attic stairs. I heard gunfire, screams, splintering wood. An explosion from the lawn shattered the four attic windows.

The desperation in Ryder's voice spurred something in Farrin. Steely-eyed, she sang louder, faster. Her voice split into pieces, as if she held an entire chorus inside her and all those fierce singers were at war with the shrieking crown. The din was awful; I strained to block it out and focus only on my sisters—Farrin's song, Gemma's panting breaths. We pulled and pulled. Every tendon in my body felt ready to pop, and my talons carved tracks into the wooden floor.

Hurry, was all I could think. *Hurry, faster, die*, die, *you awful gods-damned thing!*

Then the world burst open at our fingertips, hurling us all back into the walls. For a moment I lay there in shock, my ears ringing and a white cloud shimmering around the edges of my vision. Then I saw the jagged charred spot in the center of the room. A ring of glittering ash surrounded it.

The crown was gone.

I pushed myself to my feet and ran to my sisters, heart in my throat. But though Farrin held her right arm against her chest, and it took Gemma a moment to regain her balance, they were both alive and standing. I pulled them both to me, folding them into the safety of my wings so I could feel their hearts beating against mine for at least a few seconds. We said nothing; we didn't need to. The heat of our skin, the crackle of power that still hummed around us, the way our blood roared as one through our veins—red like our father's, gold like our mother's—said more than any words could.

Destroying the anchors hadn't hurt us. Instead it had *galvanized* us.

Breathing suddenly felt easier. When I observed that my joints ached from the stress of pulling against the crown, my power rose up inside me to soothe the pain. My muscles felt newly supple, even gilded, like I was now made of unbreakable light. I stared at myself and my sisters in wonder.

For the first time since learning the truth about our mother, I felt like I deserved the title of demigod.

Another bellowing roar from Ryder jarred us from our reverie, and quick as a shot we were back in the ruined attic, the floor heaving under our feet. We raced to the door and found Talan leaning heavily against the wall, holding his head. The three knots of glittering scar tissue on his forehead—remnants of the crown—stood out like beacons against his pale skin.

"There are fucking *vines*, or trees or something, trying to tear the house apart," Ryder shouted. He stood at the top of the stairs, firing his crossbow at something I couldn't see.

Gemma, who was helping Talan stand, suddenly froze, like she'd heard a distant chime the rest of us couldn't perceive.

"It's Caiathos," she whispered. "He's panicking, and the elements near him are responding accordingly."

"What does he have to panic about?" Ryder fired another shot with a snarl. "He's a god, isn't he? Gods shouldn't be allowed to panic."

I grabbed Talan's abandoned rifle and joined Ryder. He was right; downstairs, the Lower Army soldiers were battling a writhing knot of serpentine roots.

"I'm getting tired of fighting trees," I muttered.

"We don't know how long he's been in that body," Farrin pointed out. "Maybe he's not strong enough yet to overpower his host's human panic."

Ryder grunted. "Oh, wonderful. He'll be of great use to us, then."

"Isn't your mother with him?" Talan said, already looking stronger now that Gemma was nearby.

"We've got to subdue him," I said, "get him under control. Otherwise he could end up doing even more damage than Kilraith. Gemma—"

"I'll take care of it," she said at once. "Mother might be too deferential with him."

Farrin unclipped one of the weapons belts from Ryder's waist and slung it around her torso. "Ryder and I will go with her and then head for the library. Maybe Gareth will let me try to help them along with music."

The sound of his name was like cold water crashing down on my head. In all the chaos, I'd forgotten to think of him, which logic told me was perfectly reasonable. Not thinking about one's lover while one is dismantling an evil crown was hardly some great betrayal.

And yet something about the lapse seemed ominous. My body prickled with foreboding. Suddenly it felt essential to see his face, if only for a moment.

But then another explosion shook the house, this one the largest yet. I darted back into the attic and froze. The shattered windows framed an orange sky and a lawn swarming with enemies, and the wards—the wards were gone. Columns of white smoke marked where the shivering shell of magic had once stood. A few tiny bolts of blue light skittered along the perimeter before snuffing themselves out.

I hesitated, my heart screaming that I must go find Gareth even as the rest of my body roared with battle fever. But I couldn't ignore the disaster unfolding in front of me; my training wouldn't allow it. I hurled a frantic burst of love in the library's direction—*he'll feel it,* I lied to myself, *and it will keep him safe*—and then dove through the nearest window.

Chapter 40

As soon as I cleared the house, my wings snapped open on either side of me, and I plunged into the fray at such speed that the wind pulled tears from my eyes.

I bolted straight for a quartet of Upper Army wind elementals battling the same titan I'd seen ram into the wards. They were at an impasse, wind buffeting against wind as a cyclone of dirt and stone spun up around them. The soldiers quaked with effort, their knees close to buckling; the titan's eyes flared with triumph. Knots of lightning brewed in its fists.

I put my head down and picked up speed, aiming my body right at it. Even the gossamer-looking wind titans had some physicality to them. They weren't the four Olden Winds themselves; they were simply beings who embodied their elements and could manipulate them. Though they were admittedly better at it than any human, they weren't infallible. And this one was brittle with age; when I rammed into its chest, all its bluster evaporated, and it crashed to its knees, reduced to a heaving, pale creature with a gaunt face and bones like white twigs.

I raced on, the cheers of the soldiers I'd saved quickly swallowed up by the sounds of chaos all around me. A hundred smaller battles made up the whole, pockets of soldiers engaging Oldens with magic and gunfire everywhere I looked.

A knot of swarming chimaera caught my eye. They'd killed two Lower Army soldiers and were now fighting over their corpses. Fury licked hot through my bones. I sped toward them along the perimeter of the battle, dodging and ramming into and punching through any hostile that barred my way, and when I finally drove into the chimaera, they scattered like a pile of dead leaves.

I immediately spun back to dispatch them properly, my power roaring like fire in my veins and my body responding with lethal swiftness. A jab, a kick, a brief tussle with one of them that ended when I slashed through its throat with my talons, and soon all five of them were dead. I couldn't linger over the slain soldiers and honor their deaths as they deserved, but at least the chimaera who had killed them wouldn't be able to kill anyone else.

Suddenly the ground jolted. A shock wave of power knocked everyone, human and Olden, off their feet. Only I remained standing, but I swayed to recover my balance. Cracks in the earth raced down the lawn, some finger-thin, others so large that several Lower Army soldiers near me dropped into the chasms and disappeared.

I followed the cracks up the lawn in horror. They originated at the house, which had split in two; a jagged break sliced from roof to foundation, right through the entrance hall. The west wing and much of the house's center remained relatively intact.

But an entire section of the east wing had crumbled.

My body turned to ice.

Gareth.

I launched myself into the air and sped back to the house, nearly crashing into Ryder, Farrin, and a detachment of Upper Army soldiers as they emerged from the front doors. I landed hard, skidding to a halt with Gareth's name on my tongue. "What's happened?"

“Caiathos,” Farrin said breathlessly. “I think we’ve finally calmed him down, but it was touch-and-go for a while.”

“To put it mildly, my lady,” added one of the soldiers, grimly surveying the ruined lawn.

Gareth. Gareth. I swallowed hard, forcing my mind to focus. “Can Caiathos fight?”

“Your mother thinks so,” Ryder replied. “She and Gemma are working with him now.”

“Philippa suspects that being imprisoned by Kilraith was so traumatic for his host body,” Farrin explained, “that now it’s doing everything it can to defend itself and resist Caiathos’s will.”

“Resist the will of a *god,* my lady?” another soldier asked. “Is that even possible?”

“A reborn god who isn’t at his full strength and has been tormented by Kilraith? Unfortunately I think it’s very possible, Lieutenant.”

I hardly heard them. There was something on Ryder’s face that I didn’t like, something that made my whole body prickle with fear.

“Where is Alastrina?” I asked. It seemed the safest way to ask—for me, if not for him.

“I can’t find her,” he replied brusquely, not quite looking at me. “That whole wing is in ruins. Three of the librarians got out before Caiathos…” He fell silent, his jaw working.

It was like the ground beneath me disappeared. I lost both my breath and my balance. My talons instinctively dug into the earth to keep me standing.

“We’ll find them,” I heard myself saying, as if it wasn’t me talking at all but someone very far away. I strode past him toward the doors. “I’ll find them. I’ll move all the rubble—I’ll blast it to pieces if I have to. Someone find Lady Fontaine!” I shouted in the general direction of the soldiers. “She’s a stone elemental, and she knows the house…”

I trailed off as the ground began to quake, a soft tremor the others didn't notice. I whirled around, tracking its source to the horizon, where a dark figure loomed over the distant Mistline. The figure was small, still far away, but the shape of its wings was clear, like the sails of a massive ship, and it was getting closer every second. The long silver Mistline roiled behind it, right on its heels, like the train of a cape. The Mist was *following* it.

Following *him*.

Farrin came up beside me. "What is it?"

"He's here," I whispered, my mouth going dry. "Kilraith is here. And I don't know how, but he's dragging the Mist right toward us."

A stunned silence followed my words. For a moment we were all caught in the same fist of terror. I heard Farrin's sharp intake of breath when the disaster coming toward us became visible to her ordinary eyes.

Then the brisk clip of bootheels on stone made everyone turn back toward the house. Ryder let out a small, ragged cry.

Alastrina stood at the cracked threshold of Big Deep, hands on her hips, dust in her short black hair, and a glossy raven on each shoulder. Her blue Bask eyes glittered with gold, and even in a borrowed Upper Army uniform that didn't quite fit, she was resplendent. She *glowed*.

"Kilraith's here?" she said, her voice somehow deeper, sweeter, and brighter all at once. Everything about her was a more resonant version of the Alastrina I'd known. She took Ryder's arm with a grin. "Then let's kill him, shall we?"

Chapter 41

Ryder looked down at his sister in astonishment.

"Trina," he whispered. "The transference worked?"

"Beautifully," she replied. "Though Neave and I have a lot to work on together once this is all over. She's very respectful but is also rather, ah, *emphatic* about her opinions."

"Sounds like someone else I know," Ryder said, his eyes bright.

Alastrina looked at him keenly for a moment before pulling him into a fierce embrace. "I'm all right, little brother," she said, an incredible tenderness in her rich new voice. "Everything's going to be just fine, I promise you. And don't worry about Lily," she added. "She will heal, and she will live. And once all of this is over?" A cold smile curled her lips. "Neave and I will make sure to visit the people who hurt her."

I could no longer contain myself. I felt wild, like I might soon combust. "And Gareth, is he all right?"

"He's gone to look for his mother, who has disappeared, apparently, the troublesome old bat." Alastrina took a second look at me, then touched my arm and offered me a little smile. "He's perfectly fine, Mara. And he was *brilliant* in there. I've never seen a mind quite like his."

I let out a shaky breath, blinking back tears and unable to speak. He was alive, he was *alive*. My brilliant, brave Gareth.

Suddenly the air shifted around us, blooming with heat. Farrin had her arms around a small, pale figure wreathed in fire.

Ankaret.

Her bright blue gaze was fixed on the horizon, where the Mist-cloaked figure of Kilraith was growing larger by the second. I couldn't read the guarded expression on her face. The transference had aged her; lines around her mouth and eyes made her look tired, but her fire still snapped as brightly as it ever had.

"The rest of you stay here," she murmured. "I'll keep him away from the battle."

Alastrina frowned. "After what you've just been through, you can't possibly face him alone."

Ankaret kissed Farrin's forehead, released her, and turned to look at Alastrina with fire snapping in her eyes. "Come after me, and I'll knock you back here without a second thought. I have surpassed you, and I have surpassed him. I am the last of your age and the first of the new one." She took a breath, a wave of exhaustion passing over her face, and then said quietly, "Help these people fighting for the world you created, Neave. I'll do the rest."

Then she left us, tearing down the lawn even faster than I could've managed. Each light, leaping stride was at least fifty feet long. Sparks flew in her wake, her path blasting a wave of hot air across the battlefield, and by the time she reached the edge of the canyon, her human form was gone. The firebird of Mhorghast burned in its place, wings bright as the sun. She dove off the cliff's edge and streaked toward Kilraith at breakneck speed.

For a moment none of us could move, frozen in awe. Ankaret's fiery form grew as she flew, the beat of her wings stoking her own flames.

Kilraith picked up speed, his own wings seething with storms and spreading out wide, throwing the canyon into darkness. He let out a deafening howl of despair, of fury. And then, far out over the canyon, perhaps two miles away, they crashed into each other—light and dark, fire and shadow.

In the story Farrin had told us after Mhorghast, the Unmaking—the death of the gods—had created Ankaret and Kilraith and sent them plummeting to Edyn like comets through the stars. Now, centuries upon centuries later, they battled above the canyon like two monsters out of a nightmare. Ankaret hurled a wave of fire at Kilraith. He raced toward her with his huge beaked mouth gaping open and engulfed her in darkness. She punched her way out of the shadows, scooped sunlight out of the morning sky, and flung it at him like a harpoon. He dove into the canyon's red earth and emerged with a huge slab of stone in each shadowy hand. He launched them at her; she dodged them and flew back toward him, a streak of fire in the sky.

I tore my gaze away from them, my heart racing and my stomach sick with a primal, childlike fear. It wasn't possible to understand what I was seeing, to truly grasp the enormity of it. They were too alien, too mighty. Even the gods felt more familiar.

Ryder spat out a curse. "The *Mist*."

It roiled toward us like a surging ocean, flooding the canyon with that swirling silver-gray I knew so well. Out of the corner of my eye I glimpsed Brigid, Cira, and the other Roses in formation as they battled a group of fire nymphs. Above them, a shrieking Freyda battled a small avian chimaera with two sets of naked wings. I flew over to my fellow Roses, ducking the nymphs' arcing fireballs, and grabbed Brigid's arm.

"Split up as soon as you can!" I shouted. "One Rose for each army division. Don't let them face this alone!"

I jerked my head at the Mist, which would be on us in seconds. Brigid, sweaty and blood-splattered and fierce-eyed, nodded grimly.

"Understood!" she shouted back, before spinning around to swipe her talons across the chest of a snarling fire nymph.

I took off through the resulting shower of blood and embers, darting back up the lawn with the Mist at my heels. It overtook me in seconds, and as soon as it engulfed me, all the sounds of battle warped into strangeness—muffled one moment, blaring loud the next. The Mist whispered and hissed, choking the air like smoke. It brought storms along with it. Cold rain spat hard as nails, thunder boomed overhead, lightning crackled through the battlefield like snakes of white fire. A bolt zipped right in front of me and slammed into a nearby soldier. An instant later the scent of burned flesh stung my nose.

I raced blindly toward the house, helping no one. I should have followed my own orders and fought alongside a Lower Army battalion. Among our troops, they were the most vulnerable to the Mist, the most fragile.

But I ignored every single one of my training instincts, defied all those years of duty and responsibility and sacrifice the Warden had drilled into me. I couldn't stop. I *couldn't*. I had to find Gareth. I'd waited long enough, and if I could simply hold him for a moment, even just set eyes on him and reassure myself that he was in one piece—then I'd return to battle, and I wouldn't stop fighting until the end.

By the time I reached the house, the battlefield was in ruins, turned into a giant mud flat by the relentless rain. A chimaera sprang out of the Mist, heading right toward me. I ducked its huge arcing body and then whirled about in the air and knocked it to the ground with a swipe of one feathered arm.

A new enemy came at me every few seconds. A furiant used its brilliant fists to tear away a whole section of the house's roof and fling it at me like a discus.

A fae with golden skin and silver eyes ran at me with a spear in hand and whacked me across the shoulders with it. My knees buckled, and I fell hard into the mud. I rolled out of the way right before the spear plunged into the ground, then spun around to kick the fae's legs out from under him and wrestled him in the mud. His punches jabbed me in the chest and stomach, leaving me gasping. I managed to slice one of my talons across his midsection, and when he reeled back, clutching the wound, I got my hands around his gleaming silver head and snapped his neck.

I pushed myself up, panting and covered in mud, and looked around wildly. How in the name of the fucking *gods* was I supposed to find Gareth in this chaos?

There was Alastrina, charging into a line of armored fae with an entire stampede of birds and wolves behind her. Mother and Father fought together back-to-back, surrounded by a circle of snarling, muscular lycans that were proving no match for them.

I looked away quickly, a boiling black anger suddenly tightening my throat. Every feeling I had for them was in conflict. I was glad they were alive, but I hated how happy they looked, how they fought together so seamlessly after all these years apart. I longed to go fight them, show off all I'd learned. I hoped they would disappear after this battle was over, go spend years gazing adoringly at each other somewhere even more hidden than Wardwell so I'd never have to see them again.

Focus, Mara.

Gemma and Talan flanked Caiathos, guarding him as he wrangled the Mist's storms. He looked much calmer now, more settled in his host's skin, dignified even in the tattered rags of his captivity. He raised his muscular brown arms to the skies and parted the rain as if it were curtains. When a lightning bolt shot down toward him, he grabbed it in one hand and wrestled it into the shape of a sword. A slithering reptilian chimaera leapt for Gemma, but she tore a root from the wet earth and lashed the chimaera with it like a whip, cutting the creature in half. Another one bounded up after it, but Talan intercepted it before it even got close to my sister and beheaded it with one savage swing of his sword.

Farrin's singing underscored everything. I couldn't see her in the gloom, but her voice was strong and shrill, reminding me of a Rose's battle cry. Ryder would be with her; Ryder would let nothing touch her. As I raced around the house, searching for Gareth, my sister's music poured strength into my limbs, soothing my panic. *Courage*, it told me, told us all. No storm, no hissing Mist, no shrieking chimaera could dim the glory of her voice.

Then, at last—

I found him.

He was running down the back lawn toward the river. My breath caught when he slipped in the mud and fell face first into the slop. But he wasn't alone; his friends from the university were with him, helping him back to his feet. I started flying after them, heedless of anything but him. What was he *running* toward? He should have been in the house, or at least with some Upper Army soldiers or beguilers from the transference—some kind of defense, *any* kind.

Squinting through the storm, I found my answer.

Lady Fontaine stood near the edge of a cliff, ankle-deep in mud. Not far from her, the roaring river poured over the cliff into the canyon. She was fighting a trio of stone nymphs, returning the rocks they hurled with some of her own. *My mother is a stone elemental*, Gareth had told me as we'd sparred at Rosewarren. A stone elemental and a captain in the Upper Army—but now, years later, she was a sloppy, unfocused mess. Her aim consistently went wide; a nymph's hurtling stone caught her on the shoulder and sent her tumbling into the mud.

The fool. If she wasn't careful, what with all this rain and mud, and the river roaring so close by—if she didn't stop scooping up boulders so near the cliff's edge—she'd cause a landslide and bury herself in sludge. I didn't like the woman, but I certainly didn't want Gareth's only remaining family member to die.

I'd almost caught up with him when a voice rang out.

Mara.

The sound was so loud it felt like it was coming from inside me. I stopped, hovering above the ruins of a shattered pine. No one around me seemed to have heard the voice. The battle raged on undisturbed.

Mara, I need you.

My heart sank. I knew that voice. It belonged to Ankaret.

I looked back toward the river. Upper Army soldiers had engaged the nymphs, drawing them away from Lady Fontaine. Gareth and his friends were still running toward her through the storm. Stupid, brave, dear Gareth, with his shirt plastered to his skin and his trousers coated with mud. The back of his neck was bare and unprotected; the sight of that little patch of skin tugged at my heart. He didn't even have a sword.

Mara, hurry.

Ankaret's voice was more urgent now, a note of panic inside it. I couldn't ignore her. Gareth would never want me to abandon the larger fight. He would never even think me capable of it.

You're so full of goodness that you lift up everyone around you simply by existing.

My brave Mara.

I'd seen him, just as I'd wanted to. That would have to be enough.

I turned away from him, hardly able to swallow around the tight lump in my throat, and flew through the Mist toward the sound of Ankaret's voice.

Chapter 42

I'd never in my life flown faster than I did that day, soaring through the Mist and across the canyon like the finest arrow shot from the finest bow.

Hostiles burst out of the Mist to bar my path. A harpy even larger than the doomed Nerys swiped at me with her foot-long talons. I dodged the blow and whipped my own talons across her belly. The thin black cyclone of a wind titan lashed out at me, trying to knock me off course, but my wings were stronger than he expected. I rammed my way through the swirling wind and shattered his cloud-cloaked skull with my own.

Nothing and no one would stand in my way.

I was a Rose, and I was Kerezen's daughter. The Warden had spent years forging me into a weapon, and with my mother's blood in my veins and the triumph of the anchors' destruction still buzzing in my fingertips, all the most Olden parts of me were flaring to life. The Mist urged me on, whispering against the slick feathers of my wings. It knew me; it welcomed me.

Suddenly the glow of fire bloomed up ahead, burning a hole through the Mist.

Ankaret.

I picked up speed. The sooner I reached her, the sooner I could help her and fly back to Gareth. Not even all this gorgeous power streaming through my body could quell the terrible acid feeling brewing in the back of my throat, like I was going to be sick. With every beat of my wings that carried me farther away from Gareth, the feeling intensified, threatening to choke me. *Something bad is happening.* That was all I could think. *Something bad, something bad.*

Then, without warning, I burst out of the Mist and into darkness; the air was clear, but there was hardly any sunlight, even though, beyond these canyons, it was a bright winter morning. I stopped short, hovering at the Mist's edge while I took in the scene before me.

On a flat plain of red dirt and scrubby pines, surrounded by a ring of roiling Mist, Kilraith had Ankaret pinned to the ground. He was massive, easily twice the size of the entire priory. His dark wings stretched across the sky, crackling with storms and blocking out the sun.

Ankaret was sizable herself but still dwarfed by him. Her brilliant light shuddered like a flame in harsh wind, shadowy talons trapped her wings, and at the heart of this battle of light and darkness was another, smaller one. Two pale figures, human in form and comically tiny compared to their larger selves, dueled in a clash of swords so bright it hurt to look at. The blades crackled like lightning—one wreathed in flame, one tinged with darkness—and one clearly outmatched the other.

As I watched in horror, Ankaret's knees buckled. She fell hard into the dwindling inferno of her fire. And she didn't rise again.

The world moved slowly then, as if it knew what was about to happen and wanted to delay the inevitable, maybe out of some warped sense of pity for the creatures wriggling in its grasp. Kilraith brought his sword down toward Ankaret's neck; the great dark bird above him raised his wings as if ready to dive toward its prey. Ankaret was pleading with him, her voice faint: *Not like this. Look at me. Don't you remember?*

I couldn't move; all my power and strength, and I couldn't move.

How was he still so powerful, even with four anchors gone? And why had Ankaret called me and no one else? There must have been a reason, but it was all happening so quickly, and I didn't see what I could do, how I could help. If even she couldn't overpower him, then what hope did I have?

Alastrina was right, I thought wildly. Ankaret shouldn't have engaged him, not so soon after the transference. She was too weak; she needed time to recover. We should have given her *time*.

Gods unmade. The old curse seemed suddenly baleful as I watched Kilraith's sword arc through the air. The gods had indeed unmade themselves, and it had led to this. This day, this fight, this moment.

But then, with only the space of a short breath to spare, Ankaret rolled to the side, and Kilraith's blade plunged into the earth. She surged to her feet and threw herself at him, wrapping him into a fierce embrace. The firebird of her power twisted out of Kilraith's talons and reared up with a keening cry.

"*Remember!*" Ankaret shouted. Her voice boomed, nearly knocking me out of the sky and making my ears ring painfully, like an enormous bell had been struck right beside my cheek.

And then—

Then, in a single soundless instant, the entire canyon, the entire *Mist,* filled with images. Hundreds of them, thousands, appeared on the canyon walls and above the pines and throughout every inch of the Mist like the reflections of countless mirrors.

I saw a boy and a girl, pale as snow, each with long white hair like horsetail clouds, growing up together in a place I didn't recognize. In this place, the violet sky was spangled with unfamiliar stars, and on the horizon glittered a vast city.

I saw the same boy and girl, now a man and a woman, entwined in each other's arms on a blanket of flowers, naked and ecstatic, eyes locked on each other.

I saw so many things I didn't understand. Or rather, I could identify them—a war, a school, a cottage by the sea, a city floating in the clouds—but I didn't understand what any of them *meant*. What were they, and *where* were they? I knew none of those buildings, none of those mountains.

And then I saw the Unmaking, and the shock wave just after it that ravaged the far north, turning it into the Unmade Lands. I saw twin white comets riding the shock wave down to Edyn, one landing softly in a quiet bay lined with caves, the other plunging into the coldest depths of the ocean—separated from his love, trapped in darkness for an entire lonely age.

And I realized, tears burning in my eyes and my breath punching in and out of me like fists, that this was them—this was Kilraith and Ankaret, and these images were windows into the life they had once lived. My overwhelmed mind recalled everything that Farrin had told us in those long, hard days after Mhorghast's fall, and suddenly I was able to comprehend the true, tragic scope of what these two creatures had been, what they had become.

They loved each other, Farrin had told us one afternoon, quietly, as if divulging a grave secret. She'd been holding Gemma's hand. I'd stood by the window in Farrin's bedroom, listening with a soldier's attention.

In those few seconds it took for the comets to fall to Edyn, they lived an entire lifetime.

At the time, I'd skimmed over these details, focusing my attention on what would come next rather than what had come before.

But now, faced with this evidence—surrounded by it, overwhelmed by it—Farrin's voice returned to me. During that fall from the skies, she'd told us, time had moved differently for Kilraith and Ankaret. What would seem like a mere few seconds to our eyes had been centuries to them.

And now, watching these impossible memories, I truly understood what that meant. The Unmaking had somehow opened a doorway into a whole other world—or created an entirely new one—and the gods' unwitting newborn creations, Kilraith and Ankaret, had lived there. Not just lived there; they'd lived a *life* there. They had learned and loved under that alien purple sky, and then, decades later, they'd been torn from it, separated, and dropped into the seas of Edyn.

I couldn't catch my breath. These memories were too intimate; I felt like a child peering through a keyhole and seeing things she shouldn't. And yet I couldn't look away. If Gareth were here, his mind would have captured every detail. But I was the only witness. I had to remember this. I had to *understand* it.

Was I interpreting the images correctly? Had these impossible beings—the only two of their kind—truly lived in another world, or were these images simply representations of things I couldn't comprehend? Had the world they'd lived in, the life they'd shared, been only as large as the space between them, their language and habits and customs all their own and no one else's?

My tears spilled over. I knew that feeling. When Gareth and I held each other, sweaty and exhausted and happy after loving each other to pieces—when his head lay on the pillow next to mine, and our legs were tangled together, and we memorized each other's bodies with sight and touch—that was when my world was smallest. And yet it didn't feel small when I was in it. It felt vast, timeless. In that world, nothing could hurt me. In that world, I was home.

Our home.

"We loved each other," Ankaret said. Her voice was softer now, but I heard it just as clearly as if she were whispering to me and not to Kilraith. She held his face in her hands and smiled. "Don't you remember? I do. I can never forget."

"And you think I can?" Kilraith's voice was in shreds. The sound made me squirm. He sounded too small, too human. For almost a year, this creature had haunted every moment of our lives—and now here he was, looking lost and pitiful. Looking like a simple heartbroken man.

I wanted to scream at him. Why had he done all of this, then? Why wage a war when he could have spent his time finding Ankaret and reuniting with her?

"Then why have you done this?" Ankaret said, echoing my thoughts. "This war, this violence. Why, when this—*this*"—she looked around at the shimmering tapestry of memories—"this is the man I remember? He was gentle. He never would have—"

"That man is dead," he snarled, tearing himself away from her. "He died centuries ago in a dark sea."

"It must have been so cold, so lonely." Ankaret stepped closer to him. A tremor rippled through the memories surrounding her, as if they were physical things tethered to her body.

Kilraith stared at her as if she'd struck him. My breath hitched when I saw his face.

"You can't imagine," he said hoarsely. "I thought I would die. I wish I had."

She drew him to her, shifting them both so that his back faced the spot where I hovered, uncertain and overwhelmed. I began to think that maybe I understood why she had called for me.

"You could have come to me." She touched her forehead to his. "Why didn't you come to me?"

"You were with *them*. The humans." His voice twisted on the word. "They'd gotten their claws into you. You loved them so much you'd forgotten who you really were. I had to destroy them."

"Destroying people I loved? This was how you hoped to awaken me?"

"And it worked. You became yourself again. And now look at you." He stepped back to regard her, their hands joined. "As you were born. As you were meant to be."

Ankaret was quiet for a moment. The firebird at her back dimmed slightly, bowing its bright head.

"So much anger in you," she said sadly. "Tormenting the gods who made you. Tormenting the creatures they made. Our kindred. And yet you would see them slaughtered. You would destroy everything that keeps them safe and watch two worlds obliterate each other."

"No, Ankaret," he rasped, his eyes glinting. "The Olden world will triumph, and the human world will fall. Don't you see? It is the greatest final punishment we can deal the gods who made us and then abandoned us. The humans are not *worthy* of your love."

"And you are? You, who have battled me as if I am just as much your enemy as they are?"

"I never intended to kill you. I only wanted you to understand what must be done. And you keep *fighting* me, Ankaret. These humans have poisoned you against me. Would you truly choose them over me?"

Ankaret's sadness hit me as surely as if she'd struck me. She stepped back from Kilraith and said, "Choose them over the man I loved? Never. But you are not the man I loved. You're right. The man I loved is dead."

Then, so quickly it took me a moment to understand what I was seeing, the firebird surged forward, engulfing Ankaret's body, and plunged her fiery wings into Kilraith's chest.

I cannot do this alone.

Her voice resounded through my head, and the despair in it left me reeling. But at any moment Kilraith could recover from his shock and fight back, and his fury would overpower her sadness, and this time his sword would not miss. I saw it all unfolding in my mind like a bad dream, and I could not allow it to happen.

So I flew at them, right at Kilraith's back, which Ankaret had presented to me so helpfully. I'd done this before, I told myself, or at least something similar—with my sisters, I'd torn apart the host body housing Jaetris and revealed the gilded egg of Mhorghast.

But this was different. This was not a feeble human body barely held together by an exhausted and tortured god. This was Kilraith at his full strength, and I didn't have my sisters at my side. I had only the Mist at my back, and Ankaret's licking fire, and the power that lived inside me, which I drew upon with every scrap of will I possessed.

In the instant before my talons hit Kilraith's body, a single thought occurred to me: *This will hurt.*

Then I slammed into him, my talons sinking into his flesh like knives into hot butter. The dark bird of shadows overhead thrashed in anger, lightning shooting out from his wings to coil like whips around my forearms, and Kilraith's scream was so loud that it nearly made me lose my grip. But somehow I kept going, pressing my talons deeper and deeper into his body, until I felt the burn of Ankaret's fire against my skin.

The pain was searing, unthinkable. My vision went white. And in my desperation, the only thing I could think of—the only thing left to me—were the four precious syllables of my sisters' names.

Gemma.

Farrin.

I called out to them with everything I was—every muscle, every breath, every memory.

I imagined us as the women of mere moments ago, tearing apart a crown in an empty attic as everyone we loved fought nearby.

I imagined us as the children we had once been. Three little girls, hand-in-hand-in-hand, running through the gardens of Ivyhill and shrieking with joy, because we were playing hide-and-seek with our parents, and they were so clever with their hiding spots, but we would find them all the same. When we were together, we could do anything. We were unstoppable.

And then, as I clung to these images in my mind, my sisters, remarkably, answered me.

I felt them hear my call, and I heard them respond with *their* every muscle, every breath, every memory. Something had happened in that attic, something new and wonderful. Destroying the anchors together had formed new cords of power between us, connecting us in ways I didn't understand.

Images unfurled before me, beside me, *within* me. I saw Gemma on the great house's steps, helping Caiathos stand as Talan held them both, lending them his strength. I saw Farrin, singing tirelessly on the ruined lawn as Ryder shielded her with his body and his sword. And though they were fighting their own battles, they were also there beside me, helping me fight mine.

I'm here, came Gemma's voice.

You aren't alone, came Farrin's.

I sensed their bewilderment as keenly as I felt my own. How this was happening, and if it would last, none of us knew. Maybe this vivid connection would fade; maybe it was only the union of Ankaret and Kilraith, the violence of their power, that gave it life.

But for now it was real, and it was ours. My mind touched my sisters' minds, and their memories opened to me in a cascade of colors and sounds. I was Gemma, wrenching the Three-Eyed Crown from Talan's head, my heart breaking to hear his anguished cries. I was Farrin, navigating Kilraith's version of Ivyhill, desperate to find Ryder somewhere in the flames.

The echoes of their pain, their anger, their helplessness, turned my bones to steel.

I understood now what had to be done. I couldn't let go of Kilraith—not for a second, not for a breath—even though his anger, and Ankaret's fire, was searing my skin. I had to hold open his ruined body and keep him from thrashing away. I had to give Ankaret time to destroy him from the inside out.

We're right here, said Farrin, her voice as clear as a bell in my mind.

We won't let you go, said Gemma, fierce and close, as if she were right beside me.

When I forced my eyes open against the scorching air, I no longer saw Ankaret's familiar pale form. I could see only the firebird pouring itself into the bloody maw of Kilraith's mutilated chest. His arms lit up, his legs, the shreds of his torso. Every vein turned a scorching bright gold.

"Kill me," he said faintly, the sound nearly lost beneath the firebird's roaring flames. "Yes, my Ankaret. Kill me. Let's make her rage. Let's ruin her."

Her. The word slipped into my pain-fogged mind and right out again.

Listen to me, Ankaret said. *All three of you, listen.* Her voice was suddenly right beside me. No apology there, no regret. Only a command, and I felt my sisters listening too. *I will not leave any of you. Not yet. Not until everything is finished, and there is so much left to do. Do not fear, no matter what you see. I am stronger than him. I am everything he should have been and more. Thank you for helping me. I could not have done this alone. I could not have borne it.*

Just do it, I wanted to scream at her, *and hurry.* But I couldn't speak, couldn't breathe, couldn't even be sure that I was still alive.

You are alive. Gemma.

And then Farrin: *You're so strong, Mara.*

As I watched, tears streaming down my face, Ankaret's fire filled Kilraith completely, consuming everything he was and everything he had once been. I watched him light up from the inside—every bone, every vein, every hair incandescent with flame—until I could see nothing of the body I'd helped rend apart. The bird of shadows and storms was gone. The images of their memories disappeared. All that was left was fire.

Suddenly everything grew quiet. I could hear nothing—not the battle, not my sisters, not even the sound of my own screams.

Then an explosion at my fingertips threw me across the canyon. I rolled to a stop on a flat stretch of pebbled earth, pushed myself up with shaking arms, and looked behind me in a frantic daze.

Ankaret and Kilraith were gone. In their place was a huge black gash in the earth, up from which drifted a single column of smoke.

Numbly I inspected my body, but I was unhurt—no burns, no blisters. Only a bright pink tinge to my skin, a faint sizzling sound in my ears, and a few scratches from where I'd hit the ground.

Gemma? I thought, shaking my head a little. *Farrin?*

But they didn't answer; whatever power had joined us was gone, or at least exhausted.

For a moment I could only sit there in astonishment. Then my panicked mind came screaming back to me.

Gareth. Get Gareth.

Gareth's mother, standing near the cliff, fighting with mud and stone.

Gareth, running right toward her.

I staggered to my feet and launched myself into the air through a wave of dizziness. I had no sense of how much time had passed since I'd left him on those cliffs. It couldn't have been long, I told myself, rounding a bend in the canyon. The Mist was still thick, shrouding the cliffs in silver. Maybe Gareth was right where I'd left him. Comets and gods and a purple-skied otherworld—nothing was impossible anymore. Maybe days had passed for me and only seconds for him.

Then the house finally came into view, and everything inside me went quiet and still.

An entire section of the cliffs near the river was gone. A landslide of rocks and mud had cascaded down the ruined cliff face from Big Deep's lawn to the river below.

And lying on the riverbank, a bright red gash on his forehead and his lower half buried in rubble, was Gareth.

Chapter 43

There it was. There was the reason for that acid burning the back of my throat. *Something bad.*

My body had known before my mind did, as though loving Gareth, and him loving me, had made us one person. My body had known with the same instinct that had told me at ten years old, as the Warden's carriage bore me away from Ivyhill, that I would never be able to go home again. And my body knew now, as I landed hard in the muddy water and sloshed toward him.

He's fine, I reasoned. *He'll have a headache when he wakes up. It wasn't that far a fall.*

But my body knew. I felt sick as I crouched beside him. I wanted to be sick.

My training was the only thing left to me. *Assess the damage, Mara.* The rain and mud plastered his shirt to his skin. His hair was soaked and red. He was very pale: blood loss. His arms were broken in several places, and probably his legs as well, but they were covered in stones and cold mud, and I didn't dare move him. That was what I kept thinking. My speed, my strength—none of it mattered. If I moved him, I might kill him.

Unless he was already dead. But I couldn't hear the signals of his body that would tell me whether he was alive. Everything was so loud and roaring, even though the storms had stopped and the skies were clearing. Then I realized the roaring was my own blood, my own hard breathing.

"Gareth," I said. His name felt like tar in my mouth. I touched his cold face. "Gareth, can you hear me? I need you to open your eyes. Can you please look at me?"

It was foolish to just sit there and talk to him without checking all the things I knew I should check, and I still couldn't hear the sounds of his body—the drum of his heartbeat, the in-and-out rhythm of his lungs. There was nothing. Maybe, though, this was simply because I couldn't seem to calm my breathing. It was so *loud*.

I touched his neck, then his wrist. I placed my ear against his chest and listened. Some kind of bird was calling out far above us. Maybe Alastrina or Ryder had told it to search for survivors.

"Gareth. Please." I could hardly breathe for crying. A pressure bore down on my chest like someone was trying to smother me. "No, Gareth. You have to come back. You must come back to me. I know it hurts, and I'm sorry."

I wiped my face, but all that did was drag mud across my eyes. "I'm going to count to three," I told him, "and on three, you'll open your eyes, and we'll call for help. My mother—she'll be able to heal you like she did in Wardwell. Remember? Gareth. *Gareth*."

I kept coming back to his name, as if saying it enough times would do something extraordinary. But still he lay there, and still he didn't move. I dragged the curves of my talons carefully down his body. Maybe this was an illusion. Maybe a figment was toying with me.

Suddenly I wanted to make a fist and bring it down on his shattered chest.

"You idiot," I whispered, crying harder. "Why did you run after her, this woman you didn't even love? This woman who didn't love you? *I* love you. Didn't you see the mud, how close you were to the cliffs? Didn't you understand the danger? I love you. I will always love you. Come back to me."

I could no longer hold myself up. I lay down in the mud beside him and covered him with one of my wings. If I hid him well enough, maybe no one would ever know, and that not knowing would have the power to undo everything. Maybe I would fall asleep here and wake to find this was a dream, some horror wrought by Kilraith's cruelty.

I watched Gareth's throat for a pulse that never came. And then I started to hear noises from above—the faint sounds of battle, someone shouting commands, another person calling for help. A falcon's familiar cry pierced the air. Freyda. I knew that call; she was searching for me.

But I didn't want her or anyone else. If someone came to find me, they would see Gareth, and if they saw him, somehow I'd have to bear the pity on their faces, the sounds of their grief, and their pity was useless, and their grief was nothing compared to mine. If even my sisters dared to tell me they were sorry, I'd lose my mind with rage.

Unsteadily, I stood and turned away from him, blood pounding in my ears. I wouldn't look at him again. I couldn't look at him. That wasn't my Gareth, there on the ground. Not my Gareth, with his smile and his sparkling eyes and his brilliant mind and all his patient love for me. I pushed myself up into the air without really understanding that I was flying or where I would go. I only knew that I needed to be far away from anyone who would be able to look at my face and see my broken heart.

A wave of shock crashed into me with each rapid beat of my wings. Lightning flashed all around me, illuminating the Mist with garish light, but all I could see was a vast encroaching darkness, a tide coming to drag me out to sea. Gods, I wished it would. *Drown me. Crush me.* I sobbed his name. Gareth, Gareth, *Gareth.*

The idea came to me as I sucked in a desperate gasp of air.

I would go to the lake.

Thinking of it brought me a wild kind of peace, the kind of peace only known by a desperate mind. On the shores of Lake Voroth, twelve years ago, I had made my first kill.

And now I would make my last.

Chapter 44

By the time I arrived at the lake, I was so cold I could barely feel my toes. The numbness was nice; I didn't particularly want to feel anything anyway.

My flight north from Big Deep was already a blur. I had no sense of how long I'd been in the air or if anyone was coming after me, but that hardly mattered. Soon there wouldn't be anything for them to find. They would have chased me all this way for nothing.

The question remained of how I would do it. I hadn't given this much thought while in the air. All I'd been able to do was keep myself moving north and try not to think about Gareth. Now I was circling the lake and thinking of him anyway, my eyes swollen from crying and my chest hurting as if something was determined to squeeze me to death. No matter how hard I tried to imagine Gareth as he had once been, the only image I seemed able to recall was that of his dead body buried in mud.

For a moment I considered just pulling my wings in and letting myself drop into the water. But that wouldn't work. My instincts would kick in, and I'd start swimming. To drown, I would need someone to hold me under the water. And who was strong enough for that?

I could hunt down a chimaera, and stand there and let it disembowel me. But I feared my training wouldn't allow me to simply not fight something that was attacking me.

A sad knot of laughter lodged in my throat. I'd sought out danger all those times, not caring if I lived—hoping I wouldn't—and still I couldn't figure out how to kill myself properly.

Then the moonlight gleaming on my smooth black talons caught my eye.

There was an idea.

I held my hands out in front of me, turning them over and over and considering my talons' sharpness, their beautiful crescent-moon shapes. If I used them on myself, death would come quietly. The pain of slashing open my own throat would be fleeting, and it would all happen too quickly for my power to start healing me. I could do it right there on the shore and let the lake feed on me. My blood in the water would attract all kinds of creatures, and by the time anyone found me, I'd be nothing but bones.

The thought brought me a warm sense of peace, like there had been a hole somewhere deep inside me in this exact shape and now I'd finally found the thing that fit inside it. Gareth, and everything he had been, and everything I'd lost still dug between my ribs like a knife, but soon that knife wouldn't matter.

My eyes filled with fresh tears as I descended toward the shore. Every loss I'd ever known would soon be gone. All of this heartache, this grief, this gods-awful unrelenting *exhaustion* that had become easier to bear with Gareth in my life—it would all disappear. I would be able to rest. And whatever happened to this world that had taken so much from me would no longer be my responsibility.

My sisters would understand, I told myself. I'd hardly been a part of their lives anyway. I pictured their faces and tried not to feel anything. It was easy, now, to not feel anything.

And Brigid, and Cira, and all the Roses who cared about me—well, they were used to death. No one was better equipped to deal with loss than they were.

For every reason there was not to do this thing, I quickly found a rebuttal. Suddenly everything felt so easy.

Gareth wouldn't want you to do this.

Well, he was dead. I made myself think the words over and over. He was dead, and for no good reason. He died trying to save a woman who hated him. The unfairness of it lodged in my throat. *He died, and he is dead.* If I had died instead of him, he probably wouldn't even have contemplated doing something like this. He would have felt some sense of responsibility to his friends at the university, or to Farrin, or he would have told himself, *She would have wanted me to live a happy life,* and believed it.

Tears streamed silently down my face. Yes, maybe that's what Gareth would have done. But I wasn't him. I was me, and this was one loss too many. I was finished. This had finished me.

But then, as I neared the shore, a dark figure at the lake's edge took shape, and I realized I wasn't alone. The Warden was here. She looked awful—haggard, gaunt, like entire layers of her had been scraped away.

And she was bringing a knife to her throat.

A flash of anger tore through me—she had stolen my plan, and she was ruining it; could she never just *let me be*?—but in the end I couldn't stand by and let her die. What would her death do to the Roses bound to her? If it killed me, so be it; I would welcome the help. But I would not allow any more Roses to die because of her.

I dove toward her, my wings pinned against my body, and rammed into her just as the blade met her throat. The knife went flying into the water, and so did she. I skidded along the shore and bumped to a halt twenty yards from where she'd been standing.

The Warden stormed back toward me through the shallow water, her heavy black gown, far too big for her now, clinging to her body. A bright slash of red marred her white neck, but it was shallow, and she no longer held the knife.

I rose to my feet, shaking with fury. I didn't want to be furious. I was tired of feeling all these terrible things. They were so much more plentiful and tenacious than the good ones. And with Gareth gone, I couldn't imagine ever finding those again.

"What's wrong with you?" I said. "Why were you doing that? Have you lost your mind?"

Her black eyes were wild. "Leave, now."

"Answer my questions."

She struck me. I glared at her, my jaw stinging. "You can't hurt me anymore."

"Is that right?" She laughed, then gestured at my avian body. "Evidence would suggest otherwise, child." Then she really looked at me, her eyes narrowing. "Why are you crying?"

I couldn't find the words, and I didn't want to give her the answer anyway. She didn't deserve to have yet another part of me.

But she saw it as plain as day on my face.

"Ah," she said. "Your *lover*. Is he dead, then?"

The delicate scorn in her voice was obvious, but I couldn't bring myself to feel angry. Her words simply knocked the breath out of me.

"Yes," I whispered.

Her mouth twisted. I thought I saw on her face a flicker of sympathy, like some piece of her, somewhere, was sorry, but then it was gone.

"What a waste this all was," she said. "We could have spent these last few weeks in happiness, you and I. Instead you threw all of that away for *him*."

Something silver glinted on the beach only a few feet from us. The waves had pushed the Warden's knife back to shore. She saw it at the same moment I did. We both lunged for it, but she was the slightest bit faster. Once more she brought the blade to her throat. I threw myself at her, knocking her flat. I grabbed her wrist and held it still. The knife hovered between us, locked in our grip.

"What's *wrong* with you?" I didn't understand the deranged look in her eyes—where it came from, what she was thinking. "You don't have a successor in place. If you die with all of us still bound to you—"

"You would die along with me," she said simply. "All of you would die. And wouldn't that be a relief?"

Yes. The word stuck in my throat, unsaid. "Why would you do this? Why would you even consider it?"

"Has it never occurred to you, Mara, that you're not the only one who longs for death?"

The words were meant to chasten me, and they did. My throat went hot with shame. "Madam—"

"I did try everything else first. But then you and your sisters, all your friends and lovers…you were so determined to end this war. And it seems that you did. So now I must do this. It's the only path left to me. To *us*."

I didn't understand. I gripped her collar in my fist—an empty threat, but I didn't know what else to do. "At least give the others the dignity of an explanation. If it were only me bound to you—"

"You would have let me do it, isn't that right?" Her voice was soft, her eyes glittering. "You would have stood there and watched me draw the blade across my throat, and you would have been glad."

"To die? Yes. To lose you?" I swallowed hard, disgusted with myself, with the strange, mean life I had lived. "I should want that, but I don't. Despite everything, I love you still. You took me from my mother and replaced her, and everything I am, everything I know, is because of you."

"Well, not *everything*. Let's be honest with each other, Mara, here at the end."

A chill swept through me. For the first time since finding Gareth's body, I felt something other than grief and anger.

I felt fear.

"What are you talking about?" I said evenly. "Stop stalling. Explain yourself to me."

"Don't worry about your sisters. They mean nothing to me now. But I'm not a fool. Surely you can't think I'm ignorant of what all of you really are. Demigods." She laughed a little, closing her eyes. "Such power inside you. It would have been perfect, if you'd just gotten out of my way. We wouldn't be doing this right now. Maybe your Gareth would even still be alive."

"What would have been perfect?" I shook her a little. Her grip on the knife had relaxed. She was no longer fighting me.

"You, at least, I will grant the— What did you call it? The dignity of an explanation." She opened her eyes and touched my face. I couldn't read the expression in her hard, glittering eyes. "Kilraith and I made an agreement years ago. I would help him win his war. In exchange, my Roses and I would be spared and granted protection in his new world. The Order would no longer be necessary. We would be free."

I stared at her. "You did *what*?"

"I am very old, and the position of the Warden is even older. The magic that binds all of you to me is ancient. Few beings would have been strong enough to serve as an anchor for him. But I was, and am. And I had all of you to protect me, and the ear of the crown as well. There was no safer place I could be. But then you and your sisters stole the others from him, one after another. And *she* found one herself and left it right there in the open for you to find. Do you know what these losses did to me? How they tore at me, how angry he became? Can you even imagine?"

I could. Even in my shock, I was beginning to understand. "The black lake under the full moon," I whispered. The moon above us cast half her face in shadow. "We could never find an anchor here, not in all our searching. Of course we couldn't. The anchor is *you*."

Her smile was soft and sad, and a little cruel. "Professor Fontaine really should have put the pieces together. I was worried when he came here, even though it was at my request. I wanted to keep an eye on him. But he never suspected a thing. I suppose he was distracted." She clucked her tongue. "It seems to me that you both would have been better off if you'd never known each other."

I wanted to slap her, grab the knife and start cutting, bring her to the brink of death in the most painful way possible. But I needed her to keep talking.

"What else did you do for him?" I demanded. "You served as an anchor of the *ytheliad*, fed him power. What else?"

"The funny thing is," she murmured, no longer quite looking at me, "I don't think she would have let me do it just now. You stopped me, but if you hadn't, she would have. I've tried many times to kill myself, just like you. But every time, she manages to stop me. She is quite fond of you Roses, as she should be. Goddess of the Unknowable. And who is more unknowable than we are?"

She laughed quietly. Her eyes drifted closed once more. "She's getting stronger every day. I have to do it, Mara. I need you to see that."

She again. Both the Warden and Kilraith had mentioned a mysterious *she*. The answer was taking shape in my mind, but I didn't want to believe it.

"Stop these riddles," I said. My voice sounded hollow to my ears. "Tell me what you mean. Tell me exactly."

"Do you think your professor was the only person capable of engineering a transference?" the Warden said bitterly. "And I didn't even have help. I didn't need it. I examined his notes. Very messy, very fussy. Too many variables."

Her words sank in slowly, confirming what I had feared.

"Zelphenia," I whispered. "She's inside you."

"She was hardly a wisp of a thing at first, and glad for the offer. It took me *years* to track her down. And I thought it was terribly clever of me. Something to fall back on. If Kilraith betrayed me, I'd have a god to help me."

Suddenly I needed answers to a hundred new questions. "How did he never find out?"

A faint smile toyed at her lips. "He underestimated the depth and power of my binding magic—what I can hide, what I can trap and contain. He underestimated me. Many men do. The Warden is up at the Mist, guarding her chicks. No grander than a schoolteacher. For centuries, they took our sacrifice for granted. They won't be able to anymore."

"You didn't send us to Falkeron to look for Zelphenia," I said, understanding at last. "You sent us to curb our progress with the anchors, to distract us from the war."

"The Blessed Abbot was to occupy you with useless texts and false trails until I sent for you. I didn't know what had happened there. I would never have sent you into such danger if I had."

"And yet you would kill me now, and all the other Roses, without explanation, without warning. And the others in Aidurra and Vauzanne—will you kill them too?"

"Dismantling only one branch of the Order would leave two others still in chains," she replied evenly. "I am bound to my sister Wardens as surely as you are bound to me, and the Mist, the Wood, the Crescent are bound to each of us in turn." Her eyes gleamed with triumph. "What I do, I do for us all."

My stomach churned to think of it: hundreds of Roses dying in an instant. And with the Wardens gone, the Mist would vanish. Aidurra's Crescent of Storms would disappear. The Knotwood of Vauzanne would shrivel up and die.

Edyn would have no protections left against the Old Country.

"The other Wardens," I whispered. "Do they know?"

She laughed. "Of course not. They haven't the spine for this."

"But you're connected, the three of you. Surely they've sensed your intentions!"

"Another advantage of working with the goddess of the unknowable. My hapless sisters sense only what I wish them to perceive."

I was almost too furious to speak. "You're evil. What you're doing is evil."

"It wasn't supposed to happen like this. Kilraith was supposed to win, and we would have been free. But now?" She laughed again, tears spilling down her cheeks. "Kilraith is dead. The war is over, or it will be soon enough, and our last chance at freedom is gone. Everything will go on exactly as it always has. And I can't let that happen. I cannot condemn any more girls to this life of servitude. I will not."

"Instead you'll condemn them to death?"

"These Roses, yes, but no others. Isn't that a beautiful thought, Mara? Don't you see? We make this sacrifice so others won't have to."

"Neave is still alive," I said tightly, "and Caiathos, and my mother. If this Order dies, they'll create another one. They will build a new Middlemist and bind others to it in our stead. This *sacrifice* will be a waste of life."

"And these are the gods you were so intent upon saving?" The Warden couldn't stop laughing. "No, they won't bind any others. They are mere shadows of what they once were, even your precious mother. And even if they could, they won't have the chance."

"It wasn't Kilraith destroying the Mist," I whispered, realizing it with dreadful certainty. This was the worst revelation of all. "It was you. Everyone driven mad by the failing Mist, all the work we did to stem the bleeding—"

"Kilraith," the Warden said, her voice curling. "Kilraith was a broken creature blinded by a desire for revenge. He could never have done what I did."

Suddenly every strange behavior I'd observed over the last several months, every outburst, every sign of fatigue made a terrible kind of sense. The Warden had served as both an anchor to a curse and a host to a god. And with that power she had been unraveling the Mist from the inside, undoing gods-made magic as old as the world.

This was unthinkable, impossible. It was no wonder that she had been slowly falling apart.

She was watching me closely. "You don't approve of what I've done. I'm not surprised. You have *their* blood in your veins. Of course you want to defend their decisions, continue their legacy of cruelty."

I shook my head, my mind scrambling for a solution. "There has to be another way to reform the Order, something other than total destruction!"

"There isn't."

"I don't believe it. You're so lost in your own anger that you can only see paths forged by violence. You're no better than Kilraith."

"And if you refuse to see the truth—that what I've done, and what I will do, is the only acceptable response to generations of bondage—then you're no better than the feckless gods who brought us here."

She glared at me, her black eyes sunken in her white face. I held her gaze and refused to blink.

Finally the Warden sighed. A light somewhere inside her seemed to go out.

"I'm tired, Mara," she said, all the vitriol gone from her voice. "Aren't you? Help me do this. Release us both. The one thing Zelphenia has been good at since I found her is keeping me alive. Even with her meager strength, she manages that one thing because of what my body has given her. This body that has never been my own from the moment I was born. But now that you're here, you can end this for me. She can stay my hand, but not yours. She can't touch our binding magic. It's too mighty for her, Mara. *We're* too mighty for her."

Suddenly a scorching power spiked through my body, forcing me to move. I started pushing against the Warden's wrist, driving the blade inexorably back toward her throat.

Panicked, I tried to yank my hand away from her, but the binding magic wouldn't allow it. It was the same insistent feeling that changed my body from woman to bird and back again, the same sour charge that guided me back to the Warden when missions took me far from the priory.

I couldn't fight it. The rose tattoo on my thigh burned like a brand. I smelled smoke, I smelled lightning. And I watched through furious tears as my hand pressed the blade into her neck. My strength was nothing compared to that of the magic that bound me to her.

"I hate you," I whispered. "You've taken everything from me. And now you won't even let me die by my own hand."

She smiled up at me past the blade of her knife. "Even now, you are mine. Remember that, Mara. Think of it as we take our last breaths. You are not his, and you never were."

"You're wrong," said a voice beside me, hard and steady and impossibly, terrifically real. "She belongs only to herself."

I nearly lost my grip on the Warden's wrist as I watched the owner of this miraculous voice kneel down beside me. He smiled grimly at me, mud-spattered and bandaged but alive.

"I look worse than I feel," Gareth said. "And fear not, my darling. I've brought friends."

CHAPTER 45

I was dying. I was dead, and I had passed into the Great Dominion. That was the only explanation.

"Gareth," I said, his name barely a breath. "But you're dead."

He blinked at me in surprise. "I'm not."

It was the most ridiculous conversation. Everything felt so absurd that I wanted to laugh.

But the Warden had no patience for impossible reunions. My body suddenly seized, and the binding magic within me drew taut as a wire. It pushed me down toward her, pressing the knife blade deeper into her throat. Bright red blood tinged with gold trickled down her neck and into the mud. So much red and so little gold. My heart sank. I took this to mean that Zelphenia was indeed very weak, the balance between them skewed heavily in the Warden's favor.

"Don't look at him," she rasped, "look at *me*. Kill me, Mara. We'll die together, and we'll both be free."

It was something about the mad light in her eyes, the desperation with which her will suddenly pulled against mine. As I stared down at her, fighting her with all my tired strength, I saw the truth as clearly as if she were whispering it into my ear.

Zelphenia was the goddess of the unknowable, mother of demons and beguilers, specters and revenants. So much of her power lay in the realm of death. And the Warden had wanted to punish me, to summon me back to her for this very moment, this final task.

"You knew I wouldn't come to you if he were still alive," I whispered. "You made him appear dead to my eyes."

"I would have killed him properly if she'd let me," the Warden hissed. "But it was enough. Here you are, and here we'll die."

It was too much to bear, this betrayal. I watched her through my tears, hating that this was the final image she would have of me but unable to stop crying.

Gareth wasn't dead—he was here, he was *alive*—and still I was locked in this deadly embrace. If I relented for even a moment, the Warden would win. The knife, wielded by my hand, would cut open her throat. Every Rose would die. The Mist would fall.

But I couldn't fight her forever. Maybe if I hadn't spent so much of my strength helping Ankaret; maybe if I'd stayed with Gareth's body and not run away from anyone who might see me and wish to help; maybe, maybe...

I wept bitterly. I'd done everything wrong. Everything was wrong, and I'd never again be able to touch Gareth, or even look into his eyes and see how obviously and completely he loved me. I'd killed him. I'd killed everyone.

"I love you," I whispered, my arms trembling with the effort of pulling against the Warden's wrist. I was drenched with sweat; my whole body shook. "Gareth, I love you."

"Don't do that," he said sternly. "I hear that good-bye, and I reject it."

He reached for me, but some kind of shield had formed around the Warden and me, and it pushed him back with a bright flash and a snap like lightning. The Warden blew out a ragged laugh. No, she wouldn't let him touch me. Not now, when she was so close to winning.

Gareth hissed and shook out his hands, then came as close to me as he dared. "All right, Mara, I need you to listen to me. Gemma and Farrin are here, and your mother and father, and Ryder and Talan, and Alastrina, and Caiathos. And Ankaret. We're going to help you. I just need you to hold on for a little longer."

My mind felt sluggish as I listened to him, like I'd forgotten the familiar sounds of these words. I nodded helplessly.

Out of the corner of my eye, I saw him hold up his hands. He was cradling something inside them, something brilliantly gold and as small as a songbird.

Listen to me very carefully, Mara, said the thing in Gareth's hands.

I nearly burst into tears. "Ankaret," I gasped out.

The Warden's eyes widened, then narrowed. She let out a furious cry, and her whole body jerked under mine, pulling me closer. My arms nearly buckled; the knife's blade sank deeper into her skin.

I'm going to move the root of her binding magic into you, Ankaret said. *You will carry it now, not her. She will die, and you will live. Our own kind of transference. It is not a perfect solution, but it is what we can manage right now. Do you understand?*

I shook my head. "You can't. She won't let you."

You watched me die—you helped me do it. And yet here I am again, reborn, just as I promised you, and still you doubt me.

"Foul creature," the Warden hissed, poison in her voice. "Get away from her. We are beyond you now. It's too late to stop us."

Ankaret ignored her. She crawled lightly onto my shoulder, easily passing through the Warden's shield. Her arms and legs were slender as twigs, and stubby little wings of fire illuminated her back. With every movement, tiny whorls of ashes floated around her body.

It is true that I am still weak, Ankaret said, *but the others are going to help me. The only thing you need to do is stay strong and resist her will.*

I couldn't speak, couldn't wrap my mind around what she was telling me. I shook my head wordlessly.

I need you to let me in, Mara. I will not do this without your consent.

"Gareth," I said, a sob bursting out of me.

I felt him shift closer. "I'm here. Mara, I'm here, and I always will be."

"I can't do this."

"You can." This time when he tried to reach for me, nothing stopped him. He touched the curve of my wing, and the Warden bellowed in frustration. Whatever she'd done to keep him from me, it seemed she could no longer sustain it.

Gareth wrapped his arms around me and pressed his chest against my back, between my limp and trembling wings. I felt his lips on my nape, beneath my hair.

"I'm right here, Mara," he said. "I've got you."

It was a sweet but futile thing to say. He didn't have me. The Warden did. But the sensation of his body curving against mine, when I thought I'd never be lucky enough to feel that again, was better than anything I'd ever known.

"I thought I'd lost you," I whispered.

"Never. *Never.*"

"I can't do this. Not even for you."

"Certainly you can. Look at you, you're doing it right now."

I drew in a deep, shuddering breath, and when I let it out, I felt how easy it would be to keep going, to relax all the way down to my fingertips and let the Warden's binding magic take hold of me. My eyelids were heavy. Keeping them open was like shoving against something inexorable and immense.

"I'm so tired, Gareth," I said.

"I know, darling."

"No, you don't know. I'm *tired.* Of all this, everything that's happened, everything I've done…" Their names came to me as whispers: *Petra. Posey. Crellin.* Everyone I'd lost and every life I had taken.

"I don't want to do it anymore." The words left me on a thin breath of air. "I don't want to do this anymore."

"Don't say that. Don't you say that to me."

The way his voice broke tore at me, but that changed nothing. I meant what I'd said. I let my eyes fall shut. Ankaret pressed her tiny warm hands into the down of my shoulder.

"Everything that happened to you in Mhorghast," I said quietly. "Everything you did…do you never want to escape from it?"

Gareth's arms tightened around me. "Of course I do. But if I gave in to those feelings, everyone who hurt me would win."

"And so what if they do? Defiance alone is not a reason to keep living."

Saying the words aloud was a relief. Suddenly I felt almost weightless. It would have been so easy to let that feeling bear me away.

"No, but this is." Gareth put his hands over my heart. "You and me, and everyone who loves you. Your heart and all its goodness, your immeasurable courage, how deeply you care about everything and everyone around you, even at the expense of yourself. Your *life*, Mara—that's a reason to keep living. Your rare and extraordinary life."

His impassioned words were weakening my resolve, and that made me furious. I didn't want my resolve to weaken. I wanted him to say, *You're right, Mara,* and let me go.

"I'll never be able to leave the Mist, or Rosewarren," I said. "Do you understand what you're asking of me? I'll be responsible for it, for all of them. And I'll be trapped—just as I am now, but even worse. I'll be bound to my duty, ensnared in it, just the same as she has been."

"No you won't, not in the slightest." Gareth's voice was ragged, as if he were struggling to hold himself together, but his hold on me was strong, his breath on my neck steady and warm. "By her own doing, she has always been alone. But you won't be. We'll figure out a way, all of us, to make things right. We have Ankaret to help us, and three gods who will grow stronger every day, and we'll forge alliances with Olden scholars, and I'll read every book that has ever been written. We'll find a solution. We'll rebuild everything, including the Order."

I shook my head. More work, endless work, and the unknown dangers that would come as two worlds licked their wounds, and no promise of relief. I couldn't bear all of that. I wasn't strong enough for it, not anymore.

All I wanted was to go home.

That was what I'd wanted more than anything for as long as I could remember. And here at the crossroads of my life, with the Warden's will scraping mine raw on one side and an endless stretch of days unfurling on the other, it was the purest thing I could think of: Ivyhill, and all its parks and hothouses, the vines grown by my mother's hand, every cheerful shuttered window that I'd painted on the walls of my room at the priory.

Suddenly I was ten years old again, my heart in pieces as that fearsome black carriage took me farther and farther away from everything I'd ever known. That heartbroken girl had hoped something marvelous would happen one day, sweeping away every pain she had suffered. On that day, she would be able to go home again. She had held on to that hope for years, far longer than she should have. Some spark of it still lived inside me, and now I was considering stamping it out.

"I just want to go home," I whispered. "If I do this, I'll never be able to. Ever."

"Then we'll build a new home, together," Gareth said fiercely, "and we'll make it just as it ought to be. We'll fill it with happiness, years and years of it."

Our home. "Our home."

"Yes, darling. Mara, my love." He kissed my hair. I felt his tears on my neck. "Our home."

I hovered at the edge of something colossal, refusing to blink. The world shimmered before my eyes.

When I said her name, I could barely feel my tongue. "Ankaret?"

Yes, Mara?

I took a breath and blinked at last. Tears spilled silently down my cheeks. "Do it."

She obeyed immediately, skimming down my arm with her long firebird's tail streaming behind her. She wound herself around the spot where I gripped the Warden's wrist, faster and faster until the shape of her disappeared and became simply a spinning ring of fire.

"Mara, don't let her do this!" The Warden was insensate with anger. It jolted through me like poison. "This is the only way! Our *freedom*, Mara!"

I closed my eyes, pulling back against her with all my strength. My hand and her wrist were now fully wreathed in fire; we were in it up to our elbows, and it kept expanding. The Warden writhed, trying to buck me off of her, but Gareth was holding on to me, hands clasped at my waist and his face buried in my neck.

And as Ankaret's fire raced through me, and through the Warden, and then back into me again, a feeling beyond pain took ahold of me—a white, quiet feeling, like the highest reaches of the sky—and suddenly I could see the entire beach. I saw Farrin holding on to Gareth's waist, and Gemma holding on to hers. I saw Talan and Ryder, my parents, fierce-eyed Alastrina, and solemn Caiathos, muttering to himself as if in prayer.

They made a chain of bodies, digging their heels into the earth and holding onto me with all their power. Tears streamed down Gemma's face. Farrin sang under her breath, her brow tight with concentration. I felt their heartbeats crowd against mine; I heard the thunder of their lungs. They poured their power into the river of Ankaret's fire and held onto me, keeping me upright even when everything in me longed to fall.

Don't let go. Farrin's voice, and then Gemma's. *Don't give in. We love you.*

"Stay here with me," Gareth murmured against my hot skin. "Stay with us, Mara."

I was burning, everything I knew was burning—but instead of becoming ashes, all the inner pieces of myself shifted, expanding, and my bones turned unbreakable and golden. Soon my skin would peel away to reveal the old magic beneath—this ancient power of binding that was now mine to carry—and as my mind began to buckle under the stress, it recalled a line from one of my old books at Rosewarren, one of the first I'd been tested on during those early years of training.

Aelum: A fundamental substance, invisible to everyone but the gods. The basis of all magical life.

That was what Ankaret was doing, I thought, feeling strangely calm. She was moving aelum from the Warden's body into mine, shifting the very foundations of our bodies. Distantly, as my vision turned black, I heard the Warden start screaming. Even after everything she had done to me, I found myself wanting to comfort her. *My heart and all its goodness.*

Then, all at once, it was done. The world turned cold and dark around me. I fell into its quiet gladly.

CHAPTER 46

I came back to myself a day later, or maybe a hundred. When I opened my eyes, I had no sense of time or place, or whether or not I still had a body.

After a few moments, I decided that wherever I was, there was no danger here, and a few moments after that, I comprehended that I was in a bed, and that Gareth was beside me.

I couldn't see his face, didn't have the strength to lift my head, but I could smell him, how warm and clean he was, and that he must have been reading recently, because the earthy scent of old books was on his skin. He was caressing my upper arm with his thumb—slow, gentle strokes—and that was when I realized that my feathers and down were gone. I was myself again, at least for now. I didn't know how to feel about that; gladness felt too simple.

I pressed my cheek against Gareth and curled my fingers into the soft linen of his shirt. His arms tightened around me; I felt his breath in my hair. The wonderful quiet made it easy to find sleep again.

⟡

My progress was slow, slower than it had ever been. But then, my body had never received such an infusion of power before. It was like someone had reached into me and moved my insides around to make room for a whole *new* set of insides—which, I supposed, was exactly what had happened.

Everything ached. Weeks passed before I could leave my room, which was one of the largest guest rooms at Rosewarren—it was easier for the healers to access than the barracks, and boasted large windows that could be opened in the afternoon to let in the fresh winter air.

Every day someone came to me with a report, delivered under the watchful eyes of Freyda, Nanette, or Welma, who had come straight to Rosewarren when summoned. Most often it was Brigid who came to see me, but sometimes it was Cira, and sometimes my sisters. They told me about everything that was happening at the priory, and down in Fairhaven, and at Ivyhill and Big Deep—everywhere the war had touched.

The Middlemist had returned to its proper location, leaving behind a tapestry of shattered lands and ravaged woodlands. Refugees were slowly returning to their homes; an enormous effort was underway to rebuild all the buildings that had been lost. Soldiers from both armies constantly ran supplies from the capital to their assigned towns.

One Tuesday morning, Farrin brought reports from Vauzanne and Aidurra and read them to me—my eyes were one of the last things to heal, and it hurt every time I tried to focus on something for longer than a few seconds.

"The Knotwood, like the Middlemist, has fallen back behind its traditional borders," she told me, as I lay in bed trying to concentrate on the sound of her voice. "The Crescent of Storms has too, and has also calmed significantly. No more hurricanes, only the ordinary lightning storms that Aidurrans living near the Crescent have been dealing with since its creation."

I listened to her with my eyes closed, my lips pressed together as if that could somehow shut out all other noise.

With every day that passed, I could feel more of what was happening at Rosewarren. Every Rose on patrol, every Rose in the stables grooming the horses, every Rose laughing with her friends as they lounged among the roots of the Heart Tree—I could sense them all. Wisps of feeling brushed constantly against the edges of my awareness. Mostly it was a muddled wash of color and sound. But if I concentrated hard enough on one particular feeling, I found that I could focus my attention on a single Rose or a specific location for a few seconds before losing my mental grip.

"...and both Arora and Joseline will visit Fairhaven next week. They plan to meet with Ankaret before coming here to see you."

The Wardens of the Aidurran and Vauzanian Orders, respectively. Hearing their names gave me a thrill of nerves.

"Not once in all my time here have I ever met them or even seen them," I told Farrin. "Nor have I ever met the women under their commands."

She looked surprised. "I wonder why. Surely everyone would have benefited from all three Orders working closely together."

"I asked the Warden about it once. She told me she didn't approve of their philosophies and that they'd all had a terrible argument, one they'd never been able to come back from." I looked down at my hands. "Now, of course, I don't believe anything she ever said. I'm sure she was planning all of this for years and had to isolate herself from them before they could find out the truth and try to talk her out of it."

Farrin said my name quietly and touched my arm. Only then did I realize I was crying.

"I'm tired of crying," I said, "and I certainly don't want to cry for her, but being angry at her doesn't feel any better, and thinking of how much I loved her is worst of all. I'd really rather just not feel anything."

I leaned against Farrin's shoulder, wiped my face, and gazed at the blurry white window.

"How do you even begin to recover from the blow of someone you love disappointing you so completely?" I whispered.

Farrin drew in a deep breath. "I'm still working out the answer to that one."

"You mean with Father."

"Mm. And Philippa too."

I was quiet for a long time before speaking again. "I wish I'd been there to help you after Mother left."

"I don't," she said at once. "I'm glad you didn't see Father like that. It was bad enough that Gemma and I had to."

I felt a little flare of anger come and go. "Well, at least I would have been home."

Farrin squeezed my hand in apology. "That's true."

"And we would have been together, all three of us. It might have been easier in some ways."

"Well," she said, resting her cheek against the top of my head, "we can be together now."

Gemma made me promise that the first time I took a walk outdoors, she could be there to escort me.

On the morning of that first walk, as I practiced striding about my rooms while Welma examined my gait and Nanette scanned my face for signs of pain—and while Freyda glared at both of them, on guard for any behavior she didn't approve of—Gemma burst in, beaming in her furs, and hurried over to embrace me.

"You," she declared, pulling back to touch my face, "look wonderful." Then she offered me her arm and smiled with such bright, genuine happiness that I felt all my nervousness melt away. "Shall we?"

⟡

Several inches of snow blanketed the grounds that morning, but Brigid had seen to it that a few potential walking routes had been shoveled clean.

"So you won't have to trudge," she'd told me over tea the afternoon before—and then stared at me in horror as I burst into tears.

"Someday I really will stop crying," I assured her.

"I certainly hope so," she replied. "For now, have a cookie."

So I walked through the grounds, leaning heavily on Gemma's arm, and tried to remember that pleasant tea, or anything pleasant at all.

On the surface of my new life, of this new Order, nothing was wrong. Nesset and Danesh were running drills in the training yards. Cira flew overhead on her way to a patrol, calling down to us cheekily before disappearing into the nearby Mist. As we passed the stables, we saw Talan holding up one of our youngest littles so she could knock snow off the branches of a pine. The snow scattered down all over them, and she shrieked happily. Her friend, waiting impatiently at Talan's side, tugged on his coat for her turn.

And yet I felt on edge, like something monumental had changed, something even bigger than what had happened to me. It seemed that I no longer fit here, in this place to which I was now even more tightly bound than before.

Gemma watched Talan and the littles fondly, her face soft. "It already feels happier here."

Her words were like rain on parched earth. I drank them up greedily. "What do you mean? How? Tell me."

"The air is lighter. There's noise all the time—happy noise, sounds of life. Everything always felt so hushed and dour before." She paused near the aviary and helped me turn back around to see the house. "Listen."

I did, and at first all I could hear was the wash of sound that underscored my every waking moment. But instead of letting that current overwhelm me, as it so often did, I made myself concentrate on specific things: the priory's windows, some golden with lamplight, others thrown open to let in the air; two of our cooks sitting on a wooden bench outside the kitchens, gossiping about some man who lived in Fenwood and shaking with laughter; the snuffling horses in the stables; the distant clatter of someone running through the house; Freyda, alighting on the priory's highest tower to enjoy what she could of the sunlight.

And the nearby littles, who were now crowding around Talan to gaze reverently at the bird's nest cradled in his hands.

"None of the eggs are broken," he told them. "Isn't that lucky? Now, let's put them back where they belong."

I swallowed hard, feeling like my heart was ready to burst from my chest—but whether from happiness or sadness, I couldn't tell.

"I'm not going to cry today," I told Gemma firmly.

"You can if you want to," she replied. "I cry almost every day."

I looked at her in alarm. "About what? What's happened? Your pain—is it getting worse? The healer who helps you with your panic—is she still proving helpful?"

"It's not, and she is, so don't get that look in your eyes."

"What look?"

"The one that says you want to give my healer a talking-to. Sofi takes excellent care of me."

Sofi. I hadn't known her healer's name was Sofi. Realizing that put a knot in my throat. Even after everything my sisters and I had been through together over the last several months, even with how utterly we loved one another, there was still that distance of years between us. Letters and monthly visits were no substitute for growing up together under the same roof. I felt that loss keenly with every breath.

I tightened my arm around Gemma's, pulling her a little closer to me. "Then why do you cry almost every day?" I asked.

She glanced at me. "It will make me sound silly."

"And what if it does? I certainly don't mind silliness. In fact, I could probably use more of it."

"I think I know just the librarian for that," she said with a sly little grin.

I stifled a smile, my cheeks warming. "Don't distract me. Tell me."

"Well, then," she said carefully. "Don't misunderstand me, I love Ivyhill, and I'm happy to manage the estate in Farrin's stead. The work she does in Fairhaven is important, and she's brilliant at it. I think she and Ryder mean to live there permanently. And Ivyhill has become something of a waystation for people traveling back north to their homes. We've opened up a permanent hospital there, did I tell you?"

"You didn't. Gemma, that's wonderful."

"It is. But…" She sighed, looking up at the sky for a moment, and then at the Mist, tame and quiet, shimmering over the nearby treetops.

"Mother comes and goes often," she said, "now that she doesn't have to stay hidden at Wardwell. When she isn't helping Alastrina and Caiathos search for Jaetris and Zelphenia, she helps at the hospital, and she's tremendous at it. And Father's quite involved with the rebuilding efforts in the heartlands. They're both doing good things, and it's not as though they're *constantly* there."

She took a deep breath, let it out slowly. From inside the aviary came a quiet flutter of wings and the soft trill of a dove.

"It's just that I don't think I can stay there forever," Gemma said quietly. "Maybe if they weren't ever there, or if they were dead, or… not that I *want* them to be dead. I certainly don't. I love them," she added, then looked at me earnestly. "I do love them."

"I know you do. But…" I hesitated. It seemed like an awful thing to say, and yet I needed her to hear it, and I needed to say it. I'd been turning over the feeling of this thing for days, ever since talking with Farrin. "After everything that happened, it would be all right if you didn't."

"That's just it. Everything that happened." Gemma dabbed her eyes with her gloved fingers. "I love that house so dearly it hurts me sometimes. I stand there and look around at it and see memories everywhere—the good ones and the bad. And lately it seems to me that there's more bad than good. And the best ones…" She gave me a watery smile. "They all involve you and Farrin. And neither of you are there, so why should I be?"

She sniffled, looked up into the trees, and blinked hard. "And if I have to see Mother and Father waltzing around the house all gooey-eyed one more time, I'll scream. How can you be happy that two people have found each other again and at the same time almost hate them for it? How can you love a person so much it makes you cry and also wish you'd never have to see them ever again?" She looked at me hopelessly. "Does that make any sort of sense?"

"It does," I replied, "though it being sensical doesn't make it feel any better."

"Do you love them?"

"I do," I said truthfully, "but if I had to live with them, I'm not sure how much longer I would."

She laughed and hugged me, her pinned-up curls smelling like honeysuckle and meadow grass, even in the dead of winter. When she pulled back from me, she was no longer crying. We continued toward the aviary, arm in arm.

"Where will you go?" I asked her. "You and Talan, if you won't stay at Ivyhill."

"I haven't the faintest idea. Maybe we won't *stay* anywhere. We've become rather adept at traveling together. And anyway, it doesn't matter where we go. Home is wherever we are, together." Then she gasped, her eyes shining, and released me to duck into the aviary. "Oh, hello, you beauty!"

She held out her hand to a snowy owl—the familiar of one of our newest recruits—who after a moment started gently nibbling her fingers. I watched them, still reeling from her words. She had said them so simply, and yet to me they seemed extraordinary.

Gareth had told me something very like that as he'd held me on the shore of the lake.

Then we'll build a new home together.

We'll fill it with happiness.

At the time, I'd been so delirious with pain and sadness that the words had seemed lovely but distant, like a star to wish upon.

Now though, with Gemma's declaration hanging triumphantly in the air, Gareth's words took on a new shape in my mind.

I looked back at the priory, its red-brick walls towering over the snow. Could such a place truly ever be a home? I had lived there for years, slept and eaten and loved and mourned there, but a *home*?

I listened to the distant chatter of my Roses. If I closed my eyes and let my focus drift without direction, I could almost imagine that this was not a base of operations for soldiers but merely a house—rambling and drafty and old, with strong walls and snug nooks and centuries of stories inside it.

Hushed and dour, Gemma had called it—but it wasn't anymore.

Our home.

I opened my eyes, my nose tingling. I sniffed hard and wiped a hand across my face.

At my elbow, a white-gold light flickered gently. "Beautiful, isn't it?"

"Ankaret." I found her sitting on a bench near the aviary wall, gazing up adoringly at the perches full of birds above her. She was small, sparrow-sized, and nearly translucent, and it had taken days for even an ember of her to reappear after what she'd done for me at the lake, but she had kept her promise; she had come back to us. "I thought you were in Fairhaven with Farrin."

"She was, and she will be again. But she fears she no longer has the stomach for governing." Ankaret sighed, making a face. "*I* no longer have the stomach for it. It is difficult to speak properly when she—*I* am this new. She will get better at it." Then she glanced up at me. "You will too."

"Better at what?"

"Becoming *your* new self."

The thought made me suddenly weary. I leaned against the wall and asked a question I'd been too terrified to voice to anyone. "Do you think we'll ever manage to free all the Roses? Is such a thing even possible without ruining everything?" I thought of the Warden's face, my throat clenching up. "Without death?"

"There is still much to do," Ankaret said slowly. "We must negotiate a lasting peace between the realms. If there is ever to be no more Middlemist, or Knotwood, or Crescent, we must determine an alternative that will require no one's service to maintain it. Or," she conceded, "it is possible we will need to completely separate Edyn from the Old Country, if we cannot forge a peace. And we can do none of this without Jaetris and Zelphenia. We must find them, help them grow strong again."

I nodded, gazing glumly at the priory. "There is so much left to do."

"There is. But already there is less than there was. And look."

She held up her small white hand. On her palm, in a tiny pile of ash, a new shivering flame sparked to life. She pressed it against her heart as if to imbue herself with it, and right there before my eyes she started glowing a little bit brighter.

"Every day we grow stronger," she said, smiling up at me. "And on the days when that is not enough, we will find our strength in each other and wait for morning to come again."

"You say that as if it's so simple," I told her quietly.

"Words are simple. Courage is not. But you, dear Mara, are abundant with it. Know that, and let the knowing comfort you."

Gemma came up beside me and slid her hand into mine. "She is wonderful, isn't she?" she said to Ankaret, beaming up at me. "My brave sister."

I held her to me in silence until the feeling of tears passed. Ankaret flickered softly on her perch. We watched the snow begin to fall.

⟡

When I arrived at Big Deep, I was thinking longingly of nighttime and its quietness, and of Gareth in my bed.

The days were long now, and tiring, with messages coming and going constantly from the capital, from Vauzanne and Aidurra, from Ivyhill.

Researchers from the university were studying the Mist and its health and documenting their observations with painstaking thoroughness. Gareth, stationed at Rosewarren, worked with them day and night. They needed to be managed, their work analyzed and compared to similar studies being done at the Knotwood and the Crescent of Storms. We had to know for certain that there was no more danger, that the Mist was stable.

There were meetings upon meetings, both intimate and grand, of the royal councils and Olden delegations, scholars and mediators, military commanders from all three continents, my mother and Alastrina and Caiathos.

I was present at most of them, when my duties permitted, and felt uncomfortable at every single one.

My new mantle of Warden sat strangely on my shoulders. I refused even to take the name. I was Mara to all my Roses and allowed *Madam* only on the direst of occasions. This made me feel like even more of a child next to Arora and Joseline, and though they were kind to me, like stern but well-meaning aunts, I never stopped searching for doubt in their eyes. Was I strong enough and wise enough to oversee the Order alongside them? Was I far enough removed from the Warden to be trusted? And now that the root of the Order's binding magic rested in me, would I someday turn, just as she had, and endanger them all?

I wondered constantly what they really thought of me.

At times, I wondered what I really thought of myself.

In those first fumbling days, when both my mind and my body were exhausted, only two things were absolutely clear to me. One was that I had never been more thankful for my sisters.

The other was that I loved Gareth Fontaine more than I ever thought myself capable of loving another person.

Now, standing in the ruins of Big Deep, I watched him direct a crew of workers who were dismantling what was left of the house. Everything salvageable was to be sent away for use in the rebuilding efforts. The rest would be burned, and the land itself, stripped bare, would remain in Gareth's name.

But apparently the workers had found something in the rubble that they weren't sure how to categorize. I didn't let myself listen to their conversation, though I easily could have, and waited for Gareth to come to me.

He did so with a frown on his face, gazing in bewilderment at a charred item in his hand. Then he looked up at me, scratched the back of his neck, his mouth twisting, and sat down heavily on a slab of stone.

I joined him. "What is it?"

"My mother's medals," he said after a moment. He held up the piece of ruined wood. Only a few ribboned brass medals remained, though there was room for at least twenty.

Gareth twisted one of them gently around his finger. "She had many more, but I suppose they're gone now. She was so proud of them, polished them every day." He stared at them for a long time and then said, with a sad little laugh, "I can't decide if I want to burn the godsdamned things with all the rest of it or hang them on my wall."

Suddenly his face crumpled and he started to cry. "It's stupid, isn't it?" he said, gesturing at himself. "I hated the woman."

I opened my arms to him. "Not stupid. Come here."

He set down the medals and then grabbed me and held on to me desperately, his face buried in my neck. I stroked his hair. Soon my collar was wet; it was strange that this evoked fondness in me, and yet it did. The feeling of his tears was like some secret, precious tenderness.

"I didn't expect to care when she died," he mumbled into my shirt. "I didn't expect to care about the house either. I didn't expect any of this. What a warped thing to feel. The last thing I saw of her was her eyes, wide and terrified as she fell." He paused. "Do you think that if she'd lived, she ever would have apologized to me? For any of it?"

I considered the question. Both my parents had apologized to me; they'd even done so on the day I'd been taken from Ivyhill, my mother sobbing out her remorse as I'd climbed into the Warden's carriage. Even the Warden herself had apologized from time to time. It wasn't that their regret was pointless, exactly. I was glad of it. But I was also beginning to realize that I didn't need it.

All I needed was right there in my arms, and in the stacks upon stacks of letters from my sisters that I kept at my bedside. I received new ones, and sent my own letters in response, almost every day.

"Maybe she would have," I said at last. "Would that have made you feel any better?"

"No. Yes. Maybe. I don't know."

I pulled back from him and smiled. "Here sits the brilliant professor, utterly stymied."

"Oh, don't poke fun at me. I'm too fragile for that." His eyes, though, tired and bleary as they were, held a glimmer of humor. "Feel sorry for me instead, please. I need to be coddled for a while."

Delighted to see him smile, faint as it was, I was glad to play along. "Describe for me what coddling means to you."

"I'm not sure I should, not here," he said, glancing over his shoulder at the workers. "The more obscene language they could handle, but the soft bits I'm not so sure about."

"The soft bits?" I raised an eyebrow at him.

"Not *those* soft bits." He lifted my hand to his lips and kissed it. "I meant how lovely you are, and how much I adore you, and how looking at you, even through glasses that desperately need cleaning—"

I grinned softly. "I wasn't going to mention it."

"—looking at you makes everything better."

For a moment all I could do was that very thing—look at him. Reacquaint myself with the lines of his face, the green of his eyes, that impudent, smitten smile. I leaned in and kissed him softly, then stood, holding out my hand to him.

"On your feet, Professor," I said. "Let's go home."

Acknowledgments

It's a strange thing, finishing a series. I'm glad to have reached the finish line, and yet I hate to say good-bye, and I'll miss the Ashbourne sisters with all my heart—especially Mara, who surprised me many times while writing this book. Her story unexpectedly became my favorite of the three Middlemist installments. Her stoicism, her resilience, her sadness, and her longing for home all resonated with me profoundly. I'm delighted to share her story with you, and I'm so very grateful to everyone who supported me as I wrote it.

First, I must thank my brilliant editor, Annie Berger, who has been an utter joy to work with over the past several years. Together we've ushered two trilogies into the world, and the experience of doing so is one I'll cherish forever.

Thank you to my agent, the incomparable Victoria Marini, whose steadfast belief in my work often renews my courage to keep making it.

The entire crew at Sourcebooks continue to passionately champion my work, and for that I'm endlessly thankful. Special thanks must go to Jocelyn Travis, Mary Altman, Maranda Seney, Siena Koncsol, Angela Craft, Alexandra Derdall, Emily Luedloff, Margaret Coffee, Valerie Pierce, Jennifer Steinhagen, Madison Nankervis, and Molly

Waxman.

Looking at all three of these beautiful books side by side reminds me of how grateful I am for the keen eye and design sense of art director Stephanie Gafron and the talent of artist Nekro.

To my splendidly eagle-eyed friend Alison Cherry—thank you for being the most diligent, most hilarious, and most I understand what you're trying to say here because I love you and I know your brain but consider this instead copy editor a writer could ask for. You make my books better, and I adore you.

I remain uncertain as to whether or not I could have finished writing this book without my dear friend Kate Dramis cheering me on. Kate, thank you for the writing sessions, the Connie Thoughts, the unhinged voice texts, and for regularly reminding me that sometimes brains lie.

Thank you to my family and friends, whose patience and love brighten every day. And, since this is the first time I'm writing acknowledgments as an auntie, thank you to my precious nephew for greeting me with a smile every time I visit and for appreciating my skills as an improvisational composer. I never thought I could love a tiny human as much as I love you, but here we are.

About the Author

Claire Legrand used to be a musician until she realized she couldn't stop thinking about the stories in her head. Now she is the *New York Times* and *USA Today* bestselling author of several novels, including the Middlemist Trilogy, the Empirium Trilogy, the Edgar Award–nominated *Some Kind of Happiness*, the Bram Stoker Award–nominated *Sawkill Girls*, and *The Cavendish Home for Boys and Girls*.

Website: claire-legrand.com
Instagram: @clairelegrandbooks

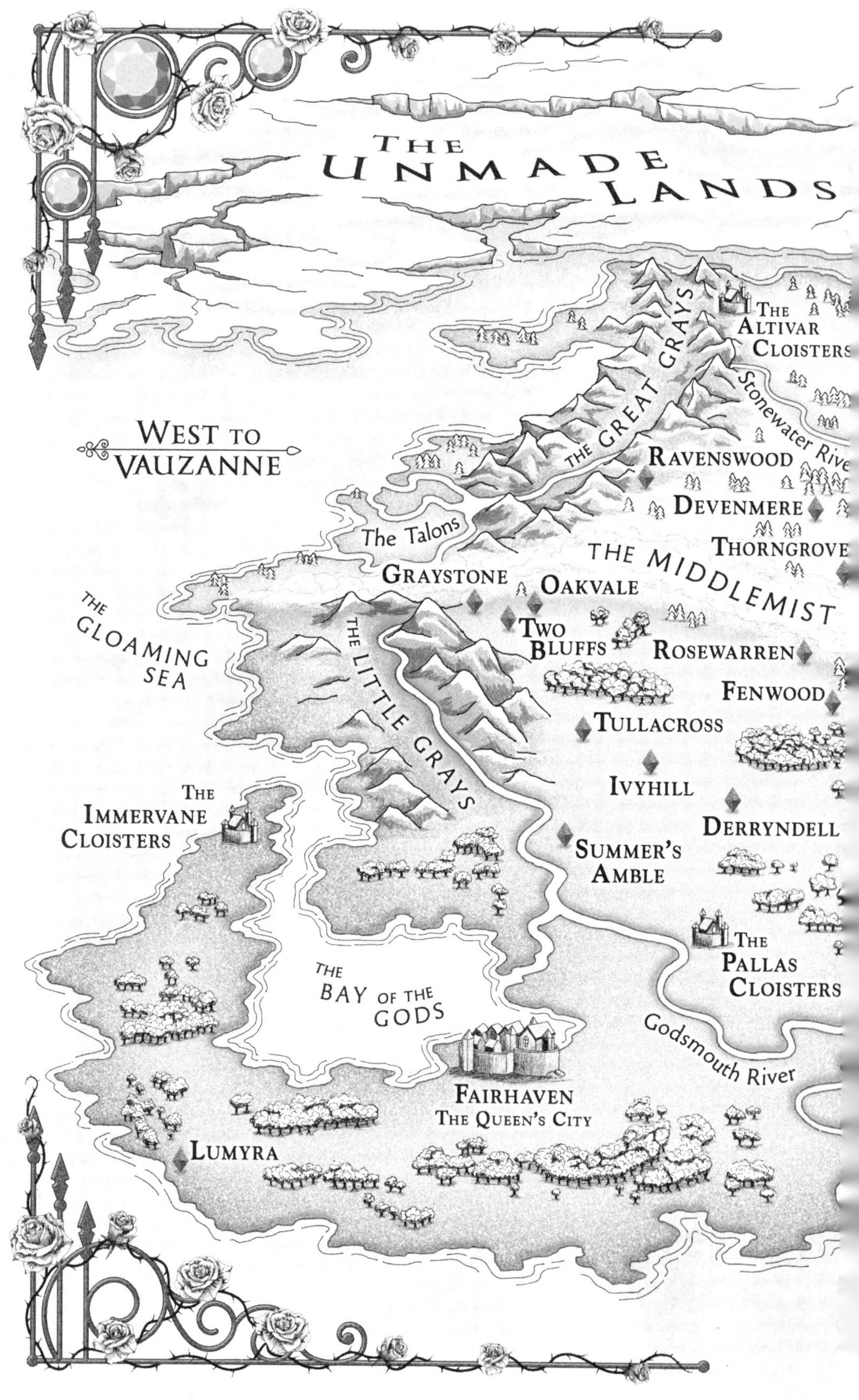

The Unmade Lands
The Altivar Cloisters
The Great Grays
Stonewater River
West to Vauzanne
Ravenswood
Devenmere
The Talons
Thorngrove
The Middlemist
Graystone
Oakvale
Two Bluffs
Rosewarren
The Gloaming Sea
The Little Grays
Fenwood
Tullacross
Ivyhill
The Immervane Cloisters
Derryndell
Summer's Amble
The Pallas Cloisters
The Bay of the Gods
Godsmouth River
Fairhaven
The Queen's City
Lumyra